THE KINGS OF HELL
HARKYN

By Alexis Maree

THE KINGS OF HELL
HARKYN

Cover by Alexis Maree | Edits by Fluffy Fox Publishing | Proofreading done by Adrianne Normanton

CONTENT WARNING

This book contains scenes of dark natures that may trigger some readers – e.g; torture, graphic sexual scenes, assault, and coarse language. Not all possible triggers have been mentioned. By reading further, you, as the reader, are continuing with the understanding that this book has darker tones and that not all possible triggers may have been mentioned. The author and any who contributed to this work cannot and will not be held accountable for a reader's actions, reactions, or state of mind after reading this book.

OTHER BOOKS BY ME

<u>ALEXIS MAREE</u>

THE KINGS OF HELL SERIES:

The Kings of Hell — Cole

The Kings of Hell - Adrik

The Kings of Hell — Malik

<u>T. MAREE</u>

THE LEAH REYNOLDS SERIES:

Sins in the Silence

Sins of a Daughter

Sins of the Past

Sins of the Enemy

Sins of the Forbidden

Sins of the Blood

STANDALONES

Falling for the Mountain Man

Colorful

<u>LUNA MAREE</u>

L'Amour Island

Her Sir & Sire

THE KINGS OF HELL
HARKYN

DEDICATION

This book is dedicated to those who did not let their past and their upbringing dictate who they became.
To those who identify as survivors, and not victims.

She wears strength and darkness equally well.
The girl has always been half goddess, half hell.

- Nikita Gill

THE KINGS OF HELL
HARKYN

ACKNOWLEDGEMENTS

As always, a big shout out to my family. I spend hours tapping away at a keyboard talking to the voices in my head—sometimes arguing with them—and pouting when they give me the silent treatment, and you never judge me for it. Thank you for allowing me to chase my dreams, and supporting me all the way.

I'd like to thank Adrianne, my alpha reader, for your constant encouragement. You are my own one-person cheer squad, and you have no idea how invaluable your encouragement is. Thanks for all you do, all the effort, and for keeping me on track.

To my sister, K. Thank you for your quiet support, encouragement, and believing I am worth investing in. Thank you!

To my ARC team who have been so wonderful in your efforts to review and encourage me when I've needed it. Thank you for being so patient.

And last, but certainly not least, thank you to Rochelle at *Fluffy Fox Publishing* for keeping me on as a client and editing the mess of a draft I hand to you every time, and helping me turn it into what it is now. You're amazing!

THE KINGS OF HELL
HARKYN

ALEXIS MAREE

THE PROPHECY OF THE NINE

From the first to the last, the Brothers Nine will fall…

The first will face death and prevail,
The second shall follow her blood trail.

The third will endure his deal of time,
The fourth need only await his sign.

The fifth will betray his woman of binding,
The sixth will save she he must be finding.

The seventh will take her to keep her safe,
The eighth will have to rely on Faith.

The ninth alone is left to find,
She who was taken, now hidden by design.

From first to the last, the Brothers Nine must fall,
Or chaos reigns, and they will destroy it all.

THE MARK OF THE FOURTH

4

THE KINGS OF HELL
HARKYN

PROLOGUE

Heaven, Hell… and the whole messy bit in between.

Where to begin explaining things?

Let's start with the phrase *peace on Earth*. I honestly wasn't sure there had ever been a time when there had truly been peace on Earth. It was a lie perpetrated by sanctimonious, puritanical, prissy, self-righteous, dipshit Angels. They talked about the possibility of peace, but only if they could get rid of us unnatural abominations who tempted humans into committing sins and damning their souls for all eternity.

The holier than thou fuckers had been working an angle from the beginning, and we'd stupidly missed it. When we'd realized their game, it had been too late to change things. Demons were the scourge of the underworld; we were the nightmares of humans, known to be waiting in the darkness to snatch them away and torture them for the actions humans believed were sins.

Honestly? We didn't give a shit what you did with your life.

If you were a good person who tried hard to help others and live by a set of morals that didn't make you a total dick-bag, odds were, you were good. However, that then meant you were headed to Heaven when you died, and it wasn't all it was dressed up to be. I wasn't totally sure what happened to the humanity attached to the soul when it reached Heaven, but it couldn't be great.

If you ended up with us in Hell, though, things weren't much better. Your humanity was stripped from you, layer by layer,

13

until we could mold you into one of us. Basically, if you were human, you were screwed.

But Witches?

Sure, they were technically human, but they had a little something extra going on.

For centuries, we thought they were extinct, wiped out by our foolish attempts to gather them en masse and use them against our opponents. When I say *we*, I don't just mean Demons—the Angels are to blame, too. It was only recently we learned that a Witch's soul was environmentally friendly and completely recyclable. At the end of their life, they did not meet Death and have their life weighed to measure the good and bad they put out; therefore deciding where they went—to the attic or the basement. They bypassed the whole system and slip-streamed right back into the soul-pool to be reborn on earth.

Now knowing that Witches were still among us, we were doing our best to find them. We wouldn't repeat the same mistakes made centuries ago—or at least us Demons wouldn't—but we had more than just that reason to look for Witches again.

When my brother, Cole, met Tomika, he set in motion a chain of events that would affect us all… the nine Kings of Hell.

From the first to the last, the Brothers Nine will fall…

It was the prophecy none of us had seen before but probably should have, and it had come into effect. We were all thrown by it. Each of us was destined for a Witch, a mate who would be tied to us forever. We were yet to find out *why*. All we knew was that it was happening, and thus far, the prophecy had been spot on—and a little confusing.

Until a few months ago, none of my brothers knew that *I* had known Witches still existed more than two years before Cole met Mika. I'd kept it to myself for a few reasons. The biggest of which was that I couldn't keep away from my Witch, and I was terrified I'd do something to take advantage or hurt her. She'd been seventeen, barely old enough to think for herself, but something inside me had recognized her for what she was, even though I hadn't known about the prophecy.

In a moment of panic and a desperate attempt to hold onto my restraint, I'd made a blood promise with her.

I gave her my Word.

The Word of a Demon King wasn't like any other promise. If I didn't keep to the deal, I died. She'd been too tempting to me, too addicting, too... *everything*. I'd barely kept my distance as it was, and I was at the end of my rope. So, I'd hurriedly given her my Word and promised to stay away. It was stupid, and I hadn't been thinking clearly when wording it. That led to four *long* years of watching her from the shadows to make sure she was okay and ease the ache in my chest at knowing I could never hold her or speak to her again.

I know. I'm an idiot—my brothers were very vocal on the subject.

But now, Witches are in more danger than ever, and I can't leave her on her own in case she's taken. Angels are hunting Witches ruthlessly, caring less and less if they're seen by humans, leaving the rest of us to be the ones who keep to the rules. Rogue Demons have sided with our enemy in what I see as an ill-conceived plan to take over the thrones of Hell. Nephilim are flying close too, making us all a little wary, and Death himself seems to have it out for Witches. Reapers are more than happy to snatch a Witch's soul, even if she's not totally dead, and that makes us all nervous. Our only conclusion so far is that Death doesn't like the fact Witch's seem to circumvent his system. The origins of Witches are hazy, and no one really has an answer for where they came from or how they came to be. One day, they were simply there, healing Angels and Demons and trying to keep the world balanced.

See? Chaos.

It's not safe for Witches anymore. Those with the know-how and skill are going into hiding for their own good, while others are out fighting the good fight. Those are the ones who need protecting more than any, and my mate just so happens to be one of them.

There, I think you're all caught up.

Remember

Angels = Pretentious morons, built like porcelain models who are puritanical assholes.

Demon Kings = Scorching hot masters of seduction who wield incredible power, sexual prowess, and staggering good looks.

CHAPTER ONE
HARKYN

Hindsight was a real bitch.

My heart was pounding, my mouth was dry, and every inch of my soul screamed at me to move, to do something, to take her. Anytime I moved to act on the age-old instinct, a heavy weight around my wrist tugged at me hard, reminding me I had no choice but to keep my distance.

Either that or die.

I watched as she laughed, that gorgeous smile and those deep dimples flashing, her arctic blue eyes glittering with humor and warmth. There was something about her pale skin that glowed when she smiled, and it made every muscle in my body lock up tight. The lighting in the restaurant was dim and warm, giving the place an air of intimacy—I hated it.

She smiled again and ducked her head, long lashes sweeping down to conceal her eyes, but it wouldn't do any good. If the man across from her—Doug—had been paying even the slightest bit of attention, then the shape of her eyes, the exact shade, and that one speck of gold in the otherwise arctic blue of her right eye would be forever imprinted in his memory. As she shook her head, her long, platinum blonde hair slid like silk across her shoulders. It was curled in large, loose curls, and it softened her appearance some. Not that she was a hard woman, not at all. She stood at five-foot-six and was petite yet curvy. She looked feminine to her core, and to me, the delicate tattoos that decorated her skin only enhanced that femininity. It was the hardness in her eyes sometimes that made her look older and more cynical than she should at twenty-one years old.

Dimitria—or Tria, as she liked to be called. My mate.

My gaze traveled down her body to her chest where her dress hugged her tightly, and once again experienced the stab of painful arousal that shot through my body. Everything about her got to me, everything made me want her more than anyone else I'd ever wanted before or since meeting her.

The gold chain that came to rest just above the swell of her breasts gave the impatient beast in me the smallest sense of satisfaction. The black pendant at the end of it was engraved with my sigil, the symbol for the fourth King of Hell. Since giving it to her, I'd never known Tria to take it off, and it allowed me to soothe the more animal side of me.

And those tattoos...

I knew each and every one of them that graced her skin, every curve and swirl, every line, every symbol of protection. Where my tattoos covered me from the tops of my hands, up my arms and across my chest and back, they looked more like a shield than decoration. Every gentle line on her was artwork and only went to make her that much more beautiful.

The sound of her laughter startled me out of my thoughts again, and I refrained from looking at the man across from her who was about to die painfully if he tried to touch her one more time.

Only years of watching this kind of thing prevented me from tearing his throat out at the dinner table.

That, and this stupid Word.

I'd been beating myself up about giving my Word to her since we discovered the prophecy… but it was pointless to keep doing it. We hadn't known about the prophecy four years ago, and at the time, I'd been overwhelmed with the need to protect her, even from myself. My self-restraint had been dangerously lacking, and I'd worried I'd seduce her and do anything to tie her to me.

I would have. I'd been a threat to her in that moment. Not that I would have hurt her—that wasn't a possibility—but I'd wanted her too much and she'd been young. *Too* young.

I'd spoken without thinking, pushed by my need to protect her from myself that I'd made a blood oath on the spot and hadn't properly considered the repercussions. Not that I'd really thought there would be any. Who knew we'd be mates? I grimaced. I guess… we were supposed to have known. Our mother, Lilith, had been onto us for centuries to read the damn books, to grow our knowledge about our origins and the workings of Hell. But then she and our father had taken off, and we'd all kind of… let it slip.

Had she known? Or had she simply wanted us to be up to date on our lore and magic? I wish I knew. It would all be so much easier if she and our father were here, but no one had seen them in— well, too long to count.

Shaking my head, I stilled when Tria's eyes skimmed over my corner of the restaurant. I was shadowed, sure, but that alone wouldn't hide me from her. She was a Witch. I'd had to resort to hiding behind a large plant so she wouldn't see me. It didn't matter though, she sensed me. I knew she did. For the last four years, I'd hidden from her while still watching over her, and more often than not, she felt my presence and looked for me. I wondered if she knew who was looking over her, and a part of me hoped she did. I had made her a promise to stay away, but I needed her to know I hadn't abandoned her, that I hadn't forgotten about her.

I gritted my teeth for the next half an hour as she and Doug finished their dinner. When they were done, he took her hand to lead them out of the restaurant. Following behind them carefully, heat burnt my wrist whenever I got too close. It was a warning that I was risking my life.

Hiding carefully in deeper shadows, I watched as they approached her car. It was a rental. She hadn't owned a car for three years, and instead preferred to ride her motorbike. But for the purposes of her job, she sometimes rented a car.

"I had a great time tonight," Doug said. His smarmy grin as he leered at my mate made me want to tear it off. I even flirted with the idea of ripping his face from his head Hannibal style, but I knew that wouldn't win me any points with her.

"I had a great time too," Tria agreed with a slow, sexy smile, her lashes rising slowly, a mix of innocence and sin no man was immune to.

"Easy, brother."

I didn't bother to turn around at the sound of Nova's voice as he shadowed beside me, concealed from my mate as well as I was. I was clenching my teeth so hard I figured I'd need one of my new sisters to heal me once they cracked.

"Easier said than done," I responded. Even in my mind my voice was twisted with a snarl.

"It doesn't have to end here," the walking sphincter disguised as a human male suggested, leaning in closer as he traced a finger up Tria's bare arm. She smiled wider, sexier, leaning in towards him as he continued to leer down at her. Fuck, I hated watching this part.

"Oh? What did you have in mind?" she asked in a low purr, the promise of sex winding through every syllable she spoke.

"How about dessert? My place?" he asked, sliding a hand around her waist to her lower back, hauling her close to him. I was going to be sick; I was sure of it, either that or burn this city block down with hellfire.

The chain on my wrist burned painfully when I took an instinctive step toward her, ready to tear that dickwad to pieces for touching what was not his. My hands actually ached with how tightly they were curled into fists. Donovan placed a restraining hand on my shoulder to keep me from revealing myself.

"Mmm, that sounds like fun. I'm feeling a little wild," Tria murmured, sliding a hand up Doug's stomach to his chest, her other hand sliding down his thick arm to his wrist.

"What are you thinking?" he asked, edging her backwards so she was pressed against the car.

Don't kill the fuckwit. Don't kill the fuckwit.

"I'm thinking close confines," she began in a suggestive tone, and the asshole moaned his agreement. "And maybe handcuffs?" she added as he leaned in closer.

Nova's hand squeezed my shoulder tightly, both to restrain me and in comfort. All it did was make me want to tear his arm off and beat this fucker to death with it.

"Naughty," the soon-to-be lifeless dick-bag said with a satisfied chuckle.

"And then maybe, if you're really bad, I can call your wife?" she added.

Doug stilled, his mouth too close to hers, and frowned. "What did you just say?"

"We should probably call both of your wives, actually," Tria added.

Douchebag Doug stared at her open-mouthed, his expression turning from shocked to outraged.

"She hired you," he snarled, his grip on her arm tightening to the point where I knew it'd leave bruises. I was seconds from lunging at him—my impending death be damned—when Tria reefed him towards her and brought her knee up hard and fast, using his forward momentum to knee him in the nuts. Douchebag gave a pained whine as he doubled over, and Tria stepped up behind him, pulling out a pair of handcuffs from what appeared to be nowhere and slapped them over his wrists.

"Fuck, that was beautiful," Nova said with pure joy and relish, and I had to admit, seeing the fucker on the ground did wonders to relieve my fury.

"She's definitely got a way about her," I agreed, my mouth still sour with how much that dick had touched her.

Douchebag Doug wheezed and groaned, and Tria stepped away from him once he was properly cuffed.

"No, neither of your wives hired me, nor did your pregnant girlfriend. And when I say girlfriend, I really do mean *girl*friend. Come on, Doug, she's barely nineteen."

"Who the fuck hired you to find me?" he snapped, trying to look imposing from his bound position on the damp concrete.

"The investment firm you've been embezzling from for the past five years before you ran off to enjoy your stolen money," she answered with a shrug. Doug sucked in a sharp breath, and he paled beneath his fake tan.

Tria smirked in satisfaction. "Yes, Doug, they know it was you. They wanted to handle this more in-house, you know? They didn't want their clients and shareholders worrying about double-dipping assholes like you running off with their money."

Doug groaned and leaned awkwardly against the car, his breathing returning to normal. "Who the fuck *are* you?"

"I'm no one to you. I was just hired to find you, and I've done that. Your ride will be here soon. I'll get paid and never think of you again."

"So, you're a bounty hunter," Doug surmised, glaring.

Tria grinned and shrugged. "I've never been fond of labels, but sure."

"How? You're not old enough," he spat.

Tria raised an elegant eyebrow and shook her head. "That didn't seem to be a problem when you wanted to sleep with me."

"Fuck off," he snarled.

"While we're on the topic of you sleeping with women far too young for you, and you stealing money, I wanted you to know that your women won't go empty handed," Tria added, pulling her cell phone from her tiny handbag. She checked something on the screen before sliding it back inside.

"What the fuck are you talking about?" Doug snapped, his temper growing now that his pain seemed to have receded some.

Tria shrugged and looked nonchalant. "Your bosses agreed to give them each a generous payment for any information they could provide on you or your whereabouts. Considering I found you, I'd say what they provided proved quite helpful."

Doug opened his mouth to speak, probably to spew obscenities, but the sudden flash of blue and red lights drew his attention and his eyes grew comically big.

"Oh, look! Your ride is here," Tria said with enthusiasm, her smile wide.

"Let me go," Doug demanded sharply, and then turned his attention to her. "Get me out of these cuffs and get me out of here. I have money, millions of it. I'll pay you to get me out of here."

"I don't want your money," Tria answered with a look of disgust.

"Then what *do* you want?" he asked desperately as the cop car parked on the other side of the road.

"Nothing you can give me. I don't like you, Doug, or men like you. You take advantage of women you profess to love. You also break your promises, and I hate that in a man," she added.

The impact of those last few words hit me square in the chest, and I knew at least some of that was directed at me, even if she didn't know for sure that I was watching her.

"Tria," a voice called. Dimitria stepped away from Doug and plastered a friendly smile on her face as the plain-clothed officer stepped towards her, his partner behind him.

"Hey, Graham, good to see you," she greeted, shaking his offered hand. "Tony," she added, nodding to the other officer.

"Good to see you, too. You got us another one, huh?" Graham asked, looping his thumbs through his belt as he looked down at the glaring Doug.

"Douglas Penrite. Charged with embezzlement, fraud, and a host of other offenses I can't be bothered to name."

Tony let out a low whistle and grinned. "Sounds like a good pay day for you."

Tria smiled. "Well, I'm beat, and I need to go scrub the feel of his hands off me," she said with a theatrical shudder.

"Fucking bitch," Doug muttered from the ground. Tria opened her mouth to speak, but Graham leaned down to reef Doug up by his bound wrists, causing the man to yelp in pain.

"Sorry, did that hurt?" he asked, clearly having meant to hurt him. Doug glared, but smartly kept his mouth shut. "Thanks for your help again, Tria. You have a gift for finding people," Graham added as they began walking Doug to their patrol car. "No doubt we'll see you again soon."

"Night, Graham. See you later, Tony. Good riddance, Doug!"

Doug was roughly shoved into the back of the patrol car, so

whatever he shouted back to Tria was lost behind the door, but the glare he shot her way spoke volumes. Tria kept grinning and waving until the cops pulled away.

I watched her carefully when she sighed and let her hand fall to her side, her eyes scanning the sidewalk. She looked tired as she rubbed her eyes and grabbed her keys from her handbag.

"You good, brother?" Nova asked as Tria slid into her car.

"I'm good. You can come relieve me in a few hours."

Nova slapped me on the shoulder once before he disappeared, and I kept myself shadowed as I followed Tria's progress to her home. She'd lived in this city for the last six months, but she never stayed in one place for long. I surmised that she must feel safer moving around rather than staying in one place, but otherwise I didn't really know why she moved so much.

We arrived at her home sometime later, and I watched from a small distance away as she turned off the car and sat in it for a few moments. She looked... sad. It broke my heart, and I wanted so much to make her feel better. Her stunning eyes swept the street around her and rested on her apartment on the third floor, and I could tell she wasn't sure she wanted to go in. Without thinking, I tried to brush her mind to get a better idea of what she was thinking, and at once fell hard to my knees, a searing, burning pain began stabbing at my brain like hot irons jammed deep. It was only by sheer will and millennia of withstanding pain that I didn't make a sound.

My head ached something fierce, and the edges of my eyes were still blurry when I tried to open them, but it was manageable. I forgot that my Word prevented me from touching her mind, too. I'd only ever forgotten three other times over the years, but it was instinct to try to reach out to her. I couldn't help myself.

By the time my vision cleared, and the pain subsided enough for me to climb to my feet, she'd already entered her building. I staggered forward quickly, wanting to go with her. I counted to thirty before I shadowed into Tria's apartment, again having chosen a spot she wouldn't see me. Her home was bare, devoid of personality. Other than the multitude of plants she'd brought indoors and the minimum amount of furniture needed, her place was empty. It wasn't bad or uninviting. My mate had done her best to try and make this house a home for however long she'd be in it, but it lacked something I couldn't put my finger on. Tria's habit of moving so often had taught her not to keep a lot of possessions. I wondered if she was running from something, or looking for something.

Tria sighed and tossed her tiny bag and keys onto the bench and leaned against the wall as she took off her stiletto heels. Once they were off, she was much smaller and my arms ached to hold her close.

Without a word, Tria went about her routine of getting ready for bed. It took strength gained from years of restraint that I remained outside the bathroom as she showered, but just being in her space was enough for now. I listened to the water and slid onto her bed, burying my face in her pillow and breathing deeply. Okay, so maybe I was a creeper, but I *needed* her. I couldn't touch her, not physically or mentally, and my body and soul ached to be with her every second of every day. Moments like this were all I had. There were brief fractions in time where I was able to drag her scent into my lungs. I could almost feel what it was to hold her in my arms again. My blood thickened and heated at the scent of her, and I cursed under my breath. I was torturing myself, but if I stayed away too long, that in itself was torture too, only she suffered as well. I knew we'd formed a bond all those years ago—our minds—so any time I spent away from her hurt her as much as it did me, only she didn't know why... and I had no way of telling her. If I asked any of my brothers to go to her and tell her why I wasn't there or what we were meant to be, it would act as a form of communication from me to her. It would break my Word and kill me. I'd sworn to never communicate with her again, that included through them. All I had were scattered minutes like this.

When I heard her shower turn off, I mentally cursed and forced myself to get up. I hurried to my corner of the apartment where I could see her but she wouldn't know I was there. On some level she was used to my presence which was why I assumed she didn't realize she could actually sense me all the time.

Dimitria exited the bathroom a few minutes later, dressed in a pair of black cotton panties that showed off the long length of her legs and a cut off T-shirt that bared her toned stomach. My already stiff dick hardened painfully at the view of her hardened nipples pressing into the material of her shirt, and I had to close my eyes to stop from reaching for her.

Fuck!

She wandered around her house with a small watering can, giving a drink to the various potted plants in her apartment, humming to herself as she went about her chore. The plants seemed to grow in her presence, they came alive in a way they just didn't when left on their own. I desperately wanted to sink into her mind and feel what she was feeling at that moment. She looked so content. I ached to feel that way again.

After another ten minutes, Tria checked the locks on her doors and windows before turning off the lights and crawling into bed, the bedside lamp the only light that stayed on. She'd been that way forever, never able to sleep in total darkness. I wondered if it made her feel less alone, and inwardly cursed. Until I found a way to break my Word without dying, I guess I'd never know. My heart pounded as she curled up on her side and closed her eyes. I could picture myself wrapping around her, holding her close and protecting her. The feeling was so real I could have sworn she was in my arms. She frowned suddenly and looked down at her pillows. When she leaned down to smell them, I mentally swore. Fuck. Could she smell me there?

She sniffed it again, but instead of looking suspicious or worried, she sank into the pillows and breathed deeply. My breath caught as I watched her gather comfort from my scent on her pillows, my heart clenching and gut somersaulting. She dragged in another deep breath, and I watched her entire body relax into the mattress.

She was asleep mere minutes later, and I stepped out of my hiding space to look at her closer. This was the only time I got this close to her. It was torture being here and not touching her, no doubt about it. But it was a torture I'd suffer as long as it got me close to her.

Hours later, she was still in a deep sleep. Any time she moved, she took the pillow that smelled like me with her, burrowing close to it. She looked so small and vulnerable in her sleep; she was practically swallowed by her bed. It was a real struggle not to slide up beside her and wrap her up.

"Let me take over now," Donovan suggested suddenly as he shadowed in beside me. I hated that I had to rely on my brothers to look over her, that I was forced to leave them alone with her. I knew deep down none of them would dare touch her or introduce themselves to her, but there was this irrational part of me that screamed and clawed at me. She was *mine!* Not theirs… and they weren't allowed to be near her.

But I had no choice.

"Go on home, brother. Let me take over for a little while and you get some rest."

I sighed and jerked my head up once in acknowledgement, knowing he was making sense. It hurt to watch her and never touch her, never *see* her see me, but it was better than trying to stay away all together. I had tried that in the beginning, but it never lasted long before I was running back to her, my soul aching just to be in her presence.

"You call me if something feels off or if she's in danger," I said, knowing the reminder wasn't necessary, but unable to simply leave.

"I've got her, Harkyn, but you'll be the first to know if she needs anything."

With a grateful nod at my brother, I drank in the sight of Dimitria curled up beneath the sheet on her bed, that platinum hair spread out like silk on her pillow, and left.

It hurt to leave her behind, but Nova was right. I needed rest. My circle of Hell was doing well, but I was falling behind on some of the upkeep and it needed my attention. I needed to sleep. Not that there was ever much of that anymore. I hadn't had more than three hours of sleep a night since I'd made that fucking promise to my mate, and I'd spent every waking moment regretting it, and then arguing with myself that it had been necessary.

I was grateful Nova could even spare the time.

Calixta, Mika, and Sawyer had all been pooling their power and resources to try and find Mika's sister. I was of the opinion that the Angels already had her which was why we couldn't find any trace of her, but I didn't feel like me voicing that would win any points. Until anyone found actual proof one way or the other as to where her sister had gone, everyone was hoping for the best. The last trace anyone was able to find was that she was in the same city as my mate. No one knew if it was by force or sheer coincidence, so until they found her, Nova was staying put. He went looking here and there, but Mika's sister knew how to hide, and he wasn't about to waste time when he knew he'd only find her if she wanted it.

To burn off steam and to feel useful, he was here helping me look after my mate.

I shadowed back to Hell and directly to my office. The desk was piled high with folders and paperwork, and I grimaced. It annoyed the shit out of me that we were immortal beings, but even we didn't get out of paperwork. Couldn't someone come up with a better system? I made a mental note to talk to my new sisters and get them to put their heads together. Maybe they could find a way to help us make things run more smoothly down here.

Knowing I couldn't put it off any longer, I moved to my desk and sat down, reaching for the folder on top.

"Ferin!" I called out as one of my Knights walked by my office.

"Sire?"

"Have you got some time?" I asked, putting the file in the correct pile.

"I can make some," he answered without hesitation. Ferin was one of my favorite Knights along with Eryd and Link. They were dependable, loyal to a fault, and always ready to help.

"Hand this lot of new recruits to Lynx and tell him to get started on their training. I want them done by the end of the month. Have the new Demons work on them. When you're done with that, come back and I'll have a new pile for you," I said. Ferin took the pile of about thirty newly molded souls and bowed his head before spinning on his heel to do as I asked. Out of all of us, Cole was usually the busiest as generally people weren't truly *evil* to land in Hell. Cole, Adrik, Malik, and I were generally busier than our other brothers. Things started to temper off from my circle through to Donovan's, then started increasing again from Cassius's circle to Corvin. It seemed people were either bad but not evil, or truly evil. The in-between was much rarer.

For every human we received, there was a file, a complete report on their every sin on Earth, and if they'd done anything to try and redeem themselves. Most days, all paperwork did was remind me that humans were the true force of evil in the world—not my kind. From these folders, I could see the work that needed to be done and could then ascertain how long it would take to tear the humanity from the soul and make it into a Demon.

I started skimming over the file before me, making notes where needed, and before I knew it, Ferin was back and the pile to my right was significantly higher. These souls had been waiting in the Pit for quite some time, but now it was time to properly rid them of whatever they'd done to land themselves here and make them ready to become Demons.

I handed over the new pile and yawned loudly, cracking my knuckles. It had been several hours, and I was tired, but I knew sleep wouldn't come unless I was bone tired, and so I got back to work, trying to banish the memory of crystal blue eyes and deep dimples from my mind.

CHAPTER TWO
DIMITRIA

I shouldn't have been surprised that my dreams had been filled with *him* again.

His smile, his eyes, that throaty chuckle that had once set off butterflies in my stomach. Dreaming of him only made my memories of the way he touched me so much more vivid, and I ached in a way I shouldn't. We hadn't spent much time together when we'd known one another, and yet I'd felt as if I knew him in a way I'd never know another soul. It didn't bother me that he was a Demon, not the way it should have. I'd never felt a connection to another person as intensely as I had with him, and it left me feeling homesick for that feeling again.

It took considerable effort to force myself out of the welcoming warmth of my bed after dreaming of being wrapped in his arms all night, but I was determined to keep moving, to not sink into that dark place where he no longer existed and I was left to face the world alone—again. I'd been alone most of my life, so being on my own was nothing new. But I'd never felt *truly* alone until the day he left me.

Har—nope. I shook my head and gritted my teeth, slamming the mental door shut. I'd promised myself I'd never think his name again... It hurt too much.

Forcing myself to move, I went about my morning, getting

dressed and brushing my hair, throwing dirty clothing into the hamper, and preparing to take it to the laundry downstairs.

As much as I tried not to think about him, I couldn't help myself. I wasn't sure there'd been a single day since he'd walked away when I hadn't thought about him, where he was, what he was doing, or if he was okay. Did he miss me? Did he wish he hadn't done the awful things he'd done?

Probably not.

I shook my head as I started brushing my teeth. I could have sworn last night I smelled him on my pillow, *that's* how pathetic I was. The man put me through my worst trauma, and then just… *left*. Sure, I'd told him to—screamed it, actually—but what man ever actually listened? He had to be the first one in history, and I hadn't really meant it. I mean, at the time I had, sure. I'd been upset, scared, shaking… but since he'd left, I was only half of my true self, and I hated admitting it. No, my entire worth and existence was not based on the opinions or presence of one man—one Demon. But I also didn't lie to myself. I'd fallen in love with a Demon King all those years ago, and he'd up and left me when things got tough. It hurt to remember those days, to realize he'd left me just like everyone else in my life had already done. I'd honestly thought he was different, that what we had was special and strong and so unique it had to last.

I rolled my eyes at myself in the mirror and spat into the sink, taking a moment to rinse out my mouth. When I stood, I looked myself over quickly and sighed. I hadn't changed that much since I was seventeen. I looked a little older, and I'd experienced more of life, but overall, I was the same girl I'd been back then.

My gaze traveled to the gold necklace I never took off, a pang of melancholy twisting in my gut. I knew this necklace backwards and forwards. It was gold all over with an onyx pendant. The pendant itself had a strange symbol in the back, a beautiful design with a sigil I didn't recognize and hadn't been able to decipher in four years.

He'd given it to me years ago. He'd said if I ever needed him, I could hold it and say his name, and he'd hear and come for me. I'd only ever had to use it once, and it had led to him leaving me forever.

I shook my head to get rid of the echoing screams and roars from that night and sucked in a sharp breath. There had been many lonely nights where I'd been tempted to call to him again, to beg him to come back, but pride hadn't let me. Pride, and this nagging voice in the back of my head that told me it would not be a good idea. Not sure what I'd even say to him if he did show up, I listened to that voice and refused to call, but I couldn't bring myself to take the necklace off.

I had a life now, one I was proud of, one I liked. I lived for a purpose. I got justice for those who couldn't rely on human laws to properly deliver, and I made sure those around me benefited from my skills. As much as a part of me missed him, I could survive without him and still have a fulfilling life. I just had to keep busy and force myself to stop dreaming about him or I'd waste away.

Drawing in another deep, cleansing breath, I raked my fingers through my hair and put it up into a rough ponytail as I left my bathroom. I had the morning free to do some chores before searching for my next job. I needed to make a stop by a clinic soon to see if there was anything I could do to help, a way to burn off some of the need to heal that had only been increasing lately. Usually that meant Angels and Demons were injured nearby, and considering this feeling had been building for weeks, it meant it was time to move on soon. I never could stay in one place too long.

I volunteered at local free clinics and hospitals when the need to heal became too great. It afforded me the opportunity to shake hands with someone and pass on a little healing energy, or hold someone's hand who was asleep or unconscious and heal them then. I was very careful not to be caught. The last thing I wanted was for people to see me healing and then word get out that I was a Witch or some kind of freak. It was part of the reason I moved around so often. It was also safer to keep moving. That, and I just couldn't seem to find a place that felt like home to me. I hadn't felt like I was home for four years, and it hadn't been because of the foster family I'd been living with, but rather the Demon King I snuck out to visit.

I huffed impatiently at myself. There I went again, thinking about him. Would there ever come a day where he wouldn't encroach on my thoughts? *Probably not*, I thought miserably.

Forcing thoughts of the Demon King from my head, I grabbed my basket of dirty washing and laundry powder and left my apartment. I was just locking the door behind me when I sensed I was not alone. I tried to keep my actions fluid and normal, but I was very aware that someone else was here, and that someone was *not* human.

A shiver of awareness tried to snake its way down my spine, and I let out a slow breath to calm myself. He was behind me, about four apartments down the hallway, and he was watching me. He knew I knew he was there, and that in itself was worrying. The power that rolled off him was immense, and it reminded me of the night that I met—for fuck's sake! I had to stop thinking of him and comparing everyone I met to *him*.

"Have you got something to say?" I asked, deciding to tackle this head on. I positioned myself to face the being, gathering power within myself and preparing to throw everything I had at him if he wanted to take me. I'd been warned long ago that there were those from Heaven or Hell who would try to take me if they discovered I was a Witch. I had been very careful to conceal myself from that first meeting, and I'd never slipped up, so I had no idea how this one had managed to find me, but I was not going to go with him without a fight.

"Sorry, I didn't mean to frighten you," he answered, his voice smooth and rich, a weapon in itself.

I studied the man before me. He was built wide and tall, tattooed, sexy, but casual. His short hair suited him, his face covered in a light scruff that looked purposefully grown. Bright green eyes shone back at me, and a knowing smirk tilted the corner of his lips. He was gorgeous, there was no doubt about it.

"I'm not frightened," I finally replied. And I wasn't. I knew how to use my power, and I would use it now if I had to.

"I can see that," he returned, taking a slow step towards me.

"Unless you want to find yourself thrown out of a three-story building, I suggest you keep some distance."

He raised an eyebrow in surprise, and his smile widened. "You have fire. That's good."

"Save me the flattery. What do you want?"

The man sighed and stepped forward again, and this time I dropped my basket at my feet and squared off, preparing to fight. He stopped and held up his hands at once in retreat.

"Sorry, I'll stay here. I just didn't think you'd want the whole floor hearing our conversation."

"I know everyone on this floor, and they're already gone for the day. Speak or leave."

He grinned and dropped his hands to his side. "My name is Tamas, what's yours?"

"If you've found me, then you already know, so I'll ask again. What do you want?"

"You're right," he answered. "I know your name is Dimitria, but you go by Tria. I know you're a bounty hunter. I know you help those in need regularly and you do it without the need for recognition which is very noble."

"Just get to what you want," I ordered, unnerved that he knew so much about me.

"I know you're a Witch."

My breath stilled in my lungs, and I let it out slowly. Of course he knew I was a Witch, that's why he was here. I just hadn't heard anyone say it in such a long time that it took me by surprise. I didn't say anything to that, I just waited.

"Right… you want to know what I want," he continued, scratching his head. "Look, this is going to sound weird, and like a lie… but I want to protect you."

"Yup, that does sound like a lie," I agreed, unimpressed.

"I know, but I also know you'd sense a lie, so I figure you'll hear it now," he replied quickly before carrying on. "I only want to protect you. Things out in my world are getting hairy, and Angels are being ruthless in their hunt for Witches. I don't want you to end up as their prisoner, so when danger started getting too close, I decided to take it upon myself to look out for you." The words themselves were ludicrous, and I wanted to scoff and laugh, to tell him to piss off and never come back. But I couldn't deny the ring of truth I heard. He meant what he said. How could that be? I studied him long and hard.

"You're a Demon."

He shrugged. "Something like that."

He was avoiding answering that one directly, and I let it go for now. "Did… did *he* send you?" I asked, licking my lips nervously.

There was only one other being I knew of to have this kind of power, this kind of presence, and it was too much of a coincidence that I smelled him on my pillow last night, and then another like him showed up today.

"Did who send me?" he asked, raising an eyebrow. His expression was totally impassive, and I couldn't tell what he was thinking one way or the other. I opened my mouth to explain but thought better of it. If *he* hadn't sent this guy—Tamas—after me, then he could be an enemy, and I didn't want to end up in some kind of power struggle.

"No one," I answered. "Look, while I appreciate your offer of protection, I'm going to decline. I can look after myself, thank you."

He smiled and shrugged. "I'm sure you can. But I found you, which means it's only a matter of time until Angels find you."

"Why do you care if they get me? What does my freedom do for you?"

"It would be better if you came with me," he said and then shook his head. "But since I know that won't happen, your freedom up here at least prevents them from gaining power with another Witch."

"And you expect me to believe you won't try to take me to Hell by force?" I asked, watching him carefully.

He shrugged a shoulder and put his hands into his front pockets. "I won't take you anywhere against your will. I just want to keep you safe. If you believe anything, believe that."

I didn't *want* to believe him. I mean, how could I? He was some kind of underworld Demon who apparently wanted to keep me safe at a time where Angels and Demons were in an arms race with Witches as the ammunition—and he wasn't going to take me for himself? And yet there was that ring of truth in his voice again. I felt it in that way I always knew when others were lying. "Even if that is true, I don't want your protection, nor do I want you hanging around. You can go now," I said before I bent down to pick up my basket.

He nodded as if he hadn't expected anything else from me and sighed. "Can you at least—I don't know, check in with me? I've taken a lease on the apartment at the end of the hall and I'm only here to make sure you're safe. I can give you a way to contact me if anything should happen and you need the backup."

All this kindness for apparently nothing was rubbing me the wrong way.

"Thanks, but I have backup if I need it." And I did. I just didn't think there'd be a time when I'd ever use the necklace again.

Tamas looked like he wanted to say something else, but after studying me a moment longer, he sighed and stepped aside, making a sweeping motion with his arm as if telling me I was free to go.

Keeping my guard up and defenses ready, I stepped past the Demon with my washing in hand and started down the stairs, keeping my senses alert as I went. It wasn't until I reached the laundry room that I let out a breath of relief. What the hell? Why was a Demon so interested in keeping me safe? While I believed it benefited them that Angels do not get a Witch on their side, I didn't believe that was his only reason for being here. There was something else going on I wasn't aware of yet, but I had a sinking feeling it wouldn't be long until it all came to light. I could only hope that when it did, I was ready for it.

CHAPTER THREE
HARKYN

Four Years Ago...

There was no *fucking* way.

I paused mid-step, my eyes wide and body still as I expanded my senses to make sure I wasn't imagining things... but it was real. There it was, powerful and intense, filled with rage and frustration, tangled with hopelessness and the need to run away. I could taste each emotion infused in the burst of energy so acutely, it was almost my own.

A Witch.

I hadn't sensed a Witch in many, *many* years, and yet I knew without a doubt the angry burst of energy that washed over me was from a Witch. How? Not just because Witches were supposed to be dead, but how was *I* feeling the emotion in that explosion of power?

Ignoring the barrage of questions that assailed me, I closed my eyes and sensed her out, looking for the direction in which the energy was coming from. The moment I had her location, I shadowed, determined to get to her before anyone else. I checked around me for signs of Angels or Demons, but none seemed to be present. The moment I arrived near her location, I carefully scanned the area. Could this be some kind of trap? Was I truly lucky enough to have found a Witch out on her own? Excitement began to grow within me as my search for anyone else came up empty.

No one. We were alone.

Looking around, I frowned. It was an empty field on the outskirts of town. There were a few dilapidated buildings somewhere in the distance, and as I scanned the area, I saw a sign.

Rodgers Real Estate – Gated Community Coming Soon!

Right, so the whole area had been abandoned or bought out to make way for new houses for rich people.

The sound of soft swearing caught my attention, and I moved further out into the field until I saw her.

The Witch.

I stayed back to observe her more thoroughly, still in shock. How was she here? How did she even exist? Donovan had said once that he believed some Witches had escaped the hunt and had gone into hiding, but we'd never seen any evidence to back that claim up. Faced with an actual Witch… I was beginning to think he was right.

She was young with white-blonde hair to her shoulders. In the moonlight, it looked silver. She was maybe five-foot-six with a feminine figure. Desire curled low as I watched her move gracefully. Despite the ripped jeans she wore or the black cardigan and heavy black boots, she was beautiful.

When she spun to pace the other way, I could see the dark eye makeup she wore and the way she roughly wiped away a few stray tears. Yep. The anger and helplessness coming from her was intense. I wondered why she wasn't protecting herself better, why she didn't cloak herself. Did she know how? Had her family failed to teach her?

Scanning my surroundings one more time, I finally relaxed a little, accepting we were alone. Wrapping myself in shadow again, I transported myself mere feet from her. The moment I appeared, I heard her swift intake of breath, and I hissed as a small zap of power hit me in the shoulder.

"Sorry!" she cried and then gave a choked sob, running her fingers through her hair. I took notice of her crystal blue eyes, and from the moment I saw them, something happened. The Earth itself seemed to stop turning, sounds around us disappeared. There was only her and those amazingly clear blue eyes.

Mine.

The thought tore through my head in an instant, and I had to actively plant my feet on the ground to prevent myself from going to her and kissing her, branding her, marking her in some way so she knew she was mine too.

What the fuck?

I had *never* had a reaction so strong to a woman before. *Never.*

"Are you hurt?" she asked, her words snapping me out of whatever trance I'd been in. "I'm so sorry," she said and bit her lip, looking frustrated all over again.

"I'm… fine," I answered, not even feeling the small sting anymore.

"Are you sure?" she asked and then began pacing. "Because I just don't seem to have control anymore. I can't do anything right. You frightened me, appearing out of nowhere, so I jumped and zapped you without thinking. And earlier tonight, I got so mad I almost set the house on fire. I mean, technically I *did* set the house on fire, but somehow, I was able to reverse the process," she explained hurriedly. Her voice was sharp and quick, twisted with so many emotions it was hard to dissect one from the other. "You don't seem scared," I pointed out, watching the woman's chest heave as she continued to rant.

She glared at me and shook her head. "Why would I be scared?"

"Because I appeared out of thin air."

"So?"

I smirked at her attitude and edged closer. "Do you know what I am?"

Her breathing slowed as she looked me over from head to toe and back again, and I'd be blind to miss the flash of interest across her face. She brushed back the fall of her white-blonde hair, her crystal blue eyes analyzing me.

"Well, you're not human, and for that I'm grateful," she finally answered.

I raised an eyebrow as I took another step closer. "Why?"

"Because if I hurt you, the likelihood of you dying is much lower," she clarified before she pivoted and started pacing again.

"Why would you try to hurt me?" I asked, moving closer until I was mere feet away.

"That's the thing," she said, spinning to face me with a sarcastic, self-deprecating laugh. "I wouldn't *try* to hurt you, but I could. I can't control it sometimes. I lose my grip on it when I'm mad or at my limit, and tonight I have no tolerance for anything."

I tipped my head to the side as I considered her and frowned as she ducked her head, the curtain of silky silver hair sliding forward to momentarily obscure her expression.

"You mean your magic?"

"Magic? Is that what it is?"

I frowned deeper and shook my head as realization began to sink in. "You have no idea what you are, do you?"

She scoffed and linked her fingers together on top of her head as she tried to drag in deep breaths. "A freak? Some kind of mutant?" She turned to face me, her eyes wide and full of questions and pain. "I feel everything, you know? People around me. *All the time*. I feel what they're feeling as if they're my own emotions, and it's driving me crazy. It will drive me completely nuts one day; I know it will. Sometimes I can block it, but other times, like now, when I'm mad or upset, the wall in my head, it just… it crumbles and I have no defense against anything."

There was a curious tugging in my heart at her words, at her helplessness, and was hit with the strangest urge to console her. "Right now," she began in a cracked voice. "I can feel your sympathy, that strange tug in your chest to help me, a feeling you don't understand because you're not used to it."

I nodded slowly because she was right, and I forced myself to shield my emotions better. I hadn't had to do it for so long, it took me a moment to slide that barrier back into place.

At once I saw the way her shoulders eased and she paused, her eyes wide. She was just some random Witch, but the sheer hopelessness coming off her was almost wrenching. What the fuck?

I didn't want to care for her. She was a Witch, a commodity my brothers and I could use to boost our power against the Angels. She would be another weapon in our extensive cache, so it shouldn't matter how she *felt*.

Even as I thought the words, they didn't sit right, and I inwardly snarled. I hated the idea of feeling anything more than attraction for her—to feel meant she would become a weakness—but I couldn't deny the way her tears twisted something inside me. What the *fuck* was going on?

Ignoring this problem for now, I decided to focus on another, and that was that she needed to learn to conceal herself, or a goddamn Angel was going to take her away.

"I—your feelings... they're gone. I can't feel you," she whispered.

"I am shielding myself," I explained.

Her eyes widened, and she gave a small, tired laugh. "You can do that?"

Nodding, I considered her carefully. "I can."

Tears glistened in those incredible eyes of hers and she sniffled and ducked her head. "You have no idea how nice this is... to be in someone's company and *not* feel. The silence. The peace..." She trailed off, closing her eyes in bliss and dropping her head back so she was facing the night sky.

I couldn't do anything except watch her, watch the serenity that passed over her face. It was like she'd been in agony for forever, and this was her first time feeling *nothing*. I couldn't imagine the kind of hell she had to have been in if she'd never learned how to shield herself. She was a full-grown woman who had felt the emotions of those around her since she was born... the hell she had to have been in was almost impossible to fathom. The fact that she was still coherent was nothing short of a miracle and a testament to her strength.

How? How had she never learned? Why didn't she know what she was? How did she not understand how to use her magic? She didn't seem alarmed by my appearance in her life, and she knew I wasn't human. And yet she wasn't running for the hills. Did she know others like me, others who weren't human? If so, why had none of them not shown her how to hide herself?

The questions in my head continued to bounce around and around, but my eyes never left her face, watching the way a small smile curved her full lips. The slim column of her throat drew my attention, and for a moment, I could imagine burying my face against it, dragging my nose upwards so that I could breathe her in. The vision of nipping and biting the skin there made my cock come to life, and I had to push down the need.

"I can help you," I offered before I really thought it through. She was a Witch, a rare asset, but more than that, I was hooked on her. I couldn't force my feet away, my mind seemed to be locked into one gear—help her. Parts of me came alive in her company. Pieces I didn't know where there were now humming in her presence, making me feel as if I'd found something incredibly important in this Witch, something I didn't quite understand but was rare nonetheless.

She gave another disbelieving laugh and shook her head before lowering it back down and pacing away again. "No one can help me."

"You said it yourself; I'm not human. I don't know how many other non-humans you've met, but I can help you get a handle on this."

She paused and considered me, and could tell how badly she wanted to believe me. "How?"

"You'd need to let me into your head," I answered quickly, pushing aside my own questions of *how* I felt her emotions so clearly.

She blinked at me in surprise and then scoffed. "No."

I sighed. I knew it would be a fight to get her to listen and do as I said. "I know it's not ideal, but I don't know how to explain it. I have to *show* you."

"Convenient," she snapped and spun the other way.

"I am far stronger than you, little warrior. I could take your mind over by force if I wanted to," I pointed out.

She glared at me, but otherwise my threat did nothing to stop her pacing. "Typical male. Apparently taking things by force isn't just for humans."

The implications of her words hit me, and I sucked in a sharp breath, tasting the air around her and anger bubbled beneath the surface of my skin. A sudden and irresistible urge raged through me with the need to tear apart whoever had hurt her. The force of my rage should have pulled me up short, but the edges of my vision were tinged red with the need for blood and vengeance, there was no stopping it.

I stepped towards her quickly so that when she spun to pace the other way, she ran right into me. She stumbled and would have fallen if I hadn't grabbed her wrist to steady her.

"What are you—"

"Who hurt you?"

She gaped at me. "Hurt me? No one hurt me," she answered, but she was lying.

"You implied that a human male had taken you by force. I can smell blood on you, and you are in a state of distress. Those things together do not paint a pretty picture, and so I want a name," I explained in a low voice before I lowered my head so she would be forced to look into my eyes. "Who. Hurt. You?"

The Witch slowly shook her head and licked her lips before taking in a steadying breath and letting it out.

"No one. At least, not in the way you're thinking."

I glared, and she pressed a hand against my chest. The feel of her small hand startled me enough that I looked down at it, stunned by the reaction I had at her touch. She wasn't even touching skin, but I felt the heat from her hand through my shirt like a brand. Why wasn't she struggling to get away? Why wasn't she trying to fight to get me away from her? Why did holding her like this feel so... right?

"What happened?" I demanded in a low growl, dragging my gaze back to hers.

She hesitated. "Why do you care?"

When I continued to glare, she swallowed hard and eased back slightly, but I refused to let her go until I had answers.

"I... I got into an argument with my—with someone. That's all. I called her some names and she... she slapped me. I cut my cheek on my tooth, but that's all. I left after. I was upset and I could feel my handle on my emotions slipping. When that happens, I can't guarantee someone else won't get hurt. My frustration started a fire, but thankfully I was able to reverse it before anyone else saw."

I considered her words but didn't let her go. She was telling the truth, and yet she wasn't. There was something she was excluding, and I wanted answers, but I had a feeling she would be reluctant to tell me.

"You-you said you can help me not feel things from those around me?" she asked softly, looking up at me with a shimmer of hope in those arctic blue eyes. I studied her a moment longer, trying to gauge if I could trust her words or not, but the longer I stared, the more I lost my train of thought. Her almond-shaped blue eyes were so pale, but there were veins of darker blue in them, and her right eye had a tiny fleck of gold in the upper right quadrant. I wasn't sure I'd ever seen a more beautiful pair of eyes in my entire existence. The feel of her in my arms made me want to pull her closer until we were one in the same. There was an urging inside me to make her mine, to keep her, to make sure she was safe from all harm. I'd never felt anything so powerful in my life, and while a part of me was suspicious of it, somewhere in my core I knew it was natural. With her, feeling like this, it was as it was meant to be.

"Did you hear me?" she whispered.

"What's your name?" I asked instead, not stepping back. I wasn't even sure if I was capable at this moment. Something about this Witch had me hooked, totally and completely sunk, and the strangest part was I didn't give a flying fuck. I was happy being trapped here in her eyes, in her company.

She considered me for a long moment before her lips softened into a small smile. "Dimitria. You?"

"Harkyn."

"Harkyn," she repeated, tasting my name on her tongue. Hearing it from her mouth had me tensing and my dick hardening in my jeans. For fuck's sake, what the hell was wrong with me?

"Dimitria," I whispered, testing how her name felt in my mouth. Those pale eyes of hers flared and her lids grew heavy as she focused on my mouth. The air between us was suddenly heavy, charged, full of possibility. What the hell was going on?

"Harkyn, will you help me?" she asked quietly and then drew in a slow breath before easing back slightly. "Will you show me how to control my emotions, so I don't hurt others?"

Slowly, I nodded and relinquished my hold on her, hating the immediate sense of loss and acute sense of wrong that hit me. There wasn't supposed to be space between us, we were supposed to be in contact, we were supposed to be melded together in some unbreakable and indefinable way, I just knew it. How I knew it was a mystery, but I did.

"We can't do it here, you've used a lot of magic in this area as it is, I don't want to risk us being found," I answered, clearing my throat. "Will you trust me to take you somewhere else?"

She hesitated only a moment before she threw back her shoulders with determination and lifted her chin. "Yes. I can feel that you mean me no harm."

Smiling softly, I held my hand out and she took it. I drew her in closer and wrapped my arms around her.

"What are you doing?" she asked breathily, but there was no protest in her voice.

"I am taking you somewhere safe. Hold onto me tightly," I instructed. She did as I said, and I held her tighter before I shadowed us away from there. In seconds, we came to a stop in an old, abandoned house, far away from that field.

"Woah," she whispered, a tinge of panic in her voice.

"Just breathe. The first time shadowing is a little rough," I told her. She staggered but gripped me tightly so she wouldn't fall. I waited as she got her bearings.

"Where are we?"

"Hopefully somewhere we won't be traced by others. I need to show you how to shield yourself from being found before I show you how to protect yourself against what others are feeling. Are you ready?"

"Why do I need to hide myself?"

"You're a Witch," I explained with a shrug.

She stared at me in disbelief, but instead of scoffing or arguing, she nodded slowly. "Okay."

I was momentarily stunned by her easy acceptance and stepped back. I could get into all the details later and ask all the questions I needed answers to. The most important thing now was that she was protected.

"There are those who would seek to take you and use your magic for their own gain. You are lucky no one has found you yet, and I can only attribute that to the fact we thought your kind were all dead, and a colossal coincidence that no one has ever been nearby when you've lost control like tonight."

"And-and who are *they*?" she asked.

"We'll talk about it all later. Right now, you need to protect yourself before we're found," I explained and steadied myself. Over the next half an hour I explained the basics of a cloaking spell, how it was performed, the words spoken, the specific finger movements for the conjuration and how long it would last. It took several tries, and I kept my mind open and senses alert for any sign of Angels or other Demons nearby who might have picked up on her magic as she attempted to shield herself. When she finally got it, the smile that lit up her face was near blinding. "Thank you," she whispered in awe.

"It's nothing, really."

"No, it's *not* nothing," she argued and shook her head. "I've never done anything with my magic before, nothing but chaos, and it's a kind of chaos I can't control. You showed me how to handle it tonight, how to take control. Thank you."

Her pure wonder and appreciation had that tugging inside me pulling harder, and I smiled my acceptance of her gratitude, feeling a little odd with the spread of warmth bloom across my chest. "You're welcome."

"Can you-can you show me how to protect myself against what everyone is feeling? I'm so lost, and I'm so tired of being affected by it all the time."

"Can you feel me?" I asked, genuinely curious. I stepped in closer to her. Her blue eyes watched me with interest, and the thrumming of her pulse in her neck pounded a little faster as I slowly eased down my guards. The blood began to rush in her veins and excitement sparked within her. As my guards lowered completely, she sucked in a sharp breath and her eyes widened, pupils blown wide. There was a delicious pink stain flooding her cheeks, and her heart rate kicked up several notches.

She nodded, licking her lips quickly. "I feel that."

Tension mounted between us, heat and unspoken desires built

and built until the ability to breathe was becoming a chore.

Just as I was about to yank her to me, Dimitria launched herself at me, and I caught her midair, my hands on her backside as she wrapped her legs around my waist. Her need was as acute as mine, and I'd never been one to turn down a good fuck. Something told me sharing this woman's body would be unlike anything I'd ever felt before.

I lifted my head as she crushed her lips to mine, and I was fucking *gone.* No one had ever tasted better than this Witch, I was sure of it. The weight of her in my arms was perfect, the feel of her hands in my hair was like she had always meant to be there. I took command of the kiss, slipped my tongue into her mouth, and was pleased when she kissed me with equal fervor. I staggered blindly forward until I had her pressed against a steel beam and adjusted her so that hard ridge of my erection pressed into her center. She gasped against my lips, and I rocked my hips, hungry for her.

Fuck, yes.

I felt her hunger for me and fed off it, knowing she was doing the same with me. It was a vicious cycle that wouldn't stop until we were both sated. Her hands slipped between us and tugged at my shirt until she could slip her hands beneath it and touch my bare chest. Every stroke of her fingers lit a fire within me I couldn't explain, and I kissed her harder and deeper, hungry for something I'd never had before.

"Brother, I need you."

I growled at the sound of Cassius's voice in my head at a moment like this. I was tempted to ignore him, and if it hadn't been for the fact that I felt his injuries and knew he was in a fight, I would have. But... my brothers were my brothers, and in the end, I'd always be there for them. If he wasn't contacting anyone else, there had to be a reason for it.

Tearing my mouth from Dimitria's, I pressed my forehead to hers and took a moment to get my breath back. "I… I have to go."

"What?" she asked, understandably confused.

"I—someone needs my help. I can't—I have to go."

"But, we were…" She trailed off, and the color in her cheeks deepened.

I grinned in satisfaction and barely refrained from taking what she was so readily offering, consequences be damned. "I know. But I have to go deal with this. I can take you home and come find you tomorrow? I can help you with your shields then," I offered. She pouted, and I leaned forward to nip her lower lip. Dimitria gasped and I kissed her again, hard, deep, craving her like I'd never craved another.

"Harkyn!"

Swearing under my breath, I pulled away and lowered the Witch to her feet. "Come, I'll take you home. What's the address?"

She told me, and I wrapped my arms around her, my body raging at me that we'd been interrupted. She gripped my shirt tightly and I lowered my head over hers and cleared my mind, shadowing us to her home. When we stopped, I was staring up at a large house with a high, black wrought-iron fence. Fancy. Someone down the street shouted at someone else before the sound of glass breaking followed. I looked at a house further down the street where a man shouted drunken obscenities and threw another glass bottle.

Humans.

It was weird for a house this nice to be on a block where other inhabitants acted like that, but I couldn't say I'd ever be an expert on humans and their actions. I shook my head and turned away when I saw the blue and red flash of the police car headed up the street and looked down at Dimitria. Her gaze was on the wrought iron fence, her eyes wide and gaze mournful.

"Are you okay here?" I asked, not liking that look on her face.

"Yeah. It's home, you know?" she answered and shrugged as she stepped out of my arms. I watched her as she took another step towards the gate before turning back to me quickly. "You promise you'll come back for me?"

The sliver of uncertainty in her eyes damn near killed me.

"You couldn't keep me away," I promised, still able to feel her in my arms, her lips on mine.

She searched my face, and a smile tugged at her lips when she was satisfied I was telling the truth.

With one last look at her beautiful eyes, I shadowed away from her.

CHAPTER FOUR
DIMITRIA

Four Years Ago...

It had been two days since my run in with Harkyn. I'd had time to think over everything that had happened, and now I had some questions.

What the heck was he, firstly? Where did he come from? How did he find me? What did he know about Witches—if that's really what I was—and could he teach me more about my magic? I'd tried over the last two days to erect a kind of shield in my head as he had done when he wanted to block me from feeling his emotions, but the only time I had any real success was when I was feeling calm and could catch my breath. Which wasn't often with everyone's emotions taking a battering ram to my head every damn day.

I was curious as to *what* he was. Obviously he wasn't a Witch. He said my kind were thought to be extinct, and he hadn't included himself in that sentence. What had happened to the other Witches? Was I in danger?

The questions pounded in my head almost as strongly as the feelings of those around me, and so I grabbed a notepad and pen and began writing them down in preparation for when he'd come for me again…

If he came for me.

He'd said he would, and he'd seemed to mean it at the time, but it had been two days and I hadn't heard a peep.

I sat back on the blanket I'd remembered to bring out to the empty field tonight and tipped my head back to look at the stars. This was my favorite spot. No, there wasn't anything amazing about it, there was no view or cool tree or anything really. There were just wide-open spaces with a beautiful view of the midnight sky above, where light pollution didn't obscure the stars. Best of all, there were no other people. I came here almost every night to get away from everything and to not *feel* everything all the time. It was exhausting, always being bombarded with the emotions of others, never quite knowing what *I* felt because it was mixed too strongly with others around me.

Out here, I could breathe, I could think, and I could actually get a sense of what I wanted. Mostly, I just wanted to get away from this life and these people. Most people wanted millions of dollars to buy fancy cars and a mansion, to travel and explore, and buy all the things they've ever wanted.

Me?

I wanted to buy a large plot of land in the middle of a forest surrounded by nothing but nature with a running stream and a cute little cottage. Maybe a dog or two? I'd never had a pet, but at least that would stave away any loneliness that might crop up. I just wanted solitude and peace. Was that so much to ask?

The wind changed subtly, and my thoughts drifted back to Harkyn and the way he smelled, the way he tasted, the strength in his incredible arms as he lifted me with such ease and pressed me against that steel beam. My cheeks warmed as I remembered the way he rocked his hips against me, the hardness in his jeans throbbing against me, the small groan he made as his tongue slipped into my mouth. I'd *never* been kissed like that in my entire life—as if he'd starve if he didn't devour me on the spot.

I'd replayed our moment together a million times in the last two days, and every time it left me blushing and aching for a repeat. Only this time, I didn't want any interruptions. Harkyn wasn't like anyone I'd ever known, and not just because of his power. The way he carried himself with such confidence was so attractive, but when he smiled, when he looked at me as if he saw more than anyone else ever did, it was heady.

He was very sure of himself—the way he moved, the way he touched me. I had a feeling there wasn't anything he did poorly, and feeling that confidence in him made me feel... I struggled to find a word that accurately described how it felt. To be in his arms, to let him take the lead and know he wasn't about to hurt me and that I could trust him to know what he was doing. There was a certainty deep inside me that said he'd never force me into anything, and to feel that was a real shock. I'd never been so sure about anyone in my life. The feeling was foreign.

I closed my eyes when I swore I could still smell him, and my lips curled upwards gently. There was something so comforting about that scent. It was crazy. *I* was crazy. My body felt alive. Wired. My blood hummed in my veins like I was about to get up and speak in front of a crowd, only there was no accompanying nausea or impending panic attack. There was just anticipation and need.

Desire for him washed over me. It made my body ache and throb, and I let out a long breath to try and get a hold of myself. It wasn't until the scent of him grew stronger that I realized these weren't my feelings. Or at least, they hadn't started out as just mine. I jumped to my feet and spun around, my gaze clashing with his gray-green eyes from where he stood several feet away. I couldn't have stopped the smile on my face had I tried. The smirk on his lips had my belly flipping, and I had to force my feet to stay where they were.

"You're back," I whispered.

He nodded and slowly stepped forward, the muscles beneath his black shirt rippling, his dark hair loose around his shoulders. I'd never seen a man in real life pull off long hair the way he did and not look weird or feminine. But *nothing* about Harkyn was feminine. Nothing about him looked soft. Every part of him fit together as if he'd been tailor made.

"I said I'd come back for you," he answered.

"It's been two days. I wasn't sure if you were going to—you know…" I trailed off, my mouth drying.

He considered me and tilted his head to the side. "You have trust issues."

I snickered and shrugged. "Doesn't everyone?"

His smile was slow and made my heart flutter nervously. "True."

I twisted my fingers together nervously when he remained where he was and bit my lower lip. I wanted him to come closer. I wanted to feel his heat, feel his arms around me. I wanted him to kiss me like he had done the other night, so powerfully that I'd lose my breath.

"Why are you so far away?" I asked.

He swallowed hard, his stunning eyes looking me over from head to toe and back again. I was wearing my usual jeans with rips at the knees and a plain gray t-shirt. I wasn't much to look at, but I wondered if my casual attire put him off somehow.

"I don't trust myself to be any closer," he admitted. I frowned and opened my mouth to ask why when the heat in his eyes registered and my cheeks burned with understanding.

"Oh."

Harkyn chuckled low, and the sound made butterflies flutter in my stomach and my pulse to pound harder. Licking my lips, I took a slow step forward and watched his gaze sharpen. I took another step, and then another. His eyes locked on my every move, his body winding tighter and tighter the closer I got.

"What do you think will happen if you get too close?" I asked, barely believing I had the guts to say it aloud. The gray of his eyes became more of a quicksilver, and I shivered at the way his breathing escalated. He was holding onto his restraint by a thread, but I didn't want him controlled. I might not know everything I wanted to know about him, but there was time for questions later.

"Little warrior, you had best be sure of your next moves. I am not adept at denying myself the things I want. And I want you with a desperation I'm not familiar with."

A thrill raced down my spine at those words. "Little warrior? You called me that last time too. Why?"

"You have not felt true peace since you came to be on this Earth, and still you persevere. I know a thing or two about pain and torture, and you have withstood what would have crumbled many. Surviving that deserves such a title, I think."

A curious melting sensation took over in my chest at his words, but I pushed it aside. I wasn't used to compliments like that, and right now, I had other things on my mind.

"Harkyn?"

His gray-green eyes bored into mine. "Yes?"

"I don't want you to deny yourself what you want. Or deny me of what *I* want," I whispered, barely able to believe I'd said it. His fists clenched at his side and his jaw tightened, something like a small growl resonating inside his chest.

"Dimitria," he said in a warning tone. I loved the way he said my name.

Shaking my head, I took a step towards him, and almost cried out for joy when he took the other, his strong arms whipping out to surround me and drag me to him. His mouth crashed down on mine, and I was ready for it. Pleasure and relief warred with each other in my head that I was finally back where I wanted to be, and that I hadn't exaggerated how incredible it was to kiss him, how amazing it felt to be with him again.

His hands slid to my ass where he lifted me into his arms, and I wrapped my legs around his waist. Excitement shot through me at the way he did that, the girly side of me giving a squeal of delight.

I had questions for him—so many questions—but they could all wait. I hadn't been able to stop thinking about him for two days, and if I could scratch this itch, if I could have him for this night, I could think straight later and ask everything I needed to know. Some deep and primal part of me *demanded* I have him, that we have this moment together, and I didn't want to argue with it. One moment I was wrapped in Harkyn's arms, and the next he was lowering me onto the blanket I brought with me. The moment my back hit the ground, he was on me, pressing the hard evidence of his desire against my center so that I gasped and gave a low moan. His forearms were braced either side of my head, one of his hands on my leg bringing it high up around his waist. I let instinct take over and I rocked against him, delighting in the way it made him moan against my mouth. He lifted his head to look down at me as his hand slid up my thigh to my stomach and under my shirt. I sucked in a breath, torn between pleasure at the feel of his hand on my bare skin, and the heat and need in his eyes. That was all *for me.*

"Harkyn," I whimpered, barely recognizing my own voice.

"Just feel, *cara,* I am with you. I will bring you nothing but pleasure," he encouraged, lowering his mouth to mine again. I was absolutely certain he knew just how to bring a woman pleasure.

His hand closed over my bra-encased breast, and I shivered at the unfamiliar feeling, but I wanted more. I was feeding off his desire for me, using it to enhance my own like a user looking for their next high. He was intoxicating, addictive, and I needed *more.*

I tugged at his shirt, desperate to feel him, and I gasped when with a click of his fingers, his shirt was gone, leaving him hot and bare chested above me. I tried to look at all of him, but there was so much to see, and I wanted him close again. Every part of him was sculpted, ridged, muscle gliding beneath tanned and tattooed skin.

"Bloody hell," I whispered in awe. He chuckled lowly and leaned in to kiss me again, and my wonder at his physique took a backseat to how amazing it felt to kiss him. His hand trailed down to the top button of my jeans and I tensed. He paused, having obviously felt it and looked down at me with searching eyes, waiting for me to give him the green light. A nagging tugged at my mind, and I decided I had to be honest with him about something.

"Uh…" I trailed off, trying to get my breath back so I could think and speak clearly through my need for him.

"What is it, *cara?*" he asked, raising a hand to brush my hair back from my face. That melting sensation came back in my chest, and I cleared my throat.

"You seem very, uh, experienced? And, uh, I don't want to disappoint you…" I stammered, not sure how to say what I needed to say. He stilled in a way that had my gaze flying back to his. His expression was blank, his eyes searching me, and I realized he was looking for something. He swallowed hard, a dawning feeling of unease and dread creeping over him.

"Dimitria, are you a virgin?" he asked.

"I—well, yes. But I want to—"

"How old are you?" he asked, cutting me off. Something in his tone told me it was not the time to play games, and I sighed.

"I'll be eighteen in six months," I answered hesitantly.

Harkyn's expression morphed into one of shock and then denial. "You're *seventeen?*"

I gnawed on my lower lip and bobbed my head once. "But I don't care that you're older or anything. Seriously, it's not a big deal, and I'll be eighteen soon anyway," I hurried to say.

Harkyn groaned and dropped his head onto my shoulder in dismay before he rolled off me and waved his hand so that a shirt covered his bare chest again and dropped a forearm over his eyes.

"I'm sorry, I just—I thought I should tell you. I wasn't teasing you and it wasn't something I was purposely keeping from you," I hurried to explain.

"It's fine, *cara*. I am the one who is sorry. I should have seen it, should have known," he said dejectedly.

"But I—does this mean we have to stop?"

Harkyn sighed and dropped his arm to look at me. I was sitting next to him, wishing there wasn't so much space between us.

"You're too young."

"In years, maybe," I corrected.

He nodded. "That's true. You do seem older than others your age, but you're still seventeen. I can't—*we* can't do this."

Embarrassment burnt my cheeks and I stood quickly, hurrying to fix the button on my jeans and tug my shirt back down. I could still feel him hard and throbbing between my legs. I could still feel his hand on my breast and his lips on mine, tugging, nipping, devouring.

"Dimitria," he murmured softly, but I kept my back to him, allowing my hair to come down like a shield between us, hiding my face from him. I felt like *such* an idiot!

"*Cara*, stop," Harkyn said again, and I could tell he was standing now. When I didn't look at him but continued to fuss with my clothes, he took my hand and tugged me to face him. I didn't look up though, I was too humiliated.

He sighed heavily and used one hand to cup my chin and tilt it up, and I got the full impact of those green-gray eyes.

"I didn't mean to embarrass you. I just… you deserve all the years you can get to be young. You deserve time."

"I know myself, Harkyn. I'm a pretty self-aware person. I know what I want and what I can handle. I want *you*," I explained, jerking my face carefully out of his grip. His hands fell to my hips where he gripped them tightly, and I crossed my arms over my chest.

"I want you too, *cara*. Never doubt that. But we cannot do this. Not now. Not yet."

"And what I want doesn't matter?" I asked, shooting him a sharp glance.

"Of course what you want matters. But I am old, Dimitria. Much older than you, and I have a personal code I live by. I will not be with someone as young as you are. I am sorry."

I frowned and looked him over. "You look like you're in your mid-thirties."

He grinned. "If that were the case, I would still be twice your age. But I am older than that. Much older."

I shook my head, not believing him. "How old?"

Chuckling, he ran a hand through his hair and sighed. "At a certain point you stop counting."

My eyes widened at his words, at what he implied, and I frowned. "Harkyn, what are you?"

He searched my face, and I caught the first signs of uncertainty there.

"Are you afraid to tell me?" I asked.

"I'm afraid you'll look at me differently and tell me to leave you alone. I don't want to go; I don't want to never see you again. I want to be around you as much as I can. I don't know what it is about you, *cara,* that makes me feel so drawn to you. Now knowing your age I'm more than worried. But I can't deny that every cell in my body screams at me to always be near you."

That was probably the most incredible thing anyone had ever said to me. Ever. I swallowed hard and let out a long breath. "You came back for me, Harkyn. No one has ever done that. I won't run from you, I promise."

He looked torn up at my words, and then disbelieving that I wouldn't run.

"Tell me," I urged.

Sighing, Harkyn stepped back from me and let his arms fall to his side.

"I'm a King of Hell, ruler of the fourth circle."

CHAPTER FIVE
HARKYN

Present Day

I walked down the stone halls, passing wooden door after wooden door, the shrieks and screams from behind them barely registering. It used to strike me as odd that a soul could make noise without the human flesh suit it had resided in on Earth, but I'd given up trying to figure out many things that happened here. Our mother, Lilith, had been instrumental in setting up the system of Hell, the tools we used, and the process we worked. At one point we'd all asked the questions, but after hundreds of thousands of years, things became more about muscle memory than actually remembering the why's and the how's of Hell. The fourth circle of Hell—my circle—was a confusing, circular maze. The hallways were thin in some areas, they branched off unexpectedly, jackknifed back the other way or broke off in many directions. It was done like this on purpose to confuse and disorient. While there was no chance of a prison break from any of the souls trapped here, I had designed it this way in the beginning because I hadn't been certain Angels wouldn't find their way here. I knew now though, after so many years of being here, that it was impossible. Only a Demon, or their mate, could shadow themselves here. Angels did not have that ability. My maze was not confusing for me or many of my older Demons as we knew the layout like the back of our hands, but I'd come to like how difficult it was to navigate for anyone else.

After catching up on that mountain of paperwork and delegating work to several of my most trusted Knights, I was happy to see things were running smoothly and the backlog of souls in need of stripping of their humanity was considerably less. It would never be empty, my intake was never ending, but at least it wasn't threatening to cause a massive problem anymore.

I paused at a sharp junction in the hallway and turned my head to the left, my gaze falling on a partially open door. I felt the soul inside—or rather, the last shred of it that remained. A soul was only a soul when it had humanity attached to it. While the soul did not take the form of the human it had once been, its consciousness was still attached and an active part of it. The consciousness was aware of everything that happened and was going to happen, and it felt every slice of the sharp tools used to strip it away, piece by piece. Hence the deserving torture they suffered in the afterlife.

I stepped to the door and pushed it open, watching my Demon as she used the tools I'd supplied and removed the last scrap of its human essence. Once the humanity was removed, it reverted back to its original form.

Pure energy.

I watched as the Knight stepped back to admire her work, and I stared at the bright ball of shining white light, the nearly translucent sheen that shimmered across its surface making it look almost like clear flowing water in a sphere. The sphere itself was no bigger than the palm of my hand, but the power in it was truly humbling.

Once the energy was in this form, it could be transformed into *anything,* as long as one had the know-how to do so. Neither I nor my brothers knew how to turn these balls of energy into anything other than Demons, but the possibilities never ceased to amaze me. God himself had created this. If some of the books were to be believed, this was what the essence of God looked like. He created Man from Himself, in His own image, and had therefore infused some of Himself in His creations to make it possible.

I was partial to believing this, only because my brothers and I were the only ones capable of making more Demons from these spheres of energy, and when we did so, we added a drop of our own blood to the mix. This allowed us to make them in *our* image, but to also provide us with a link to them which allowed us the control we needed to run Hell.

"Sire?"

I turned my attention to my Knight, her bright eyes watching me curiously, concerned.

"Did you need something from me?" she asked, putting down the torture implement.

I shook my head. "No, I just wanted to watch. This is the part I like the most."

Looking pleased, she nodded, turning to study the shining ball of energy. "It is impressive and satisfying."

I stepped forward and took the ball into my hands, feeling the thrum of it reverberate up my arms and throughout my entire being. It was like a mild electric shock, but instead of being painful or causing muscle-spasms, it was invigorating.

"Would you like me to take it to storage to await transformation?" my Knight asked.

I shook my head. "I'm headed that way now, I'll take it. You can go on to other work now."

She bowed her head once in respect before leaving the room. I stared at the ball of energy, transfixed, and then lowered it. I wondered briefly how a Witch's soul would look. I'd never seen one myself, since they never got sent to Hell, but they had to be different from the others in order to prevent them from being judged and simply recycled.

Shaking my head when images of Tria's crystal blue eyes flashed in my mind, I took the energy ball and started down the halls again, making a small detour to where we stored the spheres in preparation for making Demons. This room existed in a secondary realm inside each circle of Hell. Regular Demons could only enter so far to add one of these spheres here, but only a Demon King could remove one. It was a security feature someone thought up a long time ago when we became aware of the Rogue factions.

I entered the realm and moved seamlessly along the rows filled with these balls of energy and placed it on an empty shelf before leaving. There were millions in there waiting to become Demons, but we took our training seriously. I wasn't about to allow half-assed Demons to run about, and neither would my brothers. We each took a certain amount out every decade and we trained them brutally for that time. One could consider it another form of torture, but we were in a never-ending war with Angels. We needed soldiers who could hold their own and protect Hell and its inhabitants.

"Donovan, how is my mate?"

My brothers had been very insistent that I take some time away from constantly guarding my mate and see to the mess my realm had become while the others took turns helping me to guard Tria. They were right to do this, although it didn't stop me from feeling frustrated and helpless not being with her. Hell could not run efficiently if we constantly left things for long periods of time. Not to mention our Knights and other Demons needed firm leadership, and that meant showing up on the regular to make sure they all remembered who was in charge.

"Malik is looking over her for me. I had to see to an issue."

Frowning, I sought my brother's location in my head and shadowed to him at once. That hadn't been the plan. Why were they changing plans without first consulting me? Anger began to simmer in my blood so by the time I appeared in front of Donovan at his desk, I was ready to boil over.

"What do you mean Malik is looking after her? You agreed to do it," I asked, trying to be reasonable.

Donovan looked up from the paperwork in his hand and frowned. "I have been away from my realm longer than you have, Harkyn, and I need to get things sorted. I've popped in here and there to try and keep on top and to make sure things are running smoothly and they are—for the most part—but while I'm here and not searching for Mika's sister, I need to put in some effort."

I drew in a slow breath. "I know," I began, forcing myself to be calm. "But you are supposed to tell me of any changes *before* you make them. This is my mate, Donovan. She is everything to me, and all matters regarding her are for *me* to decide, not you, and not anyone else."

Donovan opened his mouth to argue and then snapped it shut, his eyes searching. "You know what? You're right. I'm sorry I didn't inform you of the change earlier. I'm assuming you're okay with it now?"

Glaring, I sighed and jerked my head sharply

. "Yes."

Donovan smiled and slapped the paperwork down on his desk. "Good. Have you seen Corvin or Devlin around?"

I frowned and shook my head. "Corvin said he had something to take care of, and Devlin said he was going with him to help sort it out."

"And neither of them have asked for help?" Donovan asked, pulling down a heavy box off a shelf to shuffle through it.

"Not that I know of."

Donovan frowned and looked up at me. "Do you know what they're up to?"

I scoffed and crossed my arms over my chest. "No one does. Those two fuckers might as well be joined at the hip. They're always leaving us out of whatever they're doing and never explain. Corvin is the worst for it, but Devlin does his fair share of incognito work."

Nova hesitated, his expression troubled. "Should we be worried? I don't like being kept out of the loop like this, and with how things are going at the moment, I feel like we're in the calm before the storm. They can't continue keeping shit from us."

I shrugged. "Try to force the information out of them, I dare you."

Nova flipped me the finger and I smirked. Trying to make Corvin or Devlin talk when they didn't want to was less than pointless. All of us could be stubborn up to a point and none of us would speak if we didn't want to, and Corvin and Devlin were no different.

"Any luck on finding a way to break your Word to your mate without dying?" Nova asked, but his tone was rich with knowing. It was my turn to flip him off and he grinned, putting away the box he was looking through after grabbing a folder from it.

Honestly, I had no fucking clue what I was going to do or how I was going to get close to Dimitria again. I'd fucked up by giving her my Word. Wait, no. That wasn't entirely true. It had been necessary at the time to save her from me, but I could have taken the time to word it better. I should have taken a breath and not let my anger and near feral desire to claim her obscure my clear thinking. *That's* where I'd fucked up.

"Fuck it, I'm going to go relieve Malik," I muttered aloud, taking a step backwards.

"Malik has it handled for now, and you have a realm to run," Donovan reminded.

"Fuck work. I need to be with my mate."

Donovan considered me and flicked his gaze away before sighing. "Would you like some help looking for something that will help you break your Word without dying?"

I frowned and shook my head. "How? We've all looked, we've all tried."

"Have you tried the basement?"

I grimaced. Hell's basement was a mess of discarded ideas, tools, and other implements. There were, however, old books down there that could maybe help, and at this point, anything was worth a go.

"No, I haven't tried there yet," I admitted with a sigh.

"Come on. Let's go into the basement and see if there's anything down there that will help," Donovan suggested, getting to his feet. Having someone to go through all that junk with was a bonus, and I trusted Malik to look over Dimitria until I could take over later tonight.

I nodded to Donovan and led the way to the basement while my head filled with thoughts of Dimitria again.

Fuck, I missed her.

~

DIMITRIA

After finishing my laundry, I left the building with my phone and wallet in my pocket, ready to go for a coffee. Luana's Café was only a few blocks away, and I loved the coffee there. The owner, Luana, actually lived in the same building which was why I'd gone to it in

the first place—supporting local businesswomen and all that. From my first sip, I was hooked.

Cutting down a side-street, I was a few feet inside a small alleyway when I had that feeling again, the one that told me I was not alone. I looked towards the end, expecting to see Tamas again, but was greeted with a new being. While I'd never had any firsthand one-on-one interactions with an Angel before, I knew that's exactly what I was looking at now. She was beautiful, unnaturally so, with rich, dark skin and short shaved hair that brought out her bone-structure. I was so momentarily stunned by her unavoidable beauty that I temporarily forgot the danger she posed.

"Witch," she said, her voice husky and intriguing.

"Did you just call me a bitch?" I asked, purposely mishearing her.

"I do not like games, and I have no time. I am giving you the chance to come with me now before force is necessary. Trust me, coming voluntarily will guarantee you a much more comfortable experience with my superiors."

A cold chill rippled over me, and I looked around for a quick escape. "I don't know who you are or who you're looking for, but I'm leaving," I said, backing up a step. There was a whoosh of air as I turned my back on her, and she was suddenly standing in front of me, her rich brown eyes emotionless and steady.

"I said I don't have time for games. Come now, or I'll take you anyway," she warned.

"Didn't you hear that all work and no play make Angels batshit crazy?"

At the sound of the new voice, I stepped back quickly and twisted to the side so I could keep both creatures in sight. Tamas had joined us. He was leaning against the opposite wall a few feet away, his shoulder propped against it and one ankle crossed lazily over the other while he surveyed us as if we were nothing more than a passing curiosity.

"Filth," the Angel hissed, her expression morphing into one of hate.

"You say the sweetest things," he returned, pressing a hand to his chest as if he were choked up.

The Angel gripped a silver handled blade she pulled from out of nowhere and moved into a fighting stance. I wanted to get the hell out of there. We were in close quarters, and I was about to be in the middle of a fight between an Angel and a Demon.

"You can leave, you know?" Tamas said to the Angel, slowly pushing off the wall to step closer, his movements slow and lazy as if he hadn't a care in the world.

"As can you," the Angel hissed out.

"Actually, I can't. It's complicated, but basically, that Witch is under my protection which means she can't go anywhere with you."

"The Witch belongs to no one and will come with me. If you value your life, you'll leave," the Angel warned. I edged slowly to my left, hoping neither of them saw my small movements. While I wasn't interested in going with Tamas, he seemed to be the lesser of two evils. I inwardly snickered at my words. A Demon was the lesser of two evils, really?

Tamas gave a low chuckle and I stiffened when he produced a black blade from out of nowhere, his expression turning serious. "You know who I am, Angel—*what* I am. This is more of a chance I've ever given any of your kind. Leave now and live to fight another day. You make one move toward the Witch, and you will die."

The Angel bared her teeth in a low hiss. "Never."

Tamas sighed and shrugged as if dealing with her was no more than a nuisance. "Suit yourself. Tria, I apologize for the violence you're about to witness."

I opened my mouth to say something—anything—but was left speechless when both beings rushed toward one another with supernatural speed. They clashed hard, and I gasped and scurried out of the way. Wings erupted somewhere in there, beautiful and white, before they were gone just as quickly. There was the sound of fighting, grunts and curses, flesh hitting flesh. I held my mental barriers higher to prevent myself feeling the pain they were inflicting on one another. What was I meant to do? I wanted to run, to get the hell out of there and away from it all, but my conscience wouldn't let me leave Tamas after he'd come to help me. Sure, his motives were likely corrupt, but it didn't negate the fact that he could get hurt preventing an Angel from getting their hands on me.

I looked around quickly to make sure no one was witnessing this fight and gathered my magic. I waited, watching the fight with sharp eyes, and the moment Tamas stepped back from the Angel, I threw my magic, hitting the Angel square in the chest. She gasped and flew backwards, her head hitting the brick wall with a sickening thud.

"Turn around, Tria," Tamas ordered without looking at me as he advanced on the Angel, blade raised. I spun around in time, but it didn't stop me from hearing the wet sound of the blade sinking into flesh, or the gasping sound from the Angel. My stomach twisted and I closed my eyes and focused on my breathing as memories tried to assail me of past violence I'd been witness to. There was a whoosh of sound, like the sound of giant wings taking off, and when I took a cautious look behind me, the Angel was gone leaving nothing but a blood smear, and Tamas staring at me with concern.

"Are you hurt?" he asked, keeping his distance.

I swallowed hard and turned more fully to look at him before I shook my head. "No."

His expression cleared and his shoulders relaxed when he was sure I was okay. Confusion jumbled my thoughts as I looked at the Demon before me, and I frowned.

"What the hell do you want from me?" I demanded.

He raised an eyebrow and shook his head again. "Nothing. I just want to keep you safe."

"But why? I'm no one to you, and yet you know so much about me. You even knew I didn't like violence and prevented me from watching you kill an Angel. How do you know all this and what do you get out of it?"

Tamas considered me thoughtfully, and I watched him for the slightest sign that he was about to lie. After several long moments that dragged on, he sighed and took a slow step forward. When I didn't back up, he took two more until he was only a few feet away.

"You want answers, and you are more than entitled to them. But things are precarious right now, and I'm not free to tell you everything or I risk the safety of others. I'm involved in a very complex situation where, if you asked the right questions and had more information than you should at this time, I would risk the life of someone else. I want to be honest with you, but I cannot risk the safety of others. Can you believe that?"

I blinked at him stupidly for a moment. That certainly hadn't been what I had expected him to say. He was caring, concerned, and honest. None of these qualities were what I expected when speaking to a Demon. Sure, I'd seen them in the Demon King all those years ago, but I thought that was a fluke, and over time I thought maybe it was an act. Now?

I grimaced and ran a hand over my hair before tugging it loose and running my fingers through it. I wanted to go back to bed after all this crap, but it was still morning and my days off were rare.

"I believe you," I finally answered. I did. I didn't trust that I believed him, but his words were true and honest, and my gut was telling me he didn't want to hurt me or take me away.

Tamas's shoulders relaxed, and he drew in a slow breath. "Thank you."

I smiled softly and looked around, a little lost about what to do now. I cleared my throat and straightened up, considering him. I had questions, ones I'd given up thinking I could get answers to, but maybe Tamas could help? "I'm headed out for a coffee. Care to join me?"

Tamas's eyes brightened at my offer, and he smiled. "I'd love to."

CHAPTER SIX
DIMITRIA

We entered the coffee shop, the small bell above the door signaling our entrance. I glanced around, looking for a spare table. I knew the minute Luana saw us by the wave of excitement and lust that hit me. I guess she'd noticed Tamas.

"Prepare yourself," I warned Tamas as Luana bounded over to us, a giant grin on her face and an excited energy rolling off her. She had always been happy and pleasant to me whenever I came in, trying to make sure I knew I was welcome here. If I was the kind of person who had friends, I could imagine us hitting it off. I liked her. She was hardworking, loved her twin boys, and worked hard for everything she got.

"Well, hello there, honey; I'm glad you could make it in today," Luana greeted happily, holding out her hand to Tamas. "I'm Luana."

Tamas's lips twitched, and his eyes roamed over her with interest. "Tamas."

I watched Luana's breath catch and her interest increase and shook my head.

"Can we get a table for two, Lu?"

Luana slowly dragged her attention back to me and blinked twice before seeming to come back to herself. "A table? S-sure," she stuttered and turned away from us to lead us to our spot.

We followed in silence, and I flicked a glance at Tamas to see his eyes on the woman's backside. I elbowed him, and he widened his eyes at me with a look of feigned innocence.

"Can I get you anything?" Luana asked once we took our seats.

"A jasmine and green tea please, and the biggest slice of chocolate cake you have," I ordered. Luana beamed and turned her attention to Tamas who was looking at her with an expression I could only consider 'adult content.'

"Choose for me, lovely Luana. I'll devour anything you want to give me."

A wave of Luana's lust hit me and I reinforced my mental barriers.

"Umm, okay," she stammered. She clumsily collected our menus, spared Tamas a bewildered smile before she hurried off to get our orders.

"You're shameless," I said, leaning forward on the table. Tamas chuckled low, and I had to admit, the sound did something to me. "I can't help it if women find me attractive. And your friend? She's fucking gorgeous."

"She is," I agreed and braced my forearms on the table, not bothering to correct his assumption that we were friends. "And if you go near her and hurt her, physically or otherwise, I'll see to it that your dick never works properly again. Understand?"

Tamas's eyes went comically wide, and I curled my lips in satisfaction as his legs shuffled beneath the table in what I suspect was an attempt to shield his manhood.

"Understood," he answered and cleared his throat.

"Good."

Luana was a good woman with beautiful kids and had struggled to make ends meet for years. She wasn't lucky in love, and like hell I was going to let Tamas swoop in and break her heart. I knew what it was to have my heart broken by one of his kind, and I'd save her from that same fate if I could help it. We might not be friends, but she deserved to have someone look out for her.

"Now, what the hell happened out there?" I asked, nodding out to the streets.

Tamas sighed and got comfortable in his seat before he leaned forward too, mirroring my position.

"What do you know about the war going on between my kind and those fluffy fairies?"

I snort-laughed at his description of the Angels and he smiled, humor brightening his eyes. I finally settled back in my seat and sighed, shaking my head.

"Practically nothing. I know there is a war, I know it's not good for me to end up with either side, and I know you'll all do just about anything to get a Witch. I have no idea how many of *my* kind are out there, I've never met another Witch."

"There are a few reasons Angels want you," Tamas began and seemed to consider his words. "The main reasons they want your kind—at least the ones we're aware of—are that your kind are the only ones capable of healing a Demon Blade wound. Our knives are lethal to them, the only way to heal it is by getting the blood of the Demon who stabbed them, or have a Witch heal it. As we're very reluctant to hand over our blood to those fuckers, you can understand why they want you."

I pondered this for a moment, interest lighting up inside me despite my best efforts not to get involved. I'd never had any real answers my whole life. I'd gotten a few answers four years ago, but then everything had gone to hell in a handbasket. "Do Angel Blades hurt your kind the same way?"

Tamas's lips thinned and he nodded. Right. So his kind wanted mine for the same reasons the Angels wanted me.

"What else? You said there were other reasons."

Tamas nodded. "Healing, at least in our opinion, is the main reason. But also, if they're able to get a big enough coven, then the Witches can do considerable damage to us. Your magic is nothing to sneer at, and when you put a group of you together, there's not a lot that can stop you. We believe they're building an army big enough to take out the Kings of Hell."

My breath caught sharply in my lungs at those words, and I knew I'd frozen up. The Kings of Hell? That meant...

"Here are your drinks," Luana interrupted with a cheery tone, and I jumped in my seat.

"Uh, thanks, Lu. How's work today?" I asked, taking a moment to process the information Tamas had just told me.

"Busy, so that's good. How's your day?" she asked, but I caught the way her eyes slipped back to Tamas.

"Not bad," I answered and forced myself to pay attention to the conversation. "Tamas just moved into our building, and he caught me as I was leaving and asked me if I knew where he could get a good cup of coffee, so I brought him here."

"Aww," Luana drew out the word in an 'aww shucks' kind of way and beamed.

"She didn't say anything about the view being just as delectable, though," Tamas added, his tone layered with innuendo, his green eyes unwavering from her face.

I wanted to throw my drink at him and tell him to stop hitting on her, but if what I sensed coming from Luana was any indication, then she was relishing this kind of attention. She was a beautiful woman, there was no doubt about it, but I knew when men saw that she came with two boys, the cowards tended to run the other way. Tamas didn't know about the twins, but she deserved to be looked at as the stunning woman she was.

"Oh, wow," she responded in a breathy voice. Tamas grinned knowingly, that smirk sexy as hell and eyes speaking of long, hot nights between the sheets. Seriously, it should be illegal for a smile to say so much.

"So…" I trailed off, feeling monumentally awkward.

"Right," Luana said, snapping out of it and taking a step back. "Uh, I'll be over there if you guys need anything else."

"Thanks, Lu," I said with a small laugh.

"I'll remember that," Tamas added. Luana's steps faltered and she glanced at him with a flustered expression before moving for the counter again.

"Limp dick for the rest of your life, Tamas," I reminded.

He laughed, and not just a small chuckle, but a loud bark of laughter where he threw his head back. The kind of laugh that came from deep inside. I watched, momentarily struck dumb and then shook my head, unable to hold back my own smile.

When he moved his attention back to me, he was wiping away tears at the corner of his eyes, his grin wide.

"I haven't laughed like that in fucking ages."

I shrugged, trying not to like the guy. He was a freaking *Demon* for crying out loud. It was bad enough that I had fallen in love with one years ago, I was not allowed to have best friend vibes for another. Just… no.

"What's that?"

I frowned at Tamas and he indicated with a nod of his head to the necklace I'd been absentmindedly fiddling with.

"Oh, umm, it's just a necklace."

Tamas raised an eyebrow and leaned closer, his eyes on the pendant. "You expect me to be honest with you, and you won't do me the same courtesy?"

"What makes you think it's anything more?" I returned, trying to dodge the question.

His eyes fell back to the pendant, and he shrugged before leaning back in his chair in a deceptively lazy manner. "I recognize the symbol. It's Demonic, from the fourth circle of Hell. For you to have it means that someone high up in the Demonic hierarchy gave it to you. I can only think of one Demon who would, actually. I was just curious as to why you had it—and how."

My heart thudded in my chest at this revelation and I wanted to run far and fast, but at the same time, shake him until he told me where the Demon King was and what he'd been up to these last four years, and why he stayed gone. His green eyes studied me curiously, but I couldn't read anything more from him; not his tone, not his aura or general vibe. Nothing told me what he was really thinking.

"Someone gave it to me years ago," I finally answered, my voice rougher than normal.

Tamas nodded slowly, his expression thoughtful and shifted in his seat. "Do you still talk to them?"

I shook my head. "No. They're gone now, and they're not coming back."

Tamas opened his mouth and then closed it, seemingly struggling for words. "Because you asked them not to? Or because they refuse to?"

I shrugged. "Both, I guess. I shouted at him to go away, and he did. He hasn't been back since…" I trailed off, looking down at my hot mug of tea instead of the Demon across from me.

"And, do you *want* him to come back?"

I thought about his question long and hard, and Tamas didn't rush me to answer even once. Did I want my King back? Or would I be better off with him out of my life for good? He'd known I was a Witch when we met, he'd helped me shield myself, helped me learn to heal, given me texts on conjuring and spell craft. He'd taught me a lot of what I knew now, and he hadn't once tried to take me to Hell with him. Why not? Tamas had said there was a war going on between Angels and Demons, and that both sides were scouring the Earth for any signs of Witches so that they could take them as their own. If that was the case, then why hadn't he taken me when I'd been young and inexperienced in magic? Or was it that there was something so fundamentally unlovable about me that kept him from taking me with him? Something that kept him away even now? Tamas's question rang in my head again. Was Tamas asking because he could reach out to my Demon King and ask? I inwardly flinched. No, thank you. He was gone. He was powerful and fierce. If he wanted to find me at any point these last four years, he could have. He'd chosen to leave me alone, and I wasn't going to say anything that would tempt Tamas to broach the subject with him.

I shook my head and cleared my throat, pulling myself out of those thoughts. "It doesn't matter what I want. He's gone, he's obviously not coming back, and I'd like to drop the subject now," I answered, straightening in my seat and forcing a note of finality in my voice.

More than two hours passed as we talked, and I was informed about everything there was to know about the war between Angels and Demons and how my kind got caught up in the middle of it. While I reminded myself to constantly question everything he said, at the end of the day, it seemed legit, and he seemed to honestly believe everything he was saying. I wasn't on the side of Demons, hell no, but after hearing about how all these wars began in the first place, I was definitely not on Team Angel either. Those assholes could stay up there with their pearly gates and halos for all I cared. I just wanted to be left out of it.

"I should get going," Tamas said after a while.

"Thanks for what you did today. You know, in the alley?"

His lips tilted in a half-grin and he got to his feet. "Like I said, I only want to protect you. If you insist on staying up here on the surface, then that's where I'll be too."

"There's an option for me to go with you to Hell?" I asked, slowly getting up as well.

He considered me seriously for several seconds and nodded slowly. "There would be strict rules about where you could go—for your own safety—but yes, it's an option."

"Huh," I said interestedly. "How about we leave that as a last resort?"

Tamas grinned. "Agreed."

We stood in silence a moment longer and I watched his gaze travel back to my necklace. "You know," he began slowly and shoved his hands back into his front pockets. "That necklace, it's unique. For the Demon in question to have given it to you, it means he cared a lot about you, about your safety. If he hasn't come back for you all these years, then there's probably a good reason as to why. He wouldn't have given that to just anyone. You're important to him."

My heart pounded hard at his words, and something deep inside me wept at hearing them. I wanted to believe him, I really did, but hoping for something as unlikely as that was only going to set me up for heartbreak. I'd accepted what we were and what we weren't. I didn't want to feel all that rejection again.

"Thanks, Tamas. I'll see you around," I replied, trying not to sound too dismissive.

His lips quirked up knowingly and he nodded once. He turned his attention to Luana as she cleared the table next to us and his expression heated.

"I hope to see you around, Luana. Being in the same building might have some benefits," Tamas said, stepping close to my friend—closer than I thought was necessary—and smiled suggestively.

"True," she returned thoughtfully. "If you ever need to borrow a cup of sugar, you know where to find me."

Tamas's grin was slow and sexy, and Luana practically purred in return, her eyes telling him without words how welcome he was in her home—and her bed.

"You know, I think I forgot to go shopping this week. I expect I'll need some neighborly hospitality sooner rather than later."

"Well, helping each other out is what good neighbors do. If you happen to need any help this week, I'll be available tomorrow after four," Luana added innocently.

Tamas grinned again, and I felt like a total voyeur watching the exchange happening between them.

"Good to know," he added in a low voice.

The tension between them built before Tamas winked and stepped away. We both watched him saunter out of the café, and it wasn't until the door closed behind him that Luana let out a long breath and sank into the chair he'd vacated. She pulled a menu from a neighboring table and began fanning herself with it.

I burst into laughter, and she couldn't hid her humor as she shook her head. "I thought for sure I was going to burst into flames. Did you see how he looked at me?" she exclaimed, her chest rising and falling as if she was winded.

"I did. And I gotta say, I've seen adult rated content with less sexual tension than you two had in a single conversation."

"You watch porn?" Luana asked curiously, momentarily sidetracked.

"Read it, actually. I misspoke. Smut books are so worth the

investment when you're single and lacking a sex life," I replied without shame.

Luana laughed breathily and flicked a glance back to the door as if expecting to see him there. "Did that really just happen?"

I smirked. "Yes. And I think you've got yourself a booty call tomorrow after four."

Her eyes widened and she got up suddenly. "Shit, I need to clean the apartment. And shave, and do my hair, and do some serious self-care tonight."

I laughed again and shook my head as she stood up. She took a single step away before turning back to me, her expression curious.

"I'm not stepping on your toes here, am I?"

I frowned and tipped my head to the side in confusion.

She smiled awkwardly and waved her hand in the direction of the door. "With Tamas, I mean. You two came in together, you've been here for over two hours talking. Are you into him? Cause honey, if you've got the hots for him, I'm happy to step back—"

"Luana, stop," I interrupted, holding up a hand. "I appreciate the solidarity, but he's all yours. I was just being friendly in the most basic sense. The minute he walked in and saw you, you were on his radar. You're not encroaching on my territory *at all*."

"Really?"

"Yes," I answered with amusement. "You can feel free to enjoy him, just—"

"Be careful?" she finished for me, a small affectionate look on her face.

"I get the impression he's not one for the long-haul," I added with a one-shouldered shrug.

She made a dismissive sound and waved the small hand towel in her hand. "When a man who looks like that wants a ride in my bed, I'm taking him up on it. I don't want a permanent man, so this works out perfectly."

I laughed and grinned. "Well then, enjoy."

Luana bent down to hug me. "I intend to."

I shook my head and smiled as she stepped away to clear more tables and then sighed. I was exhausted and wanted to go back home. Maybe I'd soak in the tub before bed tonight so I could get a good night's rest before job-hunting tomorrow.

I waved to Luana as I headed for the door and turned back in time to accidentally knock into a woman just leaving.

"Oh, shit!" I gasped as her coffee cup splashed all down her arm before falling to the floor.

"Ouch!" She hissed and began rolling up the white sleeves of her blouse. I felt the pain radiating off her and without thinking, took her arm in my hands at once. I poured healing energy into her quickly, examining the rest of her.

"Are you okay? I'm so sorry, I didn't see you."

"No. I mean yes, I'm fine. I don't think I'm that burned," she assured, and I continued to move my hands as if I were checking her over, but I hurried to heal what I could.

"It doesn't look like it, no," I agreed, happy to take the pain away quickly. "Luana, can I grab another of whatever this was?" I called out to my friend as one of her waitresses came by with a mop. Luana waved to acknowledge me, and I looked back to the woman.

"Oh, you don't need to do that. It was an accident," she assured.

"I do. I should have been paying more attention."

When I was through healing her, I let her go and ran a hand through my hair. The woman before me watched me curiously, and I took her in. She was about an inch or two shorter than me with black hair twisted in some fancy knot at the base of her neck so that her hair rested mid-way down her back, and her eyes were a beautiful shade of dark green. Something about her nagged at me, and when I looked down at her arm to make sure there were no burns, I caught sight of a mark there. I reached out to take her arm again and she tipped her head to the side.

"Don't worry, you got it all."

I frowned and looked up at her. "What do you mean?"

"That's a birthmark," she said, referring to the star-shaped mark on her inner elbow. "But you healed me of the burn."

Her words took precious seconds to sink in, and I dropped her arm and stepped back at once. "Who are you?"

She didn't *feel* like an Angel, and she didn't look like any Demon I'd ever seen before, but I guess they came in all forms.

"Someone who wants to help you," she answered.

I shook my head. "You're the second one today. I'm not buying it. I need to leave."

I moved to push past her, an escape plan already forming in my head. Her hand snaked out and she gripped my wrist. When I turned to look back at her, she dropped my arm at once and shook her head.

"You don't need to be afraid, I'm just like you."

I raised an eyebrow. "Just like me? And what am I?"

She smiled kindly in understanding. "A Witch, of course."

CHAPTER SEVEN
TAMAS

I shadowed into the Arrival Room, a smirk still on my face at the thought of the delectable Luana. It had been a while since I'd gotten laid, and that woman was several shades of stunning. From her darker skin, that incredible head of hair, those penetrating gold-like eyes, and that smile? How the fuck was a woman like her single? I almost salivated on the spot thinking about her delectable curves just waiting for a man to grip as he took her in bed in every possible way. I shook my head. Seeing her and knowing she was single only cemented the fact in my head that humans were all complete morons. Did none of them see the smoke show Luana was?

I knew from a brief brush against her mind that she had twin boys, so maybe that was the problem. I didn't find it to be an issue, but human men in particular had always shown a certain reluctance to being with a woman with kids. I had the suspicion it was because her kids would always come before them, and they didn't like that.

Like I said—morons.

A door opened in the hallway, and I looked up in time to see Donovan exit his realm. I looked around us quickly before he jerked his head at me to follow him. No one was around, but that didn't mean we'd always be alone, and this conversation was better had behind closed doors.

"How did it go?" he asked as he closed the door behind me. Donovan's realm changed often, but for right now it looked like a modern human house with cold colors, metal and steel fixtures, black tables and gray walls. The phrase *bachelor pad* came to mind.

I didn't like it.

"It started off rocky but ended well. I tried to talk to her at first, but she refused to listen to me," I began.

Nova nodded and crossed his arms over his chest. "We were expecting some resistance. Did you get her to listen?"

"Yeah," I answered before sitting on a small black leather couch in the corner. I grimaced—it was uncomfortable as shit. "She, uh, she was leaving the building and some Angel appeared and tried to take her. I was there, so I dealt with it."

Donovan looked concerned. "So, they know where she lives?"

I shrugged. "It's possible. But she was outside and down a small alley, so maybe they just happened to spot her and didn't see what building she came out of?" I suggested.

Donovan didn't look convinced, but as no other Angels appeared to try and take her, I was going to assume I was right.

"We know from Harkyn that she doesn't like violence," Nova reminded.

"I know," I answered and stood up to look for another chair. "I warned her and gave her time to look away when it came time to dispatch the Angel. I even gave the fucker a chance to leave unharmed—she didn't take it. I think for Dimitria, seeing me put actions behind my words and protect her without forcing her to come with me helped make her trust me a little. Maybe I should thank the Angels for sending a soldier at the opportune time."

"We'll send them a fruit basket," Nova deadpanned.

I grinned. "Anyway, she invited me for coffee and we got to

talking. She has a Token from Harkyn," I added, referring to the necklace I'd seen her wearing.

"A Token? So, she could summon him at any point, and he'd have no choice but to answer. Fuck," Nova swore and dropped his arms to run one hand over his head.

"I don't think that'll be an issue," I answered and sat on the two-seater modular, propping my feet up. When this one proved to be no more comfortable than the other I had just moved from, I rolled my eyes. The fuck was with all this crappy shit?

"Why not?" Nova asked.

"She seems to think that he doesn't want her, that he left and has had every opportunity to find her over the years. I get the feeling she's letting pride keep her from calling him."

Nova nodded and let out a long breath. "But she's still wearing the Token."

I understood his worry. She might not *want* to call Harkyn, but if she got desperate enough one day, it was hung around her neck within easy reach. If we didn't find a way to break Harkyn's Word without killing him first and she called him, he'd have no choice but to answer and then he'd die.

"Did you talk to her about Harkyn? Say anything specific?"

I shook my head. "I wanted to start off slow. None of us are sure what will activate his Word into killing him. We never said his name, but I made reference to the Kings of Hell and that I knew of the Demon who had to have given her the pendant."

Nova thought about this for a moment. "Did she hold animosity towards him? Did she seem frightened or to hate him?"

I moved to the couch by the liquor cabinet and sat down, frowning. Okay, he had to have purposely picked the worst furniture ever created. This one was far too soft and had no support whatsoever. The damn thing was going to eat me.

"No," I answered and struggled to get to my feet when the couch tried to swallow me. "She seemed sad. Hurt maybe? There was understanding and frustration, but no real anger towards him. I tell you, if we can find a way to break this Word, I think he has a real chance at making things right with her quickly," I explained and decided to pour myself a drink.

"Will she accept your protection?" Donovan asked from his sentry by the door.

I nodded and poured three fingers of scotch. "I think so. She seems much more at ease with me now."

Donovan seemed to accept that answer, but I could see the wheels in his head turning a mile a minute. The guy worried too much about everything, but I couldn't blame him. He felt responsible for Mika's sister who he was yet to find and bring to safety, and the more time that went past, the more likely it was she'd be killed or captured by the enemy. I inwardly flinched at the state Mika would be in if her sister died.

"You know," I began slowly and leaned a hip against the liquor cabinet. "Harkyn will be pissed if he finds out we went behind his back like this."

Nova shrugged. "We have no other choice. If we asked him for permission to speak to her for him, it would be the same as him sending her a letter or calling her up. He promised to stay away from her and have no form of communication that would interfere with her life—or something like that. Going behind his back is the only way to try and get her on his side again and hopefully we can figure out how to break his Word."

"I know," I assured and looked around the room for somewhere else to sit. Donovan and I were working on this alone, purposely keeping the others out of it. The less who knew we'd made contact with Tria, the better. Nova had been forced to lie to

Harkyn and tell him Malik was guarding her when she and I had been out for coffee. Donovan was positive that keeping my name out of any associations with Tria was important to keep Harkyn in the dark, or he'd begin to piece things together and the idiot would unintentionally kill himself.

"If this works, Harkyn won't give a shit that we went behind his back, he'll just be happy to have her by his side. I'm assuming he had no signs of pain while I was with her?" I asked, taking a sip of my drink. Fuck, that was good stuff. Humans screwed up a lot, but over time, they'd seriously perfected making a good scotch.

Nova shook his head. "I was with him for most of it, I didn't see any sign of pain. As soon as you said you'd left Tria in her apartment, I told Harkyn that Malik had left. He's with her now."

I spotted a high-backed chair off near the fireplace—the same looking one we *all* had in our realms—and sat down sighing contentedly. Finally, a piece of furniture that was actually comfortable.

"Okay, so our first attempt at making contact was successful. I've rented an apartment down the hall from her, so I have an excuse to be close by. Until we know what to do, we'll keep taking turns looking after her and hopefully something will give," I summed up.

Nova nodded and I raised my glass in agreement before taking another drink. Damn, that *was* good.

After another long silence, I looked back to my brother who watched me with raised eyebrows. "What?"

"You can leave now," he said.

Rolling my eyes, I grinned and downed the rest of my drink before putting the empty glass on the table and sauntering past him to the door.

"You need new furniture, brother. This shit sucks."

CHAPTER EIGHT

HARKYN

Four Years Ago

I was in Hell.

Not literally—Hell was rather nice for me—but I was in my own personal torture scenario, and it was totally of my own making. Fucking morals and self-imposed rules!

I groaned as I paced along the empty field where I'd first met Tria, watching the sun begin to sink. I had been helping Tria understand her magic for over a month now, and while I loved watching her get a handle on her power, it was also torture beyond what I knew how to inflict. The scent of her made my mouth water and caused my blood to thicken and rush. Her skin was soft and smooth, almost impossible to resist touching. I loved the sound of her voice, of her laughter, and I couldn't get enough of her smile and those deep dimples that flashed every time she did. I could watch the downward sweep of her lashes as she tried to conceal her emotions from me over and over again and never tire of it. And the way her pupils blew wide and the ice blue in her eyes melted into the bluest flame when she wanted me? Fuck. I could live off that look alone for a millennium.

But she was young—*too* young.

That begged the question: Why was my connection to her so

strong? Why did it feel like, in some incredibly impossible way, that everything about her was made to tempt me? It felt like she was created *for* me, everything about her called to me unlike anyone else ever had. What was it about this Witch that was so different from the rest?

What I found to be more alarming was that I couldn't even bring myself to sleep with another woman since meeting her. I'd tried. The night before I met Tria, I'd slept with a human, Renee, and that was the last time I'd had sex, and that was just over a month ago. I couldn't remember a time I'd gone longer than two weeks without sex, much less a whole freaking month. I'd been approached several times by females of all sorts, but the thought of touching any of those women, of tasting their lips and sharing their bodies, was almost repugnant now. All I had to do was think about Dimitria for me to be hard as a rock and desperate to have her.

I wondered if it had anything to do with what had happened when I helped Tria learn to block herself from feeling everyone's emotions. I hadn't been able to tell her how to do it, showing her was much easier, and it had required trust from her that I wouldn't wander into her mind or plant seeds of suggestions that weren't there before. It had also required me to trust her not to go wandering either. I didn't want her to see what was in my head, and in letting her in, she'd have access to my brothers if she dared to go looking. It was a big thing, which was why maybe that *extra* thing had happened. After I'd shown her how to block emotions, there's been a pathway forged in my mind, one that lead to her. I had *never* experienced a connection with anyone like that apart from my brothers. I had been created with those tethers to my brothers already there. I didn't know what it was *not* to have them. But a psychic link to Tria? In her mind? I was astounded it had happened and entirely clueless as to how. I considered asking my brothers, but that opened up the way for a lot of questions I wasn't ready to answer yet. We might not share every detail about our lives, but we at least made an effort not to lie to one another. And broaching a topic to do with Tria without telling them of her existence as a Witch teetered on that line. For now I was simply… omitting certain facts.

But that connection to each other was there now, and Tria knew it too. When we'd shared our minds, there'd been this *feeling*. This indescribable heat. It was something altogether new that burned a trail from me to Tria, that linked us, bound us in some inexpressible way, but felt inordinately strong despite its tenuous appearance. I felt Tria now, in a way I hadn't been able to before. I could sense her more acutely, I could feel her emotions, her impressions, and when she let her guard slip, her thoughts. We'd been flirting with a dangerous line these last weeks, stepping into each other's dreams, visiting, playing with temptation without breaking the rules. In our minds, it felt less real, as if we could do things in our head I'd said no to in the physical world. But I knew better. I knew that some things in a psychic realm were as real as if they'd happened in real life, and I'd been resolute not to cross those boundaries.

Sure, sometimes I felt like I was holding onto my morals by the skin of my teeth, but I held them, nonetheless. Maintaining my stand meant that I had to find other ways to quench this insatiable need to be in her presence and feel her skin against mine, and so there was rarely a night in the last several weeks where I did not fall asleep with her in my arms. Sure, I was in my realm in Hell and she was safely in her own bed, but I sent myself to her and wrapped myself around her, holding her close. I knew she felt me there when it never failed that she fell asleep within minutes of me surrounding her.

Knowing I gave her that sense of safety, that she trusted me, felt like a medal of honor. I wasn't sure why, but knowing she felt so safe with me made me feel thirty feet tall and fucking invincible. It gave me the strength I needed to keep my hands to myself and simply teach her about her magic and the world she was irrevocably wrapped up in.

Sighing deeply, I faced the setting sun and drew in a deep breath, feeling my raging needs settle and my heart rate finally even. I'd come here tonight a mess, borderline desperate and crazy for her. My need for her grew daily, and sometimes I feared how full-on those needs were. Reminding myself of who she was and what she was coming to mean to me, let me get a handle on it. The sound of approaching footsteps reached me, and I closed my eyes and felt for her. She was here.

Contentment fought with desire for dominance, and I forced myself to get a grip. She was here, that was all I needed to know. She was busy often, so most of our catch ups happened at night, but that suited me just fine. I was turning to face her when the smallest scent of blood reached me, along with a sharp stab of pain from her. I spun, my eyes darting around looking for the reason she was hurt but found nothing. When I caught sight of her, her head was hung low, her arms wrapped around her waist, and I observed her brushing a tear off her cheek.

Fear and denial over what her injuries could mean battered at me, and I was in front of her before I even thought to move. She inhaled sharply and staggered back, her wide blue eyes snapping up to my face. I reached for her arm to steady her, my gaze catching on the smeared eyeliner.

"Harkyn," she whispered almost in surprise. I was early today, and it was clear she hadn't expected me to be here yet. She had to have been caught up in her injuries not to have noticed me here.

I scanned the rest of her, looking for where her pain was coming from. "Where are you hurt? How?"

"I—nothing. Nowhere, I'm fine," she lied, tugging her hand back.

Lie.

Glowering, I stepped into her space and pulled her against me again while simultaneously pushing into her mind. She gasped and I felt her feeble attempt to throw up a shield to keep me out, but ever since we'd forged a mind link, neither of us could keep the other out anymore, not if we really wanted in.

"Stop," she insisted, but I felt the way she was trying to conceal her pain.

"Tell me," I ordered, pushing further into her head. Snippets of memories echoed around me, but none of them indicated what happened to her.

"Harkyn, stop!" she shouted, wrenching herself out of my arms. I stopped and looked down at her, my chest heaving with uneven breaths, my blood boiling at the idea of someone hurting her and me not being there to protect her.

"Speak. Now," I growled, low and deep. Something had happened, I felt it all over her. She smelled wrong, other scents combined on her, and her fear reeked most of all.

"I-I don't want to talk about it," she whispered. I made another sound in my chest and she glared. "Stop growling. I have a right to my privacy."

I invaded her space, and she tipped her head back to look at me, the ice in her eyes burning bright in defiance.

"Not when the secret you are keeping is hurting you. What the hell happened, and who hurt you?"

"Why? Are you going to kill whoever hurt me?"

"Yes," I answered immediately. "But not before I torture them for several years first."

Tria shook her head and made a sound of disapproval and stepped around me. I spun and followed her, scanning the rest of her. I felt the pain in her chest, bruising and aching. Other parts of her were sore too, but lessening with every step, as if she'd been healing herself the whole time and hadn't finished before she arrived at the clearing.

"Dimitria," I said again, softening my voice a little.

She sighed and stopped walking before she dropped her head back to look up at the sky. The sun was low now, almost gone, the bright orange making her white-blonde hair glow red in the fading rays.

"I don't want to talk about it. Can we drop it, please?" she asked, not bothering to turn towards me. I stepped around her again, and when she finally locked her eyes with mine, I searched them for a long moment. She was upset, she'd been scared, she was in pain—although it was fading. It didn't sit right with me that she'd been hurt, and worse that she refused to tell me who'd hurt her. I dropped her gaze and let my eyes run over her again with a keener eye. I caught the faint smudges around her neck, like someone had wrapped their hands around it. Rage began to burn through my body, and I dropped my gaze lower to the redness on the swell of her breasts. I could *feel* the pain on her breast and the sharp stabbing pain in her rib telling me she'd probably suffered a fractured rib that was almost healed now. There was a smudge of blood in the corner of her mouth, like she'd been slapped or cut the inside of her mouth on her teeth.

"I am not going to let this go. Tell me."

She sighed tiredly. "I don't want you to kill anyone."

"Fine, I'll just maim them a little," I answered with a shrug.

Her lips quivered at my joke, and she ducked her head, shaking it. I gently slid my finger beneath her chin and tipped her head back so she had to look at me. Fucking hell I was gone for this girl. What the hell was happening to me?

"You've been in my head, *cara,* you know the man I am. I am not the kind to sit by and let those I care for be harmed. You need to tell me who hurt you."

She studied me carefully, but I felt no give in her, no need to tell me what had happened. Tria had been handling problems in her life all on her own since forever. She didn't need anyone fighting her battles, and she didn't want to rely on anyone to do it. Once again, the term of endearment I'd given her fit all too well. *Little warrior.*

"If I tell you, will you promise to not harm them? That you will not orchestrate a series of events to cause them harm or allow one of your minions to go after them and hurt them like you wish to?"

Humor grew from deep within me that she knew me that well, but so did hope. She was going to trust me with the information and to not act on it. I gritted my teeth as I considered what she was asking, and debated on whether or not I could keep a promise like that. It was in my blood to dole out pain and violence, to seek and render retribution onto those who deserved it. To sit by and do nothing was... unthinkable.

But could I do it?

"I could get the information from your head," I reminded.

"Not without completely breaking my trust in you and ruining what we have. I trusted you in my mind, you trusted me in yours. Don't make me regret that now," she returned, her voice softening with vulnerability towards the end.

Fucking, *fuck*.

"Someone hurt you, *cara*. And you want me to promise I will not seek revenge?"

"Revenge, retribution, justice… however you want to dress it up. Yes, I want you to promise me."

Damn, she was good. Could I know and do nothing? Could I *not* know and still be as helpless? Which was worse?

Grinding my teeth, I blew out a sharp breath of annoyance and set my jaw. "Fine. Tell me who hurt you, how, and why. You have my word I will not cause them pain or allow anyone else to do so on my behalf."

"And any other little avenues I haven't thought of. I will tell you with the understanding that you'll do nothing about it except hug me," she added.

"Fine. Yes. Just get on with it," I demanded.

Tria sighed and stepped around me, and I followed her as she pulled a blanket out of her bag and laid it out. She tugged me over and forced me down onto the blanket. Sitting with my legs stretched out in front of me, she stood above me. I waited as she looked up at the darkening sky, the last rays of the day stretching out above us, losing the fight against the encroaching velvety blues.

I watched when she swallowed hard and began unzipping her hoodie. The small button up shirt below was done up haphazardly, and my eyes were glued to her fingers as they carefully worked them free. My breath caught as inch after inch of creamy white flesh was revealed and she pulled the shirt open. My gaze flew to the already purpling bruise on her ribs, and my vision tinged with red. It took several beats for my eyes to move along to the black lace bra. There was no shot of desire at the sight of the lace cupping her breasts, the fading blue finger marks there only made me want to fly into a rage. The picture her injuries painted before me was not pretty, and I had to swallow several times before I could form words again.

"Who?"

"You promised, Harkyn."

"Who?" I snapped, holding onto my control by my fingernails. Her crystal blue gaze met mine and she stepped so her legs were either side of me before lowering herself onto my lap. I gripped her hips at once and she pressed her hands to either side of my neck, her thumbs brushing the edges of my jaw as she looked up at me pleadingly.

"I need you to take a breath and come out of your anger for me. Please?" she whispered.

The echoes of violence clung to her, the smell of blood and a human man were thick and I struggled to maintain my control.

"What. Happened?" I clenched out.

She licked her lips and shook her head. "It's not what you think. I wasn't raped," she hurried to say.

Some part of me relaxed deep inside, but not much considering the injuries she'd sustained. "But you almost were, weren't you?" She ducked her head, and I had my answer.

"Who?"

"I got away, that's all that matters."

"Dimitria, tell me what I need to fucking know, or I'm going to lose my control. Talk!"

She stiffened in my arms, and I regretted scaring her at once. I wrapped my arms around her and pulled her close, so that I could draw the scent of her shampoo into my lungs and close my eyes, letting the familiar aroma calm me. Her thumbs began to stroke back and forth along the edge of my jaw.

"I'm a foster kid, Harkyn. Do you know what that means?" she asked.

"It probably means your parents are dead," I finished for her. She was born a Witch; it ran through bloodlines. I couldn't imagine Witch parents allowing their magical child to be left to the foster system if there was any other choice.

She shrugged. "I don't know. They dropped me off at a firehouse when I was four and never came back."

Anger built upon anger, and I kept my eyes closed and the scent of her in the forefront of my mind so that I would keep my promise.

"Who hurt you, *cara?*"

"Being a foster kid... everyone knows it. I don't get along with anyone at school, I'm usually a loner. There was this guy who thought I'd be desperate enough for attention that I wouldn't turn him down. He cornered me after school and didn't like it when I said no."

I kept my eyes closed, but it didn't stop images of me breaking some nameless, faceless dickbag into a thousand bloody pieces. I felt the truth of her story... but there was one piece she wasn't saying.

"Your mouth," I said, slowly pulling away to look down at her. Those blue eyes of hers were sad, and I gently brushed at the tiny sliver of blood in the corner of her mouth. "This wasn't caused by the guy; I can feel it. Who did this?"

She hesitated and glanced away from me. I waited patiently. She didn't want to tell me, but I wasn't going to let it go until she did.

"His girlfriend walked in and saw us. She didn't want to accept what her boyfriend was capable of, so she slapped me and called me a whore. He blamed me too. By tomorrow, there'll be a new rumor about me floating about the school."

Breathe in slowly. Hold it. Breathe out slowly. Repeat.

I forced myself to follow my own instructions for several minutes, and Tria didn't interrupt me or rush me once. I think she felt how close to the edge I was and gave me the time I needed to simmer my boiling rage.

"And you want me to let this go?" I asked carefully, afraid that if I spoke any louder I'd start shouting.

"Yes," she said in earnest.

"But—"

"He's a stupid boy, and I'll be done with school in less than six months. Let it go."

"He's not just a boy, and he's not stupid. He's fucking dangerous, Tria."

"Maybe," she accepted and ducked her head. "But he's seventeen. I need you to back off and let me handle it."

"Are you going to report him?" I demanded. I wasn't fond of human rules and laws as they often favored the culprit over the victim, but she had to do something.

"I will. There are cameras in the science room because of some of the chemicals kept there and Bunsen burners—that's where he dragged me. I will take the headmaster there tomorrow and report him."

I searched her voice for any sign of hesitancy but was glad when I found only grim resolve. She wasn't going to let him get away with assault if she could help it. Dragging in another deep breath, I pulled her tightly to me again and closed my eyes, fear of losing her shaking me to my core. She was too fragile, too *human*. There was so much that could take her from me. I wanted to hide her away, to take her to Hell with me. But deep down, I knew that wasn't safe yet either.

An idea came to me, and I pulled away from her, summoning an item to me from my realm. She frowned at me, and I showed her my closed fist. After a moment, I opened it to reveal a gold necklace inside.

"What's that?" she asked, surprised.

"It's mine. I want you to wear it."

"Uh, I can't. I mean, if that got lost I'd never forgive myself," she answered, leaning back. I looped it over her head and pulled her hair free until it rested between her breasts. I was momentarily sidetracked from the task at hand, and with great regret and reluctance, buttoned her shirt again. The marks at her neck were gone now, and the ones on her breast were fading fast.

Clearing my throat, I pulled my thoughts back on track. "If ever you find yourself in a situation where you're scared or hurt, or you need me, just hold this necklace and call for me. If I've got a block in my mind or something prevents you from reaching for me, this necklace will do the trick," I explained. She looked at me skeptically and I smiled softly and slid my thumb over her cheek. "Please?"

She sighed. "You're sure it will work?"

I nodded. "Yes, just hold it in your hand and call my name. I'll be summoned to you at once, and I'll take that as my sign that you want me to interfere."

"Really?" she asked, a smile tugging at her lips.

"Really."

Dimitria studied the gold pendant with my sigil on it and then looked back up at me, her expression turning warm and serious. "Thank you, Harkyn."

Leaning forward, I closed my eyes and pressed my lips to her forehead, cupping her face with my hands. I wished desperately to kiss her properly, but for now, this was enough.

"Only for you, *cara*."

CHAPTER NINE
DIMITRIA

Present Day

She was a Witch.

I frowned at myself in the mirror as I brushed my hair, running over the events of yesterday afternoon. The woman I'd healed in the coffee shop was a Witch like me. Or at least, that's what she claimed to be. I felt her honesty, and there was something about her that called to me, something familiar although I knew I'd never seen her before. She had been calm and collected, a small knowing smile on her face. She'd known what I was and had looked for the perfect moment to bump into me. I considered our conversation once we stepped out of the coffee shop.

"I'm sorry I tricked you this way, but I had to be one hundred percent sure you were a Witch so that I could warn you," she began, adjusting the bag on her shoulder.

"Warn me about what? Who are you?"

She smiled in understanding. "My name is Trinity. I am a Witch like you. I've been searching for Witches for years in order to learn from them, but recently I have been searching for another reason. Witches are being hunted, our existence has been discovered once again by Angels and Demons. I have helped several Witches to a safe haven away from both sides where they don't need to fear being kidnapped and used."

I blinked at her in surprise and considered what to say. She knew about Angels and Demons, she knew about the war, she knew we were being hunted—all things Tamas had told me.

"Okay, say I believe you. What do you want from me?"

She looked around us and indicated for me to step away from the door and further into a small alcove. "You are in danger, They know where you live. You need to get out of here, and I can help you escape. Trust me, you don't want to be at the mercy of the Angels," she whispered.

"And the Demons?" I asked, raising an eyebrow.

She hesitated a moment and frowned. "It's odd to consider them the lesser of the two evils in this situation, but they are. Despite that, you don't deserve to be kidnapped and held against your will by them either. Let me help you."

Again, I paused and considered her words. Was she for real? Could I trust her?

She sighed and flicked her gaze around us quickly as if afraid we'd be seen. "Look, it's not safe to talk here," she began, pulling out a pad and pen from her purse. "Meet me at this park tomorrow at ten, and I'll explain everything. I can answer any and all questions and then you can make up your mind whether or not you want to leave."

"And if I don't?" I asked, taking the paper she handed me with the address on it.

Her smile was sad and she lifted a shoulder in a small shrug. "I won't force you. This is about you having the right to your freedom, so your choice is your own. But I would urge you to think long and hard about it before you turn down my help, because I won't come back. I'm on the run, I'm being hunted for helping Witches escape, I can't risk returning here."

Nodding, I tucked away the piece of paper and looked her over again. She

*was calm and confident, something about her reassuring and powerful. I
had no proof, but I believed she was a Witch.*

*"I'll meet with you tomorrow," I agreed. She smiled, her bright eyes
softening in relief.*

"I'll see you there. Make sure you're not followed."

Which brought me to now.

I tied my long hair back in a ponytail and secured it with a tie and
blew out a heavy breath. A Demon and a Witch found me on the
same day I was attacked by an Angel. Trinity was right. I was
being hunted, and it was likely both sides were closing in on my
location. Tamas knew where I was, which meant other Demons
probably did too. It was only a matter of time before the Angels
clued in, and if yesterday's demonstration was anything to go by,
they'd take me without permission.

My gaze fell on the gold chain on my chest and my heart twisted
again as it always did when looking at it.

Harkyn.

Tears pricked my eyes as I allowed myself to think his name for
the first time in years, and I took a moment to breathe through
the pain it caused. It had been four years, and I'd been seventeen.
Surely, I should be over him by now? I'd loved him. I knew that
and I admitted it. But… he'd left and never come back, so there
was no way he loved me the same way. I'd come close on several
occasions to calling him to me using the necklace, but a few
things prevented it.

First, was the inexplicable sense that it wouldn't be a good idea.
The second was that I had no idea what I was going to say if he
showed up, or if I'd just burst into tears. Third, I was too hurt to
reach out first. I'd dreamed about calling him to me, how I'd

stand on my righteous high ground and condemn him for his actions, for leaving me, for never coming back. I'd rip into him with fire and venom and tear him down with my words and tell him we were one hundred percent done and he could take his damn necklace back because I didn't need it or him anymore. Or... maybe I'd just throw myself at him and tell him it was all okay, I forgave him, I was sorry I'd yelled and I could understand why he'd done what he'd done and was over it. I'd ask him to hold me close, to make the memories go away and just make me feel safe the way he'd been able to do any time he showed up. I had forgiven him a long time ago, not that he'd ever asked for it. More for myself, I guess. I'd thought about what he'd done, and while it had been horrific and violent, I could understand and I forgave him.

Shit. I was still in love with him all these years later, and no matter how hard I tried, I couldn't stop. I'd tried venturing along that mental pathway many times over the years to reach for him, to feel him, but it was like there was a disconnect somewhere and I was blocked from finding him. It hurt to think maybe he'd been the one to put the block there, but maybe there was another reason I was yet to discover.

Blinking, I dragged my gaze from the necklace and tucked it beneath the thin material of my shirt and straightened up. I needed to leave or I'd be late to meet up with Trinity. I needed to get some answers and take some time to decide what I was going to do.

After tugging on my fingerless leather gloves, I quickly grabbed my jacket, helmet, bag, and keys before leaving the apartment. I hurried to the small undercover parking area the tenants were given until I spotted my 2023 Suzuki Hayabusa. My motorbike, my pride and joy. No, it wasn't the fastest bike out there, but it held its own, and she was *beautiful*. I spent a pretty penny when I bought her brand new, and I'd done a lot to keep her running smoothly since then. This was my ride, my getaway, the one constant in my life. Grinning, I slid my small bag strap over my neck so that it rested across my chest and slid on my jacket, taking the time to zip it up properly.

Throwing one leg over the bike, I started it before twirling my hair up so that it tucked within the helmet before settling it over my head. My blood was racing with excitement. I hadn't ridden in a few days and I missed it. It never got old.

I pulled gently out of the structure, looking both ways before I pulled onto the street and let joy flood through me. I had a little time before my meeting with Trinity, I was going to take the long way.

By the time I showed up at the park Trinity had specified on her note, I was a few minutes late, but nothing to worry about. I kept my eyes peeled and senses flared as I headed towards the park bench where I sensed her. She was sitting there, twisting her fingers as her gaze skittered around the park before resting on me. I caught the way her shoulders relaxed, and she waved at me as I got closer. I couldn't sense anyone else nearby, but it didn't mean I wasn't ready to fight and get the hell out of there if this was some kind of trap.

"Hi, I wasn't sure if you were coming," she greeted as I got closer.

"Sorry I'm late. I haven't ridden my bike in a while and I decided to take the scenic route and lost track of time," I explained. She smiled in acceptance and indicated for the bench again. I sat as she did and removed my gloves and shoved them into my helmet. "Thanks for coming anyway. I know it's a lot to take in and you might not believe me," she began.

"No, I believe you."

"Oh?" she asked, frowning.

"Yesterday I met both an Angel and a Demon, and then you showed up. I don't really believe in coincidences like that."

She nodded slowly, the wheels in her head turning and she looked away for a moment as if she wanted to say something but wasn't sure if she should.

"What?"

Trinity sighed and considered me. "I saw you having coffee with that Demon, Tamas?"

"You know who he is?" I asked, frowning.

She hesitated. "I do… Do you?"

"He… he's a Demon. He said he had an interest in keeping me safe. He'd rather take me to Hell, but he knew I would hate that, so he said he had to look after me on the surface instead."

Trinity nodded slowly, considering my words. "And that's how he introduced himself? As a Demon?"

I shrugged. "I know he's not *just* a Demon. He feels far too powerful for that, so I'm assuming he's some upper-level creature. Why?"

Trinity shook her head. "It's not important, really. But you were talking with him, so do you have an interest in siding with the Demons?"

"I'm not siding with anyone," I hurried to say, but even as I spoke, I knew the words weren't true. I wasn't going to side with the Angels, I knew that without knowing how. Siding *against* the Demons—Harkyn—wasn't going to happen. But was I going to side with the Demons and their King? If Harkyn showed up today and begged me to go with him, would I?

Trinity seemed to catch my dilemma, but she didn't call me out on it. "If you came with me, Dimitria, you wouldn't have to choose. This war is between them, and we're just stuck in the middle. We have no place in it."

"How do you find Witches like me?" I asked instead.

"I... have a friend who helps," she explained, but it was obvious she didn't want to go into detail.

"A friend?"

"Yes, but he's not important right now. I have a safe place for people like us where we can live without fear of being found and taken. Would you consider going there?" she asked.

"If you want me to go with you, I'd want to know who this friend of yours is. For all I know, you're working for the Angels and this is some elaborate trap to take me to them without a fight."

"It could be," she agreed with a small nod. "But it's not."

I raised an eyebrow, not believing her. No, I didn't believe she was working with the Angels, her voice rang with truth, and her aura was clear of guilt and lies. But I wasn't about to put my life and wellbeing in the hands of a stranger and not know who was helping her.

Trinity sighed and looked around us. There were people in the park, but they were a good distance away so there was no fear of us being overheard.

"I will introduce you, but I want your word that you will wait to hear me out before you make any judgments and disappear. Do you promise?"

I hesitated, not sure I could trust her, but what other choice did I have? She knew I was here, where I lived. If she had more help, she could take me with her at any time even if I didn't want to go. She didn't seem the kind to take anyone against their will.

"I'll wait for you to explain, but I won't guarantee not to leave after," I answered.

"You have every right to leave if my answers don't satisfy you. Just... give me a chance," she urged. Drawing in a deep breath, I nodded, but I made sure to draw on my power to be ready in case. Her gaze flickered over me as if she knew what I was doing, but she didn't say anything.

There was a sudden surge in power around us, and I looked around warily for the cause of it. Something powerful had just arrived, but it was carefully hidden.

"Okay, Lev, show yourself," Trinity called. My gaze snapped to a grove of trees a short distance away, and my mouth fell open at the sight of the man coming towards us. He wasn't wearing anything special—jeans and a dark gray T-shirt—but he was unnaturally beautiful. His symmetrical features, black hair, high cheekbones, cleft chin, and bright blue eyes reminded me of Henry Cavill, only he was *more*.

I knew at once I was looking at an Angel, and as if to prove it, he rolled his shoulders and for a moment, massive white wings shimmered behind him before disappearing again. I stood at once, my heart beating hard as he came to stand beside Trinity who also got to her feet. She held a hand out to me as if telling me to wait.

"Don't go, you said you'd hear me out," she reminded. My gaze never left the Angel, and he considered me carefully, his expression not telling me one way or the other what he was thinking.

My body tensed and was ready to run at a moment's notice. "Then explain."

"This is Leviah, and yes, he's an Angel."

I gave a look that said *duh,* and she smiled and continued. "Lev and I met a few years ago. Some Angels took me to Heaven against my will, and I was fighting every inch of the way. I had

been hiding Witches, and they wanted to know where. They..."
She trailed off, her expression shuttering, and I felt the backlash
of her pain as she relived a memory. She licked her lips and raised
her chin before continuing. "They tortured me for the
information, but I refused to tell them anything. Lev, he got me
out of there, but not before they branded him a traitor."
I listened, not sure I bought Lev's innocence yet.
"They sent garrison after garrison to hunt him down, and we
evaded them where we could, or killed when we were forced to.
Lev gave up his home and his family to save me, and he earned
my loyalty," she continued.
"But... he's an Angel."
Trinity raised a perfectly shaped eyebrow at me and cocked her
head. "And you were having a coffee with a Demon only hours
after meeting him. What did he do to earn *your* loyalty before
you extended him that courtesy?"
"He saved me," I defended, frowning. "An Angel tried to take
me. He gave the Angel a chance to leave, but she refused, and he
saved me from being taken. He could have whisked me away
multiple times, but he didn't."
"So you were sitting in a coffee shop hours after meeting a
powerful Demon, laughing and talking like you were best
friends, all because he killed *one* Angel?" Trinity asked.
I crossed my arms over my stomach and glowered. "You weren't
there."
"No, I wasn't. But you trust him, you saw something in him that
made you feel safe, and I understand that. If I didn't believe in
your judgment and give him the benefit of the doubt, I would
have called Lev the moment I saw you with him and he would
have dispatched the Demon the second he left the coffee shop."
I shifted my feet and looked between the two of them again.

"You're asking me to go with you when you have an Angel on your shoulder, and you expect me to believe you're not going to hand me over to them once I'm with you," I pointed out, moving my helmet to my other hand.

"You wear a Token from a King of Hell around your neck, and still I believe you when you say you're not on the side of Demons," Trinity said, her eyes flicking to the chain that rested on my shirt, obviously having come out at some point.

I frowned and stepped a little closer. "You know what this is?"

She nodded. "It's a Token. They're rare, and very helpful if you're with them. It ties you directly to one of the Kings and allows for you to summon them to you at will. The Kings are powerful, and not the kind of Demon I want to run into."

A Token. It had a name. I gripped the pendant and looked down at it, feeling my heart twist again at the memories that assailed me. Lev moved, and I looked up in time to see him now in front of Trinity, his arm barring her from stepping forward, his blue eyes on my chain.

"Please, let it go," he said as if speaking to a bomber with their finger on the detonator.

I dropped it at once, realizing they must have thought I'd been about to summon Harkyn. "Sorry, I wasn't going to call him."

Trinity edged around Lev again and frowned at me. "What is that feeling coming from you now? When you think of him, it's almost like..." She trailed off, her expression slowly clearing to one of surprise. "Oh."

I cleared my throat uncomfortably at this line of questioning and straightened up. "So, you could get me out of here and take me somewhere safe?" I asked, changing the subject.

Lev and Trinity shared a look before he eased back and she nodded. "Yes. It's a beautiful place, peaceful, and the community

116

we have built is amazing and secure. But it would mean being cut off from everyone here. You would not be able to come back and—" Her gaze flicked to my necklace again. "You'd have to leave that behind."

The immediate refusal in my mind was sharp and unexpected and I had to blink several times to clear my head. What the hell? I'd never taken this necklace off since he'd given it to me, but the thought of throwing it out or passing it on had never once occurred to me. Being forced to leave it behind was not a thought I wanted to contemplate. But...

"I see you have some thinking to do before you make a decision," Trinity interrupted softly.

"There's a lot to consider," I admitted.

"That's fine. I want you to be sure. Take the next two weeks to think. I can't stay here any longer than that or I risk being found. Think long and hard, Dimitria. I won't be coming back once I leave," she urged.

"You said that yesterday. Why?"

She sighed. "You are being hunted. You said so yourself, all in one day you met a Demon and an Angel. They're closing in on your location. You can run on your own, many do and some of them are still free. If you don't come with me, fine, but you definitely need to leave, and the sooner the better. But they are focusing their search on you for now, and I can't let myself be caught up in that. There are too many who need me and who still need to be found."

I nodded my understanding, my mind swirling with information and considerations. What was I going to do? She was right, of course. I was being hunted, and I needed to leave. The only question seemed to be, did I do it alone? Or was it smarter to go with her so I could be among other Witches?

"Here," Trinity said, stepping forward with a scrap of paper. "I got a phone yesterday after we met. This is the number. I'll have it for the two weeks I'm here, then it's gone. If you want to talk more or you are ready to leave, message me on that and we'll organize how and when to go."

I took the paper with an unsteady hand and tucked it into my pocket, nodding slowly.

"Don't rush this decision, Dimitria. The quicker you choose, the better, yes. But be sure before you commit," she urged.

"I will," I said and cleared my throat when my voice came out strained. "And thank you for trusting me."

She smiled kindly and nodded. "I hope you can learn to trust me." With a nod to Lev and another smile to Trinity, I turned on my heel and started away from them, my head a mess of questions and possibilities. What was I going to do?

CHAPTER TEN
HARKYN

The feel of her soft skin beneath my fingers sent shocks of electricity through my body, making my blood sing and breath quicken. She was sex personified in my arms as she rocked against me, her ankles crossed behind my back, her fingers digging into my hair and tugging. The taste of her on my tongue was an addiction I would happily let ruin my life, as long as I got a taste every single day. Those sounds she made in the back of her throat as she arched against me, urging me on with her body, would be ingrained in my memory forever.

Dimitria.

Her name became a chant in my head as she continued to move against me. Her mouth was fused with mine, her heart beating out the same rapid beat as my own. Our breaths mingled, our souls cried out for us to merge, to be bound once and for all. I needed her like I had never needed anyone else. She was it for me, my life, my reason for existence, and she fit in my arms like she'd been molded just for me.

Dimitria.

I ached with need for her, to hold her, to touch her and feel her in my arms again. I hadn't thought it was possible to fall in love before, especially not in as little time as a few weeks, but I had, and distance had done nothing to lessen it. Being apart from her for so long had made my craving for her much greater, but it had made me appreciate who and what she was, and how perfectly we fit.

Her lips moved from mine, her heat disappeared from me, and I reached blindly for her as she pulled away. No, no, come back! I needed her, I needed her with me. I couldn't do the distance again. I couldn't! I—

"Dimitria!" I shouted, shooting up in bed in a sweaty mess, my heart pounding hard, my chest rising and falling with every uneven breath. *Dimitria*. I could taste her. Smell her. My hands near vibrated as if I'd just held her in my arms.

"Fuck," I swore and fell backwards onto the bed, forcing myself to take in deep breaths and steady my erratic heartbeat.

Frustration began to grow inside, and I wanted to rage. I had no one but myself to blame for the position we were in, but *for fuck's sake!*

I scrubbed a hand angrily over my face and forced myself up again, grinding my teeth against the frustrating helplessness. Donovan and I had scoured the basement looking for something that might help, but it was a never-ending void. I'd need years— decades, even—to properly search everywhere down there, and I didn't have that kind of time.

Out of nowhere, there was a rush of pain from Adrik and I touched on his mind briefly to see if he needed help only to find that he was—here. I frowned. Adrik and Cali were supposed to be in the Amazon with Cali's Aunt Penny, curing remote villagers of diseases. What were they doing here? Through Adrik, I knew Cali was hurt too, and I ran out of my room and down the stairs to my door. I wrenched it open in time to see Cole and Mika charge through their door, Mika already forcing her hair into a ponytail, her wide eyes locked onto my brother and Cali.

"What happened?" Cole asked as Adrik helped Cali to the floor before falling down beside her. Both of them looked like hell. Adrik was bleeding heavily and burnt painfully in several large patches, Cali too was bleeding, but she looked burned as well, although not quite as much as Adrik.

"We tried breaking into Heaven," Adrik admitted through gritted teeth.

"Weren't you two supposed to be in the Amazon?" Sawyer asked as she joined our group, followed closely by Malik.

"We were—are—but we had an opportunity to break in and didn't want to waste it," Cali answered unevenly as she tried to breathe through the pain. Mika knelt beside Adrik, and Sawyer beside Cali.

"Heal her first," Adrik said, trying to push Mika's hands away, and she rolled her eyes.

"Your mate is being seen to, so shut up and let me heal you," Mika insisted, slapping his hand away when he tried to block her.

"As ever, your bedside manner is wonderful, Mika," Adrik replied dryly.

"What happened?" I asked, getting a closer look. Cali's left arm was covered completely in a burn, and there were several nicks and cuts to her skin in other areas. I'd never seen injuries like this before from Angels, and that's who I assumed attacked them upon their break-in.

"Heaven is protected against break-ins. They have several traps ready to go if someone who is not meant to be there tries to enter," Adrik answered, gritting his teeth as Mika closed her eyes and began healing him.

"We set one off, and when we tried to escape, another caught us up," Cali continued, grimacing and panting. "We could hear

Angels on their way, and thankfully we weren't so far in that we couldn't shadow out. We barely made it."

"What was the trap?" Cole asked.

"Holy oil and some kind of flame. It wasn't fire; it was something else and it fucking hurt," Adrik answered with a hiss.

"Shouldn't you have expected traps?" Malik asked, watching his mate work.

"We'll know better for next time," Cali assured, closing her eyes as she breathed through the pain.

"Next time?" Adrik asked, turning a fierce glare on his mate. "There won't be a next time."

Cali sighed heavily as if they'd had this argument a million times, and I was pretty sure they had. "Not this again." She groaned.

"We're done trying to get in there, Cali. It's not worth it."

"It is to me!" she shouted, glowering.

"Your life is not worth your word. You promised an Angel you'd find his mate—a mate I'm not even sure exists," Adrik began.

"She exists. I felt her. *You* felt her," she argued, shifting so Sawyer could help heal her back.

I looked at Cole who shared the same exasperated look as I did. The women had their own code they lived by, but they never seemed to understand that at the end of the day, we didn't care about anything else *but* them. Nothing was worth their life, health, or happiness. Nothing. And yet they continued to do things that put themselves at risk.

"We'll talk about this later," Adrik growled.

"No, we won't. There's nothing else to discuss," Cali sniped.

Adrik glared at her, and she glared right back.

"Hey—woah. What happened to you two?"

I looked up to see Tamas exit his realm and pause to look at what was going on.

"They broke into Heaven," I explained
.

"We *tried* to break into Heaven. We barely made it through the first gate," Adrik corrected.

"Oh. Okay... well, do you need me here?" he asked, edging away. "I've got a hot date."

I frowned and opened my mouth to call him back when he grinned. "Awesome, bye!" And then he was gone.

I closed my mouth and stared at the place from where he'd disappeared, not sure what was going on with him lately. He disappeared often and never really answered where he was or what he was doing. Mostly, it felt like the shithead was avoiding me, which had me on alert. What was he up to? That was another thing that bothered me—Donovan. He was back for now, seemingly taking a break from searching for Mika's sister, and he'd been taking over a lot of my hours watching over Dimitria. He insisted it was so I could get my circle running smoothly, and I appreciated it, but I had a nagging feeling something else was going on. Whenever I found myself with some free time with which I wanted to go see Tria, there was always another job someone needed help with or some Rogues to go dispatch. I was beginning to suspect it wasn't a coincidence.

"So, any luck with your mate yet?" Cali asked, dragging me back to the current situation.

"No, not really," I answered with a shrug.

"Donovan mentioned going into the basement?" Adrik asked, looking a lot less pained now. "How did that go?"

"Hell has a basement?" Mika asked, blinking in surprise.

"Yes, it's fucking huge," I replied. "I'll never get through it all. It'd take me decades of serious searching to get through it, maybe longer."

"What's down there?" Cali asked, intrigued.

"Things from the beginning. From when our parents were here on their own. Books, failed experiments, just random crap," Malik replied with a shrug.

"Woah," Sawyer whispered in awe. "Things from the beginning? Like *The Beginning*?"

Malik grinned at her and brushed a kiss across her head. "Yes."

"Can we see it?" Cali asked, looking intrigued.

"Will it keep you from trying to break into Heaven?" Adrik asked, raising an eyebrow.

Cali opened her mouth to snap at him, seemed to think better of it, and then nodded. "For now."

Adrik studied his mate, and I watched the two stare the other down before he cocked an eyebrow and smirked. "Fine. We'll take you down there."

"Really?" Mika asked, excited.

"Sure," Cole agreed, getting to his feet before helping his mate up. "If it keeps you three out of trouble, you can camp down there."

The women shared a look before climbing to their feet.

"Follow me, I'll lead the way," Malik volunteered, leading the women to his realm.

"What about the Amazon?" Sawyer asked Cali.

"We can still help there, we'll just come back here often to look through the basement," Cali explained with a conspiratorial wink at the other Witch. Mika linked arms with her, and together the three of them lowered their voices as they walked and talked.

I stepped up beside Adrik as he got to his feet and considered him. "You know they're going to look for anything about Heaven to help her break in, right?"

Adrik grinned and nodded. "Yep, they're going to try. The basement is fucking huge—they're not aware of *how* big it is—I don't think they'll have much luck. You know the basement makes using magic more difficult than usual, and they'll need to know specifics in order to perform a summoning spell for anything they're searching for, so they'll have to do it by hand. In the meantime, my mate is safe. I'll take all of the delaying tactics I can."

I shook my head and grinned as he slapped me on the shoulder once and hurried to catch up to the others. I watched as the small group disappeared behind Malik's door, my smile fading. As amusing as it was to watch my brothers try to navigate life with their mates, I couldn't help but stare after them with wistfulness. I wanted to be one of them so bad it hurt. I knew who my mate was and where she was. We'd completed one of the four bonds already, and yet I was no closer to being with her than Corvin was to being with his.

CHAPTER ELEVEN
DIMITRIA

"Do you have to follow me?" I asked with a frustrated sigh as I took a seat beside a man mostly obscured by the giant newspaper he was reading.

Tamas lowered the paper and raised an eyebrow as he removed his moronically big sunglasses. "Angel activity has increased significantly in this area over the last few days. Unless you want to accompany me to my realm in Hell, yes, I have to follow you."

I frowned at him, but it didn't last as a smile broke through and I chuckled at how absurd he looked.

"What?" he asked, the corners of his lips turning up.

"You look ridiculous. The glasses, the hat, and the trench coat? Did you get your style from old P.I. shows?"

"It's a look, and I was meant to follow you incognito, so I thought I'd give it a go," he defended.

"You can literally hide from humans and Angels in the shadows, you don't *need* a disguise."

"Don't hate on the outfit. I think I pull it off nicely," he added, shaking out the paper to read it again.

I couldn't help it, I laughed. "Pretty much *no one* reads a newspaper anymore, and certainly not one from—" I leaned forward to check the date and snickered, "1984."

"I miss the eighties," Tamas responded absently as he continued to peruse the paper.

Sighing, I shook my head and got to my feet. "Alright, Columbo. If you insist on following me—"

"*Columbo?*" Tamas interjected, aghast.

"—then you should do it in the shadows so you don't draw attention to me. Also, stay out of my way. I have a job to do, and I don't want you interfering," I continued as if he hadn't spoken.

"*Columbo?* Really? You couldn't have thought of anyone better looking?"

I continued talking, doing my best to ignore him. "I can look after myself. If I need you, I'll call for you. Deal?"

"You could have at least called me Eliot Ness," Tamas continued to complain, looking wounded.

"Do we have a deal?" I asked, pushing my point.

"It's like you've never heard of Joe Mannix or Thomas Magnum," Tamas lamented, folding up the newspaper.

I sighed and rubbed my forehead. "Tamas, do you understand what I said? Can you agree to that?"

"I mean, I would have even settled for Sherlock Holmes or Jim Rockford," he grumbled, crossing his arms over his chest in a full-on pout.

"For Christ's sake, Tamas. Answer me, or I'll bind you to this chair," I threatened. He continued to pout in silence and I made a sound of impatience and rolled my eyes, putting my hands on my hips as I struggled for control.

"Sherlock, did you hear me?" I asked, gritting my teeth.

Tamas beamed up at me with a satisfied smirk, and with a wave of his hand was wearing the Sherlock hat and had a tobacco pipe in hand.

"I'll follow in the shadows. I'll watch over you," he agreed with a wink.

I scanned around us quickly to make sure no one saw his little trick and shook my head. Tamas got to his feet, smirking, and I rolled my eyes.

"And Thomas Magnum? I'm sorry, but Tom Selleck is so much sexier than you, and you can't pull off the mustache like he can. Also, we're not in Hawaii, and you're not wearing the signature Hawaiian shirt, so that was never going to happen," I argued, sliding my hands into the pocket of my leather jacket to grip my phone.

There was a strange sound beside me, and when I looked up, Tamas was standing beside me with the most ridiculous mustache that did *nothing* for him, and wearing the shirt. I couldn't have planned it better. Before he could react, I pulled out my phone— camera app ready—and snapped a picture of him. His face fell and I laughed and skipped away from him.

"Delete it," he insisted, moving quickly to catch up with me as he changed into his regular clothing of jeans and a plain T-shirt.

"Nope!"

"I can melt the phone in your pocket from here," he warned.

"It wouldn't do you any good," I said, grinning. "I am a bounty hunter. Video and photo evidence is crucial, so everything from my phone automatically backs up onto a secure server."

Tamas looked horrified, and I laughed. "Now, stay in the shadows like a good Demon bodyguard, and I won't be forced to spread this photo around."

Tamas glowered at me, but after a moment his scowl was replaced by a sinister grin and a mischievous glint in his eyes.

"Alright, if that's how you want to play this... let's play."

And with those ominous words, he disappeared into the shadows. Wherever he went, I felt him, but I couldn't see him. Pushing away the little twinge of apprehension, I turned down the footpath and continued on my way to catch up with a client.

~

Tamas followed me everywhere I went. It would have been frustrating if he didn't have a way of making me laugh so damn much. He was like the brother I never wanted. His threat to play lingered in the back of my mind all the time, and it wasn't until almost a week later that he started to dole it out.

On the first day, he followed closely, but allowed me to work without interference. I think he was getting a feel of what it was I did and how I did it. The bounty on this one was small, but hey, it paid the bills and put gas in my bike, so I wasn't about to snub my nose at it. It took me two days and I was done.

Day four had me on a new job, only I was using the honey-trap technique in a high-end cocktail bar. Although I hated the skeevy pervs that fell for it, it was an effective trap and it worked ninety percent of the time. This time it didn't, but through no fault of my own. For some reason, Tamas took it as a personal offense that the guy I was trying to lure away from the bar was getting up in my personal space and dared to grab my ass. No, I didn't like this part of the job, but I had precautions in place if ever they decided not to take *no* as an answer. When Tamas came yelling across the room for the guy to get his hands off me, the target ran, and I was forced to tackle him in the middle of the dance floor with a flying leap that tore my dress. I still got paid, but I had a feeling I wouldn't be welcome back in that bar anytime soon.

I had thought Tamas would apologize afterwards for almost costing me my bounty, but instead he decided I needed reprimanding for putting myself in these positions and allowing men to touch me. After telling him to pull his head out of his ass before he burrowed so far up he could give himself a tonsil exam, I left him on the street and took my motorbike home.

The next day he brought me motor oil for my baby as an apology. I never could turn away free things for my bike, so he was forgiven as long as he promised not to interfere like that again. He accepted before strutting down the hall to Luana's apartment where she yanked him inside by the neck of his shirt.

Trinity called later that night to see if I'd had time to think, but I told her I needed more. What she was asking of me was a big thing, and I needed to consider all the repercussions. I already admitted to myself that I could trust her, that she was genuine in her quest to protect fellow Witches, so all that remained now was whether or not I was going to leave.

On the seventh day since Tamas began inserting himself into my life, I had another job, but this time he insisted on being allowed to help. I think on some level he found my work interesting and couldn't wait to be a part of it. Unable to dampen his child-like enthusiasm, I set *him* up as a honey-trap. I mean, the mark was a guy—Tamas didn't know this—who'd managed to defraud several elderly couples out of their retirement money, and I couldn't wait to see him put away. It might have done Tamas better if he knew that going in, but I wanted a little payback for him ruining *my* honey trap. The joke was on me though, because as it turned out, the guy we had tracked down was gay, and Tamas backed our mark up against the bar and made out with him like he was trying to suck the oxygen from the man's lungs. After the arrest, I had so many questions and Tamas just laughed. "I've been alive practically since the beginning of time, I've done everything there is to do. I prefer women, but do you really think I haven't had my fun with men before? The Spartans were surprisingly interested in experimenting."

I couldn't have been more shocked had he slapped me in the face. Did Demons regularly test out the other side of the menu? Was it a thing, or was Tamas a trailblazer? Had Harkyn tried it? The question bounced around in my head, and I found I didn't hate the idea if he had.

After that, Tamas decided not to interfere directly with my marks, but set his mind to trying to distract me when I worked. On day ten—after I'd caught him leaving Luana's apartment where she stood looking *very* satisfied—we got started on the job. I was sitting at a lunch bar with a silver fox, pretending to laugh at his sexist joke. I was taking a sip of my water disguised as a martini when I caught sight of Tamas entering the establishment. I choked on my water, almost spraying it on the man across from me. Tamas was wearing fluorescent shorts that clung to his—I'll admit—impressively sculpted thighs, a cut off tank top, a rainbow headband, and sweatbands on his wrists. He looked like a very gay, jacked up marathon runner.

On day eleven, he was making out with some woman at the neighboring table when he was interrupted by the woman's husband which resulted in a bar fight, he graciously let the other guy win.

I was tempted to be mad at him for kissing another woman when he was sleeping with my kind-of-sort-of-friend, but Tamas wasn't one to settle, and Luana knew that going in.

Then on the thirteenth day, he pretended to be blind, 'accidentally' groping the mark as he passed by us.

Over and over again, Tamas showed up in ridiculous outfits, disguises, and pretended to be a multitude of people, and several times it made me laugh so hard I cried. I hadn't had so much fun in a long time, and it made me a little sad to realize I hadn't been as happy as I thought I had been since losing Harkyn. I'd been living a half-life, and I was lonely. Tamas had agreed to watch over me, and he was supposed to be waiting in the shadows, not becoming my friend. I wanted to be annoyed at his insertion into my life, but all I felt was grateful. It hurt to be reminded so often of Harkyn, but having Tamas around somehow made me feel a little closer to him, like he wasn't actually gone from my life. *But he probably would be soon.* The voice in the back of my head reminded me, and I inwardly winced. Trinity's deadline for deciding if I was staying in town or going ended tomorrow… I had a choice to make.

It had been a long day, and we were walking in companionable silence back to my building as had become the norm over the last two weeks. I had a question I wanted to ask, but I wondered if I should.

He caught me looking and smiled. "What?"

I clasped my hands together in front of me and shrugged. "Since you've started hanging around, I realized I haven't had this much fun in a long time. Why did you do it?"

He frowned. "Do what?"

"All of it. The costumes, the characters. Why not just follow me silently in the shadows like I thought you would? Why interact when it wasn't necessary?"

He considered my words for a long time, and I wondered why it was such a hard question to answer. I got the sense he was choosing his words carefully.

"Since we met—I don't know, we seemed to click and you're like the little sister I never wanted but got landed with and then was forced to look after for the rest of my life."

I snickered at his explanation, and he smirked.

"Seriously?"

He nodded. "I mean, I started looking after you because—" He broke off and his face cleared of expression, and I got the sense he'd been about to say something he was trying *not* to say. "There were good reasons to look out for you, and I was happy to do it."

"You mean the reasons that, if you tell me about them, I'll ask questions that could somehow cost someone their life?" I asked, raising a disbelieving eyebrow.

"Yes," he answered and cleared his throat. "As for making you laugh? I got the sense you didn't do it much, or at least not in a way that meant you really felt it. I wanted to give you a reason to."

I didn't want to feel gratitude towards him for his reasons, but damn it, they were pretty good reasons. "Are all Demons like you? Do all of you care like this? Because the stereotype paints you all as *very* evil beings," I asked as we followed the path around a corner.

"The Angels were sneaky, manipulative bastards who had the forethought to get their hooks into humans from the get-go. They started poisoning their minds against us, that stupid book was written, and humans just... needed a villain. We were it."

I nodded slowly. Harkyn hadn't been bad, he'd been *very* good, too good to me, really. Until that night. Tamas was proving to be an incredible friend. I didn't know many Angels—one, to be exact—and I didn't really *know* him. From what I could tell, Angels definitely seemed to be the bigger assholes of the two. Lev was Trinity's Angel friend, but in our small interaction, he seemed very protective of her, putting himself in front of her when he thought I was about to summon Harkyn to me. If what Trinity had said could be believed, he'd killed several of his own kind in an effort to free her and protect her since. So, not all Angels were bad.

I shook my head as it began to pound. Why did it all have to be so difficult?

"Have you thought about finding him?"

I frowned and looked up at Tamas who nodded to the necklace I was playing with again.

I dropped it and shrugged. "No. He's so powerful. If he wanted me in his life, he'd have come for me by now. I know I told him to go away, to not come back, but considering the circumstances, I would have thought he'd have at least tried to contact me in the last four years. But he hasn't. I won't plead for his attention or affection. His actions speak loud enough. He doesn't want me, so I'm not going to beg him to want me."

Tamas seemed to think about this for a moment and turned to look ahead of us. "What if something is keeping him away?"

I frowned. "If you know who we're talking about, then you know how powerful he is. I can't imagine anything being powerful enough to keep him away if he really wanted to see me again."

Tamas opened his mouth, but I held up a hand, forestalling his comment. "I really don't want to talk about it. Can we drop it, please?"

Tamas hesitated and sighed. "Just... one more question?"

I wrapped my arms around my waist and indicated for him to go on. He'd done a lot for me over the last two weeks, the least I could do was answer some questions.

"Did you love him?"

I stiffened at the odd question but nodded all the same. "I did— do? I don't know. I'm always thinking about him, even after all this time. No matter how pathetic that makes me, it's the truth. I loved him, but I never told him. I was so young, and we hadn't spent that much time together. Only a couple of months. I didn't want him to think it was a stupid teenage crush, and I was terrified if I told him, he wouldn't love me back."

Tamas took that in, and we walked in silence a little longer before he sighed. "He loved you."

I came to an abrupt stop. "What did you say?"

He turned to face me, his expression resolved. "He loved you," Tamas repeated, crossing his arms over his chest. "I know who he is, and four years ago he was an absolute wreck. He's a little better now, but still not as he was before meeting you. He loved you. I'd say he still does."

My heart grew and simultaneously broke at his words, and my eyes began to sting at the thought. Tamas stepped closer to me as if to hug me, and I stepped back, extending my arm out to keep him away. He paused, his lips thinning and brow creasing in protest.

Drawing in a deep breath, I forced the pain and hope away and tried to reinforce my emotional walls. If Harkyn wanted me, if he loved me, he'd have come for me by now. I couldn't imagine anything being powerful enough to keep him away, so really, Tamas's words meant nothing.

"I don't want to talk about this anymore," I whispered, my voice hoarse.

Tamas opened his mouth to protest, but he studied my face a moment longer and closed it before nodding. "Let me walk you home, then I'll get out of your hair."

The last of the pain eased away, and I stepped up beside him again, struggling to keep my mind from going down memory lane.

I was about to talk about his time with the Spartans to change the subject and lighten the mood when Tamas suddenly used his arm to swoop me behind him and throw out a wall of fire at the same time. I gasped and looked around him in time to see four Angels screech in agony. Pain radiated from them and I reinforced my barriers, shocked to see their wings flicker in and out of view.

"I need to get you to safety!" Tamas yelled.

"No, I can help," I shouted and stepped around him, drawing my magic from my core.

"Tria, no——" Tamas began but was cut off when an Angel appeared out of nowhere and sent him flying through the air to crash into a lamp post. I didn't hesitate in throwing my magic at the Angel, warping it so it acted as giant ropes that wrapped around his arms and legs and yanked him back to the nearest tree. The Angels on fire were still screeching, but I could see the flames lessening. "Tamas!"

"I'm here," he remarked calmly, if a little breathless. He jogged up beside me and sent another wave of fire at the Angels who were just beginning to extinguish before there was the sound of a guttural, bone-chilling roar behind us. I turned in time to see four Demons headed for us, their faces and arms scarred in purposefully made patterns. Gasping, I threw out my magic which sent them flying backwards, but it wasn't enough.

"I need to send you away," Tamas shouted.

I glared. "Don't you *dare*."

Growling impatiently, Tamas kept himself in front of me, his eyes scanning around us at the surrounding dangers. Sending me away wouldn't do him any good, I'd just come back whether he liked it or not. I was an asset here, I wasn't about to leave him to handle this mess alone.

The Angel bound to the tree was making his way free, the Angels on fire were still a good distance away, but the other Demons were running for us again.

"They're Demons, why are they trying to hurt us?" I demanded.

"They're Rogues. They don't work with my kind," Tamas

answered, putting one hand out in front of him towards the running Demons, his other still focusing flames on the Angels. I threw my magic out again, this time infusing in it the command to keep them down. It wouldn't last for long, but intent was eighty percent of using magic, and if I wanted the Demons to stay down, all I had to do was tell my magic to make it so. I didn't know any conjurations to make them stay yet.

"You'll never keep her safe, Demon filth!" The Angel at the tree shouted, continuing to attempt his way free.

"Uriel, I see you've decided to creep out of your hiding place. Over your fear of my brother, then?" Tamas returned in a voice full of malicious glee.

"I was never afraid of your pathetic brother," Uriel snarled.

"Except that every time you face him, you run away for years at a time. We haven't seen you in over two years since your last encounter," Tamas added, his gaze flicking to the Demons I'd thrown away.

I tried hard to block out the sounds of pained screeching from the Angels and looked around for any humans who might be witnessing this. That would not be good.

"You'll be dead soon, Demon King, mark my words!" Uriel threatened, and I didn't like the shiver that worked its way down my spine when I could taste his belief in those words.

"Demon King?" I asked, turning to Tamas.

"Stay alert, I need a minute," he ordered sharply and closed his eyes, not answering my question. I spun around, looking out for unknown dangers while my mind refused to let go of what Uriel said. Tamas was a Demon King? Like Harkyn? How many were there? Why would he hide this from me?

The Angel at the tree was working his way free and the Demons I'd thrown out were almost on us. Licking my lips, I turned to

Uriel and added to my conjuration that had kept him bound to
the tree, and he swore at me.

"You're as bad as he is, Demon whore. All of you will pay for
your alliance with his kind. You could have had a life in Heaven,
and instead you chose the bed of the spawns of Satan."

"It sounds to me that you're a little jealous. What's the matter,
Uriel? Do none of the Witches want to sleep with you, and you
hate the Demons for knowing how to get a woman into bed?" I
teased, more out of reflex than a need to insult. I was near
terrified, and my mouth tended to get mouthier when I felt
cornered.

"You'll burn, Witch, and I'll be the one to set you alight," Uriel
ranted. What the hell was wrong with this Angel?

Tamas gave a low snarl of displeasure when the air seemed to
take on an electric, threatening feel. My skin came alive with it,
and I checked my hair to see if it was standing on end in case we
were about to get struck by lightning. An ominous rumble of
thunder sounded overhead, and I gasped. The night had been so
clear only moments ago, how were there clouds gathering so
quickly?

"Is that any way to speak to a lady?" a new voice drawled, and I
turned as lightning flashed across the sky, illuminating the
creature before me. He was *gorgeous,* and the giant black wings he
shrugged back had been the kind of thing fantasy books were
made of. His shimmering black eyes flashed as another zap of
lightning temporarily illuminated the sky followed by a low
rumble of thunder.

Uriel's eyes widened when he caught sight of the stranger and I
frowned. Wasn't this guy another Angel? He had wings.
Although they were black where the Angels' were all white. Was
he... Death?

There was a garbled, strangling sound from behind me, and I spun back to see the four Demons on their feet, their hands gripping their throats as if they could not breathe. Tamas's hand was out, slowly clenching as if he were constricting their airways from a distance. His face was set in lines of concentration and rage, and the change in him from his care-free self to this furious King of Hell was reminiscent of Harkyn the night I'd seen him change. Were all of them like this?

"Look away, Tria," Tamas ordered in a rough, uneven voice and I did so at once. I had to get over my aversion to violence, but that wasn't going to happen tonight.

The jet of fire Tamas had been throwing dissipated and the Angels continued to cry out and screech as they struggled to put it out. The stranger turned his attention to me, and I swallowed hard in fear, wondering if we were better for his presence, or worse.

There was a chilling choking sound behind me, followed by the sounds of bodies hitting the ground—lifeless. My hands shook and I tried not to let it all affect me.

"Amazarak," Tamas said after a moment, a small sigh in his voice. I turned to watch him step up beside me, a little in front as if ready to protect me against the newcomer.

"Demon King," the one I now knew as Amazarak, greeted with a small incline of his head.

"What are you doing here?"

Amazarak flicked an interested glance at me and then back to Tamas. "I felt the presence of a Witch, felt the fight between one of yours and the Angels, and I came to offer my assistance."

"You can't have," I cut in, stepping out from behind Tamas who had slowly been edging in front of me to keep me hidden. "I'm cloaked. I renew the spell every few days, and I never forget.

There's no way you could have felt my magic," I insisted.

Amazarak looked at me again, his lips crooking slightly in the corner before he looked between Tamas and me with curiosity. Tamas stiffened and I watched him as his jaw tensed. A silent conversation seemed to pass between the two of them and Amazarak looked only slightly more interested.

"Anyway, I need to take these Angels," Amazarak continued as if I hadn't spoken.

Tamas shook his head. "No."

"I apologize if you thought I was asking, but I wasn't," Amazarak added, the tone in his voice telling me we were better off letting him have the Angels.

Scowling, Tamas flicked a glance at the charred and agonized Angels. "I want them dead. They attacked us, they tried to take Dimitria, they need to die."

"And they will," Amazarak answered and then shrugged. "Eventually."

"What do you want with them?" I asked hesitantly. Did I really want to know?

Amazarak considered thoughtfully and then gave an almost imperceptible sigh. "I need information, they can give it. If you kill them, I need to go hunting for other Angels. Mostly, I want *that* one," he remarked, nodding to Uriel.

Tamas protested at once. "Donovan owes that one a lot of pain and eventually death. He's been after him for centuries. You can't have him."

"Your brother has been after him for centuries and has failed to capture him. Obviously, he does not want him as badly as I do," Amazarak countered.

"You can't have him."

"Again," Amazarak said softly, but there was no mistaking the steel in his voice, "I wasn't asking."

Tamas swore and threw another wave of fire at the Angels whose flames had just died down. I cringed when the screams started up again and swallowed the bile trying to rise in my throat.

"Why? Why the fuck do you need him?" Tamas demanded angrily.

The air felt charged again, electric, and another boom of thunder sounded overhead, louder this time so that I flinched. Amazarak's black eyes settled on us, and I watched his whole body wind tighter and tighter, but I got the impression he was struggling for control.

"Nephilim are going missing. We are too small in numbers to lose anymore, and the Angels have the answers I need," he finally explained, his voice set low, but the danger in it made the hairs on my arms and neck stand up enough that finding out Nephilim were real was pushed aside.

"Someone is taking Nephilim? How is that even possible?" Tamas asked, clearly shocked.

"That's what I need to know," Amazarak ground out.

There was a whip of movement, and we all turned in time to see Uriel break free of the bind I'd put on him. Before any of us could react, the Angel disappeared with a self-satisfied grin and a rush of air.

Lightning cracked hard and loud overhead and I jerked sharply and ducked like I could escape it. Thunder boomed so loudly it reverberated in my bones. Tamas backed up towards me, keeping himself between me and the pissed off creature in front of us.

"I am taking these ones. You have no say in the matter," Amazarak growled.

"Wait, Amazarak, maybe we can help?" Tamas offered as the

black-winged Nephilim waved his hand and the flames burning the Angels died down to smolders.

"I'll call on Cali if I need your help. In the meantime, protect your Witches better and stay the hell out of my way," Amazarak snarled. One minute he was standing in front of us, and the next there was another boom of thunder, a whoosh of air, and he was gone.

I peeked out from behind Tamas and then straightened and looked around. Uriel was gone, the Angels and Amazarak were gone, and the Demon bodies on the ground were lifeless husks. The silence that surrounded us was thick and heavy, and I struggled to put my thoughts in order. Tamas wasn't just a Demon? Nephilim were real? Who was Uriel and why did Tamas's brother want him so badly? Were Nephilim more powerful than Tamas and his kind? How had the Angels known where to attack? Were Rogue Demons working with Angels? When Tamas turned to face me, only one question came out of my mouth.

"You're a King of Hell?"

CHAPTER TWELVE
HARKYN

Four Years Ago...

"Harkyn!"

The scream in my head jolted me out of my dream so fast it gave me an instant headache. My heart was racing, my chest rose and fell rapidly with every ragged breath, and I was covered in a fine sheen of sweat. I could taste blood and fear in my mouth, and I was suddenly helpless, scared, and desperate.

Wait, no. Not me.

"Harkyn, please! Help me!"

Dimitria!

My heart slammed hard in my chest, and I sank into her mind to see where she was and what she was dealing with. I'd barely discerned the presence of two men and her pain before there was a tugging somewhere in the region of my navel. The sensation was so discerning I frowned and looked down, and without warning, I was yanked out of time and space, compressed, and warped so that I had no understanding of where I was or what was happening. Almost as soon as it happened, I reappeared, fully formed in a dark bedroom.

The scene around me was jumbled, complicated, and it only took me two seconds to take it all in, but it felt far longer.

Dimitria was on a large bed, being held down by a male. Her usual ripped jeans were gone, leaving her in a pair of white panties. Her shirt was torn roughly so that her bra was mostly revealed. There were bruises on her thighs, scratches on her waist and a large bruise forming on her face. Her platinum blonde hair was spread out on the bedspread beneath her in a knotted mass, and black eye makeup smeared down her cheeks from her tears.

The man holding her down—if you could call him that—was maybe a year or two her senior. He was tall, built solidly, and shirtless. His jeans were undone and hanging so the ends were bunched around his feet. His hair was short along the sides, patterns shaved into them in sharp jagged lines meant to look artistic. The grin and glee on his face as he held Tria down told me all I needed to know about him.

He was a dead man.

My gaze moved next to the man on the other side of the room— her foster brother. I recognized him from her memories. He was mostly clothed and sitting in a chair with his jeans lowered, his hardened cock in one hand, a video camera in the other. The satisfied grin on his face made me see red, and a thousand torture scenarios burst into my head in a millisecond guaranteeing he would die painfully.

No one else was in the room, the curtains were closed, and the room was lit only by a lamp on the bedside table. My senses flared out, and I felt the presence of two others in the house downstairs, one an older woman, and the other a man—Tria's foster parents. The man was drunk and sitting in a lounge with a beer in hand watching a game, but I knew he was aware of the screams coming from upstairs, and one touch on his mind told me he was preparing to come up for his turn.

The woman was aware too, but there was no sympathy in her, only cold anger. She blamed Dimitria for what was happening, thought she was a whore, deserving of the treatment she received if she was going to continue to dress the way she did and speak to men as if she had the right. She was pretending nothing was wrong whatsoever and was keeping herself busy.

So, two more soon-to-be dead people downstairs.

Only two seconds had passed since my arrival in the room, but in those two seconds, I knew who was to blame, who would die, and how. Time snapped back into place, and I let out a wall-shaking roar of rage.

The guy holding the camera screamed and dropped it as he tried to scramble up the chair. The man holding Tria down swore loudly, his eyes wide and mouth gaping in terror as he rolled sideways, tripping over the fabric of his jeans and falling hard onto the floor.

"Harkyn," Tria's choked sob caught at me, making me all the more furious. I spared her one quick look; she held my Token in one hand, her face streaked with tears. She hadn't been raped—but it had been close. I didn't give a fuck; these guys were dead and there wasn't a single force on Earth that was going to stop me. The taste of her terror was still thick in the room, the scent of her tears and desperation only feeding my wrath.

"Oh, God, no!" The would-be rapist sobbed as I advanced on him. I gripped him by his short hair and lifted, slamming his back into the wall before I leaned in.

"Not even close," I snarled through gritted teeth before I dug my nails into the skin at his hip. His mouth opened in pain, and I ripped upwards, the skin tearing from his hip to his shoulder in a brutal move, revealing the muscle and sinew beneath. The scream that left him was inhumane, and the feel of his hot blood on my fingers made my body hum with satisfaction.

"Harkyn!" Dimitria screamed, but it was faint, far away, too far to make a difference when the need for vengeance and pain was riding me so hard. All I cared about was the waste of oxygen in front of me and causing him as much suffering as possible.

The door to the bedroom burst open, and the foster parents stumbled inside, their mouths falling open in terror as they took in the scene. I slammed the guy in my grip into the wall hard enough to rattle him before I moved quickly, yanking her foster parents into the room. I crashed them into the opposite wall to await their turn, forcing them to remain still and keep conscious as I worked. Their time would come. Barely remembering that I was topside, I took the time to constrict the vocal cords of all those in the room to prevent their screams reaching the ears of those outside the house, guaranteeing me the time I needed to enjoy this.

I pulled the sobbing asshole up off the floor before repeating my earlier actions, digging my nails into the skin at his right hip and ripped, tearing away strips of flesh. I slipped into his mind when he began to faint and seized his consciousness, forcing him to stay awake.

"No, you don't get the easy way out, fucker. You're going to *feel* this," I warned and shoved my hand into his chest, gripped a rib, and tore it out. Another inhumane scream, and I was lost in bloodlust.

I tore out rib after rib, forcing him to stay awake, forcing his body to stay alive. When Tria's shithead foster brother tried to make a run for the window, I snagged his arm and slammed him into the wall beside his friend so he'd have an up close and personal view and forced him to wait his turn.

Nothing else mattered in that moment, just the sounds of their stifled screams, the feel of their skin tearing, bones snapping, muscles ripping apart and their hot blood bathing my skin. When I was done with the rapist, he was skinless from the hips to his shoulders, his ribs and collar bone had all been snapped off one by one, his intestines were at his feet, and I'd methodically broken every bone in his body. He was lost in an ocean of pain, so for one last gift, I tore his cock from his body and placed it in his hand.

"*Now*, you may die. But this isn't the end for us. I'll see you in Hell, fucker," I hissed, releasing his mind and body from my control. He slumped, lifeless to the ground, what remained of his skin was gray but splattered with blood. The wall and floor around him were soaked in blood and gore, but it wasn't enough, his pain wasn't enough justice for what was happening, for what had been about to happen.

I faintly recalled Tria calling my name again, but I couldn't hear it, not really, not when I still had more pain to deliver. I turned to her foster brother who whimpered, his eyes white and wide with fear as he pissed himself.

"Your turn."

~

Present Day

I set fire to the last of the Rogue Demons and sighed. I'd been going stir crazy in my realm. Every time I wanted to go watch over Tria, Donovan or one of the others talked me out of it. As far as they were concerned, the less I was around her, the less likely it was that I'd die if she accidentally saw me. It made sense, and I knew they were right. More than once I'd almost been caught and it could have resulted in my death. It didn't mean I wanted to listen. Donovan explained that there was a faction of Rogue Demons closing in on Dimitria's location. We weren't sure if it was a coincidence, but considering she was the only Witch we knew of in that city, it was too close for comfort. We'd spent the last two days hunting and destroying them along with the Angels that came to their aid. It still made me angry and sick to know Demons were partnering with the Angels against us. Yes, they were Rogues, and their beliefs were different to ours, but they were working with *Angels*. There was something incredibly nauseating about it.

I was missing Dimitria like crazy, though. It had been far too long since I'd seen her, since I'd heard her voice or heard her laugh. I wanted to be in her presence again, I *needed* to be around her again. I never went long without checking in on her. I might never be able to interact with her or let her see me, but being around her was enough to soothe the irritability I was beginning to feel.

"I think we're done here, but something doesn't feel right," Donovan said as the bodies of the Rogues finally disintegrated into ash.

"I know what you mean. Why were they here? What were they waiting for?" I asked, searching the darkness around us. Donovan opened his mouth to say something when there was a rush of wind, and we both turned to see an Angel stagger to the ground, swearing. The sight would have been comical if I hadn't immediately recognized the Angel.

Uriel.

"Fucking Witch bitch. I'll take her myself and use her against those scum Kings and that *fucking* Nephilim abomination," he swore vehemently.

Again, I felt as though I should laugh at the temper tantrum the Archangel seemed to be throwing, but this was Uriel. Donovan had been after him for years after what he'd done to Mika's ancestor, Tabitha. The meaning of his words had barely penetrated my mind when a wave of barely controlled fury washed over me from Donovan. My brother was facing the Archangel with an expression of rage it was rare to see on him, a deep well of wrath and agony building inside him and directed at the Angel before us.

He must have finally felt us and registered that he was not alone, because he spun suddenly, his eyes locking on us and widening with shock.

"Uriel," Donovan gritted out, flashes of memory and pain coming from him and hitting me square in the chest. My brother had loved Tabitha. Maybe not as a lover, but as a friend, as something else. Although, if I could believe Mika and Calixta's opinion, they believed Tabitha *had* been his mate, but that it hadn't been the right time for them to meet which was why it hurt so much to lose her. It would have been possible for them to make bonds, like their mind, body, and heart even—just like I'd done with Tria—but they would have been unable to bind their souls until the brothers before had bound their mates.

Perhaps it was a good thing she'd died when she had—not *how* she had—or Donovan would have been three-quarters of the way bound to his soul mate and would have suffered her eventual death anyway. Without the rest of us before him binding our mates, he would not have been able to bind their souls and make her immortal like us.

I was only bound by mind to Dimitria, and being forced to stay away from her for four years was, at times, unbearable. I couldn't imagine being bound by heart, mind, and body, and then suffering her death.

Uriel drew a silver blade from his belt, the sound pulling me out of my thoughts, and he glared at Donovan.

"What are you doing here?" Uriel demanded.

I raised an eyebrow. "I'm going to assume the small army of Rogues that we destroyed were under your command?"

Uriel's gaze skirted around, his eyes snagging on the piles of ash that were slowly scattering in the winds before he turned back to us.

"My kind do not work with the likes of yours," Uriel hissed.

"Why bother denying it?" I asked, stepping up beside my brother whose whole body radiated with anger. "We know you're working with the Rogues. What we don't know is why. Or how you convinced them that you were all on the same side."

Uriel sneered. "They're a testament to the true greed and gullibility of your kind."

"What did you promise them?" I continued, knowing Donovan was seconds away from going full supernova.

"Isn't it obvious?" Uriel asked, twirling the blade in his hand. "We promised them your thrones, and all the Witch whores they wanted."

Donovan moved before I could stop him, throwing a blade that hit Uriel high in his left shoulder. The Angel groaned and threw his own blade, but it went wide and missed Donovan by inches. We were both on the move, but just as Nova reached him, the Archangel laughed and disappeared. Nova snarled and let out a deep, bellowing roar. I stepped back as my brother raged, knowing all too well what he was capable of when he was pissed off. It took a few minutes, but when he was finally calm enough, I stepped closer but wasn't stupid enough to touch him.

"Let's go," I said.

"No."

That one word was small, but it held every ounce of rage and violence my brother was capable of.

I drew in a slow breath. "Let's go hunting, brother. He was *just* here, he's injured. Let's see if we can find him, or see where he just came from," I suggested. Donovan stilled and closed his eyes, and I watched as the seconds ticked by and little by little, he seemed to release the tension in his shoulders.

"He was talking about a Witch. Obviously, he had a run-in with one. He also mentioned a Nephilim, I can only guess it's Zarak. Maybe we should check in on Dimitria and call Amazarak to make sure they're both okay?"

Donovan shook his head and sighed. "You can't keep going to your mate, Harkyn. You're both safer apart for now."

"I need to see if she is okay," I reminded, getting antsy.

"Check in with Tamas. He was watching over her tonight," Donovan suggested tiredly. A pang of sympathy hit me as I watched my brother try to rein in his emotions after seeing Uriel again. He'd lost so much already and had no luck in finding Mika's sister in the last two years. He was always looking after the rest of us, looking out for us. I wanted my brother to get his vengeance, and I wanted him to be happy. He deserved it.

"Tamas, were you watching over Dimitria tonight?"

There was a pause as Tamas heard me. *"I am. She's finished work for the night and is entering her building now. She wrapped up another case and looks tired. I think she'll be headed straight for bed."*

I scrubbed a hand over my face and sighed. *"No Angel activity? We had a run-in with Uriel who was bitching about a Witch and a Nephilim before he took off like the coward he is."*

"Nope, your mate is safe and secure, nothing to worry about here. How is Donovan?"

I frowned as I replayed Tamas's words. He wasn't lying, exactly… but there was something in his voice that made me curious.

"Are you sure everything is okay?"

"Everything is fine, brother. Is Donovan and the surrounding area still intact after his run-in?"

Tamas was telling the truth, but he felt… on edge. Sighing, I looked back at Donovan and the way he stared bleakly at the space Urial had been standing. I didn't envy my brother the loss he'd suffered or the fury he felt at not having avenged his friend yet.

"Everything is still alive and standing. We're probably going hunting anyway if you care to join."

I felt Tamas's sympathy for our brother. *"Probably better I stay here and watch over your woman. But call me if I'm needed."*

Appreciation for my family hit me hard and I took a moment to swallow it. I'd made mistakes that were costing them time and effort, but none of them complained about it. They'd all been taking turns in guarding my mate, and I'd be forever grateful for that.

"Thank you, Tamas. Let me know if anything is wrong."

I felt the affirmative response from Tamas before we disengaged and I stepped close to Donovan again.

"I trust your mate is safe?" he asked quietly.

"She is," I confirmed. "Let's go hunting, brother."

Donovan was already shaking his head, but I put a hand out to stop him from stepping away.

"It will help to look, and if we stumble upon any other Angels or Rogues along the way, you'll have someone to work your anger out on. Let's see if we can pick up Uriel's trail, and pray he has no Witches nearby with the need to heal him."

Donovan hesitated, and I felt his need to tear something apart, battle with the side of him he was trying to cultivate, the side that was logical and calm, reasonable and grown. He didn't want to react in anger every time he saw Uriel, but I had a feeling that it was a pointless battle.

"You're not going to go run off to your mate?" Donovan asked, eyeing me skeptically.

I shook my head. "I want to, fuck knows I want to. But you're right. It's getting harder and harder to stay in the shadows and keep myself apart from her. If I go back to her, I might fuck up. It'll feel worth it just to hold her again, but I need to stay away until we get some answers."

Nova nodded slowly and sighed. "You're sure?"

I smiled and punched him lightly in the arm. "I can feel your eagerness for some vengeance, and I, of all people, understand that drive. Let's go get bloody. Having me with you might save your ugly mug from being Angel bladed."

Nova scoffed and tried to sound calm and amused, but I felt that river of rage still bubbling beneath the surface of his calm veneer. "Body count competition?" he offered.

"Angels or Rogues?" I asked, grinning.

"Both. Loser does all the paperwork for a week," Donovan added.

"Oh, you're on. I look forward to lightening the load in my in-tray," I agreed.

Donovan grinned at the easy-going banter before we shadowed out, sensing for the trail of a doomed Angel. Nova was putting on a good front, but if he ever got his hands on Uriel again, the Angel was going to suffer unlike any soul in Hell ever had.

CHAPTER THIRTEEN
DIMITRIA

Four Years Ago

I sat in the hotel room, my back to the headboard of the bed, my legs clutched to my chest. My hair was still damp and leaving wet patches on my clothes, but I didn't care.

I couldn't stop hearing them scream.

Movies got it all wrong. The men and women playing roles in horror movies and thrillers just didn't have the real deal to their shouts of terror. Yes, Harkyn had done something to lower the decibel of their cries, but I'd heard them, I'd heard them all.

I closed my eyes and a tear tracked down my cheek, but I immediately opened them again when the vision of blood and the sounds of snapping bone became more vivid behind my closed lids.

I couldn't stop shaking no matter how hard I tried. Blood, flesh, and skin had been *everywhere,* coating every inch of the room, some of it even landed on me. And their screams... The inhumane sounds of agony, the pleading and sobbing continued to echo in my head on some grotesque loop. I'd seen violence before—seen men beat women, seen a foster sibling stab their foster parent. I'd seen broken bones and felt what it was to be hurt myself. But nothing, *nothing,* could compare to the kind of violence I'd witnessed.

The Harkyn I knew—or thought I knew—hadn't been there tonight. When I'd grabbed the necklace and pleaded for his help, it had been a last desperate attempt not to suffer the rape I knew was coming. I hadn't thought Harkyn would arrive and literally strip them of their flesh and make them plead and beg in such a way I was sure to hear in my nightmares for the rest of my life. I'd tried to call him off, begged for him to stop and let them go, but it was like he couldn't hear me. My words had no effect. I'd tried reaching him in his mind, to soothe him and calm him, to beg him to just take me out of there and leave them, but the block in his mind had been unlike anything I'd encountered before. It wasn't there to keep me out of his head, but rather to *protect me* from what was going on in there.

I flinched as another memory of his harsh words and gleeful expression filtered across my mind. What he'd done was beyond terrifying, beyond comprehension, but it had been the *joy* on his face as he made them hurt that I couldn't get over. He'd *liked* causing them pain, he'd enjoyed hearing them scream, beg, and plead. He'd been determined to wring every ounce of pain from them that he could before moving onto the next.

No one had survived. No one had been spared.

Harkyn had started with Isaac, my foster brother's friend, and maybe it was only five minutes, maybe it was days, but his torture seemed to go on forever before Harkyn let him go. Then Jeremy, my foster brother. Much like with Isaac, Harkyn made sure he knew why he was being tortured and what was going to happen to him. I'd never seen someone so scared in my life; I'd never felt such fear—it was chilling.

My foster parents had begged and pleaded for him to stop, to leave their son. As usual, they defended him. He was just a boy who had made a mistake, boys would be boys, he'd learn, they'd made sure he never did it again. Even in the face of such a monster like Harkyn, they hadn't been capable of admitting that their son was a psychopath in the making.

By the time Harkyn turned to them, I felt in control of my body and had tried to stop him. Not because my foster parents deserved to live or have me protect them in a way they'd *never* done for me, but because I didn't want Harkyn to keep doing this. I didn't want to bear witness. He was covered in blood and gore, but he seemed to relish in it.

With a gentleness I hadn't known he was capable of at the time, Harkyn had gripped my upper arms and put me back on the bed, and before I could get up again, he waved his hand and somehow, I was stuck there. I could move, but not off the bed. It was as if there were some invisible force field keeping me in.

He started with my foster father first. I knew Harkyn had gone into his mind, and with every passing second, with every thought and memory he took from my foster father, his expression darkened, feeding the rage inside. For the first time, I saw my foster father pale and start to cry, but he wasn't to be spared either. His torture seemed to last longer than either of the first two, and my foster mother sobbed uncontrollably.

I was near catatonic when he started on her, and she suffered worst of all. Harkyn seemed to think as my step-in mother, that she had a greater duty to protect me, to defend me, and she had not only failed in her duty, but had even allowed things to happen. His disgust with her was beyond what he felt for the others, and the fact that she was a woman made no difference to Harkyn. She was a bad soul in need of punishing in his opinion, and he punished her brutally.

When at last he allowed her to die, I couldn't move. I'd been rocking back and forth on the bed, lost in my mind in an attempt to distance myself from what I'd been forced to witness. When Harkyn turned back to me, he was soaked in their blood, and he didn't look the least bit ashamed. With a wave of his hand, he cleaned himself up and then did the same with me, but I still couldn't move.

The silence that surrounded us was both full of chaos and mixed emotions, and yet empty, void of anything to say or think. There was nothing but static. I wasn't looking at the man I'd come to love, the Demon King I'd fallen for. I was looking at a stranger I could not reconcile with the creature I'd spent the last few months falling for.

"We're leaving," he said, his voice rough and thick, shattering the silence. Hearing him speak to me was like the catalyst to set me off, and I burst into tears. His eyes looked pained as he stepped towards me, and I shuffled away from him quickly, keeping as much space between us as possible. He froze, his eyes locked on me as I moved to the opposite edge of the bed.

"Dimitria."

"Stay away from me!" I screamed, my chest heaving. I couldn't breathe, I couldn't feel anything but terror and panic. What the *hell?*

"Tria—"

"Who are you? Wh-what did you—I can't," I stammered, hot tears streaking down my face fast and uncontrollable.

"Just come with me so I can get you somewhere safe," he suggested, making a move towards me again, but I couldn't be near him. I leapt off the bed to keep space between us—glad that I could leave now—but something hot and wet squelched beneath my feet and I gasped and looked down. It took precious seconds for my brain to fully comprehend what I was standing in, and when it did, I screamed. My feet were sunk in about an inch of flesh and blood, squishing between my toes and under my feet, and horror took me over completely.

Harkyn hurried to me, and I scrambled away from him, acting on nothing but instinct. He was powerful, horrible, and capable of the kind of violence I hadn't known existed, and he was getting too close. I slid in the mess, stumbling backwards and hit the ground hard. The blood around me sent me into a terrified panic and I couldn't do anything but cry and scream.

Harkyn was there, but I couldn't see him, couldn't do anything more than kick and beg him to leave me alone, to not touch me. He tried to calm me. I felt him in my head trying to soothe me, but I was lost to the terror. The next thing I knew, I was curled up on the floor of a shower with hot water beating down on me. I don't know how long I had been in there, a long time if the redness to my skin was anything to go by, and I was alone. My face felt swollen from tears, my throat raw from crying and screaming, and I ached from being curled up in the same position for far too long. It took me a long while, but I managed to pull myself up on wobbly knees and turn off the water before I wrapped myself in a towel.

Looking around, I could see I was in a motel bathroom. I didn't know how I got here or where *here* was exactly, but that was beyond my control right now. *Adapt, accept, react.*

I spotted a duffle bag on the basin, and I recognized it as my own. Without giving it much thought, I forced myself to dress in a pair of long cotton sleep pants and a black racerback tee. My hair was dripping wet, and I did the best I could to dry it with shaky hands before I started for the door. I listened intently for several seconds, scanning around me to see if anyone was nearby, and when I was sure the coast was clear, I stepped out. I was definitely in a hotel room. There was a queen-sized bed in the center, bedside tables, a TV bolted to the opposite wall, a bar-fridge and a microwave and toaster on the counter. Another duffle bag I recognized as my own and my school bag sat in a small chair beside the window where the curtains had been pulled closed, but otherwise I was alone.

I had two bags of belongings here, which was practically everything I owned anyway. I had to assume Harkyn was the one who packed them.

Thinking his name caused my knees to almost give out again, and I moved for the bed where I burrowed beneath the blankets and sat with my back to the headboard. I was cold, but not in a way I could fix. I was cold *inside*. My eyes burned from unshed tears, and I tried to remember what happened after Harkyn caught me, but I was blank. I'd been out of my mind with terror...

Over and over, the hours I'd spend locked in place on that bed ran through my head and I felt sick. Harkyn had *liked* what he was doing, he had *wanted* their pain and fear, wanted their tears and pleas. How could I have ever loved such a monster? I knew he was a Demon King, on some level I knew what that meant, but seeing him in action so blatantly was a shock I wasn't sure I'd ever return from. How could I ever look at him the same? How could I be near him and not fear him? How could I trust him to not do anything like that again? Why hadn't he heard me or listened when I begged him to stop? I had only wanted him to get me out of there when it was obvious I wasn't able to escape on my own.

I'd come home from school and Jeremy had snagged my wrist on my way past his room. He'd yanked me inside and slammed the door shut, and that's when I'd seen Isaac there. At once, I'd known I was in danger, but I tried to get out on my own. Nothing I did helped. I was slapped several times and forced onto the bed. I kicked and screamed for help—my foster parents were downstairs so they had to be able to hear me—but no one came. That was when I realized they knew but didn't care. I'd seen my foster brother take a seat with a video camera in hand, and I tried to kick out, but Isaac punched me in the face so hard I'd fallen backwards onto the bed and was momentarily stunned. It had been long enough for him to take off my jeans. I fought back, but he tore my shirt and then grabbed my wrists. I'd tried to get free, knowing my foster brother was getting pleasure from my pain only made my reality so much more real. I could remember them laughing and talking, Issac saying something about me being worth the money and my foster brother agreeing I would be. Isaac had paid my brother for the opportunity to rape me.

I'd never felt so desperate and alone, and I'd reached for Harkyn. I knew he was asleep, and it took a few tries before I had reached him, and by that point Isaac had unbuttoned his jeans and I yanked a hand free to grip my necklace and scream for Harkyn. When he'd arrived, I'd been so relieved, so happy to see him, and then it had all gone to hell.

The hotel room door opened suddenly and I gasped and stiffened at the sight of Harkyn as he entered. He hesitated a moment, his gaze zapping over me before he stepped inside and closed the door behind him. My heart pounded hard, and I couldn't stop the overwhelming feeling of fear that filled me.

I knew the second he felt it too, because he flinched and his expression filled with remorse. He was clean, and looking at him, I never would have known what he'd done earlier or what he was capable of. Love fought with fear and disgust and disappointment as I looked at him.

He didn't move from where he stood, and I was locked tight in dread. Several minutes passed before he finally sighed, and his shoulders drooped. He scrubbed a hand over his face and cleared his throat.

"I got your things out, anything I knew was yours. The house, I burned it. There's nothing left for you to go back to now. I need you to come with me."

I blinked stupidly as his words slowly penetrated, and I frowned. "I... I'm not going anywhere with you," I whispered, my voice hoarse.

"This isn't the time to get into it, nor is it up for discussion. You have no family here, no life. You are a Witch, you're being hunted, you need protection. Obviously, I can't protect you up here, so you need to come with me now."

"No," I snapped, anger burning its way through me. I gripped it tightly and fed it so it built hot and bright inside me. I was tired of feeling scared and helpless.

"This isn't up for debate," Harkyn growled. I could see it now. The careful mask of calm was nothing but that—a mask. He was still angry, and it was bubbling just beneath the surface.

"No," I reiterated and slowly stood from the bed. "I won't go *anywhere* with you. Not after what you did. I know who the hell you are, but you're not the man I thought you were."

"That's your problem, sweetheart, because I told you from the beginning I am *not* simply a *man*. I am a Demon King, and I am the deliverer of justice to those who end up in my realm. I never lied to you about what I am." His voice was low and full of rage and impatience.

"You lied to me everyday you played the part of this dashing hero teaching me to be a Witch. I begged you, Harkyn," I added, my voice catching as tears burned my eyes again. "I begged you to stop, but you ignored me."

"They deserved what they got," he argued hotly, not an ounce of regret in his voice.

Who the hell was he? The stranger staring back at me was *not* who I had fallen in love with. He couldn't be the same man who held me close when I needed to cry or the one who brushed my tears away so gently it made my heart flutter. There was no way he was the same person who laughed with me, who'd kissed me with so much passion and need, who had morals and integrity enough not to sleep with me because, in his opinion, I was too young.

I shook my head and wiped away the tear that snuck down my cheek. "No. I'm not going anywhere with you. You need to leave."

"I'm not leaving without you."

"Go, Harkyn. I don't want you here anymore. I don't want *you*. Leave me alone. Go back to Hell, and stay there. I don't care just stay away from me!" I yelled, letting my anger flow free.

"You are mine, *cara,* and I will not let you go now."

"If you try to keep me, Harkyn, I'll sooner kill myself than let that happen. You tricked me. You—I *begged* you to stop!" I shouted, my voice ravaged even to my own ears.

He stepped closer, his eyes burning with anger. "They were hurting you, Dimitria, and they had plans for much more. So did your foster father. That woman knew what was happening and did nothing. She even thought you deserved it. Those people were not worth the air they breathed. I did the world—and you—a favor."

"You did it for yourself!" I returned hotly. "I saw how much you enjoyed it; how much you liked hearing them scream and beg. I saw your face, Harkyn. You relished in their agony and fear!"

"So what if I did?" he bellowed, stepping closer again. "I am a King of Hell. Torture is what I do, and the people I torture *deserve* their pain."

"*I* asked you to *stop!*" I reminded. "Does it even matter to you what I want? *I* was the one being hurt, *I* was the one almost raped, and my needs were ignored there too. When you arrived, I was relieved, but you ignored what I wanted too. You put up a wall in your mind I couldn't breach, and you made me *watch*. You kept me captive as you tore into them—" I broke off and struggled to draw breath.

"I was protecting you," he ground out.

I scoffed. "You were scratching an itch. You were indulging in your favorite activity. What I wanted no longer mattered."

"You have no idea what I felt when I saw you like that," he snarled, his voice a low growl as he edged closer. I should have recognized the danger I was in right there, but I didn't. My skin felt itchy and hot, my heart was thudding hard, my body vibrating with some kind of need. What he felt was mixing with my own emotions and I couldn't push them away long enough to build up that wall in my head. I wanted to shout and yell, I wanted to scream, I wanted... *something*.

"Why should I care when you've never cared what I wanted? When I wanted *you,* you said no. When I said I didn't care about the age gap, you said no. Any time I have broached the subject of us being more than what we are right now, you always say no. And when I asked you to stop torturing them, you ignored me. What *I* want has never been a priority to you, only what you consider to be the best option!"

Harkyn was on me in a second, his mouth covering mine, his hands rough and hard. I should have been angry, I should have been scared and disgusted, but the second he was touching me, the moment his lips crashed against mine, I was gone. I was a tangled web of desire, anger, fear, and a million other things so that I couldn't decipher one from the other nor what were my feelings or his. Harkyn fell with me onto the bed so that I was beneath him, his hands trailing over my body, shaping me with his hands, his tongue and teeth teasing me to the point where I was panting. There was something else going on here, something I needed to say. I shouldn't be with him, shouldn't be encouraging this, but it was like my body had a mind of its own, it's need for him being enticed by something else. I moved and rocked, arched, and ground against him. I heard him swear, felt his body's response and the overwhelming need in him to take me. Considering the last time I was in this position with a man over the top of me, I should be screaming right now, running, trying to fight my way free, but this was Harkyn. Everything with him was different, was *always* different, and his touch only ignited within me a need I knew would never extinguish. I tore at his shirt, relishing in the sound of material ripping, and my hands skated over the hot flesh of his chest. The rumble I felt beneath my palms elicited a rush of desire within me so that a throbbing started between my legs. He rocked against me, his mouth on my neck, his teeth nipping and scraping, and I moaned. His hands slid up to my breasts and I arched again, whimpering as his fingers teased my nipples, needing more. I was blind with lust and anger, the two dangerous emotions tangling and feeding off one another so that neither of us had control or any tangible thought. The rules didn't matter, the reasons we shouldn't be doing this no longer existed within this mess of need and desperation.

"More," I pleaded in his head and my hands slid down to the button of his jeans. I got it free and had just slid his zipper down

when he growled loudly and tore away from me so quickly and with such force he slammed against the drywall, cracking it. If I didn't know any better, I'd have thought someone threw him off. He was panting, his eyes burning with hunger, anger and… fear. Swallowing hard, I pushed up onto my elbows and watched him, feeling confused. What the hell had just happened? The hands that had just been caressing me with such gentleness and need had only hours ago been tearing flesh from bone, and I'd allowed him to touch me.

What the hell was wrong with me?

His emotions were as tangled and confused as mine, but one thing was prominent in his head. He wanted me with such a desperate savagery that he'd scared himself. He wanted to fuck me; his body was demanding it. His blood was at boiling point, something inside him demanded he take me, to tie me to him somehow and keep me locked up forever, chained to his side so I could never escape.

Fear began to trickle down my spine, dampening the heat and hunger I felt for him. He was struggling. I watched the fight behind his eyes, the way he held himself completely still against the wall, his wide eyes locked on me. I didn't move an inch, too afraid that if I did, he'd lose the battle he was fighting and take me.

What I feared more was that I'd let him. All he had to do was touch me, kiss me, and I was a goner. My fear increased when I realized how much of my future was in his hands right now.

"Harkyn," I whispered softly, wondering if there was anything I could say that would prevent him from somehow tying me to him for all time.

Swearing, Harkyn reached into his boot and pulled out a small knife. I shot up at once and held out a hand to him as if I could ward him off. Gritting his teeth, he cut a line along his wrist and I gasped, automatically moving to stop him, to heal him. The cut barely registered in his head and the second I was within reach, he used his injured arm to take my forearm in his grip. I stilled, not sure what was going on. He looked down at me with such an intense look that I was rooted to the spot. Need was still riding him hard, but confusion flooded me. What was he doing?

In a low voice, he began to speak. I couldn't understand the words. They were a language I didn't know, but they were somehow... beautiful. He spoke low and quick, his eyes flaring with need, his jaw tense. I bit back a gasp when I saw his blood wind around my wrist and then back to his in a figure-eight. The moment between us seemed to draw out for ages. I looked back up to him and he stopped speaking, but before I could let go, he tugged me forward again, his other hand bunching in my damp hair and he kissed me hard. I let him, kissing him back, feeling something of a farewell in his touch. He was desperately angry, scared... and heartbroken.

When he pulled away, I gasped and looked up at him, confused. He stared down at me with searching eyes, his hand still clasping my forearm tightly, but something was happening, some inner war he was waging.

"There; you'll never have to worry about me again, but at least you'll be safe."

I opened my mouth to ask what he was talking about, but he kissed me hard and fast one more time and let me go. By the time I opened my eyes again, he was gone. I was left feeling empty, worried, and somehow more alone than ever before.

CHAPTER FOURTEEN
DIMITRIA

I woke with a jolt, the memory of that terrible night so vivid, it was as if it had just happened. Tears dampened my pillow, and I realized I'd been crying in my sleep. Muttering to myself, I wiped them away and pushed myself into a sitting position and drew my knees up. That night was the last time I'd seen Harkyn, and it haunted me. Having had time to relive that night a thousand times, I could see now the struggle he faced. He'd been very clear from our first meeting that his priority was me. He would never bend his rules to sleep with me while I was so young, no matter how much he wanted me. And I *knew* how much he wanted me. I'd been in his head, felt the demands of his body, experienced that incredibly strong pull to throw his morals out the window and do what some unknowable force was urging him to do. He'd wanted me, and still he'd fought tooth and nail to do what was right by me. I touched my wrist and admitted there was an odd kind of weight to it. No, it didn't feel heavy exactly, but sometimes I could swear there was a weight there that tugged once in a while. Whatever he'd done—that chant with his blood—I knew now it was to protect me. He had decided to leave that night, but not without seeing to my safety first. Despite my anger at him for leaving me these last four years, I could appreciate the fact that he'd made sure I was safe first.

As for the rest, as for Isaac and my foster family, I didn't believe they deserved the pain they suffered while alive, but they hadn't been good people. My foster brother would have grown to be a monster, and he would have hurt so many other women, destroying lives without a care in the world. His friend, Isaac, was just as bad. At least now they weren't able to do any damage. And my foster parents? They would never take in another vulnerable kid and hurt them the way I'd been hurt. I shivered at the memory of their last moments and felt a little nauseous.

Time and space had given me what I needed to see the events of that night clearly, and while I still didn't think they deserved what they got, not to those extremes, I couldn't say I was sorry they were gone. Harkyn had warned me that he was a man not used to denying himself the things he wanted. I knew from being in his head that he had a protective streak towards those he cared about, and those he cared about were few and far between. From what I knew, those he *did* care about could all look after themselves. I could understand now how seeing me in that position had driven him temporarily insane. I was not someone who could guard herself against the kind of assault that had been happening—at least not back then—and he'd cared about me deeply, maybe even loved me, even though he'd never said the words.

It had been four years; I'd come to grips with it and had even managed to let go of the guilt I'd been feeling. Yes, they'd all been terrible people, but I'd felt responsible for their deaths because I'd called Harkyn. It had taken a long time, but I finally came to terms with everything and moved past it. I couldn't change what had happened, and I lived every day to make sure bad people didn't get away with doing shitty things.

My heart clenched when I remembered our last kiss. He'd known it was goodbye, I'd even felt it at the time, but it had taken me several days, weeks even, to fully accept that he was gone. He'd broken my heart when he hadn't come back. I'd loved him in a way I hadn't ever experienced again. It was soul-deep and entrenched in me as if it were a part of me. I'd loved him, and he left. I was almost certain he'd been in love with me too, which always confused me as to how he could stay gone forever. I'd asked him to leave, yes—but I'd been emotional and hurting. I'd thought he'd come back after giving me some space. Obviously, he hadn't loved me enough...

I thought back to earlier tonight and what Tamas said. He knew Harkyn, and he said Harkyn loved me. Frowning, I shook my head. Tamas was a King of Hell as well. Did that make Harkyn and Tamas brothers? I remembered Harkyn saying he was the King of the fourth circle of Hell. How many circles were there? And were all of the kings his brothers?

Groaning, I scrubbed a hand over my face and leaned my head back against the headboard.

When Tamas left earlier tonight, he'd barely explained anything. I'd asked him if it were true, if he was a King of Hell, and he'd grudgingly admitted it. But when I asked why he hadn't told me, why he'd lied, if he knew Harkyn personally, where he was and why he'd never come back for me, he'd remained stubbornly silent.

My hand trailed down to the necklace that rested on my chest and my breath hitched at the idea of calling Harkyn. I didn't hate him. To be honest, I wasn't sure I ever had. I'd been scared, confused, horrified at the violence he was capable of, but I'd had time to process everything since he'd been gone. I missed him like crazy. My heart had never healed from his absence in my life.

If I called him to me now, would he answer? Would he be happy to see me? Would he explain?

You'll have to leave that behind.

Trinity's words came back to me and I dropped the Token. She was getting out of town soon, and my chance to leave was going with her. If I called Harkyn and he was happy to see me, I'd never leave, and I'd effectively be choosing a side in this war, because there was no way I could fight against him, and no way I wouldn't help him if he needed it.

If I left, I'd have to leave the Token behind, and any chance I had to see Harkyn again along with it. Could I do it? I'd gone these last four years without seeing him. I'd gone all this time knowing he wasn't coming back. But deep down, had a piece of me been holding onto the idea that we'd one day see each other again? If I left now, I'd be closing that door for good. I wouldn't risk the lives and freedoms of the other Witches in the group by looking for him or giving Demons a way to track me.

Sighing, I thought back to the other events of tonight.

Nephilim.

I mean, I had heard of them of course, but a part of me had always assumed they were either extinct or had never existed at all and were just a story to scare other Angels and Demons. Nephilim were meant to be incredibly powerful, and after seeing Zarak tonight, I had to admit he was. Even Tamas, who wasn't exactly lacking in the power department, hadn't fought the creature when he'd taken the Angels.

It bothered me a good deal to know Rogue Demons were a thing and that they'd come looking for me. Tamas said they'd teamed up with the Angels, so what did that mean? And how had Angels come close to finding me twice now? We'd been less than a block from my apartment when they ambushed us. I was sure to cloak myself from being found every few days, and I *never* missed it. Zarak had said he could sense me. Was that true, or had he been trying to appear more knowing than he already was?

Groaning, I raked my fingers through my hair and frowned. At the end of the day, I didn't like how close the events of tonight had taken me to being forced to choose a side. Tamas had made it his mission to protect me, to look after me, and if we were ever overrun more than we had been tonight, he would die protecting me. Could I live with that? No, hell no. Despite his lies, Tamas had become my friend, and I would hate to be the cause of his pain or death. But nothing short of choosing Demons and going to Hell would stop him from following me around. So what was I going to do?

My gaze fell on my phone by the bed, and I gnawed on my lower lip. Was running really the right choice? Angels didn't seem to be great, even some of their own were leaving their ranks.

Demons—not the Rogues—thus far seemed to be the safer and morally correct side in this war. I scoffed. I had come to this conclusion after having an incredibly vivid dream about the times my former King of Hell Demon boyfriend had shredded four humans, caused them insurmountable pain, and enjoyed every moment of it.

Sighing, I picked up my phone and flipped it over again and again. It was just after midnight, but I needed more information before I decided. I sent my senses flaring and picked up Tamas's aura. He wasn't in the room, but he was somewhere close by, keeping track of me no doubt. I needed to talk to Trinity, but not if he would overhear.

Whispering under my breath, I cast a spell that would put me in a bubble that would not allow for sound to escape. Flicking through the contacts, I found Trinity's name and pressed dial.

She answered on the third ring. "Dimitria, are you okay?"

"How did you know it was me?" I asked, frowning.

"Because you are the only person who has this number. Are you okay?"

I hesitated and sighed. "I'm okay, I'm just confused. I need more information about what leaving with you entails. I need to know... you. I know it's probably not possible in a short phone call, but I just can't leave without knowing who you are and what you're about," I explained, rolling my eyes at myself. I couldn't have bungled it up more had I tried.

There was a soft laugh from the other end, and she sighed. "I get it, I really do, and it's more than okay. I wouldn't feel comfortable just running away with a stranger because she offered a way out either. What do you want to know?"

I smiled. "Yeah. I guess... Did you always know you were a Witch? Did your parents teach you about magic?"

"No." She sighed. "I mean, I've always known I had magic, but I didn't know *what* I was until I was older. I was in the foster system for years until I ran away. So, I don't remember my parents. I went searching for answers and discovered what I was, what was going on in the world, and then made it my mission to help save those who had no idea we were being hunted."

Knowing she'd been in the system too made me feel a little closer to her. She could understand my inability to trust easily.

"And-and how did you learn about the Kings of Hell?" I asked, clearing my throat.

She hesitated a moment and I held my breath, wondering if she'd answer. "I read about them, honestly. I found a lot of old wiccan books that helped me learn about our world and its dangers."

"And the Kings are written down as a danger to us?" I asked, wanting to rage against it.

Trinity sighed. "Not exactly. They're Demon Kings, they run and control the legions of Hell. From most of the accounts I've read, they're not interested in turning the world against Heaven and getting as many souls to Hell as possible as religious fanatics have been saying for years. They're there to punish the wicked, which makes them seekers of justice. They do their job and they do it well. They're not evil like everyone assumes, if that answers anything."

"So, you've never met any of them in person?" I asked, fiddling with the necklace again.

"I've had my dalliances with one and seen some others from a distance," she answered.

I frowned. "What does that mean?"

She hesitated again. "Are you sure you're safe there? No one is listening?"

"I put myself in a soundproof bubble with magic just in case."

She laughed lightly, and I smiled. "Okay, that's smart. Look, the truth is, I have met one, and he wasn't what I expected. He was charming—far too good looking—and seemed to be genuine in his concern for me and my safety. But I had a mission, and he would have gotten in the way of it. I didn't need or want his protection. Not until I was taken, anyway," she answered with a heavy sigh.

"The Angels?" I asked carefully, aware this could be a touchy subject.

"The Angels," she confirmed. "They took me and tortured me. I had no way to reach him or anyone else, and if it hadn't been for Lev, then I'd either be dead or they'd still have me. They kept going on about specific Witches being meant for the Kings of Hell, and how keeping these Witches from the Demons would give them more power. They were convinced I was one of them, and that I could be used as bait."

I frowned and shuffled until I was more comfortable. "Is it true? Can you be used as bait?"

"I don't know. I don't know if I believe certain Witches are tied to the Kings in some inexplicable way, but I don't think I'm one of them. I do fear that the Kings think so, though, and that's why they'll hunt and take any Witch they find," she answered. "I just don't want to give them the opportunity to take me."

I swallowed hard at her words and tried to find a way to ask what I needed to know. "So, you wouldn't trust them to keep their word? You wouldn't consider siding with them?"

She was silent for a moment, and I liked that she gave it some honest thought.

"I... don't know. I know for sure I'll never side with the Angels after what they put me through, but I'm not sure siding with the Kings is smart, either. Remaining neutral and looking out for my own kind seems the smartest move."

I nodded and then made a sound of assent when I remembered she couldn't see me.

"Do you want to side with the Demons?" she asked softly. "You have a Token from one of them. I can't imagine he'd give it to you without some strong reason to do so. To give someone the ability to summon them in an instant is leaving themselves vulnerable if the wrong person got their hands on it."

I considered her words as I played with it and bit back a sigh.

"Did you know the Demon I was with in the café is a King of Hell as well?"

Her silence rang through loudly. "Yes."

"I thought you might have, after your reaction to learning about him when we met in the park."

I went on to explain what had happened tonight—all of it—and by the end of it, we were both silent in our thoughts.

"Dimitria, I think you need to get out of there. That's twice now an Angel or other enemies have come close to your home and found you. You said you ward yourself regularly, so they shouldn't be able to find you through any bursts of magic you're using, and yet somehow, they are. Add in the fact that you have a Token from King and another is shadowing your every move…"

"I know," I admitted and swallowed hard. "That's why I'm calling. I was trying to decide what to do. If I don't go with you, then I still need to run. Either that or side with the Demons because I have a Token from one, and am friends with another."

Trinity gave a small sigh that ended in a light laugh and I could picture her shaking her head at my conundrum.

"So, what are you going to do?"

I bit my lower lip and thought about it and tried to sense what the right answer was. Anytime I leaned towards the Demons, I was aware of what I'd be giving up, and I didn't want to lose that freedom. I couldn't stay here for several reasons, but the one that tugged at me hardest was that Tamas would be in constant danger. If things had gone differently tonight, he might have died or been captured, and that would be on my head. I also now knew he was likely related to Harkyn, and that meant Harkyn had sent him in the first place, or that Tamas could report my comings and goings to Harkyn and bring him back into my life before I was ready.

On the other side, freedom now meant running constantly, trying to stay under the radar. I'd be running from Angels *and* Demons, and considering how easily Angels were finding me now, I wasn't sure I could run on my own for long. I shivered at the thought of ending up with the Angels.

Glancing down at the Token in my hand, I swallowed hard and

let out a long breath, closing my eyes on the sudden stinging. "I need to leave, and I need your help."

CHAPTER FIFTEEN
DONOVAN

I'd kill Uriel if it was the last thing I did.

I paced back and forth in front of my fireplace, my fingers linked on top of my head as I strode angrily; first one way and then spun and did the same in the opposite direction. That bastard had managed to give me the slip one too many times. Maybe looking for Mika's sister was a waste of time. Maybe she was better off in hiding away from all of this shit. Perhaps I'd have better luck in turning my attention to tracking Uriel and luring him out into the open. If I could capture that asshole and bring him back down here to Hell, I could torture him for eternity. He deserved no less, and it had the added bonus of getting information out of him.

I closed my eyes as frustration nearly influenced me to get started on the hunt now and leave everything else behind, but just then, an image of Tabitha's deep blue eyes swimming with tears burned across my memory and I came to a sudden halt and closed my eyes in dismay. I'd promised her. She was meant to have been safe with me, and instead, her friendship with me had cost her and her entire family their lives. I owed it to her to protect her descendants, and that meant finding Mika's sister and ensuring her safety.

I had to think logically. First, Harkyn needed all our help to break his Word in a way that wouldn't end up with him dead. Cole, Mika, Calixta, Adrik, and on occasion, Malik and Sawyer, were constantly down in the basement searching through several millennia worth of junk for answers. Once we figured out how to get Harkyn his mate, then I could take off on my own vendetta. The only thing to decide was if I was going to search for Mika's sister first or go after Uriel.

"I need to speak with you." Tamas's voice was unusually serious, and alarm bells went off in my head. I waved my hand towards my door, and it opened. Tamas came in and shut the door behind him, looking worried.

"What is it? Is Dimitria okay?"

"She's fine," he said quickly and then shook his head. "At least for now. But I think I fucked up tonight, and I think it's going to send her running."

"Fucked up how?" I demanded. I swear to fucking Lucifer if he went and put the moves on her and she reciprocated, I was going to do my brother a favor and murder him right here. It would be a favor to him in contrast to what Harkyn would do.

"We were ambushed tonight near her building, Rogues and Angels. Uriel showed up, and so did Zarak," he continued. I nodded, already knowing this. "When Uriel was blabbing, he announced that I was a King of Hell."

Ah, shit.

"Okay, well that's not ideal, but it's also not a deal breaker."

"She's going to run, Donovan," he said ominously. I wanted to argue, but he'd spent the last several days getting to know her. If someone knew her by now, it was him.

"How do you know?"

"I just do. She asked about Harkyn, if I knew him, what it all meant. I know she's still in love with him. She admitted she used to be and likely still is. She thinks he just doesn't want her and won't beg for his attention. But after tonight, after that fight, she's got some kind of plan, I know it, but I don't know what it is."

"Do you think she'll use her Token?" I asked, dreading the outcome of that.

Tamas hesitated. "She seems equal parts averse to using it and tempted."

Shit. We were flying blind here, and had no idea what to do. I considered Zarak. The Nephilim had been around for a long time, he was incredibly powerful, and maybe he knew a way around our issue.

"What about Zarak? Can we ask him for help protecting her?"

"I wouldn't," Tamas said and shook his head.

"Why not?"

He stepped around me to grab himself a drink. "He was there tonight, and when I asked him what he wanted, he said he could sense me, the Angels... and Dimitria."

I frowned. "Impossible. You said she's warded constantly."

"She is," Tamas answered and took a mouthful of his drink. "But he claims he could sense her anyway. I don't know, Donovan. I'm not sure how much we should be trusting that Neph, there's something off about him."

"He does seem to be more powerful than the average Nephilim," I conceded, giving it some thought.

"That doesn't even cut it. Have you noticed when he shows up and is all mad, the weather acts up? Thunder and lightning. No other Nephilim ever has such an announcement," Tamas pointed out.

I frowned. I had noticed that, but we'd also been dealing with other issues and it had slipped my mind.

"His wings are different too; black and far bigger than the others. Then, tonight, I set fire to a bunch of Angels, and he put out the hellfire with a wave of his hand, Donovan."

My eyes widened and refrained from gaping. *That* was news, and very interesting. No Nephilim could do that—none. They were part human, part Angel, and neither species had any control over hellfire.

"He can see us in the shadows, he senses the Witches, he can touch and put out hellfire without being harmed. He influences the weather and is a fuck-load faster and stronger than any other Nephilim we've ever heard of. I'm telling you, I'm not sure it's wise to trust him with anything."

I shook my head. "But he has a soft spot for Cali. He shows up for her whenever he can," I pointed out.

Tamas shrugged. "I'm just saying, let's not rely on him more than we should."

I considered his words and nodded slowly. He had a point. Blindly trusting the Nephilim just because he'd done a few good deeds was not a smart move. We'd proceed with caution from now on.

"Is the fight the only reason Zarak showed up?" I asked, curious.

"Nope," Tamas answered and poured himself another drink. "He said Nephilim are going missing, and the Angels know something. The guy was royally pissed too, and almost struck us all down with lightning. Something is going on."

Missing Nephilim? What the fuck? First off, who was powerful enough to catch a Nephilim unawares and kidnap them? It would be something if they were killed outright—rare—but understandable. But Nephilim were now missing? No wonder Zarak was pissed. From what we all understood, he was the undeclared Nephilim leader. He was the most powerful of their kind, and they were already small in numbers. For any of them to be going missing could spell extinction for the species as a whole. None of us particularly gave a shit, it wasn't our fight, but it was worth keeping an eye on. If the Nephilim were being hunted, them something bad was in store for us, there had to be.

"What should we do about Tria?" Tamas asked after a moment, his green eyes serious. Tamas was usually a free-spirit; funny and easy going. It was odd to see him so somber and only underlined the seriousness of the situation.

I sighed and moved to the drink cabinet, pouring myself a glass too. "I think we just do what we've been doing. We watch over her carefully and make sure she's safe."

Tamas nodded slowly, and I raised an eyebrow. "What's your idea?"

He shrugged and looked down at his drink for several seconds before turning back to me. "What if I brought her down here to Hell? She could stay in my realm, or yours. She can't leave either one of ours without us opening the door for her. She can only get out through Harkyn's door. It would keep her safe, and we'd just have to be careful that Harkyn doesn't find out."

I was already shaking my head. "That's a recipe for disaster. One slip from any of us, and Harkyn would find out she's here. How do you think he'd respond to knowing his mate is cooped up in the realm of one of his brothers? He'd go ballistic. Not to mention he'll demand to check in on her at some point, and what happens when he can't find her topside anywhere?"

"Well, what's your solution?"

"I already told you," I reminded. "Keep her safe topside while we continue to search for a way out of this mess for Harkyn."

Tamas let out an exasperated breath, and I couldn't blame him. We were stuck until we could make progress on breaking

Harkyn's Word safely. Once again, I inwardly swore at my brother's choices. What was he thinking? In his defense, he hadn't known mates were a thing, and he'd done it as a last-ditch effort to protect her from himself. I understood—we all did—but it still royally sucked.

"Alright, I'm going to catch up with some of my Knights and see what they can dig up about Zarak, and I'll put a few on scouring the city for more sightings of Angels or Rogues. I'll head back up there now and keep an eye on her until you or Malik can take over for me," Tamas said with a sigh.

"We better figure something out soon. Harkyn is getting impatient to see his mate again, and if she slips up and mentions your name when he's around, we're fucked."

"I know," Tamas answered grimly.

Thinking of tonight attack, an alarm started to sound somewhere in the back of my head. I looked at Tamas who was waiting for me to say what was on my mind.

"Rogues, again?" I was more than concerned now. For the last four years we'd been systematically wiping them out, hunting them whenever we could. We wiped out tens of them at a time, and yet their numbers didn't seem to be lessening.

Tamas grimaced. "Yeah... I think there's a bigger problem there than we realized."

I inwardly cursed and shook my head. That was an issue for another night, right now, there were bigger issues.

Tamas finished what was in his glass and set it on the table before giving me a salute and sauntering out. I watched him go, opening the door for him from where I stood and closing it when he left. Tamas was right; we needed to do more. I'd put some of my own Knights on look-out duty as well, and then I'd check in with the others to see if they'd made any progress. I'd start putting together regular hunting parties for Rogues, too. Somehow, that problem had gotten out of hand, and we had to get a handle on it before it got one of us killed. My thoughts drifted back to Mika's sister, and I cursed under my breath. I wanted Uriel dead, but I needed to find her and make sure she was okay. If the Angels had her—I shook my head. I had to get to her before they did, and I had to keep her safe.

CHAPTER SIXTEEN
DIMITRIA

I kept my senses alert as I left my building a little after two in the morning, refusing to look back at the life I was leaving behind. It was a cool night, so I tugged my jacket closer and zipped it up. The moon was high in the sky, illuminating the streets so I didn't have to wander in total darkness.

After getting off the phone with Trinity, I'd hurriedly packed my bag. I'd uprooted my life so many times that there was only one duffle bag of things I needed, and my backpack. Clothes could be replaced, and I didn't have a lot of sentimental items to bring with me. My hand, of its own accord, moved to touch my necklace, but there was nothing there. I forced myself to ignore the pang in my gut at leaving it behind, but Trinity was right. If I was going to leave and hide somewhere away from all this, then I couldn't bring a piece of my old life with me that literally tied me to a King of Hell. I knew I could call him in an instant with it, but what if he could track me using it too?

After packing my bag, I'd written a note to Luana saying goodbye, and told her to keep or sell whatever was left in my apartment and to keep the profits. My place was paid up till the end of my lease anyway, so I wasn't costing the owner anything. I'd also taken the time to write a note to Tamas. He was my friend, whether I'd wanted him to be or not, and he'd risked his safety more than once to protect me. He deserved a goodbye, even if it couldn't be to his face. Inside the note I'd also left him a message to give Harkyn, and left the Token behind, allowing myself to close the door to that part of my life. It was done now; it was time to move on.

Leaving behind my motorbike hurt almost as much as leaving the Token. I'd saved for that bike for *years* and it had represented freedom to me. But I didn't want to take anything that could be used to trace me, and Trinity said we couldn't take the bike in the way we were traveling. Maybe we were flying on a private jet?

After the ambush earlier in the night, I was very aware that nowhere was safe, and kept my senses peeled for any sign of Rogues or Angels. I didn't want to run into Tamas either, but I hadn't sensed him close when I left the apartment, and he didn't seem to be anywhere near me now.

As I approached the spot I'd agreed to meet Trinity, I slowed down and searched around me again, wanting to make sure I wasn't walking into a trap or that someone wasn't following me. I came to a stop a block away and let the eerie silence of the night wrap around me, the cool air brushing across my face. I couldn't sense anyone nearby, nothing but one small, warm light up ahead that I knew to be Trinity.

Sucking in a deep breath, I started towards her at a fast pace and smiled nervously as she came into view. She turned in my direction and her face reflected her relief when she spotted me. I had a feeling she was as antsy as I was. Something about tonight held an ominous feel to it, as if this was the calm before the storm, and we were running out of time to outpace it.

"Hey," I greeted.

"I'm glad you chose to leave. I was getting worried about you," she answered as I stepped up beside her.

"Well, I had to be sure this was the right choice," I replied with a shrug.

She dipped her head in acknowledgement, her deep green eyes solemn. "I understand. Are you sure about this? You're ready?"

I straightened my shoulders and nodded. "Yes. There are a lot of reasons for me to leave, and I think it'll be safer for everyone this way."

Her gaze dipped to my chest, and she gave a small look of commiseration. "You left the Token behind."

"You said it wasn't safe to keep it, and I agree," I answered without looking her in the eye.

She was silent for a moment, and I shifted uncomfortably.

"Okay," she began. "We need to get moving then. Lev said there are a good number of Rogues in the area scouting for you, as well as some Angels. He's waiting for my signal and then he'll create a distraction to keep the Angels focused on him and not scanning the area for a sign of a Witch. We'll need to look out for the Rogues on our own."

"What signal?"

She gave a small smile. "I created a temporary spell that allows us to communicate via our minds."

I was momentarily stunned by her capabilities, but I frowned. "Why not have him meet us here?"

Trinity looked a little awkward and I realized why. "You weren't sure you could trust me?"

"If anyone can understand that, I figured you would," she replied, a sheepish expression on her face.

I did understand, and I was too nervous to care much. "I do. So, what do we do now?"

Trinity smiled in relief that I wasn't offended and straightened up. "The moment he comes to us, the other Angels will know. If they're searching for you as carefully as we suspect they are, the other Angels will be here in seconds, and we don't want to risk them following us back to our safe place. You and I will head east, and when I feel as though we are close enough to the spot we've chosen, I'll let him know. Lev will then draw the Angels west where some of the King's Demons are patrolling."

Nerves tugged at me, but I gave a sharp jerk of my head. I knew this wasn't going to be easy.

"Let's go. The sooner we're out of here, the better. Once Lev has the Angels properly distracted, he'll zap over to us and shimmer us out of here. He just wants to make sure we're not being tracked first. We have a protocol to follow in order to keep those we've already saved protected."

"Shimmer?" I asked as we started walking at a brisk pace.

"Yes, shimmer," Trinity answered. "I think the Demons call it shadowing."

That made sense. We walked quickly and in silence for a while, both keeping our senses peeled and alert for any sign of the Demons. Trinity seemed like an experienced and capable Witch, so I felt secure that she could look after herself. I'd been learning since Harkyn had given me lessons and branched out over the years to absorb what I could. Finding *real* grimoires and spell books was difficult, but I'd found a few texts over the years that helped me learn the basics. I was confident I had a chance to get out of here if Trinity was by my side.

"Okay," Trinity said as we came to a stop, and she looked around again. "I've just told Lev where we are. He's still tied up leading the Angels away. They can move quickly, so he wants to make sure they're thoroughly distracted."

"How long will we be waiting?" I asked, feeling anxious.

"Shouldn't be long," she replied, but I felt her nerves.

The more time that went by, the more my pulse raced, and my nerves increased. Something felt… odd. Almost like we were waiting for the other shoe to drop.

"Dimitria!"

I jumped at the sound of my name and turned back to see Tamas several yards away, his face like thunder.

"Shit," Trinity whispered and grabbed my hand. "We need to move. Now!"

I opened my mouth to say something—anything—but nothing came to mind. Tamas's expression was angry, but there was a shadow of betrayal that stung at me. He started towards us, but before I could say anything, Trinity spun around, magic in her hands, and threw it at him. It hit Tamas square in the chest, and he flew backwards. He was airborne for several seconds before he crashed hard onto the unforgiving ground. I winced, but Trinity didn't wait to see if he got back up. She yanked on my hand, and we ran.

I hated that Tamas was hurting—both physically and emotionally—but he had to let me go. I felt the surge of power from behind me and yanked free of Trinity's grip to throw my hands up in time to prevent Tamas from toppling us over. He was storming towards us now, furious. I knew he could shadow to us in an instant, but he seemed angry enough to need the short walk.

"Dimitria, it's not safe out there. What are you doing?" he demanded, looking both angry and confused.

"It's safer for everyone if I leave, Tamas. Please, just let me go."

His gaze moved to Trinity behind me, and he frowned. "How did you find her?"

Trinity shifted behind me but didn't say anything.

"How do you know you can trust her? Some Witches are working with the Angels. She could be leading you right to them," Tamas reminded.

"She's not. We've talked. I trust her."

"I thought you trusted *me*?" he asked, the hurt in his voice unmistakable.

"I do. You're my friend, Tamas. You're probably the only real friend I've ever had. Which is why I can't risk your safety in exchange for my own. You've protected me twice now. I won't allow a third time to be the reason you're hurt or killed."

"I won't be. Just... don't go. Please, I have a plan, I just need time," he encouraged.

"Dimitria," Trinity whispered, and I knew we needed to leave.

I struggled to move under Tamas's pleading gaze, but in the end, I had to make sure he was safe.

"I left a message for you in my apartment. One for Harkyn, too. Please see that he gets it?"

Tamas's expression darkened, and I threw out my hands, conjuring magic to confuse and disorient him. He had no chance to evade it, and I watched him stagger and drop to one knee as he struggled to keep upright.

"I'm sorry," I added, guilt trying to drown me before Trinity tugged on my hand and we were running again. There was a wave of hatred and anticipation headed for us, and one quick scan told me it was Rogue Demons. Swearing under my breath, I put on the speed, only to come to a jarring halt when Trinity yanked me back. I frowned and looked up to see a group of nine women ahead. The power emanating from them made the hairs on my arms stand on end and I stilled. My first thought was that they were some of the Witches Trinity had helped to escape, but when I saw the look of worry on her face, I knew I was wrong.

I opened my mouth to ask what we should do, but they weren't looking at us. They were holding hands, and the woman in the middle looked less than pleased to be there. Rather than looking a part of the group and participating in whatever spell they were working, their hold on her arms told me she wasn't there willingly.

Almost at the same time, each woman lifted their left hand—all except the one in the middle—their palms coated with blood. They spoke quietly and in unison, the power in the air grew to an electric point, and I realized they weren't planning to cast a spell on *us*...

Gasping I spun to warn Tamas as he staggered to his feet and took a shaky step forward just as they Witches threw their combined power at him. Again, he was hit squarely in the chest. For a brief moment, a complex and layered pattern flared to life where it hit him, glowing a bright and magical gold before it faded. I froze in fear that he was about to blow up or drop dead, but nothing happened. He groaned and staggered a little more, but that could have just been from the spell I'd cast on him moments ago.

"He's fine. We need to run. Now!" Trinity hissed and tugged on me. When I looked back to the other Witches, they were long gone. Tamas was behind us, disoriented, slightly weaker, but still determined to catch us. He seemed to be fine, and I needed to run. Shaking off the feeling of foreboding, I gripped my bag tighter and followed Trinity around a corner and up a small, paved hill.

"Lev is almost there. He'll leave the Angels in a minute, maybe less," she encouraged as we made it to the top of the hill. A small alley cut off to the right and I followed Trinity down it. It was an alley between blocks of quiet, rundown, and abandoned houses, making it the perfect place to disappear.

Tamas was still following, the Rogues closing in, and I worried he would be caught in their path, but I reminded myself who he was. He was a King of Hell. I'd seen what he did to the Rogues earlier in the night, the way he pulled their life force from them. Crap, had it really only been hours since we'd been attacked and I learned what he was?

Yes, it took a little time for Tamas to pull the lifeforce from those Demons, but he'd managed it. He could do it again, and maybe their energy would help him to get rid of the effects of my spell. Even with the number of reasons I told myself I had to keep running, my conscience had me constantly looking over my shoulder to make sure he was okay.

We almost made it to the end of the alley when I caught sight of Tamas at the other side, staggering, but still running. Why didn't he shadow to us? Did my spell disorient him so much that he couldn't anymore? Ability to shadow or not, Tamas kept running towards us, his steps uneven and jarring, but his expression was determined. Was he really so worried about me, or was he worried about losing a Witch?

"Lev is on his way," Trinity told me and tapped me on the shoulder to urge me on. I had taken a step towards her again when I jolted to a halt, my breath catching as a horde of Demons came around the corner behind Tamas. There had to be at least twenty of them. Their snarls and shouts of victory were so loud, they made my blood turn to ice.

"Tamas," I whispered in denial, knowing he wasn't moving fast enough to outrun them.

"Dimitria," Trinity warned, but even as she was trying to urge me away, I *felt* her denial that the Demon King was going to die. She might not want any part of them, but some part of her deep down didn't want them hurt or killed either. I remembered her words from our phone call, how she believed she was a danger to them. Would she invertedly hurt Tamas if she stayed?

"Trinity, I have to help," I whispered, unable to look away.

"You'll be lost to them if you turn back now."

"I can't just leave him!" I shouted, spinning back to her as desperation mounted.

Her dark eyes were filled with indecision and remorse. "There are too many of them," she insisted.

She was fighting with herself. At her core, she wanted to help him, but she was trying to use logic to keep herself separate from the situation at hand, she was trying to protect herself from the guilt she'd feel if she didn't help.

Tamas was struggling to move now, and while I expected to see fear for his life on his face, all I felt was a desperate need to protect me. He wasn't running to me for safety for himself, he was still trying to reach me to protect *me*.

"If you go back now, I might not be able to help," Trinity warned. She was supposed to go, her logic dictated she leave, yet she was still here.

"Go," I told her. "I'm going back, but you should go," I added, dropping my bags and drawing magic from my core.

"Dimitria—" she started, but I didn't hear the rest. Blood rushed loudly in my ears as I watched the Demon horde catch up to Tamas.

"No, Tamas!"

My scream echoed in the dark and dirty alleyway, but I barely registered it. The full moon lit up the alley enough so that I could see everything as clear as day when a cold wind whipped my hair across my face, momentarily obscuring my vision. The Demon King I'd come to call friend was attacked on all sides, the Rogue Demons who converged were taking pleasure in causing him pain. Time seemed to stop as I watched a Demon plunge a blade into his back from above, dragging the razor-sharp instrument down his spine. Tamas fought back with hellfire and his own power, Rogues flying backwards and into the brick wall that made up the alleyway. It was an impressive display of power considering his weakened state, and yet over in the span of a couple of seconds, he was stabbed and sliced repeatedly, the poison in them taking effect almost immediately. I was useless, frozen in abject horror and disgust. Tamas was powerful, he was *so* strong, and he was quick. I hadn't thought there'd ever be a time he would lose in a fight, but I'd weakened him with my spell. *I* was the reason he couldn't fight back.

"Dimitria, we have to move!" Trinity shouted in a last desperate attempt to get me to run for safety, but I pulled away and started towards my friend.

Tamas's pain-filled eyes met mine through the snarling and snapping hoard, and despite his pain, I saw the moment he realized what I was going to do.

"Tria, no!" he roared, but he staggered under the weight of the assault, fighting back despite his massive injuries. "Run!"

But I couldn't—I wouldn't. Despite my freedom being no more than a few steps away, leaving now would result in Tamas's death, and I couldn't let it happen, not if there was the slightest chance to save him.

I started towards Tamas, preparing to cast a conjuration to throw the Rogues off my friend, I just needed a few more seconds...

It felt like a vice was squeezing my lungs as I watched a stolen Angel blade in the hands of a particularly vicious looking Demon. He raised the blade high, and in one powerful strike, he brought the sword down. I watched as it sliced through the muscle of Tamas's shoulder, severing his arm. The residual pain I experienced from him was nothing but a drop in the bucket compared to what I knew he had to be feeling.

I ran towards my friend, raising my arms as I did so, throwing out a wave of power strong enough that it sent at least nine of the Demons whirling through the air. Tamas staggered, blood was *everywhere,* and I swear the breath of death brushed the back of my neck, but nothing was stopping me now.

Then I felt *him.*

One minute there was nothing but screaming, roaring, blood and agony. The next, a wave of hellfire rushed past me, so close it singed my skin. I gasped, blinked in surprise, and watched the fire catch onto every Rogue Demon trying to take down Tamas. They screeched in pain, but it wasn't going to kill them. Already those who had been thrown off guard by its sudden appearance were leaping onto Tamas again, but another wave came, and another, each one stronger than the last. I reached Tamas as the last one fell off. I expected them to lunge at me as I got within reaching distance, but they all seemed to stiffen suddenly, unnaturally, as if they were all puppets whose strings had ruthlessly been wrenched tight. I dropped to my knees by my friend's side as blood poured from his severed arm. Healing him hadn't even been a thought before it was an action, I was already pushing healing energy into him, trying desperately to stop the bleeding and at the same time, counteract the poison I knew would be layered on those blades.

I glanced at the eerily stiff Rogue Demons. Pain washed over them and was lined in every crease of their faces as they appeared to struggle for breath, for movement. Almost at the same time, they fell abruptly as if their puppet strings had been cut. But not before I felt it. The rush of energy, the force of their very lives being yanked from their bodies so that none remained for them.

The sudden silence was deafening, and I raised my gaze down the alley. Trinity was still there, indecision on her face as she struggled between helping me and making her escape. I couldn't blame her if she ran, not after what she told me, but I silently urged her to stay, to help me. Her expression hardened into one of determination, and she ran towards me, brushing by a lone figure in the shadows.

My breath caught at the sight of him after all these years, those haunting gray-green eyes that appeared in my dreams constantly over the last four years.

Harkyn.

Several thoughts, memories, and emotions swamped me in those few precious seconds, almost as if the last four years had never happened and I was reliving those short few months we'd spent together all at once. My breath came short and choppy, and I was shaky and overwhelmed.

Trinity skidded to the ground beside me, healing energy already pouring from her as she reached for Tamas, and I pulled my attention back to her, trying to think past the jumble of thoughts in my head.

"Trin, the others are going to show up. The other Kings," I whispered with tears in my eyes.

"I know."

"Is it safe for you? For them? You don't have to stay," I reminded, pouring every bit of my strength into Tamas who was lying unnaturally still before me, but I knew he was not dead. His pain was still too great for that.

"I told Lev to wait the second that Demon Hoard came around the bend. It's not safe for him to show up here now. I'll leave if I have to, but not a second before. I'll help you while I can. Tamas doesn't deserve to die."

Gratitude for my new friend rushed through me hard and fast, but I had no time to dwell on it when the rolling waves of pain from Tamas made my stomach heave.

"Tamas, stay with me," I whispered, brushing a hand over his sweaty forehead even as my mind struggled not to dwell on Harkyn only a short distance away. He was *here!*

"Tria…" He trailed off, licking his lips as he began to shake. *Shit!*

"Shh, don't talk, conserve your strength."

"He-he can't be here," Tamas warned.

I hesitated and frowned. "Harkyn?"

Tamas made a sound of pain and nodded, and despite the monumental agony he was in, I felt his urgency for me to understand. "He's going to die—save him."

I frowned. Save *him?* Harkyn wasn't the one bleeding, he wasn't the one stabbed repeatedly with poisoned Angel Blades—

A sudden strangled groan caught my attention and my head snapped up in time to see Harkyn stagger, see him clasp his chest and fall to his knees as if in slow motion. The light from the moon caught his eyes, and my breath hitched at that all too familiar gray-green. While seeing him again brought out in me a strong sense of exhilaration, it was dulled somewhat by the unwavering certainty that something was wrong, *very* wrong.

"Harkyn." Saying his name after all these years wrenched at something deep inside me.

"Save him," Tamas pleaded as blood leaked from the side of his mouth and the shaking in his body intensified.

"We're losing him, Tria," Trinity warned.

We're losing him.

He's going to die—save him

Who was I meant to save? The man I'd come to call my friend, or the one I'd loved and lost years ago?

CHAPTER SEVENTEEN
HARKYN

A few hours earlier...

I missed my mate.

Glowering at the building in front of me, I ground my teeth together. I missed Tria, and despite the points my brothers had made over the last few weeks, I needed to see her. They didn't understand the draw to her, the need had to be in her presence even if she didn't know I was there. I *had* to see her.

Scanning around me quickly, I couldn't find any trace of Angels nearby and shadowed into her apartment, into that same spot I always stood in so that she wouldn't see me.

The apartment was quiet. I frowned, unease washing over me. It was *too* quiet. I couldn't detect the breath of another here. Searching, I found no sign of anyone. Where was she? It was midnight. It was possible she was on a job, but the niggling doubts in the back of my head told me that wasn't the case.

I entered her bedroom and took a long look around. Everything appeared the same. Her bed was made, the curtains drawn closed. The bathroom too seemed the same, only—I frowned again, and it took me a moment to realize the reason it looked a little different. Her toothbrush and hairbrush were no longer in their normal places. Turning around, I hurried to her dresser and wrenched open the drawers and cursed. Most of her clothes were gone. Searching around me for a clue as to where she went or why, my gaze snagged on the small round dining table she had set up in a corner. There was a note on it.

I was there in an instant, but I hesitated before grabbing it, my brain taking far too long to comprehend what I was seeing. There were two envelopes, one for her friend down the hall, Luana. And the other...

"What the fuck?"

Tamas.

My brother's name was written in her beautiful handwriting, and the implications of it sped through my mind at a rapid speed.

What the fucking *hell?!*

Sure, okay. Maybe it was a coincidence and she knew someone else named Tamas, but I doubted it. I hadn't seen her in two weeks, and she didn't have any real friends. Tamas was not a hugely popular name, at least not in this country. What were the chances that this was someone else? When I considered how evasive my brother had been the last few weeks, things began to make more sense.

Had he secretly been seeing my mate?

Why?

Without taking a moment to breathe, I tore open the envelope and something heavy and gold fell out. I hesitated when I saw it at my feet, and recognition hit me at once.

My Token.

I gently picked it back up and held it in my palm. I hadn't held this in four years, but Tria hadn't taken it off in all that time either. Why now? Slipping the necklace over my head so that it rested on my chest, I opened the letter and started reading.

Dear Tamas,

I know you'll be pissed, and that's totally okay. I knew you'd try to stop me from leaving if you knew, and I had to do this. Since we met, some things have become clear to me. The first of which is that, as long as I am around, Angels and Demons will continue to find me and put in danger all those around me, especially those I care about.
You have risked your life and safety twice in the time we've known each other to keep me safe, and that last time could have been a lot worse if that Nephilim hadn't shown up. I won't risk a third time where you are injured too badly to heal or are killed.

The second thing is that I have come to realize you're my friend. I know, it says a lot about my lack of taste, but it is what it is. I don't have friends, not really, but I cannot escape the fact that you have become that to me, almost that annoying nagging brother I never wanted. I care too much about you to risk your safety. I care too much about Harkyn to let you get hurt protecting me.

I blinked down at the letter, my breath trapped and burning in my lungs. Tamas had told her about me? She knew who he was to me? What else did she know? Adrenaline coursed through my body as I continued to read.

You never came out and said it, but I put together the pieces of the puzzle myself when I found out you are a Demon King. He's your brother, isn't he? That's how you know him so well. That's how you knew he hadn't been the same since letting me go.

I lost Harkyn four years ago, and it hurt like nothing else ever has. I'd like to say I hate him for abandoning me like everyone else in my life has done, but I can't. I'll never be able to hate him. I feel too deeply for him to do that. So, you understand how I could never risk his brother's life to save my own. I won't hurt him like that.

You have been a good friend, Tamas, and I have loved our time together. I forgot what it was to laugh like we have, so thank you. I am sorry if you're mad or hurt by my leaving, but it's for the best. I bumped into a Witch the day we met, and she's been helping others like me escape from Angels and Demons so that we won't be forced to choose a side. I took time to think about it, and I trust her. She's not lying.

I won't choose a side here, Tamas, not if I can help it. I want to be free. I want to know Witches like myself. I want no part in this never-ending war.

Because of where she's taking me, these will be the last words I say to you. I can't communicate with anyone here again or I risk revealing the location of other freed Witches. I have enclosed Harkyn's Token. I can't take it with me. Please return it to him? Please, tell him that I'm sorry I ever told him to leave. Tell him that I forgive him for what he did, that I never hated him, that I was just scared and confused. Life has been lonely without him, and there hasn't been a day where I didn't regret telling him to leave. Tell him I'll carry the memory of him and us with me forever.

I am sorry, Tamas. Thank you for being my annoying, intrusive, and hilarious best friend. I'll never forget you.

Love, Dimitria.

I read the letter twice more until it all finally sunk in, memorizing every word of it. Tamas had been protecting her up here, and I had to imagine his goal was to slowly bring her over to our side without scaring her. I had no idea what his endgame was, but he'd told Tria about me, mentioned me to her so she knew we had a connection, and still she had not run.

There hasn't been a day where I didn't regret telling him to leave.

She had never wanted me to stay gone. I'd never intended to stay away forever, just until she was old enough that if we gave into temptation, I wouldn't spend the rest of eternity hating myself. I closed my eyes when they burned hot, and took in a long, shuddering breath. She still cared for me. She didn't say love, but I couldn't blame her. Still, she cared for me enough to keep protecting me.

I was torn, wanting to celebrate and cry in relief. I wanted to wring my brother's neck and hug him tightly in thanks for what he'd accomplished here...

Except, she was gone.

My building joy stopped with a harsh jolt, and I looked around. Where was she going? When had she left? Maybe I could still find her? I remembered just in time not to search for her myself and gritted my teeth. I had to remember the blinding pain in my head anytime I tried reaching for her.

Shoving the letter in my pocket, I shadowed back to the Arrival Room in Hell and took a few seconds to breathe deeply and try not to rage. I had taken two steps towards Tamas's realm when Donovan came striding out of his. His steps faltered as he took in my dark expression and his gaze fell to the Token on my chest. The second his eyes widened at seeing it, I knew he was in on this.

"What the fuck, Nova?"

Donovan had the good sense to look wary and held up his hands. But I was beyond being reasoned with. I was on overload, my emotions heightened to a point where I needed an outlet for them. I continued striding towards Donovan and didn't stop until I grabbed him by the shirt and shoved him hard against a wall.

"What the *fuck?* How dare you two go behind my back with *my* mate? What were you thinking?"

"We were thinking there were no other options. We've all looked, Harkyn. No one knows how to do this without you dying," Donovan explained, not looking the least bit worried at my anger. Barely holding back a growl, I shook him.

"She's gone, Nova. She's fucking gone, and I don't know where." Donovan frowned, his blue gaze searching. "What do you mean, she's gone? She couldn't have gone anywhere. Tamas is watching over her."

"A fucking good job he's doing," I snarled and shoved the letter into Nova's chest before pushing away from him. Nova caught the letter and I waited angrily as he scanned it. His eyebrow cocked in curiosity and when he looked at me again, it was with a twinge of smugness.

"At least she doesn't hate you."

"Where the hell is she?"

Nova paused and closed his eyes. I knew he was searching for her, but the moment he began frowning, I knew he was blocked.

"I don't understand…" Nova said, blinking his eyes open.

Cursing under my breath I turned away and shoved my fingers through my hair. "She has to have had help from the other Witch she mentioned."

"Tamas has to be looking for her, I'll just—" Nova trailed off and stilled.

"What is it?"

"I... I can't feel Tamas, either."

Apprehension traced a path up my spine, and I searched for my brother too, but was taken aback by the sudden black void. *Fuck*.

"Angels," Nova gritted out.

Dimitria was gone, out on her own with some unknown Witch we weren't even sure she could trust, and now our brother was out of contact which could only mean he was wounded with an Angel blade. If that was the case, then it was likely he was in a fight, trying to save Dimitria, and the Angels were too close to getting my mate. Fuck, they could already have her.

Shoving my fingers through my hair again, I struggled to find calm amongst the panic.

"I've called Cole and the others. The women will perform a spell to find her," Tamas assured, but I didn't care. It would be too late. There was only one thing for it, and it was going to hurt like a motherfucker, but it would be worth it if I could help her.

Closing my eyes, I braced for the pain as I reached out on the familiar path in my head to touch my mate's mind. At once, a blinding, burning pain seared through me, sending me to my knees. I think I cried out, but I was too focused on Dimitria to pay it much mind. It hurt, but it was enough that I felt her, felt her fear, her panic, her desperation. She had an irresistibly need to help, and before the agony caused me to lose the connection, I fell into the shadows and sent myself to her.

I found myself kneeling on a loose gravel path, the sharp rocks digging into my legs. It was dark, a cool wind blew through what I now knew was some kind of alleyway between houses. My stomach heaved and my head felt as though it was going to splinter, but I forced myself to push past it, to open my eyes and identify the threat to my mate so that I could eliminate it. It took me several precious seconds to get to my feet and for my other senses to engage.

"Tria, no! Run!"

My head snapped up despite the dizzying pain, and I caught sight of my mate. She was standing towards the end of the alley to my right with another woman, her white-blonde hair looking iridescent in the moonlight, those pale blue eyes of hers shimmering with unshed tears. Even terrified and sad, she was the most beautiful creature I'd ever laid eyes on.

Tamas's words finally registered to me, and I watched as Tria left her Witch friend and ran for my brother. There had to be at least twenty Rogues attacking Tamas, and she was running right for them! Worry for my brother was overshadowed by fear for my mate as she ran headlong into battle, magic shimmering in her hands as she drew it from within herself, preparing to attack.

There was an unnatural roar of pain, and I watched as a Rogue lifted a sword and brought it down, slicing through Tamas's arm. *No!*

Everything seemed to be taking a long time to happen, and at the same time, it was all over within a split second. The pain in my head lessened enough that I could think clearly. My brother was going to die if I did nothing. My mate was going to die if I did nothing.

I would die if I intervened at all.

It took me less than a second to decide what to do, and I stepped out of the shadows and drew on hellfire. At the same time, I began locating each of the Demon's in my mind's eye, latching onto their lifeforce. Careful of Dimitria, I let loose the flames, aiming for each of the Rogues attacking Tamas. I did it again and again, stepping closer with every blast, my aim precise so as not to hurt Tria.

She skidded to a stop at Tamas's side, her healing powers already at work. I took control of the last Demon and at once clenched my fist. The Rogues stiffened immobile. Remembering how much Tria hated violence, I wished there was another way to do this, but there wasn't. I yanked the lifeforce from each of them and at once felt the energy pour into me. They fell at once, their corpses lifeless and heavy, but Tria didn't pay them any attention, her sole focus on my brother.

The energy I took was overwhelming, but I didn't take it in. I held it, determined to pass it over to Tamas.

Tria looked past me to the other Witch, but I didn't care. Just seeing her alive and unharmed was a relief, and I simply took a few seconds to admire her, to revel in the sight of her again. Two weeks was too long.

The other Witch rushed past me, and I felt some relief when she slid to a stop beside Tamas as well, power rolling off her and into him.

And then it happened.

Dimitria's bright blue eyes met mine, and my world stopped spinning. Everything outside of us ceased to exist as her focus came to land on me after four long years.

No more than a few seconds could have passed before I found myself getting dizzy, and my strength leaching out at an alarming rate.

I had interfered.

This was the end.

CHAPTER EIGHTEEN
HARKYN

I was going to die.

I'd had the thought in the past, of course. Each of us had been severely injured in one way or another to the point where death was an actual possibility, but it had never before been a certain outcome. While my brothers had a chance at surviving whenever they were attacked—whether it be because they were bound to their mates or because we had access to Witches now who could heal an Angel blade wound—I knew I would not be so lucky. Nothing could be done for what was killing me.

I'd broken my Word.

I'd revealed myself. I'd interfered in her life even if doing so saved her—and I was now going to die because of it. This was blood magic; it was not something to take lightly, and there was no known cure for a King breaking their Word.

Why weren't my legs holding me? Why did I suddenly lack energy? Sure, I knew breaking my Word would mean my death, but I hadn't known *how* it would kill me.

My gaze slid to Dimitria and the Witch as they worked on healing Tamas. Blood soaked through their clothing, and my stomach turned at the sight of my brother's dismembered arm lying off to the side. He was shaking with shock and pain, and the poison on the Angel blades were taking their toll.

"Help."

I sent out the call to our brothers as black dots began to cloud my vision and my knees gave out. Some kind of groan tore from my throat unbidden, and I raised my gaze in time to clash with Dimitria's pure blue gaze. Those eyes...

Something inside me warmed and settled at having her look directly at me for the first time in years. Despite the feeling of life draining from my body, having her look at me again was exactly what I craved.

I saw her mouth move, and I thought for certain she'd said my name, but the blood rushing in my ears prevented me from hearing it. I groaned again and landed on my hands and knees, my strength draining from me as quickly as the blood from Tamas.

Tamas.

I knew he would not be able to communicate with me via our mind link due to the poison in his system, but he needed help, he needed me.

"We are coming."

That was Malik's voice answering for everyone, and relief washed over me. At least when I died, the others would get here in time for Tamas. And my mate... she would be protected now, properly. She would know everything, and they would look after her.

I began crawling on my hands and knees to Tamas. He wasn't so far away, but the distance felt longer with the sheer force of will it took for me to make it to him. Soft hands brushed my arm, and a shiver worked its way down my spine at the touch.

Dimitria.

I'd know her touch anywhere, and my body cried out at the feel of her for the first time in years.

"Harkyn," she whispered. The sound of her voice saying my name made my heart race.

"I need… to get to him," I clenched out, my breathing labored. "He said—"

"There is hope for Tamas. Help me help him," I cut her off, knowing she was going to try and help me. But there was no more hope for me. I was done for. If I could save my brother, then I would.

Dimitria clutched my bicep and I turned to look at her. She was trying to help me up, and with a pained groan, I summoned my wavering strength and let her help me. It took some time, and when I was finally standing, she fit under my arm, her head in line with my chest. She was so small. No one would know the power such a little thing wielded over me just by looking at her. I wanted nothing more than to hold her to me and never let her go, to wrap her tightly in my arms and just breathe her in, but we had no time. It felt cruel, after our years forced apart, but with the situation as it was, Tamas needed me more than I needed to hold Dimitria, but it was close.

We staggered forward, me leaning on my mate more than I would have liked. When we finally reached Tamas's side, the other woman's brow creased, and eyes closed as she worked. She was mouthing something wordlessly, but I felt the power coming from her.

Her black hair was long and tied back in a braid, her skin smooth and clear. I looked her over as something about her became familiar to me. My gaze snagged on the birthmark on her inner arm. I knew it meant something, but the information seemed as insubstantial as mist. Every time I tried to grasp it; it evaporated before I could grab hold. She looked like—but surely she couldn't be, right?

"What does Tamas need?" Dimitria asked, bringing me back to

the problem at hand.

"He needs time," I replied and slowly lowered myself to the ground beside him. As I pressed my hands into his chest, his eyes opened and he glared.

"Don't," he hissed.

Agony washed over me from him, and I clenched my teeth against it. "It will help you until the others get here."

"You need it. Save yourself. I'll live," he insisted, just as another tremor wracked his body. I frowned as his skin lost some of its color. Something else was going on here, something was wrong.

"He's not healing," the other Witch said.

"What?" Dimitria gasped in shock. "What do you mean? Trinity, he *has* to heal, he was just trying to protect me and I—what do we do?"

The woman I now knew as Trinity stared down at Tamas with remorse and helplessness. "I don't know."

"The others are on their way," I informed them.

"What?" Trinity whispered, her face paling.

I searched her expression and gritted my teeth against the next wave of weakness that sapped at me, draining me. Was I seriously going to waste away to nothing? Was my death to be so… helpless?

"The others… they're coming. We have three other Witches with us, five if you two stay and help. Together you'll figure something out," I explained.

Trinity pushed to her feet at once and stepped back.

"Trinity?" Dimitria asked confusedly.

"I—… Tria, I *can't*," she whispered, and even I felt the helpless struggle she seemed to be in.

"Then you should go," Dimitria told her. There was an edge to her voice—anger and frustration—but there was also understanding. "You tried to help and you can't. I know what you're risking. You should go before they arrive."

Trinity's large eyes shimmered with indecision, regret and fear fighting a war within her. I couldn't help whatever she was going through, I had to help Tamas. I turned back to my brother and found his eyes already on me. Ignoring the way my limbs seemed to be heavy and slow, I closed my eyes and pressed my hands against his chest and poured energy into him. The lifeforce of the Rogues should help to keep him going a little longer. It wouldn't heal him, but it would be enough for now.

The moment the transfer was complete, the world around me spun and I found myself on my back, blinking slowly up at the velvet sky. Dimitria's face hovered over me, her expression full of concern and helplessness. I caught sight of that odd speck of yellow in her blue gaze and somehow felt content with being right where I was, despite knowing I was dying.

"So beautiful."

I wanted to raise my hand to touch her face, to feel the silken strands of her hair between my fingers again, to touch the satin-soft skin and feel her warmth. But my arms would not obey my command to lift.

She opened her mouth to speak when there was a loud gasp from somewhere down the alleyway. I rolled my head to the side to see Tomika there clutching Cole's arm tightly, her eyes wide with disbelief, her skin paling. Cole frowned down at her. Adrik, Cali, Malik and Sawyer all watched her with similarly confused expressions, and then there was another sharp intake of breath, this one filled with something... else.

 Donovan stood a few feet to Cole's right, his face reflecting his shock and surprise.

"Trinity?" Mika whispered brokenly.

A smile tugged at my lips, and I sighed. I *knew* Trinity looked familiar.

CHAPTER NINETEEN
DIMITRIA

I was missing something here, I knew I was, but it wasn't important now. It couldn't be.

The Witch with strawberry-blonde hair and the male at her side looked at us and without a word hurried forward. I tensed, but Harkyn's grip on my hand tightened. When I looked down at him, nothing about him seemed alarmed at their presence.

"Harkyn, what were you thinking?" the woman asked as she knelt by him, her hand roaming over his chest. The sudden feral urge to rake my nails down the woman's face for touching Harkyn without permission froze me in place as I breathed through the abrupt and alarming urge. What the *hell* was that? If I hadn't felt her immediate healing, I worried I might have done it.

"I don't think, Cali, remember? I just act," Harkyn joked weakly.

"I know. None of you do," she reprimanded, her voice a hiss of words.

"Brother, what the hell are you doing here?" the male at her side asked, his voice a low growl.

"There was no time, Adrik," Harkyn defended drowsily.

"You're going to die now, you fucker," Adrik snapped. I frowned and opened my mouth to speak but Cali butted in.

"You can tell him how much of an idiot he is when he's healed. Sawyer!"

Another Witch hurried over as the first Witch moved to Tamas, her hands roaming over him, getting a read. The Witch known as Sawyer was at our side at once, her golden blonde hair tied back in a long ponytail, her pretty eyes filled with worry.

"Oh, Harkyn," she whispered in a shaky breath. My hackles rose immediately at the way she said his name, at the familiar way with which she looked at him, touched him. Why was I suddenly so damn possessive?

The male that accompanied her was as beautiful as the others, but his expression was wrought with worry and a touch of fear as he looked at his downed brothers.

"Malik, we might need help," Sawyer explained.

"From who?" the brother known as Malik asked, frowning.

"Can Zarak help? Or Mervyn?"

Malik looked at her, incredulous. "You want me to ask the Reaper for help?"

"Well *you* died and came back," Adrik pointed out.

"Yeah, but I was Marked. My mate was bound to me," Malik protested.

There was an awkward moment where I felt each of their eye's land on me before they flicked away. What the hell?

"Trinity... I've been looking for you." The short, dark-haired Witch announced suddenly. I lifted my gaze to look at the way she was watching my friend who resembled her in almost every way. Her eyes were bright with unshed tears, and I almost drowned in the rolling waves of relief, joy, and confusion from her. I flicked a glance to Trinity to see a similar expression on her face, but I felt her despair, her regret, and her wistfulness.

"I know, Tomika."

"I-I don't... if you know, why do you keep running? Don't you want to see me?" Tomika asked as she took a step closer, and the sheer heartbreak in her voice stabbed at me.

Trinity sucked in a breath and I saw her steeling herself, bracing herself to run. I wanted to help my friend. I did, but Tamas was slipping away and so was Harkyn. I think. He wasn't actually injured that I could see, but I felt his weakening.

"I..."

"How have you been able to hide from me?" one of the men asked, his dark blue eyes intense. Trinity looked at him, and I caught the flicker of longing in her, something I found very interesting. Each of the Demons around us were incredibly powerful, they all had that same *feel* as Harkyn, so I had to assume that they too were Kings of Hell. Trinity had to know this too, so that look of longing was interesting considering she'd already said she'd never trust a King.

"Tamas is dying," Trinity said instead. "He was attacked, he's not healing, and nothing I do is helping. He says your other brother is dying too, although I can see no injuries on him."

Tomika's gaze flicked to Tamas and Harkyn, and I felt more than saw her shock and horror at the sight that met her as she took in the dismembered arm and all the blood.

"Wait, where are you going?" Tomika asked, her gaze straying back to Trinity. Trin swallowed hard, her gaze pulling slowly from the man and back to Tomika.

"Somewhere safe."

"We have somewhere safe," Tomika said hotly, taking another step closer.

Trinity took a dragging step back, her hands held out as if preparing to ward them off. "It wouldn't be safe if I were there."

Tomika opened her mouth to say more when Cali cried out.

"We're going to have to table this for another time, Tamas is dying!"

The others started towards us, and Trinity continued to back up. Her gaze found mine, pleading. There was something else going on here, something she hadn't told anyone, but I couldn't be the only one that felt how torn she was as to whether she should stay or go. Whatever reasons she had *not* to get involved with the Kings and to stay away from Tomika—who appeared to mean a lot to her—had to be powerful.

"Go," I told her.

"What?" Tomika gasped, her gaze swinging from me and back to Trinity.

"Wait," the man with dark blue eyes called.

"Last chance," Trinity whispered to me.

My eyes stung and I shook my head. "I don't think I ever really had one. Go, run."

"Trinity!" Tomika called, her hand raised as if she could pull her back.

"I'm sorry, sis," Trinity whispered, her voice full of remorse.

"Please, wait," the man called again, running towards her now. Trinity didn't wait, she spun and ran, the man giving chase. But a second later, her running figure glowed with a shining white light, and when the light dimmed, she was gone.

The man slowed to a stop, and I had no time to sit in wonder at the realization that Tomika and Trinity were sisters before the former looked at me with confusion. "Why did you tell her to go?"

"We can deal with that later," Cali cut in sharply before I could form an answer. "Mika, I need you here. Your sister was right, something is blocking Tamas from being healed."

There was a momentary pause and then people began moving and shuffling. My gaze swung between Harkyn and Tamas, my heart torn. I wanted to reach out and take Tamas's hand, but my body refused to move from Harkyn's side, something deep within me telling me he needed me more now than ever. But how?

"What's happening to him?" I asked Sawyer as she continued to look Harkyn over. Her pale eyes met mine and then flicked to Malik, a question there. When I turned to him, his eyes were bright as they studied me.

"Don't," Harkyn growled, and I frowned down at him.

"What harm can it do, brother? You're already dying," Malik pointed out.

"And there's nothing she can do. I do not want her feeling guilty," Harkyn replied, but his voice was weak, and his eyes were struggling to remain open. I leaned over him and gently raised a hand to his face, feeling the heat of his skin beneath my palm, the scrape of his beard. Every atom lit within me at the familiar feel of him. How had I missed him so much when I'd only really known him for so little?

Harkyn's gaze rose to mine, and I felt the impact like a sucker-punch to my gut. "How can I help you?"

He hesitated a moment and shook his head. "You can't."

"She can," Malik interrupted.

"She can't!" Harkyn snapped and groaned. I waited as he settled once more and shuffled closer.

"You are dying—somehow," I began sternly. "I don't know what you were doing here tonight or why you decided to finally show yourself, but you're dying, and I'm seriously pissed about that."

He frowned and blinked slowly. "Finally?"

"Yes, finally," I repeated with a frustrated frown. "I've felt you around for years. At first, I had no idea what I was feeling, why I felt *something* familiar. It wasn't until I was writing a letter to Tamas that I realized it had to be you the entire time," I explained quickly, flicking a glance to Tamas when I heard him groan. My heart clenched and I tried to focus on Harkyn. Tamas had the other Witches, Cali and Tomika working on him, I had to stay with Harkyn. My body wouldn't allow for anything else. Harkyn was *here*. He was real and alive, and he'd come to save me when I'd needed it. I hadn't realized just how much I'd missed him until I started talking to Tamas about him, and now that he was here, every cell in my body was demanding I do everything in my power to ensure I didn't lose him again.

"You're mad?" Harkyn asked and I watched him close his eyes and drag in several deep breaths.

"Yes. If anyone gets to vanquish your freaking ass from this plane of existence, it's me, but not before I get some answers. So, what the hell is happening and how am I meant to save you?"

Silence greeted my words, and his eyes locked on mine, curious, questioning... smiling. "I'm not sure you can help me."

I frowned and looked from him to his brother and back. "Malik seems to think I can."

Harkyn glared at his brother, and I could tell the movement took effort. "Malik is guessing."

I shrugged. "If guessing is all we have right now, then let's try it. What do I need to do?"

Malik opened his mouth, but Harkyn made a low rumbling sound in his chest. Did he just *growl*?

"Not like this," Harkyn gritted out.

Malik rolled his eyes. "You may not have another chance or another way. This is it, brother."

"Just tell me," I snapped.

"You have to let Harkyn bind your souls together," Sawyer interrupted quickly.

Harkyn glared up at her and I blinked in surprise. Well, that hadn't been what I'd expected.

I opened my mouth and closed it again when I realized I had nothing to say. *Bind our souls?* "Uh, I… what?"

"You are his mate, his soulmate," Sawyer began, dragging in a steadying breath before looking up at me with brilliant whiskey-colored eyes. "You are destined to be together. There are four parts to a binding for a King of Hell, four parts of you that must be bound together so that you will be forever linked." Harkyn swore and made some vague threats, but Sawyer ignored him.

"The Angels kept going on about specific Witches being meant for the Kings of Hell…"

Trinity's words from earlier came back to me and I tried to wrap my head around it. I was one of these Witches destined to be with a King of Hell? I should hate the idea, I should want to run for my freedom now, screaming and pleading, but I didn't. I'd always felt connected to Harkyn in a way I *knew* was far more intense and powerful than the average relationship. Knowing why I'd felt so intensely towards him helped me feel a little less crazy and obsessed.

Sawyer continued explaining. "You need to bind your hearts, minds, body, and soul. The first three happen whether you're ready for them or not, it happens differently for each of us, but it has to do with your ability to trust and find common ground. The last one is done deliberately, and it's Harkyn who has to do it. There is an ancient prophecy which describes vaguely how each King will mark their mate or when, or something like that. *The Fourth need only await his sign.* That's you and Harkyn. I don't know what sign the universe is talking about, but he'll feel when it's time."

Sawyer's voice was hushed and clipped as she hurried to pass the information onto me.

I stared at her blankly for a moment, the information slowly sinking in. Glancing down at Harkyn's pale face, something inside me rebelled at the sight of this once powerful man barely able to lift his lashes to look at me.

I flicked a peek at Tamas who had stopped shaking, but he looked close to death's door. Tomika and Cali were working hard, their faces lined with concentration. Small, whispered words were exchanged between them, but their focus was entirely on the injured King.

"What will binding our souls do?" I asked Sawyer.

"We've discovered that a bonded pair cannot die. If you carry his Mark, he'll carry it too, and it will prevent a Reaper from taking his soul over to the other side. It acts as a lock, an anchor, something to hold him to you so that neither one of you can die."

"I thought he was already immortal?" I whispered, unable to stop myself from brushing his hair off his face. His eyelashes fluttered as he struggled to keep them open. I'd practically been a child the last time I saw him, angry and hurt, scared out of my mind. I'd witnessed brutality and violence on a level I had never seen before or since, and it had scared me to my core. To know it had been the man I'd been falling for who was capable of it had only frightened me more. I'd seen a side to Harkyn I'd been unprepared for and unable to properly cope with at the time. He'd seemed invincible, too powerful to stop no matter what.

"We are… kind of," Malik answered and sighed. I watched his eyes stray to Tamas, a shadow of fear sliding across his expression before his face hardened and he swallowed hard. "But there are things that can kill us."

"And… and binding Harkyn to me will save him?"

Malik opened his mouth to speak and then hesitated. "I—we think."

"You *think*? None of you have come this close to death before?"

"I have died," Malik said quickly and shoved his fingers through his hair in agitation. "I died, but I came back. The Mark works."

"Then why the hesitation?"

"Harkyn isn't dying from anything any of us have ever faced before. I can't guarantee it'll work."

I frowned and looked back down at Harkyn. He was still now, utterly quiet, and I had the feeling it was taking too much energy for him to keep his eyes open. Panic rose within me, sharp and fast, and I licked my lips quickly.

"Harkyn?"

He groaned, and I gripped his hand tightly. He was going to die if I didn't do this.

"There's no other way?" I asked softly, my eyes never leaving the man before me.

"None that we know of," Malik explained, and I felt his honesty and desperation for me to save his brother.

"But you said the prophecy mentioned he had to wait for some sort of sign. What if that time isn't now?" I asked, beginning to panic. But whether I was panicking at the thought of this working or not working was anyone's guess.

"We didn't know if it would work to save a King when I told Malik to bind us," Sawyer encouraged, reaching out to take Malik's hand.

Tears burned in my eyes as I considered what this meant, that I'd never be free again. I could run now; I was fairly certain none of them would stop me. But to run would mean certain death for Harkyn. I may have been scared of him once, terrified to be in his presence, disgusted by the ability he had for gruesome violence. But I had been a girl, young and scared of being alone.

Now?

My hand went automatically to where I was used to having

Harkyn's necklace, but I stilled when I found it bare. I'd left it behind at my apartment.

I didn't know the man—not really. But could I live with myself if I left now, knowing it would ultimately lead to his doom? Was my freedom worth the price?

My gaze caught on the shine of gold around Harkyn's neck, and my breath faltered. Gently, I removed the necklace from Harkyn and stared in wonder at the Token. It seemed to warm in my hands, and I felt as though a piece of me had been restored. Sniffling, I slid the chain over my neck before I leaned down to brush a kiss across Harkyn's forehead.

"Harkyn," I whispered, shuffling close to him. He made a noise that he'd heard me, and I let out a long breath, letting go of the necklace he'd once given me. "Bind us. Bind our souls."

~

HARKYN

I wasn't in pain, so that was something. But I was weaker than I could ever remember being in my life.

The effort to stay in the moment was monumental, and the thought of opening my eyes and talking? It was almost laughable. Until she said those words.

"Bind us. Bind our souls."

I frowned and forced my eyes open, her beautiful crystal eyes staring back at me. The moonlight on her platinum blonde hair made her look ethereal. I'd always thought she was beautiful— always.

222

"Dimitria," I whispered her name, relishing in saying it aloud to her, loving the way it felt rolling off my tongue.

"We can talk about everything later. I owe you a verbal beatdown, you owe me some answers, and the only way those things can happen is if you bind us now. So, do it. Bind us, damn it," she insisted, and I wanted to hold her close at the sheen of tears in her eyes. Was she crying over me?

Bind her. Take her now. She's asking!

I grimaced. She wasn't asking for the right reasons; she was doing this to save me. But if I didn't do this now, we'd never have a future where I could try to make up for everything I'd done.

"Harkyn!" she hissed, followed by a sharp sting to my cheek. Did she just slap me? I realized my eyes had fallen shut again and I struggled to keep them open. I opened my mouth to tell her it was useless, I was too far gone, but as she leaned forward, her necklace slid forward. I blinked at the gold chain, recognizing the black pendant with the golden sign for the fourth King of Hell. I'd been wearing it earlier tonight, she must have taken it back at some point.

I couldn't take my eyes from it, something inside me urging me to make a connection, but everything was too hard. Dimitria frowned down at me and looked at the pendant and back to me. I watched the wheels turning in her head, and then she gasped, a look of comprehension dawning across her face.

She gripped the pendant in her palm and cleared her throat. "Harkyn."

She whispered my name, but the force of it rang in my head, demanding I pay attention. "You promised me you'd come to me if I needed you. All I had to do was hold this pendant and say your name. I'm saying it now. Come back to me, Harkyn. Bind us."

Almost at once, I was overcome with an urge near impossible to resist to put my Mark on her. It burned hard and sharp within me, lighting every nerve ending until I *ached* to tie her to me. What the hell? A sharp gasp wrenched from me as the feeling settled into my being, into my very bones. My fingers curled into fists as I struggled not to take what I wasn't sure was being freely offered.

"Dimitria, this cannot be undone. Ever."

She nodded and gave me a watery smile. "Then you're stuck with me, and we'll get you an attitude adjustment. I can't live with the thought of you dying, so get on with it."

I grimaced. This wasn't the way I wanted to do it; this wasn't how it was supposed to go. She was supposed to have a say in it, damn it. She was supposed to be able to tell me yes or no, and be the one to decide when and where and how or even *if*.

Fuck.

"Tria…"

"For fuck's sake, Harkyn. Bind us already!" she snapped, her fury making her pale blue eyes almost burn silver. I wanted to grin at her fire and tease her some more, but despite the burning in me to Mark her, I felt my energy draining once again.

I carefully lifted my hand. It felt leaden, far too heavy to move, and yet somehow, I managed. Dimitria caught my hand in hers and looked at me uncertainly.

"Put my palm against your skin," I whispered. She swallowed hard and carefully placed my hand over her heart. The heat of her skin almost burned, and I felt the rapid beating. She had to be scared, worried, nervous, but she was doing this to save me.

"Last chance."

"Don't make me hurt you." She said it as a joke, but her voice wobbled and her eyes betrayed her fear.

"I'll make this up to you," I promised.

She nodded but didn't say anything as I let loose on that tightly wound instinct somewhere in the back of my head. Things from back there were far too old to look at for long, but it was an instinct I hadn't realized was there until meeting her, something ancient that would not be ignored when the time came. The moment I let my hold on it go, there was a rush of heat and power radiate throughout my body, down my arm and through the palm of my hand. Dimitria's mouth fell open, and she gasped as I felt my Mark burn into her skin and her very soul, felt it etch itself onto my palm. Deep inside, I rejoiced. I was... whole. I felt a part of something, or like a long-ago stolen piece of me was now back where it belonged.

Dimitria's heart was pounding hard against my hand, and I raised it slowly to cup her face. A tear that had been brimming in her eye fell and trickled down her cheek, and I swiped it away with my thumb.

"I am yours to do with as you will," I mumbled, my eyes falling closed again.

"Harkyn?"

I struggled to open my eyes, but they wouldn't. Somehow, they were heavier than before and refused to open.

"What's going on? Why didn't it work?" Dimitria asked, but I could no longer see her face. Unconsciousness was pulling at me, and I fought it hard. I needed to be here for her.

"Malik?" Dimitria's voice was faint now, as if it were far away, but I could hear the urgency in her voice. Whatever my brother said or did in response was lost on me as I drifted further and further away. I hoped Tamas would make it, that the Witches would figure out what was blocking him from healing. I hoped the life-forces of the Rogues I'd pushed into him had helped his strength some.

I hoped Dimitria would be okay if I never came back.

CHAPTER TWENTY
DIMITRIA

"Malik, what's happening? I thought you said this would save him?" I asked, panicking now. Harkyn had done something, I'd *felt something*, and—

I looked down at my chest where a mark like a tattoo was. The design was beautiful, but I didn't recognize the outer symbols, none except the one in the middle. It was the same symbol on the necklace Harkyn had given me all those years ago.

"I said it *might* work," Malik clarified before he swore.

"What do I do?" I asked.

"Nothing."

I turned to look at the other brother, the one who had looked at Trinity with such longing and he walked closer to us, his expression inscrutable. "He will die, and then he'll come back."

"He—he'll die?"

"You are bound together now. That Mark ensures he will come back."

"But…" I looked at Harkyn, panic still swirling inside me.

"Where are the others? Where's Cassius, Devlin, and Corvin?" Sawyer asked quickly from beside Harkyn, her gaze searching the alley as if she might find them.

"Cassius has gone looking for them. There was nothing but a void when I tried to reach them. They're injured. Cassius is going to make sure they're okay and bring them back."

There was a spattering of swearing around the small group before Malik's gaze turned to Harkyn and then back to the blue-eyed brother.

"Nova, what if…" Malik started. I didn't need him to finish his sentence to know what he'd been about to say. What if it doesn't work?

"Maybe we can call Mervyn?" Cali suggested over her shoulder.

"And have him do what?" Nova demanded.

"It's worth a try," Adrik murmured with a sigh.

"And you all just happen to know how to call a Reaper to you now?" Nova demanded with a raised eyebrow.

"Well, no," Adrik began and shrugged. "But he seems interested in preventing other Reapers from intercepting any of our souls on the other side. It reasons that he'd be hanging about when he feels one of us close to dying."

"Mervyn!" Tomika suddenly shouted, and I jumped, my eyes wide. Everyone was looking around in the shadows.

"Mervyn, come on! You're here somewhere. Don't wait until he dies to step in," Cali encouraged.

"I'm sure you're sick of hanging around us. Might as well just get this done," Adrik added.

"Come on, Mervyn," Malik called as well. I watched them all talking to the shadows, not exactly sure what to feel at this point. Were they all crazy? They were expecting a Reaper to come out and talk to them or even prevent a death from happening?

"I do not know who you are calling," a deep voice responded from behind me, and I gasped and spun. "But my name is not Mervyn."

I almost swallowed my tongue at the look of him. Talk, dark, and handsome was a phrase this man had coined, I was sure. A shiver worked its way up my spine as I took him in, from his broad shoulders and long legs, a face so chiseled it could have been made from stone. Whenever I thought of Knights or warriors back in the times of Vikings or sword fights, I pictured men like him. It helped that he wore a long black trench coat with a silver buckled vest and a sword strapped to his hip. If I weren't so terrified, I'd have thought him sexy as sin.

"Since you won't tell us your real name, you're stuck with the one the Witches gave you," Malik said in response. Mervyn-not-Mervyn raised a regal eyebrow, his expression barely changing. I had no clue as to what this man was thinking or feeling, and right now I didn't care.

"What do I need to do to save him?" I demanded.

The Reaper turned his dark, fathomless eyes on me. I watched him look me over, his eyes resting briefly on the new Mark on my chest before he dragged his attention to Harkyn on the ground beside me.

"The Mark will not save him. Not from this."

"What?"

"The fuck?"

"What do we do?"

Unanimous cries went up all around, but I couldn't speak, couldn't move.

"There has to be a way," Donovan ground out, his blue eyes practically spitting fire. Mervyn didn't bother to look at him. Obviously, the fury of a Demon King was of little consequence to him.

"It is simple," Mervyn began with a slow sigh.

"You want to spit it the fuck out already?" Cole snapped, his black eyes glittering in the moonlight. Tomika reached up to take his hand, her touch seeming to soothe him.

The Reaper looked at Harkyn a moment longer before turning to look at me, his gaze searching.

"Please," I whispered.

"He broke his Word, Witch."

I frowned and shook my head. "His what?"

"How do you know about that?" Adrik cut in.

The Reaper gave a small, impatient sigh at being questioned. "I do not owe any of you an explanation."

"What are you talking about?" I demanded, annoyed at the alternate route the conversation was going.

The newcomer looked back at me and answered. "His Word. His promise, his vow. The blood pact he made with you. He broke it, and that's why he's dying."

"What vow? What... *word?*" I demanded, shaking my head.

A puzzled expression passed over the Reaper's face for a fraction of a second. "You do not know?"

"Know what?" I shouted. "Someone explain what the hell is happening!"

"The promise he made to you," Tomika said quickly. "The one he made you four years ago. Something about never interfering in your life again. He stayed away all these years because he'd given you his Word."

"He..." I shook my head. Was that what he'd been saying in that motel four years ago? That had been in another language! "So? How the hell could that be killing him? He's kept his word all this time, so even if something like that could kill him, it shouldn't be. He didn't interfere," I argued, shocked and confused.

"It was a blood spell," the Reaper corrected.

I frowned and remembered the last time I saw Harkyn. He'd cut his arm and gripped mine. He'd muttered some things under his breath, words I couldn't understand.

"So, he didn't really abandon me?" I whispered, feeling stupid now.

"No," Adrik answered stiffly.

"And that spell he did, it made him keep his promise?" I asked, needing clarification.

"Once a King gives his Word—performs the ceremony with it—he cannot break it, or he will die. Harkyn has been able to stay close to you all these years, as long as you didn't see him, as long as you never knew he was there, as long as he didn't interfere with your life in any way," Cali explained, her eyes back on Tamas.

"So, how did he break it?" I asked, feeling my cheeks suddenly wet. Shit, I hadn't realized I'd been crying.

"He revealed himself to you tonight. We weren't here, but I can only assume he saw the attack on Tamas and you, and he felt he had no choice. He wouldn't risk his brother dying if he could stop it, and nothing short of death would prevent him from doing whatever possible to protect you if he thought you were in trouble," Donovan explained.

Fuck. *Fuck*.

I cleared my throat and drew in a deep breath. "What can I do to save him? I'll do anything," I asked, my mind and heart a whirlwind of thoughts and emotions. All this time… all this time I'd thought he'd left me. Yes, I'd been mad, furious, terrified when I shouted at him four years ago, but I'd thought I knew him better than that. I hadn't really thought he'd stay gone. No one told Harkyn what he could and could not have. I'd fully expected him to show up after a few days despite his promise to stay away. I didn't take into consideration that the blood spell he'd done could affect him. Honestly, I'd thought it was some form of protection. That's the way it had felt when he'd performed it.

Like it was a way to keep me safe, not to keep him away.

The Reaper looked at me with an expectant expression and I glared. "I'm not a fucking mind reader and it's been a long damn night. Can you just answer the question?"

Malik snickered and Sawyer sighed at her mate.

The Reaper shifted and shrugged. "You need to reverse his promise. Refuse to hold him accountable for it."

I frowned and blinked in confusion. "That's it?"

The Reaper's lips tugged in what I was sure was going to be a small smile, but then it was gone. "That's it."

"I just say, 'hey, Harkyn. I no longer hold you to your Word, you are free to interfere now,' and it—"

My sarcastic rant was cut short when Harkyn gave a loud, somewhat dramatic gasp. His back arched and a second later, he was sitting up, his chest rising and falling rapidly, his color returning quickly.

"What the—" I whispered, stunned.

"Yes," the Reaper answered unnecessarily, and this time there was a shadow of a smirk on his lips. "That's all you needed to say."

Silence met his answer.

"Fucking hell," Donovan swore and shoved his fingers through his hair as he spun on the spot and paced away. Relief washed over me from all angles, and I looked down to see Harkyn looking up at me, his eyes wide with surprise and wonder.

"You... saved me."

I shuffled and shrugged, feeling suddenly nervous and foolish. "Apparently it wasn't that hard to do."

"The binding?" Harkyn asked, frowning.

"Er... no," I answered and shoved my hands into my jeans pocket. Harkyn frowned and looked at me, then those around him. His gaze paused on the Reaper, and he frowned.

"Mervyn?"

The Reaper glowered, and I couldn't stop the small laugh that escaped me. Mervyn stepped back and swore under his breath.

"The Reaper saved me?"

"More like he gave us the instructions," Malik answered and stepped forward, offering Harkyn a hand up. Harkyn took it, grinning. I watched as the brothers embraced, thumping each other on the back with closed fists. It may have looked casual and passed as basic brotherly affection, but I felt the heavy relief washing over me from Malik that his brother hadn't died. Sawyer stepped up beside him and took his hand as he let Harkyn go, and I caught the small look of understanding and deep affection between the two.

"Reaper?" Cali asked, and we all turned to look at her pale figure by Tamas. Guilt lashed at me at once. How had I forgotten my friend? I hurried past the others to kneel by Tamas's prone and bloody figure, ignoring the puddle of deep red blood. I frowned at the signs of magic I could see on him—Witch magic. Closing my eyes, I let myself see it the same way I saw auras. There was something binding going on, something that threaded throughout his entire body but came together in some kind of knot in his chest, tangling the cord together in a mass. What the hell was that?

I opened my eyes again and felt slightly sick. There was something extra here, as if the magic had reacted badly to the poison in his system, making him worse.

"How do we save him?" Tomika asked, looking up at the Reaper. "Something is blocking him from being healed, and I don't think we have the time to unravel it."

The Reaper stepped around us to peer down at Tamas. With a

frown, he crouched beside me and raised a hand over his chest, his brow furrowed in concentration. He closed his eyes and I waited, holding my breath to see if Tamas too would suddenly shoot up off the ground, healed and alive. Seconds passed— twenty, thirty. Eventually I had to draw breath again, but no one spoke, no one moved as we waited.

When the Reaper finally opened his eyes again, he shook his head, grimacing. "It is a complicated spell. Have you studied it?" he asked, looking around at us.

"Briefly," I admitted, having only just taken a look.

"I've looked at it closely," Cali admitted and shook her head. "I've never seen anything like it. It's similar to what happened to Sawyer when her magic had been bound as a child. There's some kind of... lock?"

The Reaper nodded. "To put it simply, you've been locked out of his system. Whoever created the spell on him made it so no one can get in and heal him without the key."

"What's the key?" Sawyer asked.

"Usually the blood of the one who cast it," the Reaper explained. "Like all locks, you can always try to break into it, or *pick it,* if you will."

"But we don't have the time," Cali whispered, her expression turning desperate.

"Can you do anything?" I asked, my gaze locked onto Tamas's face, my heart hurting all over again. There was the slightest of brushes against my mind, a flutter of comfort, and I turned to look up at Harkyn. Gray-green eyes met mine, his expression blank, but I felt his awe at touching me, his fear for his brother, his need to comfort me despite it.

Send a small touch of thanks to Harkyn, I turned back to Tamas. I could deal with all that later. Tamas needed us now.

"There's not a lot I can do," the Reaper admitted.

"But there's something," I said, hearing the unspoken words. The Reaper flicked a glance at me and nodded, holding out a hand to me. I hesitated a moment before placing my hand in his. There was a twist of annoyance, of possession, and without thinking, I mentally reached out to Harkyn to ease his discomfort. Instinct drove me to calm him when I felt his need to tear me away from the other male.

The Reaper leaned over and took a blade from Tomika's boot, the woman looking at him in surprise.

"I feel your connection to this King. He is your friend, yes?"

"Yes," I admitted without hesitation.

"Then you will act as his anchor and the backdoor into his system. Your body will mirror his injuries. You will not acquire his injuries, but where he is cut, you will feel cut. Where he is bruised or poisoned, you will feel so too," the Reaper began.

"All Witches feel where he is hurt," Mika reminded.

"This will not be the same. You feel pain, yes… but you do not feel it like he does now. Once connected, she will," the Reaper explained.

"Wait," Harkyn tried to interrupt, and I felt his worry but I didn't look away from the Reaper.

"So, the others can heal him by healing me?" I cut in.

"In a sense, yes. He may still be limited once his physical injuries are healed, the lock on him does more than just prevent him from healing," the Reaper explained.

"What else does it do?" Cali asked, frowning.

"It will limit his powers, his abilities. He will still be powerful, yes, more-so than the average Demon. But he will not be of his normal caliber. That will not stop until you retrieve the blood of the one who put the lock on him. When you find that Witch, he must take her blood into his system, and it will dissipate," he explained.

"But for now, to heal him and keep him alive, you can make it so we can heal him?" I asked, more concerned with him slipping away in the meantime.

"Yes. If you are willing to bear the pain of his injuries, he can be healed. They'll need to heal you, and by doing that, they'll heal him."

"Do it."

"Just wait a second," Harkyn interrupted. "We're his brothers. We have a closer bond than anyone. Let me do it."

"You are not a Witch," the Reaper pointed out.

"What the hell does that have to do with anything?"

"The transfer will only work on one who is born to heal. Witches feel the pain of those around them all the time, even with their shields and their blocks. I can tie them together via a blood-tie which will allow for her to truly feel and experience his injuries and exactly what is wrong," the Reaper explained, a small sigh at the end telling me he was tiring of this conversation.

"Do it," I said again.

"Just wait," Harkyn argued.

"Harkyn, we're running out of time. The Reaper has been more than helpful, let's stop arguing," I cut in.

"But why you?" he demanded.

"I'll do it," Mika volunteered. "I've known him the longest, I have a strong bond with him."

"No," I cut in when I could see the other women preparing to volunteer as well. "Tamas is my friend, and he was only hurt tonight because he was trying to protect me while I was fleeing. I'll do it, you'll all heal me, and he'll be better. Let's stop squabbling over who suffers his injuries and do it already," I snapped, tiring of the arguing.

Guilt was swirling in my gut. I'd been planning to leave him behind, but he'd come after me because he knew I was in danger. I'd weakened him with my spell, leaving him open to attack from those other Witches. I had to do this.

I felt Harkyn's annoyance, but he didn't say another word about it. The Reaper turned my hand over, and with the blade he'd taken from Tomika, he cut my hand. I winced and watched as he placed my hand over the bloody mess on Tamas's chest.

"Are you ready?" the Reaper asked, his dark eyes studying. I let out a long breath and braced myself, nodding.

With a small flicker of approval in his eyes, the Reaper closed his eyes and his lips moved wordlessly as if he were whispering a chant to himself. Heat washed through my hand, and I *felt* the connection to Tamas begin, something tugging at my chest. I opened my mouth to say as much when instead of the words I planned to say, a scream wrenched unbidden from me. Pain unlike anything I'd ever felt before slammed into me, tore at me, shredded at my very insides. I thought the loss of his arm would have been the thing to hurt the most, but it wasn't, not by a long shot. The poison that now infested his body was an all-consuming sort of pain. One moment I was kneeling over Tamas, prepared to bear his injuries alongside him, the next I was floating in a sea of agony, uncomprehending of where I was or with who. I felt nothing. Not the cool night air, not the ground beneath me or the hands that touched me.

There was only pain.

CHAPTER TWENTY-ONE
HARKYN

The second she went down, I was there, catching her before she hit the ground.

"What the fuck?" I snapped at the Reaper, glaring.

"He's in a lot of pain," he defended and slowly stood. Dimitria's back arched and her mouth opened in a wordless scream. She was in agony, I felt the pain ripping through every cell of her body, but no matter how hard I tried to take it from her, there was some kind of invisible barrier preventing me from helping.

"What do we do?" I asked, my mind blank with terror.

"We need to get out of here before we get found out. It's a miracle no one has seen us yet, but we need to get somewhere safe to heal them," Donovan suggested.

"My realm," I announced, swinging Dimitria into my arms as carefully as I could as I stood.

"Let's go," Malik agreed, as he and Adrik lifted Tamas.

"I'll clean up the scene here and meet you there," Donovan told us, but I barely registered it. Between the blood pooled on the ground and my mate writhing in agony in my arms, I was barely thinking straight. I drew in a breath to try and center myself, closed my eyes, and shadowed us to Hell. The second my feet touched the black marble floor, I was on the move. I didn't need to look around the empty circular room to know we were alone, or count the red doors leading to each realm for the ruling Kings of Hell. I pushed open the heavy wooden door leading to my realm and left it open for the others, my eyes only for Dimitria. This was not the way I'd planned to bring her here; this was not how I'd wanted to introduce her to my world. Nothing had gone as planned, but I could agonize over that later. Right now, I had to get her as comfortable as possible. I ran up the stairs to the small landing that took me to my bedchamber. Unlike Cole, Malik, and Adrik, I preferred my bedroom in another area entirely.

I heard the others enter my realm, their footsteps mere seconds behind mine. Holding Tria in one arm, I waved the other to make the bed and lay her on it. She was panting, her skin slick with sweat and paler than normal, and her damp hair was sticking to her face. There was blood on her clothes from where she'd knelt in the pool of Tamas's blood. I waved the blood away too, needing to do something but helpless to do anything. I tried once again to reach her, to take away the pain or at least lessen it, but I was locked out, unable to help ease her burden.

"Lay him beside her on the bed," Cali ordered, running her fingers through her hair to put it up in a rough ponytail. Malik and Adrik hurried to do as she ordered and she pushed in front of me without so much as a word, her hands hovering over Dimitria.

"Adrik, run back to our realm and grab my bag. Malik and Cole, get to work cleaning up Tamas and then either get out or get a handle on your emotions because we need some peace in here," Cali continued.

I wanted to argue with her and tell her where to shove her demands, but I took a moment to breathe through the anger and do as she said. I forced myself to project an air of confidence and calm. I'd seen these Witches pull off some incredibly powerful magic in the past, I knew they could handle this.

Dimitria's pain battered at me again and I let it wash over me and moved to the other side of the bed where Tamas lay. Blood still poured from him, and I inwardly raged at the pain he was in, at the fact that he was near dead. Those fucking assholes had convinced Witches to put a lock on his ability to heal. The underhanded sneaky fuckers. We were going to have a good time tracking them all down and making them pay.

Adrik came running back up the stairs, jolting me out of my murderous thoughts. My gaze met Cole's briefly, and I could tell he was thinking along the same lines. He gave me a single nod in confirmation, and I drew in a deep breath.

Later. For now, I had a brother to clean and a mate to soothe. My gaze wandered over to her again as Cali began pulling out candles and telling Adrik where to place them and light them. In no time, my room was alight with the soft glow of candles, a pleasant herbal scent in the air. Tomika climbed onto the bed between Tamas and Dimitria, Cali stayed near Tria's head on the other side, and Sawyer moved further down towards her hips.

"Okay, deep breath," Cali instructed to the other Witches. They did as she instructed, and I watched as they clasped hands and closed their eyes. Power surged and crackled in the air, and I found myself holding my breath. Dimitria's pained moans were like daggers to my brain, to my soul, tearing and shredding, knowing I couldn't do a damn thing to help her.

I stepped beside Cole and Adrik, and the three of us cleaned our brother and did our best to take care of him when there was little to do. We weren't the healing sort; we didn't have the compassion or the patience for this kind of thing. So, standing above our brother as he bled out, as he writhed in pain, I felt worse than useless.

I loved my brother, I did. Malik had died on us last year, and we'd all felt what it was to actually lose one of us. As close as some of us had come in the past to dying, it hadn't ever happened. It was not an experience I was keen to try again anytime soon—or ever. Despite my fear for my brother, there was nothing more I could do for him, and so my eyes flicked to Dimitria. My mate.

We were linked, I'd marked her, and she was mine. The thought was only now beginning to sink in, and I'd be lying if I said a part of me wasn't secretly excited and satisfied with that knowledge. Years ago, we'd unknowingly formed the mind-bond. I knew that now after watching my brothers. She's trusted me in her mind, and I'd trusted her in mine despite having no reason to. Tonight, she'd asked me to Mark her, and I'd done it. We were tied now, soul to soul, bonded for all time. She was here in my realm, fighting to save the life of one of my brothers without a single thought for herself. A part of me wanted to reprimand her for it. Nothing was more important than her safety and her life, but I knew I'd be forever grateful to her for her sacrifice tonight, as would the rest of my brothers.

I wanted to go to her now, to bury myself in her mind and take away the pain she was in. I wanted to be her shield, to protect her against all the ugly in the world. Fuck knows she'd experienced more than her fair share of it growing up, she didn't need more of it now.

I brushed her mind again and stayed there this time, sank there so that I was immersed in her. Her pain was immediate and intense, and I gritted my teeth against the agony she was in and tried to soothe her. I couldn't take it for her, but I could be here beside her and make sure she knew she wasn't alone. She'd never be alone again.

"Dimitria," I whispered her name, still reeling in awe that I could reach her like this, that I could touch her mind without experiencing mind-numbing pain.

"Harkyn?" Her pain-filled whimper tore at me, and I clenched my fists tightly.

"I am here, cara," I returned, torn between joy at speaking with her and frustration that it was all wrong. Everything was all wrong. Nothing had gone the way it was meant to.

"Everything hurts so much."

The strain in her voice as she whispered to me made me want to rage, but I swallowed it and projected calm confidence, forcing myself to speak evenly, as if we had everything under control.

"The others are working on it. Feel for them. They're working as hard as they can, I promise."

"I know," she replied shakily.

"I cannot take the pain from you. I tried. I should be able to, but there is some kind of block keeping me out," I told her, wondering if she knew how to get around it.

"Maybe it's something to do with the block on Tamas?" she offered, and I swore under my breath at the way her voice wavered and more pain battered at her.

A hand came to rest on my shoulder and I flicked a glance at Malik.

"Something is blocking me from her. I can't take the pain; I can't shield her. I can't do a fucking thing," I snarled, feeling my temper slip.

"Just talk to her, Harkyn. Make sure she knows you're here. At the very least, it might distract her," he suggested. I nodded, having already thought of this, but it was hard to ignore her pain and continue talking as if she wasn't.

"How did you and Tamas meet?" I asked, desperate to distract her, but also curious. I'd barely found out about my brothers' plans to insert themselves in Dimitria's life before I'd intervened, I had no details.

"I met him at a café—a woman in my building owns it," Tria answered shakily.

"Luana?"

"How do you know about Luana?" Tria asked, and for a moment she was truly shocked.

"My Word kept me from intervening in your life in a way that would impact it or interrupt it, but I had my ways of keeping tabs on you. Despite what you may think, Dimitria, you were never alone. The moment I made that promise, I wished I hadn't."

Silence met my words, and I wondered if she was in too much pain to respond, but she sighed against my mind and I felt her confusion.

"Why did you?"

"Make that pact?"

"Yes."

I thought about what to tell her, *how* to tell her without sounding like a creep or a monster. But she deserved the truth, no matter how corrupt it made me look.

"Truthfully, I was protecting you from me."

"I know I told you to stay away after what you did…"

I knew she was remembering that night. Despite how hard I tried—and I'd tried a lot over the years—I still couldn't work up any guilt for the justice I'd delivered that day and how I'd gone about it. My only regret was that Tria had been there to witness it.

"But I never meant for you to stay gone. Not forever. I was young and scared," she admitted.

"I know. Trust me, I know." Her youth was a major factor in me staying away, and I was surprised she hadn't realized it yet. Then again, I was a Demon. Age of consent was probably not something she thought we took into consideration despite the fact that we'd talked about it in the past. Those who did not know us may consider us monsters—and sometimes they were right—but we had morals and rules we lived by. Sleeping with a human below the legal drinking limit just wasn't something we felt was tolerable... not even for universe--approved soul mates. Yes, we were capable of living forever, and at a certain point, age really is just a number, but... no. We wouldn't go there.

"You didn't answer my question," I prompted, not wanting to get into the specifics of why I'd needed to keep my distance from her. That was a conversation for later.

"Question?"

"Yes. How did you and Tamas meet? It was in Luana's café, but then what happened?"

She was trying to ignore the pain and steel herself against it as the other Witches worked to help her, and my admiration for her grew. I listened as she explained their first meeting, how Tamas had introduced himself because he knew that the second she saw him, she'd know he wasn't human. At first I was jealous. I hated the affection in her voice when she spoke about him, the feeling of friendship from her for another male was like needles on my brain. But when I examined it further, that was all there was to it. Friendship. He was there for her, and despite her not knowing if she was ready for it, Tamas provided her with a link to me, a way to contact me, to learn about me and my world without having to actually be in it.

Every time the pain became too much for her to handle, I hurried to speak, to say something else. Sometimes I was random, I brought up strange facts about the history of earth that she didn't know and would find amusing.

After several hours, her pain was lessening, and through her, I felt Tamas healing too. It wasn't until I heard a low groan of pain that I opened my eyes and turned my gaze to Tamas. He frowned and licked his lips before forcing his eyes open. I moved closer to him, and when he blinked open his eyes I smiled in relief.

"Harkyn?"

"Fucking glad to see your ugly mug alive and well again," I told him, feeling the vice that had gripped my chest the moment I saw him go down loosen slightly.

"What-what happened?" he asked, blinking in confusion. Before I even had a chance to speak, his eyes widened and he tried to sit up. "Dimitria!"

"Lay down, she's okay," I ordered, and caught sight of Adrik hurrying over to us.

"Fuck," Tamas swore as his pain finally registered. He turned his eyes to his arm—or the place where his arm should be, and he stilled. "What—"

"One of the Rogues severed it," Adrik answered the unspoken question.

Tamas took several moments to register the words before he cleared his throat and nodded. It wasn't the first time one of us had lost a limb, we knew it would come back with the help of our Witches, it just took time. "Dimitria?"

I gave a tense smile and flicked my gaze away. "She's alive. She's..." I trailed off and sighed.

"What?" Tamas asked, frowning.

I jerked my head at the space beside him and Tamas looked and froze, his mouth falling open and eyes wide. He took in the three Witches chanting around her, their expressions filled with concentration. Each of them looked paler than they had before. Sawyer was nearly swaying with weariness and Mika had a worrying complexion. Adrik and Cole hovered close to their mates, and I felt their tension. Each of them knew there was no point in trying to coax their women away from what they were born to do, and none of them would think of leaving my woman in pain while she was helping our brother, but I could understand the need to shield their mates or make things easier. I looked around for Malik, but he was nowhere to be seen.

"I thought you said she was okay?" Tamas demanded, his voice rising.

"She is—mostly," I answered and grimaced. "Look, long story short, you have some kind of lock on you. Witches performed a blood spell that prevents you from being healed. You were dying, almost dead. We called the Reaper who helped us, and he said that the only way to heal you was for someone to act as a... a surrogate," I explained, flailing on the description.

"A what?" he asked, confused.

"Someone to mirror your injuries, to take your injuries onto themselves so that they can be healed. Only a Witch has the ability to do it, otherwise, believe me, I would be lying where she is now. But the Reaper performed a kind of conjuring that locks her to you. She feels each and every one of your injuries, and through her, the women can heal you."

The shock and fury building on his face the more I explained spoke volumes about what he thought.

"Stop them," Tamas gritted out. "End the spell."

"I don't think we can."

"Fucking find a way then. I don't want her feeling this shit!"

I nodded in agreement. I'd be furious too, if I were him—I was pissed now. But I also knew how much Dimitria cared for him, and no one was going to stop her from looking after her friend.

"It's too late, and we were out of options. If we didn't, then you were going to die. You remember what it felt like to lose Malik all those months ago?" I reminded him.

Tamas opened his mouth to snap something at me, but he bit back the words. He remembered the feeling of loss, the echoing, yawning darkness we'd all felt when Malik was taken from us. That fear, the pain and loss we'd all felt was *not* something any of us were ever going to voluntarily feel again.

"How are you so calm about this?" he demanded angrily.

"I don't have much of a choice. If we don't keep our emotions in check, we'll be kicked out," I explained, nodding to the women.

Tamas nodded slowly and then snapped his head back in my direction, his eyes wide.

"How the fuck are you alive right now?"

I chuckled low and raked my hand through my hair.

"Is Tamas okay?" Dimitria whispered against my mind. The sound of her voice, the feel of her there knocked me off guard and I drew in a short, sharp breath, my soul rejoicing.

"He is awake, cara. He is none too pleased with your sacrifice, so I am sure you'll hear about it all when you wake up properly," I answered at once. There was the impression of a small smile in my mind, and I envisioned brushing my fingers across her cheek.

"Harkyn?" Tamas prompted.

"I Marked her."

Tamas frowned and shook his head. "And that overruled your Word?"

"No," I answered and shrugged. "I was dying right beside you. I Marked her upon her insistence in the off chance that it would save me, but it didn't."

Cole stepped forward to explain further. "The Reaper told her that the way to free Harkyn of the constraints of his Word and the results of breaking it was to not hold him to it anymore."

There was a small, disbelieving silence. "And that worked? Just like that?" Tamas asked, as skeptical as the rest of us had been.

I shrugged. "I'm here, aren't I?"

Tamas shook his head and frowned. "I thought for sure it would be something more dramatic."

I laughed. "Me too."

"If I had known all of this, I would have rescinded it years ago," Tria told me, clearly following our conversation.

My chest warmed at her words and my heart literally skipped a beat. Was there more to that statement than the words themselves? Would she have rescinded it because she felt bad, or because she wanted me in her life?

"Everything in time, cara."

"So, you two are bound now? She's safe, you're safe—it's all over?" Tamas asked, leaning back in the bed and wincing.

"In a way, yes. Nothing is over for me as far as I am concerned, but she is safe now. We can try to build some kind of relationship, and no one has to lie anymore. I want to talk to you about what you did, by the way," I added.

Tamas winced, and I watched him hold his breath as another wave of pain washed over him, the same pain I felt echoed in Tria. When it passed, he eased back onto the mattress and sighed.

"Are you pissed about that? 'Cause we were only trying to help," he defended.

"I'm pissed," I admitted with a small nod. "But I also understand and am grateful. You protected her, and you put yourself in danger to do so. You gave her a way to know about us, our lives, who and what we are. And even at the end, you were still going to fight to the death to keep her here and safe."

"She's your mate," Tamas said as if that were explanation enough. And it was. Despite the shit we gave each other on a regular basis, each other was all we'd ever known. All of us would give our lives for the other if ever required, and that extended to each other's mates.

I smiled my appreciation and cleared my throat, plastering a shit-eating grin on my face. "The countdown has officially begun to when you'll be able to Mark your mate."

A shadow passed over Tamas's face briefly before it disappeared and he nodded, giving me an easy grin that didn't reach his eyes. "So, is there a way we can disconnect her and just heal me now?" Tamas asked.

I shook my head and leaned a shoulder against the post of my bed. "No. You still have a lock on you. The Reaper said it will limit your abilities. You'll still be stronger than the average Demon, but you will not be as strong, and you cannot self-heal or be healed by a Witch as you normally would."

Tamas blanched. "What the hell am I meant to do? How is this possible?"

"We need to find the Witch who worked the spell. Only her blood can unlock it and get you back to normal," I explained as Tamas's expression darkened.

"How do I find the Witch?"

"We can help with that," Sawyer answered breathily, and we turned to see her leaning against a bed post, exhaustion printed across every line of her face. I hurried to her and she leaned into me heavily. Scooping her up quickly, I moved to the other side of the room to place her carefully on the cushioned lounge I had against the wall. Considering Sawyer had only known she was a witch for less than six months and had only been training for that long, I was impressed at how long she'd been able to remain standing to help heal Tamas.

"Malik, where are you? Your mate is exhausted and needs you."

"Is she okay?" Malik asked at once.

"She's fine, but she's wiped and needs to rest. Do you want me to take her back to your realm?"

"I'm here," Malik replied as he reached my bedroom doorway, his expression stormy, his eyes locked on his mate.

"Before you say anything—" Sawyer began.

"You promised me you wouldn't push yourself. You said you'd tap out when it got to be too much," he reprimanded, coming to kneel at her side.

"Dimitria needs us; she's hurting. Tamas needs us, his pain…" Tears glistened in her tired eyes. Malik cupped her face and pressed a quick kiss to her lips.

"You do no one any good if you're too tired to walk," Malik replied in a low rumble, and through our bond I experienced the mix of emotions pouring off him. Gratitude for his mate, for her selflessness and need to heal. Love for her and how she cared for his brothers. Annoyance that she had to help at all. Frustrated that she never seemed to listen. Guilty for wishing she didn't have to put herself in such a position at all, even if the people she was healing were his brother and one of his brother's mates.

I wanted to be annoyed, but I wasn't. We were all a mess at the moment. Judging by the darkening of Malik's expression, I gathered he and Sawyer were talking privately and I stepped away. Whatever they were talking about, they could keep it to themselves.

"Is Sawyer okay?" Dimitria asked, and I marveled at her ability to keep tabs on what was going on around me when she was in such pain. Tamas could hold a conversation and appear not to be

hurting because he was one of us, a King of Hell. We had perfected not showing pain millennia ago, and only really allowed ourselves to show it when we were among our family. But Dimitria wasn't like that, which made her ability to cope and handle it nothing short of miraculous.

"She is tired, she extended herself further than she ever has. She will be okay with some rest," I answered at once.

Tamas made to move, and through Dimitria I felt the breath-taking stab of pain it caused him even though he didn't show it.

"Sit your fucking ass down now," I snapped, crowding my brother so he was forced back onto the bed.

"We need to find that Witch."

"And you'll do what? Groan at her? Beg her to unlock this magic on you?"

Tamas glowered and I glared right back. "I need this shit fixed."

"And it will be, but not until you're healed, and Dimitria is free of you."

"I'm doing this *for* Dimitria, so she no longer has to feel my pain," Tamas explained.

"Every move you make, she feels. I felt your pain through her the moment you tried to stand up. I swear to fucking Dad that if you make another move that causes her an ounce of pain, I'll knock you out cold to ensure you stay down while they heal you."

Tamas looked momentarily ashamed, and I watched him drop my gaze and grind his teeth. Regret rolled off him and I let out a long breath.

"I know you're eager to fix this, but nothing can be done right now," I said, softening my voice when I was sure he was going to stay still. "We need you to lay back and get healed. Once that's done, once the poison from the blades is worked out of your system, we'll go hunting for your Witch."

After a few seconds consideration, Tamas jerked his head once in acknowledgement, his jaw tight and anger rolled off him.

I looked back at Mika and Cali and stepped closer. "How are you both doing?"

Cali didn't look at me when she spoke, and when she did, her voice was low and cracked. "We're getting there. We'll take a break in a moment to recharge, and then we'll start again."

I wanted to protest them taking a break, but I caught a glimpse of Sawyer on the couch looking so pale and shaky and kept my words to myself. Mika looked damn near translucent, and Cali was barely any better.

"I'm going to get the tea started, you'll stop when I'm finished with it," Adrik told Cali. There was no room for argument in his voice, no space for protest. His tone of voice—while soft— spoke volumes on what he expected.

Cali's lips twitched a little in the corner, but she nodded.

I watched Adrik's shoulders ease slightly in relief and he stepped past me to Cali's bag of supplies.

"Tea?" I asked curiously, making sure to remain connected with Tria the whole time.

"Different herbs help them heal and recharge faster. Since meeting Cali, I have learned what different herbs do, and I make sure to have the right ones on hand to ensure she recharges quickly whenever she pushes herself too far. Which is more often than I'm happy with."

I watched curiously as he got to work crushing herbs and tipping them into four different mugs. My appreciation for my brother spiked when I realized he was making one for Tria as well. I turned back to the bed when she brushed gently against my mind, and I stiffened when I saw her eyes on me. She was still in pain, still fighting not to show it, but she was at least able to open her eyes now.

I stepped up to the bed and looked down at her, a mess of words tumbling together in my mind, everything I wanted to say twisting together in some kind of mental car wreck so that nothing came out at all. A spark of humor touched my mind, and I knew it was her feeling my tangle of emotions. I had so much to say to her, there was so much we needed to talk about, but now was not the time. It would all wait until we were alone and we could properly hash out what happened and where things would go from here.

A moment later, Adrik finished making the women their drinks and at once, Mika and Cali stepped back. Cole was there for Mika immediately, wrapping his arms around her and carrying her away from the bed, waving his hand to create a large armchair for her to sit in.

Cali staggered and before I could help her, Adrik was there with a mug for her. He too drew up a chair for her to rest in and she fell back into it gratefully.

"Here," Adrik said, passing me a mug before moving to his mate. I took it and stepped closer to the bed.

"You need to drink this," I told her. Tria made a low moan of pain as she struggled to sit up, and I hurried to help her. Moving quickly, I shuffled in behind her and leaned against the headboard, carefully moving her between my thighs so she could lean against my chest and I could hold the mug for her.

"I could have managed," she pointed out, and I heard the awkwardness in her voice.

"I am sure you could have," I returned. It was the truth, but it didn't mean I was about to let her endure more pain when I could help.

"Let me?" she asked, echoing my thoughts. Shit. She was more in tune with me than I'd realized.

"I know we have a lot to talk about, and I have a lot of explaining to do about my life, our ways, and what being a mate means, but yes. In matters of your comfort and safety, I will always put you first, and if ever you are uncomfortable or in pain, it is because I have allowed it. Trust me, there will always be a good reason."

Tria mulled that over as I helped her to take a mouthful of the tea. She sighed gently as she swallowed the first sip, and we remained silent as she drank the rest, one small sip at a time. When she finished drinking, I put the mug aside but made no effort to move.

"Tria?"

We both turned to look at Tamas laid out on the bed, his wide eyes looking at my mate with a mix of gratitude and guilt.

"You would have done it for me," she whispered before he could say anything, but the pain in her voice was obvious.

"You still shouldn't have done it," he reprimanded.

"If not me, one of the others would have. I figured I owed you for running in the first place," she explained.

Tamas's expression darkened. "Why were you running? Where were you going? Why didn't you talk to me first? Who was that woman you left with?"

It wasn't until Tamas asked that I remembered Trinity. Mika's sister. Shit, Donovan had been looking for her for years now, the two of them had been playing cat and mouse until she'd up and disappeared. No one had been able to find her, and I'd been convinced the Angels had her and were hiding her.

Dimitria licked her dry lips, and I felt her preparing to answer, but her pain was growing so I interrupted.

"It hurts her too much to talk right now. I don't know why she was running or where she was running to. These things I'm sure we'll have answers to later on. I'm figuring she didn't tell you because she didn't want you to follow her. As for the other woman," I began and let out a long breath. "That was Trinity, Mika's sister."

Tamas's eyes widened and his mouth fell open. He looked around the room until his gaze landed on Mika, and then continued searching.

I shifted carefully behind Tria before continuing. "Donovan stayed back to clean up the mess we left behind. He should have been done by now, but I'm assuming he is trying to continue his search for her since she got away."

"Got away? How?"

I shrugged.

"She ran and used some kind of magic to disappear," Malik explained from the cushioned armchair, Sawyer sitting on his lap as she drank her tea. "I was with Donovan when Harkyn called for me to come back. He's looking for her again and has a stronger feel for her. He doesn't want to lose the trail now that he might have a chance."

"Why did she leave?" Tamas asked, puzzled. Malik shook his head, and I saw everyone else wonder the same thing. Dimitria stiffened ever so slightly in my arms, and I felt her discomfort immediately.

"Do you know why, cara?"

She didn't answer me right away, but I had a feeling she knew something.

"You told her to run," Mika said to Dimitria softly. "Back in the alley when we asked her to stay, you told her to run. Why?" There was no anger or accusation in Mika's voice, just the desperate need for answers.

Dimitria shook her head and winced when the movement hurt. "I don't know her whole story, but she is very concerned with her freedom. She knew something about certain Witches being meant for Demon Kings. I think she feels that she is a danger to others."

"Then why would she come for *you*?" I cut in before Mika could. Tria mulled that over and sighed. "She has been helping Witches disappear for years. She said it wasn't safe for Witches anymore, and that if we stayed out in the open, we'd become a prisoner of either Heaven or Hell, and neither were what we thought them to be. I'd already met you and Tamas and so I knew there were good points to Hell, but I didn't want to be anyone's prisoner, so I was going to leave with her."

"Why does Trinity think she's a danger to us?" Mika asked, her eyes focused on my mate with desperation.

Dimitria shook her head and winced in pain again. "I don't know, but she believes it. Maybe the Angels did something? She was only coming to collect me, take me somewhere safe, and then she was leaving again. We didn't know each other long enough for me to know all the details."

"The Angels?" Cole asked, frowning. Mika opened her mouth to ask another question but I cut across her again when I felt the burning pain in Dimitria increase.

"I know you're desperate for answers, Mika. I know, and I'm sorry, but they'll have to wait. Tria's pain is increasing again and we need to heal them both now. We can all sit down and talk about what happened later."

Mika looked disappointed and frustrated, but she nodded and handed Cole her empty mug. "You're right. I'm sorry, Tria. You need healing now, not a bunch of questions." Her eyes swung to Tamas, and she smiled warmly. "We'll get you up and about in no time."

Sawyer got to her feet unsteadily, and Malik watched her with a frustrated scowl. She simply smiled and patted his cheek before she made her way back to the bed.

"Are you going to move?" Tria asked.

"Nope," I returned quickly. I felt her immediate rush of humor and satisfaction, and I bit back my own smile. The women crowded close and I slid my hands down Tria's arms and the delicate, swirling patters there, marveling at her smooth, tattooed skin. I reached her hands and tangled our fingers together, closing my eyes on the feel of her in my arms. How many nights had I lain awake watching over her, my body physically aching with the need to do just this, just hold her? How many times had I wished for nothing more than to hold her hand or trace the angles of her face? It was almost mind-blowing that I was here with her now, that she was wrapped in my arms and that I could be so close to her.

Drawing her scent deep into my lungs, I closed my eyes and merged my mind with hers as the mates of my brothers began their healing once again.

CHAPTER TWENTY-TWO
DIMITRIA

The moment I woke up, I knew I wasn't alone.

No, I wasn't surrounded by Witches and Kings of Hell, but there was someone here. The room was dark, but there was a flickering orange light on the stone walls that told me there was a fire going somewhere. The bed I was in was comfortable, the covers thick and plush, and I wanted to burrow into them and never leave. I hadn't slept so well in a long time, and I felt refreshed.

Except that I wasn't alone.

I searched with my other senses to find out who was there, but I needn't have done it. I should have known Harkyn wouldn't leave me alone, not when he could finally show himself to me. I blinked to wake up a little more and thought back to the last thing I remembered. Mika, Sawyer, and Cali had worked tirelessly to heal me and Tamas. They'd taken one more break hours later before finally finishing. It was a good thing, too, since I felt the increasing annoyance of their mates—their worry and need to step in. For men of action, it had to be a form of torture to sit on the sidelines and watch their mates get weaker and weaker as they expended their energy on another, even if that other was their brother and brother's mate.

As the last of Tamas's injuries healed, I remember feeling an immense sense of exhaustion wash over me, everyone became fuzzy and their voices distant. I remembered Harkyn's grip on me tightening and his worried tone of voice before I fell unconscious. Handling Tamas's pain all that time had taken a toll.

"You're awake."

I rolled onto my back and sat up carefully, testing my body for any residual aches and pains, but was glad to find I no longer hurt. I raised my head to look at Harkyn, pushing back my blonde hair as I did so and paused. He was leaning against the back of the couch, one ankle crossed over the other, his sexy, tattooed arms crossed over his expansive chest. He wasn't trying to be sensual, not that I could tell, but damn, the man even relaxed sexy.

"I—yeah," I responded, not knowing what else to say. I tried reaching out to him, but he was very closed off and I was immediately hurt. Okay, so maybe I didn't have the right to be hurt, but why was his guard up? Why wasn't he open to me now that it was possible? "Uh, how long was I out?" I asked instead. Harkyn studied me a moment longer and pushed off the couch, walking a few steps towards me with his hands in his front pockets. "Almost two days."

My eyes nearly bugged out of my head, and I gasped. "Two *days?*"

"You scared the fuck outta me when you passed out," he said and shook his head, a wry smile curving his lips. "But the others assured me you were just exhausted, that the toll on your body was huge and you'd need time to rest."

I nodded slowly, still in shock. I'd never slept that long before. Silence fell between us again and I clasped my hands together on my lap, twisting them as I waited for him to say something else.

"So..."

Harkyn's lips twitched, and he ran a hand through his hair as he ducked his head. *That* moment, that tiny section of time where he looked bashful, confused, unsure and a little hopeful would live rent-free in my head forever. He was this huge, hulking, tattooed, sexy as sin King of Hell with power beyond anything I could do, and in that moment, he was as unsure and awkward as I was.

"Look, we have a lot to talk about. Do you need anything? Do you want to get dressed or bathe? Do you want something to eat or drink?" Harkyn asked. At the mention of food, my stomach growled embarrassingly loud, and he grinned.

"Food would be good," I admitted.

"Okay," he agreed. "I'll be right back. You can feel free to look around or just stay there if you're comfortable."

I nodded again, feeling oddly like I was fifteen and at a boy's house for the first time. Why was this so awkward?

Harkyn's lips curved upwards again before he turned on his heel and marched out of the room, leaving the bedroom door open as he went. I took a moment to look around his room and smiled. It was masculine, but not in a *Saturdays are for the boys* kind of bachelor pad. The four-poster bed I sat in was made from a rich, deep timber, the bedspread was a navy blue, and the furniture was warm and inviting. I carefully climbed out of bed, grinning when there was a decent gap between the floor and my dangling feet. I'd always wanted a bed that I had to run up and jump onto as a kid. I don't know why, it was totally impractical and I'm sure it would get annoying at some point, but it had always looked so comfortable as a kid watching movies where the character had to do just that.

I slipped from the bed and noticed I was wearing an oversized shirt that ended just above my knees, and I frowned. Realization dawned that it was Harkyn's shirt, and I couldn't help the blush that ran up my neck to my cheeks. Had he dressed me? A quick look down the neck of the shirt showed I was still wearing my bra and panties at least. I hooked the neck of the shirt with my thumb and smelled it, closing my eyes when the scent of him filled my lungs.

I'd been breathing that scent in on and off for years, and the whole time I'd been sure it was my mind making it up. Now I know it hadn't been. The carpet beneath my feet was lush and thick, but it only covered the space beneath the bed and then a little around it. The rest of the ground was a thick stone that reminded me of a medieval castle. Were we in a castle? There were no windows to give me any indication of the time, so it felt as though it was late at night, but I had no idea.

I caught sight of my duffle bag by the bedroom door and wanted to cheer. Anything I cared about—with the exception of my bike—was in there. I rummaged through it until I found my notepad and pen before flipping to an empty page. If I was working a case—a mark—I'd write down literally anything about them and how they lived in order to ascertain the kind of person they were. It helped me when I needed to find them, because sometimes I didn't want to use magic, and for the human realm, an actual paper trail of some kind was needed to prove *how* I found my bounties. While I didn't need to do more than look into Harkyn's mind to find out all there was to know about him, some habits die hard, and writing things down was a familiar chore that made me feel a little more in control of an otherwise uncontrollable situation.

My gaze skirted to the open bedroom door and curiosity got the better of me. I stepped towards it and pulled the heavy wooden door open more. Yep, it definitely belonged in an old castle. I stopped to write a few details down before I looked up to find myself standing on the top of a landing that overlooked a large

space. The wall directly beside me was covered from floor to
ceiling in climbing ivy, and at once I reached for it. I felt the life
of the plant thrumming strongly through its vines, and I smiled as
it reached for me, called to me. I hummed slightly under my
breath and touched the wax-like leaves, feeling peace steal over
me at the presence of nature in this place. I had no idea how it
managed to grow here as I was yet to spot a single window to
allow in light, but nevertheless, it was growing, and from what I
could sense of it, it was happy and healthy.

From my vantage point, there was a darkened doorway down the
stairs and to my left that for some reason had the hairs on the
back of my neck standing on end. I moved on from that and
caught sight of another fireplace, this one much bigger than the
one in the bedroom. Without going near it, I felt the magic in its
flames, in the construction of it. A huge, plush looking couch sat
before it, and I was eager to curl up on it and feel the warmth of
the flames. A side table bookended either side of it, both with
lamps on them. Upon further inspection, I couldn't see any
power points, so I had to assume they were magic lamps. The
thought of electrical points in hell made my brain momentarily
short circuit and I laughed to myself. I don't know why it was
funny, but it was.

A floor-to-ceiling library ran from the far-left side of the wall
opposite me to the far right. The only break in it was at the large
red door in the middle, where I had to assume would lead out
to… where? If I stepped out there, would there be fire and
brimstone? Would there be the tortured souls of the damned and
Demons with torture weapons?

The door opened suddenly and Harkyn strode in with a tray in his
hands. It closed behind him, but for the two seconds it was open,
I didn't see anything Hell-like, just polished black marble.

Confusion tugged at me, but it was wiped away almost at once as Harkyn came to a sudden stop, his familiar eyes landing on me.

"I wasn't sure if you were up for walking just yet. Do you want to come down here or go back to bed?" he asked.

"Uh, I'll come down," I said, wanting to see more of his home. I mean, I had to assume this was his home.

Harkyn waited as I walked down the polished stone steps, my hand sliding along the stone banister as I made my way carefully down. He indicated to the couch with a jerk of his head and I smiled and moved that way.

I closed my notebook and saw the way he noted it, but he didn't ask.

Harkyn had been gone from my life for so long, and the time I'd had with him had been so brief in comparison that I started to believe I'd made our time together into something it wasn't.

Surely I'd been wrong about how gorgeous he was, how sinfully sexy and confident, how powerful. Surely I'd made up the way he looked at me, spoke to me, the way he stared at me like he wanted to tear every inch of clothing off me and devour me whole, while at the same time restraining himself with the willpower of a god.

Looking at him now, I knew I hadn't been wrong, nor had I been mistaken about the way I'd felt about him. I'd begun to think it was a stupid teenage crush and I was blowing it out of proportion, but since seeing him in that alleyway, it all came rushing back and I knew for certain I'd been in love with him.

We'd only known each other a few months, and when we did see each other, it wasn't always for very long.

Was I still in love with him?

I shied away from that question, not ready to open that particular box of memories. He'd hurt me by running off all those years ago, but now I was left with the knowledge that it had been *because* of me he's stayed away. If I hadn't been so emotional, so scared—if I hadn't shouted at him to go away and leave me alone, then maybe I wouldn't have been alone all these years. Maybe I wouldn't have felt so rejected and unwanted. Being a foster kid meant I was already drowning in feelings of inadequacy, I already felt unwanted and unloved. When Harkyn left, it only reinforced what I'd already felt, only it hurt so much more because I'd actually begun to believe he would never leave me.

I'd thought badly of him for so long, it was a little weird to look at him now and know it wasn't his fault.

"I wasn't sure what you were in the mood for," Harkyn told me as he placed the tray down on the couch and stepped back. There was an assortment of cold cut meats, fruit, cheese, crackers, dips, and bread. Honestly, I was so hungry I could eat it all, but I was more desperate for answers than food.

Had I been making up the chemistry between us back then? Sure, I was only twenty-one, so it's not like in the last four years there had been what others would consider a ground-breaking amount of mental growth, but I like to think I'd grown a bit at least. But when I thought about Harkyn in those few months, the way he looked at me, the way it felt to kiss him, to touch him, to have him press me into a wall and almost take me then and there—had it all been in my head? Was it even possible for two people to experience that kind of heat?

Frowning, I dropped my pen and paper on the small end table and stepped closer to Harkyn instead of the couch and he stilled. "What are you doing?"

I heaved a small sigh and shook my head. "I need to know something."

"You're not hungry?"

"I am," I replied. "But I really need an answer to a question I've had for a long time first. I need to confirm something before we talk so I know where I stand."

Harkyn frowned, looking puzzled, but he didn't step back when I closed the distance between us. Up close, he was even more beautiful, and the firelight that played upon his skin made him look all the more delicious. His shoulder length hair was tied back at the nape of his neck as it usually had been, his cheeks and chin covered in that perpetual stubble that made him look rugged and sexy. There was the smallest of dimples in his chin that I had the almost inescapable urge to touch. Those long lashes of his framed his eyes beautifully and made me want to sigh with envy. I hadn't thought men like him existed, not to this kind of standard, and not in real life. I guess he wasn't really a man, but a Demon King. I mentally shrugged. Oh well, I could overlook that minor detail for now.

As I leaned towards him, the scent of him filled my lungs and I breathed deep, swaying closer, lifting my hands until they came to rest lightly on his chest. I felt his sharp intake of breath, but he didn't step away, didn't raise his hands to touch me or push me away. Slowly, I tipped my head back to look up at him and inched closer, pushing up onto the balls of my feet as my hands slid up his chest to his neck where they interlaced. I let my fingers slide into his hair from the base of his neck and pressed down lightly, urging him to lower his head. He didn't make me wait, and my breath caught as he slowly lowered his face to mine, his green-gray eyes burning with heat and need.

The first touch of his lips was tentative, a mere brush across mine. I pushed myself higher, desperate to feel him kiss me properly, desperate to see if my memory of him held up, or if I'd truly let the fantasy of him overshadow everything. Had my teenage brain been so obsessed with him that I'd made him out to be something he wasn't?

"Dimitria," he whispered across my mind, his voice ringing with tension and need, his body strung tight like he was holding himself back by the merest thread.

"Kiss me, Harkyn."

The string snapped and his arms swept around me, crushing me to him as his mouth descended upon mine. I gasped at the speed with which he moved, but when his tongue teased my lips open and slipped into my mouth, it turned into a needy groan. I responded immediately, kissing him like I'd dreamed of kissing him since we first met, since he'd put a stop to our intimacies and just became my friend.

Okay, so apparently, I *had* been deluding myself to how good it felt to kiss him. The delusion being that I was so far off the mark it wasn't funny. He was *better* than I remembered, so much better. Intoxicating was a word that came to mind, and then was swiftly melted away as coherent thought became impossible. I practically turned to liquid against him, literally sank against his hard frame, and let him take my weight. He didn't seem to mind this at all as his lips fused to mine and he kissed me like our lives depended on it. The feel of his large hands on my back made me feel small and delicate... cherished and protected. His hard frame was solid and compounded with muscles my fingers itched to trace. The taste of him brought back memories from those early days, days in which I'd felt hopeful that I'd never be alone again, that I'd found someone who would stick by me no matter what. I lightly dragged my fingers across his scalp and the groan he emitted rumbled through his chest and sent a shiver down my spine. When he pulled back a moment later, we were both breathless and my pulse pounded through every inch of my body. My skin was one raw nerve, needy and desperate for more. Wherever his skin touched mine it felt aflame with desire.

"Dimitria." He whispered my name, but there was a question there. I swallowed quickly and gently eased back onto the flat of my feet, but I didn't look away. Harkyn slowly released me, and I felt deprived of his warmth, but he deserved answers and I needed to get a few of my own.

"Sorry, I just… I needed to know if the memory lived up to the real deal, or if I had made you out to be something you weren't," I explained. He nodded slowly, the heat still alive in his eyes, and the smile that tugged at his lips was slow and sexy.

"What's the verdict?"

My face warmed and I smiled as I stepped away. "I have a good memory, but the refresher was a good idea."

Harkyn chuckled lowly, and my stomach flipped at the deep, rich sound. Was everything he did sexy?

"In that case, let me know if you need any more memory prompting kisses. I'm your willing subject."

Smiling, I stepped back to the couch, careful not to knock over the tray. My stomach reminded me once again that it had been several days since I'd eaten, and I picked up a piece of mango and chewed on it, groaning as the flavor exploded across my tongue. "Food is so good," I moaned. Harkyn grinned again and took a seat on the opposite side of the couch. I had the distinct feeling he was putting deliberate space between us. I wanted to know everything, but I wasn't even sure where to start. Thankfully, I didn't need to.

"You seem to be accepting all of this rather well. A little too well," Harkyn pointed out, a small, puzzled frown creasing his forehead. I considered his statement for a moment and then shrugged.

"Not really," I began, swallowing my food. "I just adapt. I've been in the foster system since I was four years old, and I never knew who I was going to be with from one month to the next, what that family would be like, what people would think of me." There was a sharp prick in my chest, and it took me a moment to realize it wasn't coming from me, but from Harkyn. His dark eyes were focused on me, impassive, serene, as if nothing were bothering him at all. But I *felt* his despair at the circumstances of my younger years.

"I learned early on that complaining and whining did no good. No one cared, no one was going to change things just because I didn't like them. So, I could either kick and complain every time things changed, or I could adapt to the situation, accept how things were, and react accordingly in whatever way that kept me safe."

"And that's what you're doing now?" he asked. There was an odd note in his voice, but I couldn't place it. Was he upset? Angry? Pleased?

I shrugged. "I am still trying to understand everything. I don't know all the facts, what happened, where, why, or how. I don't know how to react yet."

Harkyn considered me for a long moment, and I continued to eat in silence. I needed answers, my body needed fuel, and then I could figure out where to go from here. Was I scared? Umm, yeah. I was in *Hell,* or at least some version of an underworld, and I had no idea if I could leave—if he would let me leave—or what was expected of me now. I was very much aware that I had given him consent to *bind our souls*. Surely that had to carry greater consequences than I was currently aware of.

I leaned back to pick up my pen and paper and scrawled a few quick notes and things to ask later. My mind was a mess of things right now, so I needed to keep track of what I knew, and what I needed to know.

"I didn't know what you were to me, who you were, when I found you four years ago," Harkyn said suddenly.

I lifted my head but didn't say anything. I watched his face as I ate and kept my senses open for any signs of deception. Why he would lie about anything now was beyond me, but if my time as a bounty hunter had taught me anything, it was that I didn't need to know the reasons why people did things, just that they did, and I had to be prepared for it.

"When I found you, it was because of the burst of magic I felt from a Witch, a species of human we all thought extinct. That part is true. Our first interactions, all of it, they were all genuine. There was no dishonesty there or deceit."

I nodded. Deep down I knew what we had in the beginning was real and true, but it helped ease something in me to hear him confirm it now.

"Why did you leave? Why did you make that pact?" I asked, picking at a piece of thick cut bread so I could avoid looking at him. I was desperate for answers, but a part of me was afraid to know. I'd been so scared, and he'd been mad at me, furious at the ones who hurt me. Our last goodbye had been angry and intense, and I wasn't sure I was ready to know why he'd stayed gone, but I needed to know.

Harkyn hesitated, and I waited to see if he was going to lie, but what I felt from him was a loss for words. He was searching himself, looking for a way to properly explain, and so I let him take his time.

"The first moment I saw you out in that field, there was an incredibly powerful pull. There was something inside me that recognized you and demanded I take you for my own," he started to explain.

My face began to warm at the memory of our first meeting and his gray-green eyes rose to meet mine, the small smirk on his face telling me he knew exactly what I was thinking. I'd been seventeen, I'd never been kissed like that before in my life, never felt so consumed by someone's presence before. It had been intoxicating.

"I knew something about you was different, but I had no idea what. None of us knew about the prophecy at that point, none of us knew we were destined for mates or that Witches were involved. All I knew was that leaving you was not an option. I was addicted to you, for lack of a better word."

I nodded slowly, knowing that feeling all too well. I had been addicted to him, too, completely obsessed. He'd taken up so much space inside my head, it was a wonder I could dress myself in the morning without asking him what he thought I should wear.

"But you still left," I reminded softly.

Harkyn ducked his head and sighed heavily. "You were seventeen, Dimitria. I know you're not much older now, and those few years shouldn't make a difference, but they do. I'm old, *cara*, very old. At a certain point, age is nothing but a number humans use to track the passing of time. But it is important, and even we Kings of Hell have standards and limitations. None of us are interested in bedding children. We make it a point to never touch a human until they reach a certain age. We prefer our women to be of legal drinking age at the very least. Any younger, and it's just too young."

My face was hot now, but I frowned. "So, the second time you came to me and discovered my age…"

Harkyn groaned. "I was mad enough to tear down a warehouse. You were addictive, I was hooked on you, but your age meant there was a *Do Not Touch* sticker on you made out of bright neon lights. As much as I wanted you, I wasn't going to break that rule."

Chewing slowly, I considered this. I knew my age had been an issue for him, he'd said as much, and yet it still hadn't really rung true for me. Now, I guess I could see. He was a King of Hell and could do anything and get away with it, but he and his brothers had a rule about sexual relationships and the ages of humans, and I found that… refreshing. I smiled and shook my head at the irony.

"What?"

"Huh?"

"You were grinning, what's so funny about that?" Harkyn asked, a perplexed smile on his face.

I shrugged. "Several God-fearing religious groups on Earth will tell you that it's totally acceptable for a grown man to marry a young girl who hasn't even reached her teenage years, that God says it's okay, but the Kings of Hell say no, that it's immoral and gross," I explained, and a small laugh slipped. "Men of godly religion say it's fine, but the freaking Kings of *Hell* have higher standards and more morals than they do."

Harkyn smiled, but it wasn't full of amusement, more sad acceptance. "That's true."

"Sorry, I wasn't trying to say you're bad at your core," I hurried to say, worried I'd insulted him.

He quickly shook his head and reached out to touch my hand. "It's not you. I see a lot of the humans you're describing down here. I spend a lot of time punishing them for their crimes. I get full, detailed reports on their sins so that I can properly punish them. It's a sad reality that humans are often far viler and damaging to each other than we will ever be to them."

I considered his words and my stomach roiled uncomfortably. He was right. From what I'd seen of the Kings versus what I'd seen of humanity, humans ruled in the vicious species department without a contest.

"Anyway," Harkyn said with a deep breath, bringing us back on track. "Because you were so young, I forced myself to keep space between us, forced myself to keep my distance and to just train you. It was a torture I hadn't expected, but I endured. I loved watching you learn, watching you gain strength and confidence, watching you grow into your powers."

I ducked my head at the pride and genuine joy I heard in his voice. It hurt to hear all this because I'd hated him for years, but at the same time, it soothed old hurts I thought I was healed from.

"I still wanted you, despite ignoring my instincts to take you home and have my way with you."

I choked on a laugh and he grinned, his eyes playful. The light in his gaze slowly dimmed, and his features tightened. There was a pause, and I knew where his mind had gone to, and I sat the pen and paper on the table once more before bringing my knees up to wrap my arms around them, uncomfortable with revisiting this topic.

"I—fuck, Tria. When I heard you call for me, when I knew what was happening—" He struggled to speak, and I felt the echoes of his fear, his terror, and his all-consuming fury. "When I saw that fucker on top of you while you begged him to stop, and that fucking waste of oxygen foster brother of yours in the corner with a camera—" He cut off suddenly and pushed up off the couch to pace away, one hand spearing through his hair as he moved towards the fire. I didn't move and watched him from my seat, slowly breathing out in an attempt to calm the sudden rage and disgust in the room.

"I lost it. I know I lost it, and I'm sorry you witnessed it, but Tria…" He turned to look at me. There was a storm in his eyes, a turbulent clash of emotions that had lived there for a long time. "I need you to know something. I'm not sorry for what I did."

I swallowed hard, remembering the sound of their screams, the hot splash of blood and the roar of rage that ripped from him. The sounds of flesh being torn from flesh still woke me some nights, and the memories of that day seemed to echo between us now.

"I know it's not what you want to hear, I know it's not what you'd consider a good quality in a man that's been singled out as your mate from the universe, but it's the truth. I might do a lot of things you don't like or approve of, but you can be sure I'll never lie to you."

Drawing in a slow breath, I nodded. I knew him. Even after these years had passed, even having only known him for a short time at a younger age, I knew him. At first, I'd been horrified and sickened, a lot of thoughts had raced through my head that day and I'd panicked and said some things I now regretted, but I knew he wasn't a monster.

"You still haven't explained why you made it impossible to see me again," I reminded softly.

Harkyn sighed, his shoulders dropping in relief that I didn't fight him on his right to tear into those who tried to hurt me.

Honestly, there were times I wanted to do the same thing to some people in the world.

"I couldn't trust myself around you, Dimitria. That day, I was *so* close to taking you to Hell with me, you have no idea how soon your normal life almost came to an end. In that motel room when we kissed, I almost took you. Had I done that, there wouldn't have been anything you could have done to stop me. I wanted to keep you safe, I wanted so badly to save you from the monsters on Earth I almost took your right to your life out of your hands."

I frowned. I could hear the torture in his voice, the guilt, the shame, I felt the remanence of the fight he'd endured against himself, but something didn't add up. "That's all? You got scared you'd lock me in a tower, so you made it impossible for you to be around me ever again? How does that even make sense?" I asked, getting to my feet, my hands on my hips.

"No," he said and turned to face me more fully, his dark eyes glittering in the firelight.

"Then what? Explain it to me. Because I was terrified of you, for you, of what you were capable of. I was scared that night and I had every right to be. I didn't recognize the man before me, and I needed time to come to terms with the violence you were capable of. Surely you had to know I didn't actually want you to stay away forever. You've been alive since the dawn of time. Tell me that at a certain age, males understand what a woman means when she says certain things," I argued, annoyed, a fire beginning to burn in my stomach.

Harkyn stepped closer, the look in his eyes one I didn't fully trust but couldn't look away from. "I was protecting you."

"How?" I demanded sharply. "You wanted to protect me, so you disappeared? How does that make sense?"

"I was protecting you *from me*," he snapped, his voice a low growl as he stepped closer again. Whatever words I'd planned to say died on my tongue and he edged closer, stalked ever so slowly that it was almost impossible to notice when he'd actually moved, his eyes locked on me the entire time. The air seemed heavy with meaning, with tension and unspoken wants and desires making it hard to breathe.

"I wanted you with a desperation I had never felt before, and have never felt since. Being around you was like having my skin on fire all the time, and you were the water I was not allowed to touch to ease the ache. I hungered for you so completely that every time I saw you, all the time I spent with you, took a toll to the point I feared my restraint would snap one day and I'd rip up my rule book and seduce you."

His chest heaved as he finished speaking, his dark eyes glittered down at me with a combination of frustration and hunger. My gaze fell back to his luscious mouth, and I licked my lips quickly, the fire in my belly turning to an all-out inferno, my blood singing with the need to yank him closer and kiss him until I passed out.

"Oh," I whispered breathily.

"Yes, *oh.* I was bordering on desperation, holding onto my restraint by my fingertips and sheer force of will. You were *seventeen,* basically a child, Tria. I beat myself up constantly for thinking of you the way I did, but it didn't stop my thoughts or my fantasies."

"I was never really a child." It was the truth. I couldn't ever remember feeling like a kid.

His smile was small and sardonic. "I thought those same thoughts as a way to try and justify them to myself. Any excuse you can come up with, I said it to myself at one point or another. It started with how you always acted older, you were very mature, even more than women older than you. You were stronger and different to other girls your age. You hadn't been a child for a very long time, your life had not allowed you to be. Even the fact that you seemed as interested in me as I was in you... on and on the excuses went. At the end of the day, though, you'd been on this planet for seventeen years, and that was an inescapable truth."

Silence fell between us as I struggled to find something to say, something besides *fuck, you're gorgeous.*

"Buffy and Spike," I blurted.

Harkyn blinked furiously for a moment and then frowned. "Excuse me?"

"Buffy and Spike. They had a *huge* age gap. Although they got together when she was an adult, so maybe that doesn't count. Buffy and Angel then. She was only sixteen and he was hundreds of years old. That's an age-gap no one really blinked at."

Harkyn continued to look at me like I was crazy. "You're comparing our situation to a TV show?"

"Not just *any* TV show—*Buffy*! But if that's not your thing, then what about Elena and the Salvatore brothers? Again, teenage girl and Vampires, each over one hundred years old. Or Edward and Bella. That's a smaller age gap, but still rather big when you think about it."

Harkyn's grin grew wide and he shook his head. "Are you trying to justify the fact that I lusted after you when you were seventeen?"

"What about Rose and The Doctor? He was hundreds of years old and an *alien*, and she was only eighteen. Or Piper and Leo? Or what about Dean Winchester and Anna the Angel? Hell, Dean and Castiel even. You *cannot* tell me those two didn't have a little thing going on," I continued to rant.

"I don't know what I should think about your fixation on TV shows and books involving characters with unhealthy age-gaps," Harkyn remarked with a shake of his head.

"It means," I began and smiled, "that I am okay with an age-gap. Even one as big as ours."

Harkyn groaned and reached out to take my hands. They engulfed mine, and my heart stuttered at the zaps of awareness coursing through me at a mere touch.

"It isn't the same," he reminded.

"I know, but I didn't think it was a big deal then, and I don't now. Not for us."

"I was a danger to you, it wasn't right."

"So, you made it impossible to *ever* see me again rather than just leaving for a few years?"

He grimaced. "I acted rashly—desperately. You were standing there yelling at me, telling how you never wanted to see me again. I wanted to shelter you and protect you, and at the same time ravish you on the spot so that no one would ever mistake you for available again. I was dangerously close to losing a war against myself, and I did the first thing that came to mind. I didn't word it well; I didn't take the time to think of the consequences or if I should leave myself a loophole. I just reacted," he explained, and I heard the genuine regret in his voice.

I shook my head and we stood there in silence a moment longer as I digested that information.

"So, we've both spent the last four years missing each other, wanting to be with each other, and we couldn't because I spoke rashly and you acted without thought?" I asked, looking for clarification.

Harkyn choked on a small laugh and nodded. "I guess you could say that."

"Men," I whispered with a shaky laugh. "You all say *we're* the emotional ones."

Harkyn's eyes met mine, that sparkle in them making him look so much more care-free. I studied him carefully, marveling that he was actually here in front of me. Mostly, I rejoiced in knowing I hadn't been imagining him, that I hadn't given him more credit than he was due. I was happy to see the man I'd known four years ago was still in there, with his good heart and protective nature. *"Safe,"* I whispered to him in my mind. His eyes zapped between mine, his expression studying. I smiled and reached up to gently cup his face. *"You make me feel safe. I never felt that again after you left."*

His expression tightened, his gaze turning remorseful as he held my hand to his cheek. "Did you mean what you said before? That you've spent this whole time missing me too?"

My heart leapt in my chest, but I gripped my courage with both hands and nodded. "I did."

A weight seemed to lift from his shoulders, and I watched his eyes flick towards my mouth before his lips parted and he swayed forward. I didn't make him wait—I didn't make *us* wait. Not this time. I leaned up to meet his kiss halfway, rejoicing in the feel of him again, in the way he seemed to drown in me as much as I let myself get lost in him. It was unlike anything I'd ever felt, kissing Harkyn. He was everywhere at once—in my head, my heart, his hands on my body, his scent making me both dizzy and euphoric. I had craved this man since the moment he walked away, and I needed him more than ever. I didn't care that he'd been the one to leave. I didn't care about what he'd done in the past. I knew he was sorry; I knew what he'd done was out of love, fear, and protection. I knew his *soul*. He wasn't evil, there was no need to hesitate when the man I'd mourned and missed for four years was standing before me now.

Adapt. Survive. Thrive.

Harkyn was here now. I finally had answers as to what had happened, and I knew where we stood. I wanted to revel in this moment for a while before I thought about what was next for us.

CHAPTER TWENTY-THREE
HARKYN

The food platter clattered to the ground as Dimitria pushed me backward towards the couch. I smiled against her mouth at the way she knew what she wanted and how she went for it. I fell onto the cushioned lounge and she leaned over me, her hands braced on either side of my head at the back of the couch.

She tasted like mango, her lips soft and sweet. I could kiss her forever, but she was impatient and I loved it. She stepped closer and slowly moved so she sat astride my lap. My hands went to her hips and she gasped against my mouth as I rocked upwards. Fuck, I'd wanted to touch her for so long, to kiss her, to devour her mouth and sink into her body. I was hard as granite beneath my jeans.

"Wait," I whispered, pulling back.

"What?"

"I—are you sure?" I asked, swallowing hard. I wanted her to want this, but a part of me felt like we were moving too fast. Fucking hell, if my brothers had heard my thoughts just then, I'd have had my ass kicked from one end of the Arrival Room to the other for being such a fucking girl.

"Harkyn," Dimitria began, blowing out an impatient breath that sent a strand of platinum blonde hair flying back over her head. "I have wanted you since the first time you kissed me. I have been deprived of you for four years through no decision of my own. You've explained yourself, our situation, and we've cleared the air. I'm done waiting—are you?"

"I…" I groaned, forcing myself to take a breath. "The binding, us being mated, you don't know all the details," I tried to explain, but my dick was making it hard to think. The heat she radiated through the thin pair of cotton underwear she wore was evident, and it was driving me mad.

"Sawyer explained," Tria said. "There are four parts to the binding—heart, mind, body, and soul. We tied our souls together in that alleyway, and I'm given to understand from the information in your head that we performed the mind-bond four years ago. If we do this now, we'll be sealing the body bond, yes?" she asked.

"I—yes," I answered, frowning at the lack of panic and wariness in her voice.

"I'm assuming these bonds cannot be undone. You said as much in the alley," she continued, her hands trailing down my chest to my stomach.

"No. Mika looked into it when she and Cole first got together, and there doesn't seem to be a way out," I answered honestly. "If there was, would you want to take it?"

She hesitated a moment and dragged her crystal blue gaze back to mine. "No."

Surprise rippled through me at her blunt answer. This all felt too easy, too… I don't know. I'd been expecting more resistance from her, like with the others. The other women had fought this tooth and nail with my brothers; they had argued and tried to find a way out. I had expected the same fight from Dimitria who I knew was fiercely independent and used to doing things on her own.

"Why?" I asked, while another part of me was mentally kicking my ass. What the hell did it matter why? She wanted me, wanted this, why was I looking a gift horse in the mouth? Tria's hands slid to the hem of my shirt before she slipped her hands beneath it to touch my bare skin. I sucked in a sharp breath, my dick raging at me beneath the zipper to be released so we could get on with this.

"Harkyn, we started this relationship before either of us knew about mates and bonds and all the rest of it. I know our feelings were genuine. I know how I feel about you, how I have *always* felt about you. They have not gone away or lessened in our time apart, and I am grateful to have you back in my life now. Being a Witch, I know the way you feel about me, I can sense it, and I'm more than happy with that level of affection before moving our relationship in a more physical direction. I am not about to waste time asking questions or postponing what seems to be a pretty inevitable event for the sake of a little drama. Hear me... I want you; I have always wanted you, and I don't particularly like the thought of my future without you in it. So, the only question that remains is, are you with me in this?"

I didn't have to think about that for long. Relief at knowing she wouldn't want out if she had the choice washed away any lingering hesitations I had.

"Fuck yes I am." I bunched her hair in one hand and slammed my mouth against hers. She gave a shriek of surprise that turned into a moan of pleasure, and I was fucking *done.* My woman wanted me, she knew everything that went with this moment, and she still wanted me.

By the time oxygen became a necessity, we were both panting. I wished away my jeans—almost groaning in relief—but left myself clad in a pair of briefs so that she didn't think I was jumping the gun. Her hands tugged at my shirt and I lifted my arms and allowed her to pull it off me. The heat in her eyes expanded as she gaped down at my tattooed chest, her gaze drinking in every inch of me, tracing the tattoos along my abdomen, chest, and arms. The innocence and hunger on her face made my craving for her increase exponentially. Gently, I slid my hands up her thighs to the edges of my shirt I'd dressed her in for bed. Hesitant blue eyes met mine before she gave a small nod, and I slowly lifted the shirt over her head to reveal the white lace bra beneath it. I'd wanted to take this off before putting her to bed the other day, but I hadn't wanted her to feel violated or uncomfortable with me. The sight of my Mark over her heart soothed something deep inside me, that raging animal that needed her to be mine and only mine. I leaned forward to brush a kiss over it, and she shivered, her sensitive skin rippling with goosebumps.

"Dimitria, I have watched over you for years, so I think I already know the answer to this, but I need to know," I whispered against her mind as I leaned forward and pressed gentle kisses to her cheeks, her forehead, her lips. I peppered them across her face, wanting to mark her again and again to prove she was mine.

"What?" she asked, but judging by the rising heat in her face, she already knew.

"I left you at seventeen because you were so young. So innocent and inexperienced. Has that changed?"

Her pulse jumped and her breath shuddered as anticipation and need rose within her hard. Those crystal blue eyes of hers met mine and she swallowed hard.

"No. That hasn't changed."

Some primal, animalistic part of me roared in triumph, and I physically ached to sink into her and claim what would only ever be mine. I didn't know why it mattered, wasn't sure why it was so important and such a relief to know she hadn't been with another, but it was, and I was fucking blissed out about it. It probably made me a monumental dick bag that I was so happy to know I would be the only one to ever touch her like this, the only one ever to share the heat of her body and watch her face contort in ecstasy as we rose to new heights together. I'd be the one to show her how to please me, and I'd make damn fucking sure I pleased her.

"Cave man," she teased aloud with a grin, obviously picking up on my territorial smugness.

"Who do you think they learned it from?" I asked and kissed her again.

It was a struggle to reign in my desire to take her hard and fast right now, but I did it. I slid my hands around her waist as she settled her weight more fully on my lap. Her smaller hands slid up my arms in a gentle caress. I watched her face, the wonder, the anticipation and need flit across her face as she felt my muscles tense beneath her touch. Fuck, this was torture, but I craved every second of it. The need to yank her closer and devour her rode me hard, but I was determined that she set the pace, that she have control. Years of wanting her made it almost impossible to do, but for her I would wait, I would endure—or try to, anyway.

My eyes devoured her, my gaze tracing every delicate and fascinating tattoo that decorated her pale skin. My brothers and I all loved our tattoos, but none of the other mates had them. I loved the ones on Dimitria's skin and the way they told her story in every curve and stroke and the way the vines of them effortlessly followed the dips and contours of her body. I could see the way she wanted me but was self-conscious in her movements. I was reminded once again that she'd never been with another man and that knowledge sent the animal in my chest roaring. It was archaic, sure, and definitely hypocritical, but I loved that she'd only ever know my touch and no other man's. Gently, I rolled my hips up and encouraged her with my hands on her hips to rock back and forth on my lap. Her blue eyes widened, darkened, and her mouth fell open in a small gasp of surprise. I kept my eyes glued to hers as she began to rock against me, her hips circling and gyrating, her grip on my arm tightening. Fuck, she was beautiful.

"Harkyn." She whispered my name on a breath, and I knew the sound of it would live forever in my head, a memory I could call on whenever I wanted to hear it.

"You're so beautiful, Dimitria. So fucking beautiful," I murmured, clenching my jaw against the rising tide of pleasure. I had waited years for this moment, I would not blow it now. I knew she felt the tension in my body as I refrained from taking over, but she didn't stop, didn't hesitate, and knowing she trusted me to let her lead only made things harder for me, both in the physical and emotional sense.

"I-I feel so…" Her voice was breathy and full of need.

"That's it, *cara*. Just feel. Take your pleasure from me," I encouraged, hearing my voice deepen as I struggled to remain still and not take from her what my body was desperately demanding I take.

She whimpered again, her eyes fluttering closed and her head rolling back as she began to ride me faster. Her platinum hair fell like a waterfall over her shoulders, the sight so goddamn beautiful I wanted to draw her just like this. The feel of her heat against my confined and raging cock was sweet torture, but I was addicted to it. I'd suffer this agony forever if only to see that look on her face as she rode her way to bone-melting pleasure. She was everything to me, would be my everything. I knew we had years together yet—centuries even—but this first time, all these firsts would live forever in our memories as the beginning, and I wanted to enjoy the moment, not rush it.

"You are so sexy, baby, so beautiful. I love watching you ride me. I love the feel of your hot body against mine, the scent of your need, the heat of your pussy," I whispered roughly, and she gasped. As connected with her as I was, I felt the jolt of desire that shot through her like lightning at my words. She liked it when I talked her through it. "Ride me, baby, let me watch you come."

Tria moaned, her brow creasing as she neared her climax. *Fuck,* she felt so good against me. *So* good… too good. I gripped her hips harder as I struggled to hold back my own release, determined she get hers before we took things any further. But fuck, the way she was riding me, the scent of her in the air so thick I could practically taste her on my tongue, those little sounds she was making as she ground her hips against me were driving me towards the edge.

Not yet, not yet, not yet. Fuck… hold on, not yet.

I ground my teeth so hard I was amazed none of them cracked. Groaning, I nearly salivated at the way she whimpered and her hips jerked unevenly, her brow creasing, her eyes closed as she chased that high. So close… she was almost there…

Not yet, not yet. Hold on a little longer. Fuck, just hold on…

"Harkyn…" She whimpered, her nails digging into my arms, the bite of pain sending a jolt of pleasure through me.

"Get there, *cara,* you're almost there. Come," I encouraged, almost pleaded. Sweat beaded on my forehead, my breathing became erratic and heavy, my heart was beating harder and harder.

"Harkyn," she cried, her hips jerking. I held her tighter to me as she reached that precipice, swearing through gritted teeth as she gasped and bit her lower lip hard enough to draw blood.

Not yet, not yet—

"Fuuuck!" I roared as the feel of her climax hit me, sending me over the edge. My release erupted within my briefs as my hips jerked beneath her involuntarily. I ground my teeth together again as she moaned low and shivered against me.

Fucking fuck.

I groaned as she slumped forward and I swore under my breath.

"Are you okay? Did I hurt you?" she panted, pulling away to look down at me. I closed my eyes and shook my head, wanting to laugh at myself but also rage. I had waited for that moment for forever, and I'd fucking nutted in my clothes!

"I'm not hurt," I answered and cursed myself again.

"Then what—oh," she began and then noticed. "Did, uh… did you mean to do that?" she asked, and her voice wavered dangerously close to laughter.

I glared up at her, and her pale eyes danced merrily back at me, her cheeks a stunning shade of pink, her lower lip slightly swollen with a tiny bead of blood on it. I leaned forward to capture her lips with my own, swiping my tongue over her lip to taste her blood. She was sweet and tart, a combination I could get drunk on.

"No, I didn't mean to come in my fucking briefs. I had planned to come inside *you*."

Some of the laughter died at my words and her breathing stuttered, and I let her see every ounce of hunger I had for her. Instead of reaching for her, I swore softly again, unable to believe I fucking came in my pants. Tria's lips wobbled before they began to curve and she slapped a hand over her mouth in an attempt to conceal her grin.

"Don't you dare start," I warned. A giggle slipped free of her lips and she struggled to get her humor under control. "How about you go four years with a raging hard on that never went away and then tell me how long you'd last? The woman of my dreams was riding me, it wasn't exactly easy to hold back."

Dimitria dissolved into a fit of giggles, rolling off me and onto the couch with her eyes closed and head back as the moment overtook her. I'd have been mad if seeing her laugh with such abandon didn't make me smile and something inside me warm at the sight of it. She opened her eyes to look at me, her laughter fading off, but I wasn't ready to let it go yet. I pretended to lunge at her and she gasped and tried to crawl away, but I dragged her close and began tickling her. She squealed and started laughing again, trying half-heartedly to push me away. I grinned at the sound, needing to hear it. She surprised me by twisting out of my grip and landing on the floor, but I followed her down, trapping her beneath me.

"I didn't have you pegged for a premature King," she said breathlessly and giggled beneath me.

"What did you just say?" I asked in a mock stern tone.

"You heard me."

The tense laugh of anticipation made me want to smile, and I caged her in with an arm either side of her head and lowered my voice, bringing my face an inch away from hers.

"Run."

"W-what?" she whispered, her breath catching.

"You better run, little warrior, because if I catch you, the punishment for such an insult will not be denied."

Tria's pupils blew wide at my words and I heard the stutter of her heart. The idea of hunting my little bounty hunter made me hard as a rock all over again, and I knew she felt it by the way her eyes widened and flickered downward for a split second.

"I'm going to give you until the count of three," I warned and pushed away from her. She remained still on the ground, her tongue swiping out to lick her lower lip.

"One."

She gasped and rolled to her side before jogging away from me, the air thick with anticipation and arousal.

"Two."

She began looking around wildly before her gaze landed on the staircase. With a shriek she ran for it, and I nearly growled in satisfaction that she was headed for the bedroom.

"Three!"

Her shriek of laughter had me grinning and I flicked away the rest of my clothing, cleaning myself at the same time, and started after her up the stairs. The anticipation of catching her made my cock painfully hard and my blood sing. It was time to show my mate just who was in charge here.

CHAPTER TWENTY-FOUR
DIMITRIA

I barely made it through the bedroom door before Harkyn was on me, his strong arms wrapping around me from behind. I gave a startled laugh and tried to wriggle away, but his hold tightened and he walked steadily forward. For a second, I was airborne before landing on the soft mattress of his bed. My breath was short and jagged as I pushed myself onto my elbows and watched him crawl onto the bed, his dark eyes on me filled with hunger and need.

"I have you now, little warrior. You are mine to do with as I please," Harkyn said in a low, rumbling voice that made every cell of my body sing.

"And what would please you, my King?" I asked breathlessly. The gray-green of his beautiful eyes were nearly eclipsed by his pupil as it blew wide. My gaze darted down his naked form to stop at his long, hard cock. A shiver went up my spine at the sight of it, and heat pooled low.

"I think you know what would please me, sweetheart," he murmured as he crawled up onto the bed with me. He continued to move until I was once again flat on my back, his hands braced either side of my shoulders. His dark, shoulder-length hair fell forward, framing his masculine face and making my fingers itch to delve into the thick mass. Every breath drew the scent of him into my body and made my head dizzy with desire and my body sing with anticipation.

"Show me."

A satisfied kind of rumble sounded from inside his chest, and it set my blood on fire. With dark eyes locked onto my face, Harkyn lowered his head until his lips brushed mine. I expected him to ravage, to demand entrance and take me with the usual desperate need we succumbed to every time we came together like this, but he didn't. His lips were soft, teasing, a mere brushing of contact across mine. I leaned up, chasing his lips, but he pulled back, a satisfied smirk on his face.

"Patience, *cara*. I want to savor this."

I huffed. "Four years, Harkyn. I think we've savored things longer than necessary."

His grin was devastatingly handsome, and I found myself once again inwardly sighing like some Elizabethan damsel. It just wasn't fair he could be *that* attractive. More than that, it wasn't fair a simple smile from him—cocky or not—could garner this kind of reaction from me on command.

"After four years, a few more minutes to enjoy myself cannot be much to ask, is it? I can assure you, *cara,* you will enjoy this too. But, if putting up a fight makes you feel better, then feel free," he said before slowly dragging his lips down my neck where he nipped and sucked. My breath stuttered and my body throbbed with need, but I decided against fighting. I just wanted to enjoy the ride, and I'd take every ounce of pleasure he wanted to give me.

At feeling me relax beneath him, Harkyn chuckled low in a way that made my blood run hot. "That's a good girl. Just let me take care of you."

I raised my hands to tangle in his hair as he nipped and sucked his way down my neck to my chest. He touched the Token I still wore around my neck before he gripped the material between the lacey cups of my bra and pulled. I gasped when the material snapped, but any protest I had about him ruining the expensive undergarment disappeared at the low rumble he gave while staring at my bare breasts. I didn't have time to say anything before he lowered his head and used the tip of his tongue to flick at one of my nipples. The feeling was so unexpected and foreign that I jumped beneath his touch and arched my back. He continued to tease me, using only the tip of his tongue before doing the same with the other. My heart was pounding hard, and the constant throbbing between my legs was distracting. I *needed* him.

As I opened my mouth to tell him to stop teasing, he drew my nipple into his scorching hot mouth and sucked hard. I moaned loudly, surprised, the pleasure I received was unexpected.

"Harkyn." I said his name breathlessly, the sound of my voice almost foreign to me. Every pull of his mouth sent darts of pleasure from my breast straight to my core so that it was a constant reminder of where I wanted him.

His hand came up to cup the other breast, squeezing gently before tugging at the nipple and I arched my back again, something like a whimper escaping me. I wanted him so badly, but he was all too happy playing.

"I need more, Harkyn. Stop teasing!" I scolded. He chuckled low again, and instead of moving on, simply switched to the other breast, laving just as much attention on it as he did the other. I loved it, enjoyed every moment, but I was impatient for the main event.

"I have wanted to touch you like this again since the last time. I've wanted to kiss and lick every inch of you for what feels like forever. I want to explore every curve and dip of your body. I have dreamed about this for years, and I want to live it now," he explained, kissing down my stomach. The muscles there quivered but I rejoiced that he was moving on. He could do more of that later, but not right now.

Hooking his fingers into the waistband of my panties, I watched as he sat back long enough to drag the white cotton from my body. He could have just clicked his fingers and I'd be naked, but I had a feeling he was enjoying unwrapping me. I took advantage of the space to quickly toss away the now ruined bra and smiled a little self-consciously at him.

"Lie back," he instructed, and I did so quickly. I watched his eyes as they traced over me, almost as if he were devouring me with his gaze. I shivered and the corner of his lip twitched as if he liked that reaction.

"Spread your legs for me, Tria," he ordered, his voice set low and velvety. The heat already in my cheeks burned hotter still, but I did as he said and was rewarded with his quick release of breath, as if he'd been holding it in anticipation.

"That's my girl," he whispered, and I tried not to like those words as much as I did. Gripping my ankles, Harkyn slowly slid his large, rough textured hands up my bare legs, his fingers almost caressing as they reached my knees. He situated himself between my legs and continued his excruciatingly slow journey up my thighs. I just watched his face, the way his breathing turned almost heavy, the way his eyes became hooded and heated as his lips parted slightly. He was wholly fixated on the task at hand, and seeing that kind of attention from a man like him on me made me want him all the more.

"I want to taste you, Dimitria. Will you let me?" he asked. I couldn't believe he was actually asking, but hearing him do it had my heart flipping and melting just a little more.

"Do you even have to ask?" I whispered with a shaky laugh.

"I don't want to do anything you're uncomfortable with. If I do, tell me, and I'll stop," he explained. I knew he was trying to remind himself that I hadn't done this before, and knowing he was keeping that in mind when his body was so demanding just nudged me a little closer to that cliff I had already been dangerously close to falling off. That cliff where if I fell, I'd lose myself to him forever.

"I trust you," I assured, the weight of my words suddenly heavy with meaning. Those incredible eyes of his locked onto my face, and something inside him burned hot and bright.

"You're always safe with me, Tria. In every situation, I'll never let you be hurt or experience discomfort where I can help it. Believe that, and you'll never have to worry."

I smiled, and deep down, I knew he meant it. "I know."

Grinning, Harkyn traced small circles along the insides of my thighs and I shivered slightly in response. His smile was knowing and his eyes daring as he continued to tease me, working his fingers ever closer to my center.

"Touch me, Harkyn. Don't make me wait anymore," I urged, about to go out of my mind if we didn't move this along.

Grinning wickedly, he lowered himself between my thighs and I watched with breathless anticipation as he dipped his head and flicked his tongue out. Without making me wait; he opened his mouth and his thick tongue stroked up and down my slit before sucking on my clit. I jerked upwards with a startled moan and his forearm came to rest along my lower abdomen, keeping me pinned to the bed. His assault was not what I'd been expecting. From the slow build up he'd been working at, I'd thought I was in for countless minutes of teasing, but he didn't let up even once. His tongue stroked and plundered, flicked and sucked. His fingers slid between my thighs and gently eased inside me. I was mindless with need, and he stroked me with his fingers, touching somewhere inside that I hadn't known was there. The feel of his thrusting fingers stretching and stroking combined with his tongue and lips sucking and lapping at me, I was lost in a haze of sensation and pleasure. Any time I began to come out of it, Harkyn upped his game, mixing physical with the mental. He let me feel his own pleasure at what he was doing, how he was addicted to the taste and feel of me, how hearing me cry out, whimper, moan, and say his name had him harder than he'd ever been. He wanted me to come, he wanted to feel me squeeze his fingers and flood his tongue.

"You can do it, cara. Come for me, I've got you, let me feel you come."

"Harkyn!" I groaned as he stroked faster inside me, crooking his fingers just so as he sucked and flicked at my clit. My body became impossibly tight, my back arched, and I felt my breath trap in my lungs as I hurdled headlong into an explosion of pleasure. I moaned so loudly I wouldn't have been surprised if the others in the Hall heard it. My hands dug into his thick hair and bunched it hard, holding his mouth to me as I bucked against him, lost in the bombardment of pleasure he gave me.

"That's it, sweetheart. Fuck, you're gorgeous when you come," Harkyn groaned, his voice gravelly and deep.

I wasn't sure if I'd died or if I was floating in a state of unconsciousness when he gently pulled his fingers from inside me. I was blissed out, my body a boneless mass of overstimulated nerve endings. He kissed my center before kissing up my stomach to my breasts again. They were sensitive and I whimpered.

"Holy shit," I wheezed when I could finally find the energy to open my eyes.

"I don't think there was anything holy about that," Harkyn returned and I laughed. His grin made my heart flip, and I reached up to pull him down to me. He didn't make me wait, and I kissed him hard and deep, wanting to get him as close to me as possible. He settled between my legs and I rocked against him, feeling the hard length of his cock slide up my slick entrance. I shivered, still sensitive, but more than ready to take him.

"Are you ready, *cara?*"

"More than ready," I whispered, rocking against him again, sliding my hands up his sexy as sin abdomen to his incredibly built and tattooed chest. I made a mental note to thoroughly look over and taste each and every tattoo over the next few days, but not now.

"Harkyn——" I paused when I felt him go rigid above me. For a moment I thought maybe he'd had another. uh… *premature moment,* but when he cursed and closed his eyes in dismay, I knew it was something else.

"What?"

"It's Tamas. Cole went to check on him, and he's gone missing. Some Knights are out looking for him, one of them said they saw him and he looked a little unhinged."

"What's he doing? Is Tamas okay?" I asked, concern for my friend beginning to dampen my mood.

Harkyn's dark eyes glittered back at me, a frown turning his lips down and creasing his forehead.

"I really don't like you saying my brother's name when I'm barely an inch from sliding inside your body."

I laughed and shook my head. "You brought him up."

Harkyn sighed and regretfully pulled away. "I have to go find him. He's looking for the Witch who put the lock on him, and he's going to get himself killed."

"I'll come," I said, moving to the edge of the bed at once.

"I don't think so," Harkyn interjected, gripping me by my ankle and dragging me back to him on the bed.

"What do you mean?" I asked, puzzled.

"Tamas isn't in a good place right now. I don't want you up there where you might get caught in the middle."

"Tamas is my friend and means a lot to me. If he's hurting, then I want to help soothe him and bring him home safely."

"While I appreciate that, it's simply not happening," Harkyn reiterated before waving his hands to clean himself before standing, dressed once again in his usual black jeans and shirt.

"So, I'm relegated to the role of housewife while you go off and do the man things? Like hell! I'm a freaking bounty hunter, and I can look after myself."

"You're not equipped to handle Angels and Rogues. If you want to continue this discussion later, we will, but right now I have to go," Harkyn added, his tone telling me this was the end of our talk.

"Oh, hell no, mister! You don't get to delegate or call the shots. We're a *team,* and I am not some damsel-like waif to be ordered about."

"You could be injured or taken up there, Dimitria. This isn't about you not being powerful, it's about the danger you will be facing."

"Tamas won't want to listen to any of you. You're males. Some things call for a female, and damn it, he's *my* friend. He's hurting because I was running away and he was injured trying to save me. I owe him."

"Your debts and fights become my responsibility too," Harkyn said. "I will take care of this one."

And with that, he turned around and walked out the bedroom

door, leaving me sitting there with my mouth hanging open. Oh, he did *not* just give me an order and expect me to obey it!

Hurrying, I ran to my duffle and dragged on a pair of jeans and an old shirt before I grabbed my boots and hurried down the stairs. I stopped for a couple of seconds to drag them on, snatched up my pad and pen I saw on the end-table from earlier and shoved them into my back pocket before I hurried for the red door.

"Harkyn!" I shouted as I yanked it open. No one was there.

I was standing in a black marble hallway that was lined with several red doors. Nine, including the one I was in. My shout echoed against the walls and I glared when I could see no sign of him.

"Motherfucker," I hissed as the door across from me opened. There was a small snicker as Cali stepped out, her bright eyes laughing. "He left you behind?"

"He wouldn't even listen to my plan!"

Another door opened and Mika came out, followed by Sawyer. I frowned at the sight of all the women and then glared. "Did you all get left behind too because you're women?"

Mika grinned. "You were left here?"

I grimaced. "Abandoned is the better word."

"Don't take it personally," Sawyer soothed as we all stepped further out into the hall. "He's protecting you the only way he knows how."

"I didn't ask for it," I protested. "Tamas is my friend, he's hurt because of me, and I want to help him come home."

The women around me shared a look and I frowned. "What?"

"Do you know what you're doing against an Angel? If you were up there and confronted with one, would you know how to defend yourself?" Mika asked.

I shrugged. "I managed to hold Uriel to a tree for a while when on the surface, and I sent Rogues flying with a quick conjuration the other day. I don't know if I'd say I was an expert, but I can hold my own, at least for a while."

The women shared another small look. "We're like you. We can feel how desperately you want to help Tamas, how you *need* to be there for him. We understand that need. Our mates love us, they'd do anything to make us happy, *except* allow us to put ourselves in danger. Sometimes we have to get creative to circumvent their will in order to do what our calling demands of us, even when it makes them mad," Cali explained.

"And are you going to help me?" I asked, raising an eyebrow. Sawyer grinned and stepped closer. "Us women have to stick together down here; we'll help you get out of here."

"Really?" I asked, surprised.

"You understand he's going to be mad at you, right? As in, he might set fire to the world with how mad he'll get," Mika reminded, her eyes weighing me carefully.

I shrugged. "Harkyn would never hurt me. He'll get mad, he can yell and shout and berate all he wants. I have been looking after myself for a long time now, and there are very few people I care enough about to risk my happiness and my life for. Tamas became one of those people, and I'll do anything I can to help him."

"Even against the will of your mate?" Sawyer asked. Something about the way these women asked me questions felt like I was being tested somehow.

"This isn't about my ego or enforcing my will over Harkyn's. I know he wants me safe, and I wouldn't go against him unless it was important," I assured before drawing a steading breath.

"Tamas called me the little sister he never wanted but got landed with. He's the brother I never dreamed of having but am forever grateful to have. I *need* to help him."

Cali's expression softened and Mika grinned widely, her blue eyes sparkling with mischief and approval. Sawyer's lips curled upwards and she flicked a glance at the other two.

"Okay, if you can promise us that you can look after yourself, then we'll help," Cali said, straightening her spine. "We'll go with you to make sure you're okay and that everything goes smoothly, but we need you to make us a promise."

"What promise?" I prompted when no one said anything else.

"That you'll back off and come back here if we tell you to. We're not like the guys; we're not going to hold you back just because something is dangerous. But if we lose you, we lose Harkyn, and that's not something we're willing to risk or put our mates through," Mika explained, the seriousness of her tone drilling home her point. They were risking a lot to help me, and they'd never forgive themselves if they showed me how to get to the surface against Harkyn's orders and something happened to me. Their mates wouldn't either.

"I won't take unnecessary risks. I love Harkyn, and I'll do whatever I have to in order to protect him. Even if that means protecting myself. But Tamas is his brother. If Tamas dies because he's in pain or tormented, then I have to help him. He's my friend."

The women smiled softly, but it was indication enough that they understood and were willing to help me.

"Okay, we're going with you. There's strength in numbers, and we don't know what we're up against. If the coven who cursed Tamas is up there, then the guys will need our help," Cali answered.

I smiled gratefully and stepped closer to the women, feeling an almost instant kinship with them. They were Witches like me, mated to a King of Hell. They knew more than anyone else what it was like to be in our situation, and because of that connection, I felt closer to them than I had with other women before.

"Cloak yourself again. When you're done, close your eyes, clear your mind, and try to follow my instructions," Mika coached.

Smiling, I let out a long breath and cleared my mind.

CHAPTER TWENTY-FIVE
HARKYN

"Where the *fuck* is she?" Tamas roared, pressing another handful of hellfire into the face of the Angel he had pinned to the ground. His previously missing arm had come back, but I could tell it was still weaker than it had once been. The Angel made an unnatural sound full of pain and I flicked a glance at my brothers.

Cole, Adrik, and Malik were by my side, watching as Tamas continued to torture the Angel. Cassius stood off to the side looking as helpless as the rest of us. He'd been the one to first find Tamas, and he'd called as soon as he realized he'd need the help.

Tamas was determined to find the Witch that cursed him, and I couldn't blame him. I didn't envy the position he was in. He was still Tamas, and he was still powerful, but we could all feel the difference in him. He was weaker, less sure—angry. Something about him was… broken.

"Should we do something?" Cassius asked.

"Like what?" I asked, frowning. We'd already tried to pull him away, and he blasted us all. Sure, we could subdue him if we really wanted to, but I didn't see the point. Tamas was pissed, and if I were in his position, I can't say I'd be doing anything different.

"He's going off the rails. The females said they'd find a way to help him

track the Witch he's after, so let's go back and ask them to do something. He's going to get himself killed, or at least hurt, and the only way to heal him is for one of the women to suffer alongside him first," Malik interjected.

He was right. The women had said they could help him find the Witch he was after, but they'd all been so exhausted after the healing that nothing had been done yet. I inwardly flinched at the idea of Tria suffering the same pain as Tamas again. I already knew she'd be the first to volunteer. The guilt she felt at him being injured in the first place wouldn't allow her to let anyone else take that role.

"Tamas," I called, hoping to bring our brother back to the brink of sanity.

"I asked you a fucking question you pathetic excuse for an Angel. Where are the Witches who did this to me?" Tamas demanded, pressing hellfire into the Angel's chest and holding it there. The Angel panted hard and tried not to scream, but the pain won out and he cried out again.

"Tamas, stop. We can ask the women to help," Cole interrupted, stepping in closer.

"I won't risk their safety," Tamas growled.

"They can do it all from Hell, they'll be safe," Adrik reminded. Tamas didn't seem to have heard him, or maybe he just didn't want to. He wanted to cause pain, he wanted to hunt down Angels and inflict agony on them for the suffering he was enduring now. This was just an excuse to hurt them. Any other time I'd let him vent his rage, but he risked getting injured and not being able to heal himself. If that happened, it would result in Tria's pain again, and I'd had enough of that for the rest of my life. She'd suffered more than her fair share throughout her young life, I wasn't keen on letting her take on more.

I'd taken a single step towards him when I felt her. Gritting my
teeth, I spun around to see Tria standing several feet away—
Tomika, Calixta, and Sawyer by her side. For a shivering
moment, the sight of the four women was breathtaking.
Everything around us seemed to go quiet and still, and I *felt* the
combined power rolling off them. Even Tamas paused with his
fist in the air as he recognized that we were no longer alone.
The question of *how the fuck did she get out of Hell* vanished at the
sight of the other women. They had to have shown her.

"Tamas."

Her voice was sure and confident, not raised or edged with
anger. The sight of her standing there, tall and confident, her
platinum blonde hair loose and flowing around her like a silk cape
made her look like a goddess. Her pale blue eyes shimmered with
the need to help my brother, the warmth in her shining like an
inner light. Fuck, she was beautiful.

"Tamas, please," Dimitria whispered as she stepped away from
the other women. They let her go, but I caught the way they
looked around them. Cali nodded to them, and each woman
spread out a little. Malik shared a look of confusion with me as
the women got themselves into position, and once they settled,
there was a hum of power in the air. Cole stepped closer to me,
his gaze snapping up and around as if sensing for their energy. I,
too, searched around us for signs of the enemy, but I realized the
women were wrapping us all in a protective shield, something to
keep us from being sensed by others.

"You need to go home, Tria," Tamas ground out, his voice low
and gravelly, his gaze never leaving the burned and heaving
Angel.

"This isn't the way to do this. We can help you find the Witch
you need, but going out like this isn't the way to do it," Dimitria

counseled.

"I will do things my way. You have a mate now, go be with him and leave me to deal with this on my own," Tamas almost snarled. Instead of flinching at the venom in his voice, Tria's eyes burned angrily and her jaw set as she stomped over to him. Any pretense of gentleness vanished from her face as she strode towards him, annoyance in every step.

"Tria," I warned, edging closer to my brother. She threw a look of warning at me before focusing on Tamas again.

Malik's laughter echoed in my head. *"Is someone in the doghouse already?"*

"Fuck off. I left her behind for a reason. Your mate is one of the ones who brought her here against my will. They're actively putting themselves and my mate in danger. Perhaps you should concentrate on your own mate."

I felt Malik's humor dry up, and the tiny victory went a small way to relieving some of my anger at Dimitria.

"Go home, Tria," Tamas growled, lifting the ball of fire in his hand again.

"No."

"You're not needed here," Tamas insisted.

"I disagree," Dimitria retorted, stepping closer.

"I'm about to start torturing this waste of oxygen, and I won't hold back this time just because you're here. So, if you stay, whatever you witness is on you," he threatened.

I wanted to reach out and slap my brother, but I felt a small flutter against my mind, Tria urging me to be calm.

"I'm sorry, were you born this stupid or did you take a special lesson?"

Cole choked on a laugh and Tamas froze and turned to look at her. "Excuse me?"

"You heard me," she answered, crossing her arms over her

stomach. "You have four Witches here, ready and willing to help you track down the Witch you need, but instead, you're going to go all over creation hunting Angels to torture for information."

"Maybe it's not about the information," Tamas gritted out.

"No shit, Sherlock."

"Piss off back home, Tria. I've told you to leave, this doesn't concern you," Tamas snapped.

"Watch your fucking mouth when speaking to my mate," I growled, stepping forward. I was about ready to slap his stupid ass up and down this empty lot when Tria shot me another look. I felt her appreciation, but also her need for me to back off.

"If you want to be an idiot and risk getting hurt or dying, then you do it when you're able to heal on your own. That means you need to wait until *after* we find the Witch you're looking for," Tria pointed out.

"I'm healed, we're no longer bound, what I do or how hurt I get is of no concern of yours," Tamas snapped, turning back to the whimpering Angel.

"I'm sorry, do you remember me asking you for your opinion on this? Because I sure as hell don't," Tria shot back, moving closer so that she stood behind the Angel Tamas had bent over broken crates. Her eyes never left my brother, and I tensed, ready to step in at a moment's notice. The Angel was wounded, yes, but I didn't like how close she was getting to him.

"This isn't a matter of opinion," Tamas returned through gritted teeth.

"You're right, it's not. It's about fact. And honestly, you're being really freaking stupid."

Tamas glared at her. "Should I go get some cool water for that sad excuse for a burn?"

Adrik swallowed a smile and I sighed quietly, fed up with this back and forth.

"Now *that* was a pathetic come back, which just proves my point that you really aren't in full form. Leave the Angel and come home so we can help you find the Witch you need. Running around up here on a pointless rampage is only going to result in you getting hurt, and me suffering alongside you when you need to be healed."

"You won't suffer with me," Tamas ground out, his expression darkening.

"Like hell I won't. We're friends, Tamas. You're my brother, remember? Family is rare and treasured, or did you forget that you'd made yourself a nice little home in my heart? And now you're doing your best to put space between us. All you're doing is hurting me in the process. If you get hurt, of course I'm the one who will suffer your injuries alongside you because *I* owe you for the damage already done to you."

As much as I hated her admitting that Tamas meant so much to her—a purely selfish and territorial response—she wasn't lying. She viewed Tamas as a brother, and she hated seeing him in pain. She truly believed she was the reason he was hurt, and I tried at once to soothe her. She didn't look away from Tamas, but I felt her small touch of thanks.

"How I deal with this is up to me, not you, and not *them*," Tamas gritted out, jerking his head in our direction.

Tria sighed heavily. "Look, I don't have the time or crayons to explain this to you in a way you'll understand, and I'm sure your pain and injuries are adding to your limited abilities to process logic, so listen closely and I'll be sure to use small words so you'll understand."

Humor sparked within me even as I made sure to keep my expression neutral. Tamas was in a rough spot, and I wasn't altogether sure how he'd react if pushed too hard.

"You. Are. Fucked," Tria began, speaking slowly and clearly, enunciating every word as if he were hard of hearing. "You. Need. Help. Come. Home. Like. A. Big. Boy. And. We'll. Deal. With. This. Together."

The atmosphere around us seemed to go dead and quiet at her words, all of us holding our breath to see how Tamas would react.

"Listen to the Witch bitch, Demon filth. We all know you're fucked; you won't stand a chance out here on your own," the extra crispy Angel interrupted. Tamas's attention turned back to him, and he growled low, shaking him sharply so that his head snapped back against the broken wood and he groaned.

Tria closed her eyes and sighed loudly. "You know, everyone has the right to have a few stupid moments in their life, but right now, you're abusing the privilege. Shut the hell up, idiot."

The Angel forced a laugh, but we could all tell it was for show. He was about to be a very dead, very *fried*, Angel. He was all talk.

"It's true. You're all dead, you just don't know it yet. The Angels will prevail as we were always meant to, and the Kings and your Demons will eventually be an amusing footnote in the history of the universe," he continued to taunt, his voice rough. He coughed wetly and Tria grimaced.

"You're the reason God invented the middle finger, aren't you? Just shut up," she returned.

"Better yet, let's get back to frying you," Tamas snarled before lighting the Angel up again. The Angel screamed and Dimitria stepped back, watching the scene with dispassionate eyes. I felt her immediate revulsion at the act of violence, but to her credit, she didn't try to stop him.

Tamas's expression was one of feral anger and joy in causing pain. I knew without looking into her mind that Tria would be comparing his face now to how mine had to have looked four years ago. We were Demon Kings—we were created to torture those who deserved it—we would not feel bad for finding a way to enjoy doling out pain when it was needed.

Dimitria moved, and I was too late in touching her mind to realize what she was about to do. She slid up beside Tamas and took the Demon Blade from his scabbard.

"Tria—" I called, both in her head and out loud, but she ignored me. She stepped forward, blade raised, and plunged it into the flaming Angel's heart before stepping back. Pain tore up her hand and arm, some of it slid up her chest, and I was on the move. Through Dimitria, I *felt* Tamas's immediate horror at his hellfire flame causing her pain, and at once he put it out. The Angel on the ground fell, gasping and gurgling, but I paid him no attention as I reached Dimitria. She hissed, her face screwed up in agony as she worked to heal herself.

"Tria?" Mika called from her position, still keeping the shield above us.

"I'm good," she called, pain heavy in her tone.

"What the hell were you thinking?" I snapped, careful not to touch her where it would hurt. Tria didn't answer me, she simply looked up at Tamas with pained tears in her eyes as her body worked to heal her.

"What the fuck, Tria?" Tamas snapped, his face still filled with horror.

"You were torturing that Angel for the sake of it, and you were punishing me for not leaving," she pointed out. He opened his mouth to disagree and she glared. Tamas snapped his mouth shut and lowered his gaze, shame rippling off him.

"You're right," he muttered.

"I know I'm right, you idiot," she snapped, hissing as she looked down at her severely burned arm. I poured energy into her, hoping the boost would hasten the healing before shoving into her mind to take the pain from her. Instantly, my arm, hand, and my chest felt burned, but it was nothing compared to what I'd experienced in the past. Tria's appreciation for me fluttered across my mind, and I was careful to keep my other emotions locked up tight. Now was not the time to berate her for her foolishness and stupidity. She'd taken an unnecessary risk, she'd been hurt, and she'd killed an Angel. While they were our enemies, she was going to feel the guilt of that death. I knew it. She was a Witch, life was sacred, even that of an Angel. The only saving grace was that she hadn't used her magic to kill.

"What were you thinking, Tria?" Tamas said, apparently uncaring if he should reprimand her or not.

"I was thinking that my stupid ass friend was going to get himself seriously hurt or killed while on some ridiculous vendetta, and if I was going to end up hurt because of his idiocy, I might as well get it over with now," she returned hotly, turning back to the burns that were slowly healing on her arm.

"I have every right——"

"You have no right to risk your life and cause unimaginable pain to those who love you, all for the sake of revenge!" Tria interrupted sharply. "We love you, Tamas. Your brothers love you, their mates—me—we love you. But you're going to get yourself killed doing this, and you haven't taken a single damn second to consider how we'd feel losing you."

I inwardly grimaced at hearing her say she loved Tamas before ever saying the words to me, and her humor filtered across my mind along with a quiet laugh. I huffed. Sure, she could be happy at my misery at a time like this, why not?

"I'm more powerful than you realize, even hindered the way I am," Tamas assured.

"I don't give a shit," Tria shot back, and Cole snorted and moved to his mate who was grinning at the show before them. "You are *not* as powerful as you were, and you heard that moron," Tria pointed out, indicating to the dead Angel at her feet. At once, there was a rush of regret as she remembered how it felt to sink the blade into the now dead creature, but she brushed it off, determined to think about it later.

"He could have been lying," Tamas muttered defensively.

Tria scoffed. "You are so full of shit it's coming out of your mouth."

Adrik's loud bark of laughter drew our attention to him for a moment, and Tria's lips twitched in humor before she turned her gaze back to Tamas.

"Just admit you were being a pig-headed idiot so we can go home and do this stupid spell to help you find the Witch."

Tamas looked ready to argue, his jaw was set and fists were clenched.

"Brother," I interrupted, wishing I could take his pain as easily as I could take Tria's. *"You know Dimitria does not allow herself to care for many because she fears they'll leave her or die. Please, do this for her. I know it makes you want to rage, but please... for her."*

Tamas's gaze rose to meet mine, and I saw the war raging in his eyes as clear as day. He was furious that Witches had bound his power, made it so he couldn't access its full potential. He felt stuffed inside a container too small for him, making it hard to breathe or move when he was used to being one of the most powerful creatures in the world. He felt less than, and it was not a feeling I'd wish on any of my brothers.

"I need to find the Witch."

"And no one is stopping you," I answered quickly. *"We will help, and if you want to go hunting once you're unbound from this spell and tear apart the Angels who had a hand in this, then I'll be at your side to make sure it happens. But for now?"* I let my sentence trail off and knew he understood.

Tamas fought with himself for several moments, trying to force himself to back down. I knew that if he said he would, then he'd keep his word. Tamas wasn't usually one for trickery or deceit, and he cared for Tria deeply. As angry as he was, he didn't want to hurt her, and he knew how careful she was in giving away pieces of her heart.

Drawing in a deep breath, Tamas forced down his rage and helplessness and nodded. "Okay, Tria. We'll go home, as long as you all promise to help me find the Witch."

"Done," Tria answered quickly.

"Of course," Mika added at the same time as Sawyer.

"All you had to do was tell us you were ready," Cali added.

Tamas gave a shark dip of his head and stared down at his shoes, the muscle in his jaw ticking wildly as he continued to struggle.

"Let's go back home so we can help expedite healing Tria's wounds, then we'll get to work on a spell to locate your Witch," Mika suggested.

There was a general agreement all around, and I watched as Tria stepped forward and offered Tamas her hand. My immediate refusal to allow her to touch him unnecessarily earned me a sharp look of disapproval, and I ground my teeth together. It was just Tamas. He needed this.

As soon as her fingers closed around Tamas's hand, I shadowed us back to Hell. The usually quick mode of transport seemed to go on forever as I was overly aware of another male touching my woman, and the second our feet touched the ground in Hell, I tugged her to me and away from him.

"Possessive much?" she quipped. But even as she said it, I felt her edge closer and almost rub herself against me.

"Feeling uncomfortable, love?" I asked, raising an eyebrow.

She frowned and nodded. "I-I just needed to touch you again."

"It's the bond," I assured. "Touching another male will make you feel this way, as will touching a female for me."

Her eyes widened and her mouth parted in surprise. "Really?"

"Yes," I answered and leaned forward to kiss her. She sank against me and I drew the kiss out a little, drowning in her until someone cleared their throat loudly.

We pulled apart to see Mika standing nearby, her grin full of glee and knowing. "Want some help healing?"

"Why bother?" Cole asked and smirked. "Her injuries don't look like they're hindering anything."

Tria smiled, her cheeks burning pink, but she held out her arm. "Thanks, Mika."

"No problem," she answered, and I watched and waited as she worked on my mate. Several moments later, Cali came out with a large book.

"I was working on finding the Witch earlier and have been studying this book. We can do it, but…" She bit her lip.

"But what?" Tamas growled.

Cali sighed. "It's going to take time. The Witches are cloaked, like us, meaning we can't just find her with a wave of our hand. We need to work a spell, and it will take time to get results."

"How long?" Cole asked when Tamas swore and paced away.

"Two weeks or so. I'm sorry, Tamas. But hunting her down out there won't get you any closer either," Cali added, her expression full of remorse when Tamas kept his back turned. He paused, putting his palms flat against the wall as he hung his head, his posture screaming defeat.

"Tamas," Tria began, taking a single step in his direction.

"I'm fine—it's fine," Tamas cut in quickly, pushing away from the wall.

"You're not fine," she whispered, her eyes swimming with sympathy.

"No, I'm not," he agreed and gave a small, sarcastic laugh. "I feel like a dog that's been fucking neutered, and now every Angel out there knows I have a handicap. I'm not at full strength, I have a target painted on my back, and I can't do shit about it for at least two weeks."

"We *will* find her," Mika comforted, her tone soothing.

Tamas sighed and took a moment to try to breathe through his turbulent emotions. I shared a look with Cole and Adrik before catching Cassius's gaze.

"I need to go get drunk," Tamas muttered, shoving his fingers through his hair roughly, wincing as his once injured arm locked for a moment.

"I'll come," Cassius volunteered. "I could do with getting drunk right now, and our mother always said it was smarter to drink with a buddy."

Tria frowned. "She really said that?"

I grinned but didn't answer. I'd let her wonder a little first.

"You'll watch him?" I asked Cassius, not wanting our brother left alone for a while.

"I'll stay with him until we get this sorted," Cassius agreed, and I felt his determination to be there for our brother, even when he didn't want us to be.

"I don't need a babysitter," Tamas reminded, an edge to his voice.

"No, you don't," Malik agreed before stepping up. "But we're pissed like you, so let's go drink."

"Yeah, why not?" Adrik added, leaning down to kiss Cali's head quickly. "Let's go get good and drunk."

"Count me in," Cole added, winking at Mika.

Tamas looked around at his brothers, rage mixed with humor and appreciation. They all waited a second before he sighed, but allowed a small smile to curve his lips. Words of approval were called before Cassius wrapped an arm around Tamas's shoulders and they headed for his realm, the guys making a bunch of jokes and laughing loudly to try and bring about an air of frivolity.

"What about you?" Mika asked as she finished healing Dimitria's arm.

"Me?" I returned; my eyes wide.

"Are you going to get drunk too?"

"Uh, no," Tria answered for me, before turning to face me. She smiled and leaned up to wrap her arms around my neck, aligning her body with mine. "We were in the middle of something before we were called away, and I'd like to get back to it."

I grinned down at her, my blood turning hot at the reminder of our previous activities. My mouth watered as I recalled the taste of her, and I watched her pupils blow wide, her consciousness merging with mine.

"Alright, you two. Go away," Cali called, and Sawyer laughed.

"Don't mind if we do," I replied before sweeping Tria up in my arms, dipping my head to capture her mouth with my own. She met me halfway, and as we stumbled across the threshold for our realm, I beamed, happier than I could ever remember being before.

CHAPTER TWENTY-SIX
DIMITRIA

"You disobeyed an order, *cara,*" Harkyn reminded, hauling me up against him as he slammed the door to his realm shut behind us. "You can't tell me what to do," I reminded, leaning up to kiss him again. He groaned against my lips and spun me quickly until I found myself backed against the door. His hands slid down my side to my ass where he squeezed and ground himself against me. I wanted to whimper, but I didn't want him to know just how much he affected me. I was about ready to explode if he didn't touch me the way I needed him to.

"I can tell you what to do, and you will obey next time or I'll punish you," he warned, his voice low and rumbly so that my skin rippled with goosebumps. I wanted him so badly.

"You can't punish me either," I pointed out, leaning up to nip at his lower lip, not knowing where I got the courage to do so, but loved knowing that I could. His eyes flared with arousal, and he rumbled low in his chest.

"I can, and I think I should. You disobeyed; you should be punished."

My breath stuttered and I swallowed hard. He hummed low under his breath, and I caught snippets of what he wanted to do to me in his mind, every image dirtier than the last, each of them causing a rush of heat to pool between my legs. How were some of these even possible?

"I'll be happy to show you, sweetheart."

Anticipation rose and he ground himself against me again, his gaze locked with mine as zaps of pleasure shot straight to my core.

"Then show me," I whispered, leaning up to kiss him again.

Harkyn's moan was lost against my mouth, and I jumped to wrap my legs around him. Without breaking the kiss, I felt him move, but I didn't care where he took us, only that we were doing this. When I felt him walk up the stairs, I knew we were headed for his bed and silently cheered. He sat me on the edge of the bed and pulled away, and I gasped as he yanked my shoes off before doing the same with my jeans, letting them fall to the ground by the bed.

"Shirt off," he growled.

With shaking hands, I hurried to do as he ordered and made sure to remove my bra as well. He was naked in seconds, and my mouth went dry at the sight of him. *Damn,* he was sexy.

"So, you *do* take orders," he teased.

I grinned and shook my head. "Only when I want to listen."

"Noted," he murmured and crawled up over me, forcing me to lay flat on the bed. I wrapped my arms and legs around him at once, near desperate for him now. He chuckled lowly at my eagerness and leaned forward to kiss me again. He teased, he didn't plunder, he pulled away and nibbled and nipped at my lips, dipping low just to skip my mouth and brush kisses across my cheeks and jaw.

"Harkyn," I complained, bunching his hair in my hands. "Kiss me, and then take me."

"I give the orders here, mate," he reminded with a cocky grin.

"Then clearly only one of us is thinking properly if you're not on the same page," I pointed out. Harkyn chuckled and slid a hand between my legs, testing my readiness. He needn't have, I was so ready it was almost embarrassing.

"Fuck, yes," he groaned as he felt how slick I was. He slipped two fingers inside me, and I moaned at feeling stretched. He was a big man all over, including his hands, and I was inexperienced. I arched my back and widened my legs to take his fingers deeper as he crooked them over and over, thrusting in and out, driving me wild again.

"Harkyn," I pleaded.

"Not yet, *cara*. I need to feel you drench my hand before I share your body, I need you ready for me."

Hearing him put it into words made me spasm around his fingers and he grinned knowingly. "Yes, baby. I feel you. I want you to come for me. Let me have it."

My eyes rolled back as his fingers worked their own kind of magic, and I clenched his hair in my hands tighter. When I opened my eyes, it was to see his gaze on my face, scorching hot, focused on what made me go wild. That kind of intensity amped things up and I gasped as pressure began to build deep inside and his triumph grew.

"Kiss me," I whispered.

He didn't make me wait, his mouth crushing mine as his thumb circled my clit in short, sharp strokes and I came hard. My body grew taut, my muscles clenched hard, and I cried out against his mouth as I fell over that pleasurable edge. Harkyn was there, in my head, whispering words of encouragement and praise, words that only drew out my release.

"So beautiful," he whispered a little breathless.

"I need more, Harkyn. No more waiting, please. I want to feel you, I *need* to feel you. I want us bound closer," I insisted, my breathing choppy.

I felt the force of his joy as it overflowed from him and into me, and he grinned. Sliding his arms underneath my body, I shrieked a little as he rolled us so I was on top. Nerves hit me out of nowhere and he smiled up at me.

"I want to watch you," he explained.

"I-I don't know what to do," I answered. I mean, I knew *what to do,* but...

Harkyn seemed to understand, and his expression softened. He leaned up to kiss me, drawing his legs up behind me, his hand sliding into my hair to kiss me deeply. I let myself get lost in his kiss, let myself feel the stroke of his other hand as it cupped my breast and rolled my nipple between his fingers. Before I knew it, I found myself rocking against him, my hips undulating of their own accord, searching for that release my body was desperate for.

"Just like that, sweetheart. Keep moving," he encouraged, slowly laying back. I refused to let my self-consciousness take over and continued to watch Harkyn's expressive face. He kept his mind wide open to me, letting me feel how he felt when I moved, how much he wanted me, how sexy he thought I was. The way he saw me blew me away, and it fed into my confidence.

I was still hot for him, needy, and it didn't take long before my rolling hips brought back that familiar building tide inside. The hard ridge of his cock against my clit was driving me crazy, and I felt his handle on his control slipping with every slide of my slick body against him.

"Harkyn," I whimpered, needing more but wanting help.

"Don't stop, *cara.* I've got you, keep going," he encouraged, his voice shaky as he struggled to keep himself in check. I felt him beneath me, growing, throbbing, his need nearing its peak. I was so close to the edge when he gripped my hips and lifted me, positioning the head of his cock at my entrance. Unease began to creep in.

"Look at me, *cara*," Harkyn ordered, and I did so without thinking. His teasing smile told me he was thinking I took orders well and I felt a smile curve my lips.

"Good girl," he whispered.

The moment he began to ease in, I slowed my hips, worried about his size and how much this was going to hurt. The first time always hurt, right? Everyone said so. He slid forward an inch and my mouth fell open at the feel of him stretching me. The foreign feeling wasn't unpleasant, but it wasn't what I thought it would be, either.

"Look here, *cara*," Harkyn instructed, and I dragged my gaze back to his incredible eyes. He slid a hand to my center and I felt his thumb stroke and circle my clit, causing that wave to continue to build inside. It felt different with him inside me, tighter... better.

"Oh, *oh*," I whispered, incredulous.

"Just feel, baby," he instructed, sinking deeper. A burning began and I closed my eyes as I tried to focus on the pleasure he was creating deep inside me.

"More, Harkyn. I need..." I trailed off, not knowing what, but something. Harkyn stroked my clit faster, and I felt his mouth on my nipples even though he never moved. I gasped, my eyes flying wide and he smirked. I felt him there, stroking, tugging with his tongue, his teeth grazing. Throbbing between my legs grew more pronounced as I hurtled headlong into pleasure as he worked my body like an instrument.

"Please" was all I got out before he thrust upwards and at the same time, pulled me down over his thick, hard cock.

There was a split second of sharp, intense pain before Harkyn
shoved into my mind and flooded me with his pleasure,
quadrupling mine and overwhelming me with it so that I felt the
orgasm that had been building crash over me. Any pain I was
expecting to feel was *gone,* and I was left crying his name as he
buried himself completely inside me.

"Fuck, yes!" Harkyn groaned as I convulsed around him, his cock
throbbing deep inside where I felt him.

"Harkyn," I whimpered, overwhelmed, a little lost.

"Ride me, Dimitria. Ride my cock, *cara,*" he instructed through
gritted teeth. I blindly did as he ordered, my body still rippling
and convulsing around him even as I felt that wave begin to build
again. This couldn't be possible! I'd read romances all my life,
and they all explained sex to be mind-numbingly blissful, but I'd
never believed it. Feeling it now for the first time, feeling the
pleasure Harkyn took from my body and gave back to me, it was
truly mind blowing.

"Fuck, you feel so good, sweetheart. Your pussy was made for
me—*you* were made for me," he groaned. His lids were half-
closed as he spoke, but I felt like it was to himself, he was half out
of his mind with pleasure. The desire he'd been holding back for
four long years had finally won out, and he was lost to it. "Yes,
baby, fuck, you feel so good. You take my cock so damn well,
cara."

His words were salacious and did everything to build me up
again, to make my body throb and ache and work its way towards
another orgasm. He filled me so completely, stretching me,
every ridge of his cock made to bring me pleasure in ways I was
sure no one else would have ever been able to do. His grip on my
hips was hard, but he slid his hands to my backside where he
helped me to ride him to the tempo he needed. The feel of him

fucking me down onto his cock was almost dirty—and I loved it. He was taking his pleasure from me, using my body to give him something only I would ever be able to give him, and some warped part in my head loved it. I wanted him to take me for his own pleasure.

"Use me, Harkyn. I am yours; I want to please you. I want to feel you come," I whimpered. I might have been shocked that the words came from my mouth, but I was too far gone to really care. All I cared about was the way my words ignited something inside him, turning him almost feral with need.

"Mine. You're mine, *cara*. This body, your mind, heart, your soul. You're all mine, baby."

"*Yes!*"

I exploded around him once more, stars bursting behind my eyes as I climaxed, every inner muscle I possessed squeezing around him tightly. He moved quickly, flipping us over so he was leaning over me before he drove into my body, over and over, hard and rough, mindless with the need for release.

"Yes, yes, yes. Take me Harkyn. Come for me," I whispered to him, needing him to find his own pleasure. He pushed inside, his grip on my hips almost painful as he held my body down, my back arched and hips tilted the way he needed me as he pulsed deeply inside me.

"Fuck!" He roared the word so loudly I was sure I was temporarily deaf. I felt him release inside me, his cock swelling before he flooded me with his cum. Whether he meant to or not, he pushed his pleasure into my mind, the full force of it sending my body into yet another orgasm.

I cried out and he grunted loudly at feeling my release, his grip on me tightening, but I didn't care. We were both adrift in a sea of pleasure, one we'd been desperate to immerse ourselves in for four years.

Heat seared hot and bright inside, and I gasped at the feeling, the way it seemed to bring Harkyn and I closer, binding us together just as he'd done when he'd bound our souls. I closed my eyes on the feel of it, on the way being tied to him made me feel freer, safer, a part of something bigger than myself.

Pleasure was not the right word. It was far too tame and too average for what we'd just experienced. I didn't want to move, my body limp and exhausted, wrung out to the max. I ached, but in a good way, in a way I never wanted to forget.

"Dimitira?"

"Mmm?"

"Did I hurt you?" Harkyn whispered, his gentle fingers stroking my hips.

"I don't know, and I don't care. You killed me," I murmured sleepily. He chuckled and I pried my eyes open to look up at him. That shoulder length hair was loose around his shoulders, and I thought once again how damn sexy it was on him. Those gray-green eyes burned down at me, full of happiness and joy, fulfillment shining there.

The last four years I'd been a zombie compared to how I felt in Harkyn's presence. A piece of me had been missing, and I'd known it, but was unable to put me back together. Then he'd come back, and suddenly I could see myself being complete once again. I'd missed him so freaking much, my heart was in a constant state of aching, my soul empty and miserable without him.

Harkyn, picking up on my emotions, leaned forward to cup my face, his gaze searching.

"I'm so sorry I was gone so long, *cara*. I didn't think. I was desperate to protect you, even against myself, and I hurt us both in the process. I'm so sorry. Can you ever forgive me?"

I blinked at the moisture that gathered in my eyes and nodded. "I forgave you a long time ago."

"You have no idea how much I missed you," he said, and I shook my head.

"I think I have a pretty good idea," I said before I leaned up to kiss him. He met me halfway, and I loved the way my heart pounded hard and my soul cried out in relief. When he pulled away, I smiled and cupped the side of his face.

"I love you, Harkyn. I've loved you for years, and I never stopped loving you."

The full force of Harkyn's joy and relief almost knocked me back, and I beamed as the roaring in his soul reverberated between us. Disbelief tinged his satisfaction, but I understood it.

"*Cara,* my sweet Dimitria. I loved you from the first time we met, I just didn't realize it until later, and when I did, it scared the fuck out of me. I love you, baby, and I've loved you ever since. For always."

Tears burned my eyes at the heat that seared its way across my chest to tug at my soul. An invisible, powerfully made thread tugged tight as we were pulled closer still, and a shiver worked its way up my spine as the final bond between us was made.

Harkyn ducked his head to kiss me again, and I gave as good as I got, winding my arms and legs tighter around him. He began to move, his hips rocking back and forth as he slid in and out of me again. I moaned against his mouth, raising my hips to meet every one of his short, shallow thrusts, feeling that heat build between us again.

"Will it always be like this?" I whispered in wonder.

"No. It'll get better," he assured, kissing me hard again.

I could live with that.

CHAPTER TWENTY-SEVEN
HARKYN

"And that's what we call the Arrival Room," I explained as Tria asked me yet another question.

It had been several hours since we'd completed our bond, and we'd shared that incredible experience several more times before she'd called for a break. I had to remember that she was human in her build, and while she was a Witch and healed faster than the average human, there were still limits.

I didn't want to hurt her, but I felt as though I had to have her, as if we were making up for the past four years since being apart. The feel of her beneath my fingers, the taste of her, the sound of her moans of pleasure... I was well and truly addicted.

Tria nodded slowly and gnawed on her lower lip as she adjusted the sheet that covered her breasts and wrote something down in that notepad she'd had with her yesterday. We'd done a lot of creative and intimate things in the past few hours, but she was still a little shy being completely naked when we weren't having sex. I'd get her there, but for now I'd let her have her modesty.

I smiled at her curiosity, at the way she wanted to know about everything in this world. "There's not a lot in the Arrival Room. No windows, and no doors except those that lead to the nine realms of each Demon King."

"You each have your own room. So, this part of Hell is like...

your house?" she asked.

I smiled and reminded myself not to laugh. I didn't want her to think I was laughing *at* her. "No, not exactly. Realms and dimensions are different to normal space. Inside each of these doors is each of our homes, styled to how each King prefers it. Within each King's realm is another door leading to that King's circle of Hell. When we enter that circle of Hell, we each have our own office that has *another* door which leads us to The Pit," I explained.

Dimitria watched me with such concentration, anyone would think she'd be graded on what information she took in right now. She scribbled something down on that pad and I watched in amusement, wondering what she could be writing. Surely, she didn't need to make a copy of our conversation.

"What's The Pit?" she asked.

I inwardly sighed. I guess that was a fair question, even though I wasn't sure how she'd take it. "As you already know, a human's soul on Earth will either go to Heaven or Hell when they die, except for a Witch's soul which gets recycled," I began. Tria nodded and watched me as I explained.

"When a soul comes here, it goes to a kind of storage chamber. My brothers and I take out a certain number every decade, and our Demons are in charge of stripping the soul through torture," I continued.

I could see the protest on her tongue—the way she despised the thought of torture.

"Believe me, the ones who end up here are not good souls. They did horrible things when they were alive," I explained.

"But how can torture be a fit punishment for *all* damned souls? Surely not all of them are rapists and murderers?"

I shook my head. "No. But they are all bad to different degrees.

Just listen and let me explain."

Dimitria frowned but slowly nodded, jotting something down on her pad again. Sighing, I got comfortable on the bed and grabbed her foot, resting it on my thigh as I massaged it. She protested for a whole second before she groaned and sank into it. I laughed and thought about my answer.

"Humans die. Death weighs their soul and deems them either fit for Heaven or Hell. We take what we are given and the souls eventually go to The Pit. Think of it as a waiting room while we sort out just how bad they were," I began.

"Okay, I'm following so far," she said slowly, her intelligent eyes watching me. I was sure she was looking for any sign of deception, but I was determined to give her the whole truth.

"The soul is tortured for their wrong doings—"

"But why torture? Why do they need to be tortured?" Dimitria interrupted.

"I know this is hard for you to understand, but there is a method here," I said, trying to soothe her. She huffed an impatient breath but indicated for me to go on.

"A soul at its core is pure, it's energy, it's capable of being molded into practically anything. Now, pretend that every bad deed that qualifies a soul for Hell adds a thin layer of tissue to it, making it damaged and heavy. The more layers the soul has, the more torture is needed to rid the soul of every bad deed and make it nothing but pure energy again, any memory of the life it lived now gone. Once the soul is back to its original form, it can be molded into what we need—Demons—soldiers to defend our realms against the Angels."

Dimitria frowned a little but indicated for me to keep going.

"The blades and other instruments of torture we use are infused with an ancient kind of magic. This magic is almost alive in itself, and with each strike of the device or slice of the blade, it shaves off a piece of that build-up on the soul in a way that is a fit punishment for the evils they committed. Yes, it hurts the soul, but the soul did bad deeds on Earth that built up these layers, and the cost of those layers is pain in the afterlife. Still with me?" Dimitria drew in a slow breath but nodded, and I saw she understood even if doing so made her wary. I could understand—no one wanted to believe Demons were doing good work.

"My brothers and I look each soul over. We get a complete file on the human and the reasons they're here with us, and depending on the severity of their evil deeds, depends on which circle of Hell they end up in. Cole—ruler of the first circle of Hell—takes those who qualify for Hell, but for things like infidelity, sexual harassment, ignoring those in need, purposely spreading hate-speech and so on. Corvin—ruler of the ninth circle of Hell—takes the worst of the worst. I'm talking child sex traffickers, molesters, the men who create child soldiers and rape and pillage villages," I explained. Dimitria was nodding, which I took for a good sign. I waited a few more moments to let her digest this.

"So, for someone like Hitler—who I'm assuming is down here—when would he get free of his tortures?"

"He will never be free."

She frowned. "Why? Not that I want him to be free after what he did."

"The build-up on a soul isn't just by their actions alone, but by the resulting effect they had on those around them. For a rough example, rape might get you ten layers on your soul which would take several years to chip away at in Hell, but more layers get added if the effect the rape had on the victim created more bad things to happen on Earth. If the rapist's victim suffered a psychological break due to the attack and it caused them to go on a killing spree, murdering convicted rapists, then the *victim* gains layers for murder. But for every layer the victim gains as a direct result of the assailant's actions, the rapist gains a layer as well."

"So," Dimitria began slowly, "because of Hitler's actions, the existence of every neo-Nazi working under his name and ideals, their actions add layers to his soul?"

"Exactly," I answered with a small smile, pleased she understood. She nodded thoughtfully, and I could see her shoulders loosening slightly as it all began to make sense.

"What if someone did something bad, but then spent the rest of their life making up for it? What then? Do they go here, or Heaven?"

I continued to rub her foot and shrugged. "There are a lot of factors. Were they truly repentant? How much good did they put out into the world? Were they forgiven? Just how bad an effect did their one bad deed have and on how many people? It *is* possible to clear away these layers on one's soul while they're still alive, but it takes a lot of work and genuine regret and remorse for it to even begin to be possible. Most people prefer to pretend they never messed up and carry on with their lives."

Dimitria considered my words and flicked the pen in her hand, her notepad angled so that I still couldn't read what she'd been writing.

"Can I see The Pit?" she asked.

"No."

"Why not?"

I hesitated a moment. "You're not ready."

"What gives you the right to decide whether or not I am ready for something?"

"You can't stand violence, Tria, so no. Not even the other mates have seen The Pit," I explained.

"So?"

"So, they've been here longer and experienced what life is like here. They're not ready for The Pit yet, so neither are you."

"I think I can be the judge of that."

"You're not seeing The Pit," I argued, determined to shut this down.

"It's because you know it's wrong, isn't it? The torturing. You know it's wrong and you can't look at me and try to defend what you're doing," she pushed.

"No, it's because we do what is necessary, and you'll still see me as a monster like you did four years ago."

She paused and seemed to take in my words. "I don't believe you're a monster."

I wanted to believe her words, but it was going to take me some time to consider and really take it in, and it wasn't about to happen tonight.

"What kind of people do you think are down here, Tria?" I asked, frowning.

"Those who have sinned, those who have broken the laws of God," she persisted.

I shook my head and sighed, tempted to laugh but I held it back. Instead, I ran my fingers up and down her leg. "You're *still* basing everything you see on a book that wasn't even written by God or anyone in Heaven or Hell. That book was written by man, to control and dominate over others. At one point, it did say a lot of good things. You know, thou shalt not kill and so forth. But over the centuries, over countless translations, and edits, it turned into a weapon against those who are different, disguised as the key to Heaven," I explained, shaking my head.

She frowned and tried to take her foot back, but I kept a hold of it. I wasn't going to let her put some space between us now. "So then… who *is* in Hell? Who qualifies for it? Why does torture become necessary?"

"A soul is not a person. It's not a human being anymore," I began. "A soul is a ball of energy, a forever shifting, shimmering piece of creation that can be twisted and formed into whatever form is desired. For whatever reason, we can't make anything other than what we are. I can't take that soul and make a human; I can only make more Demons. Just like Angels only know how to make more Angels."

"Okay," she said, drawing out the word. "What does any of that have to do with why you torture?"

"When God made humans, he added something else to the mix, some kind of…" I struggled to think of a word that would make sense to her. I'd never tried to explain what humanity looked like before. "Think of humanity like… like a protective casing. It's frail and thin, but it's welded so tightly to the soul that it's almost one with it."

Dimitria nodded but didn't speak, waiting for me to continue.

"As I said before, a soul gains layers for every evil act committed. I can look at each of these layers and see what each one was for. However thick this layer is depends on how bad the act itself was. How hard it is to remove depends on how bad an impact that sin had on Earth and the lives affected by it. You still with me?"

"So…" she trailed off, thinking. "Using Hitler as an example again… he may have gotten one hundred layers for working people up into a racist frenzy, but each of those layers will take a hundred years to remove because of the rippling affect they still have on Earth?" she asked, frowning.

"Pretty close. The difficulty in removing the layer isn't measured in years, but rather pain and devastation. Every slice of a blade on his layers may equal some of the pain and devastation his actions had on Earth, but in his case, we can never keep up with it, we can never get through those layers. Even if we made some headway, the next thing we know, a neo-Nazi tattooed with a swastika is topside burning down Jewish temples taking away all the progress we made and adding more layers," I explained.

"And he can feel this?" she asked, and I was sure she was a little disgusted.

I shrugged. "The last layer to remove is humanity itself. By that point, the consciousness of the human who committed the crimes is revealed. We remove that layer by slipping it off the soul, and we're once again left with a pure ball of energy, waiting to be turned into what we need."

"And what happens to the consciousness of the human once you remove it?" she asked.

"It cannot survive without the soul. The second it is removed; it becomes nothing more than a nearly transparent wrapper that was once a human."

Dimitria swallowed hard as she considered this and I let her take the time she needed to digest it.

"You still can't get past the torture part, can you?"

"I just… I was always taught that to stoop to the levels of those who hurt us makes us no better than them," she explained.

"Humans also say that Karma will get them one day. Well, one day is when they end up here. And you can consider me and our Demons the Karma everyone waits for. You like to use Hitler as an example, so let me. Are you telling me that asshole doesn't deserve eternity burning for what he did? For all the innocent lives he destroyed?

"I…" she trailed off, looking distressed. "I just—who else ends up here? If someone cheats on their partner, do they spend twenty years here getting tortured for it? It just doesn't seem like the punishment fits the crime."

"You're still thinking that real sins are what is listed in that book," I said again, letting her tug her foot free, but I kept us close on the bed. "Everyone else involved in the judging process couldn't give a shit if you wear more than one type of material at the same time and eat all the shellfish you want while screwing every one of the same sexes before getting married. Those things don't matter to *us*. They have never mattered for us. If you do your best every day, help when you can see someone needs it, keep your promises, don't kill for the sake of killing, you're basically good. It doesn't even have to do with believing in God. No one really cares about that. It's about being good for the sake of doing good, and not allowing the circumstances of your upbringing dictate the human you turn out to be."

Dimitria was silent for a long time as she digested this, and I worried for a moment that this would be the breaking point for her. She had been so accepting of everything that had happened so far, surely there had to be something that would tip her over the edge. I knew her aversion to violence, so it would make sense if this was it.

Sighing, she gave me a pouty look and I felt my lips twitch.

"So, I can't see The Pit?"

I hesitated and then shook my head. "Not now." I could see the protest building on her lips but I held up a hand to forestall her argument. "The Pit is a lot for anyone to take in. I promise to show you everything and share it all, and I will hold to my promise. But you have to believe me when I say that I also need to protect you and only show you pieces at a time so as not to overwhelm you."

333

"But one day you *will* show me. And I don't mean fifty years down the track."

I sighed. "Yes. If you insist upon it, I promise to show you one day soon."

Her blue eyes studied me for a long moment before she nodded and smiled. "Good. Now," she said and tossed her pad and pen aside. "I need to prove to you that I don't think you're a monster, and there's something I want to try," she added and straddled my lap.

The change in topic took me aback, but I got over it quickly when I caught an image in her head of what she was thinking.

"You don't need to prove anything," I reminded.

"I know," she answered and bit her lower lip as her imagination got more graphic. Grinning, I leaned back against the pillows as she kissed her way down my chest and stomach. My cock was already standing at attention as I watched her head move closer and closer to it.

Fucking hell...

I bit my lip to stop from groaning in anticipation, but the throbbing in my cock was giving me away. Dimitria looked up at me from between my legs, her pale blue eyes alight with desire and humor as if she knew just how badly I wanted her.

"Patience, my dear King," she teased.

"Fuck patience." I groaned as her small hand wrapped around my cock. Fucking hell, had anything ever felt this good? She was still unsure, testing how things felt and tasted, cautious in her grip and touch.

"Tighter," I instructed roughly, and her lips curved in a small smile as she did as I said. My breath left in a whoosh as she began to stroke, and I reached out to push her pale hair back and over one shoulder so I could see her better. Sliding inside her mind, I let her feel my pleasure, allowed it to build her own and I smiled when her lips parted in surprise. Images filtered across my mind, ways she could touch me to bring me pleasure, things I wanted her to do with me at some point if not now.

"Teach me," she whispered in my mind, focusing on one image in particular, her inexperience making her feel self-conscious. To me, teaching her to please me and only me was far sexier than if she already knew what to do.

"Are you sure you want to? There's no rush, no pressure, we have all the time in the world for new experiences," I offered. She raised her almost silvery eyes to meet mine, her expression certain.

My cock pulsed in her hand, and she smirked and focused on the image in my head, on the instructions she could see there. I wanted her badly, but I also wanted her to take her time, to explore. Tria's tongue darted out to flick over the head of my shaft and I jerked at the feel, gritting my teeth against the need to take over.

Her hot mouth slid over the head and my eyes snapped open, my breath escaping in a long, low hiss. The feel of her velvety tongue sliding over the sensitive tip was almost enough to make me lose my mind. I watched her work, the way her head bobbed up and down slowly and she took more of my length in her mouth. I was mesmerized by the sight of her lips spread wide around me; her hand fisted at the base rising to meet her lips when she'd taken me as deep as she could. She followed the instructions in my head so well, it was all I could do not to come.

Her long lashes fluttered and then lifted, and the moment her blue gaze clashed with mine, I felt an overwhelming feeling of lust and love clash inside. I wanted to be tender and rough. I wanted to fuck her, but I wanted to worship her... to take my time and to plough ahead and get us to that explosive, inevitable end.

My fingers bunched in her long silvery hair and her grip on the base of my shaft tightened.

"Relax your throat," I instructed, my tone raspy as I tried to hold back. She struggled, and I waited, forcing myself to be patient. I felt her need to give me this, to bring me to the end of my rope with just her hands and mouth, and I wanted to give that to her. She did as I said, as I showed her, and felt her take me deeper. She lifted up, my cock shiny with her saliva. She took in a sharp breath and bobbed her head again, tongue stroking the underside of my length as she hollowed her cheeks and sucked.

"Fuck," I groaned low, the word drawn out as I fought to stay still. "That's it, *cara,* take me deep."

She worked her mouth up and down, her hand stroking, taking me deeper little by little. She was returning the favor I'd been doing all night and allowed me to feel how much she enjoyed giving me pleasure. She liked making me feel this way, liked how much she loved making me groan and moan. Feeling my reactions, hearing me praise her, made her shiver and become aroused.

I tightened my grip in her hair and felt the immediate bite of excitement the small sting of pain caused her. As she lowered her mouth, I gently rocked my hips up, trying not to do as my body was demanding.

"Shit, so good… so good, baby," I told her, unable to say the words aloud, my mouth incapable of forming words at the moment.

Her mind snagged on an image in my head.

"Do it," she urged.

"I do not want to overwhelm you or hurt you, cara. We're not at that level yet," I returned, struggling to keep control.

"I see how much you want it, Harkyn. I feel your need, and I want you to use me like that. Take control, move me how you want me, use me the way you need me," she pleaded, and hearing the way she needed me to do it almost sent me over the edge with the need to ravage her.

"Tell me if it's too much. Don't push yourself," I warned, giving in. Her excitement grew as I slid both hands into her hair and gripped tightly. She kept her hand on the base of my cock, but relaxed her mouth as I raised my hips, slowly at first before lowering. I did this again and again, keeping her face still as I fed my cock into her mouth, faster and faster, a little deeper each time. She timed her breathing to match my strokes, focusing on my speed. She sucked hard, creating suction, and when she swallowed around my cock I almost came.

"Fuck, baby, do that again, *cara*."

Dimitria took me deep and swallowed around me, and I groaned and raised my hips faster, careful not to be too hard. Over and over we did this, her swallowing around me, dragging me to the edge of my sanity slowly when all I wanted to do was drill into the welcoming warmth of her mouth.

"Cara, fuck... baby, I'm going to come," I warned, teetering on that ledge.

"Let me taste you, Harkyn. I want all of you," she almost pleaded, her hand tightening, her lips hollowing. She forced me to feel how turned on she was, how near her own climax felt just by giving me such pleasure, and I was done for.

"Tria!" I roared her name as she sucked hard, drawing out my release. I came in her mouth, my load shooting to the back of her throat where she swallowed around me. I shuddered and groaned, forcing myself to let go of her hair so I didn't force her head down and instead gripped the bed sheets beneath us.

My ears felt as though they were temporarily filled with cotton wool, and I was overly aware of my heart pounding hard and fast in my chest as my lungs struggled for air.

"Fuck." I groaned, my body going limp. Tria swallowed around me once more before she let me go, and when I managed to pry my eyes open to look at her, she was grinning like the cat who ate the canary... or was that the cream?

"What have I done? I've created a Demon of a different kind," I moaned.

She laughed in satisfaction and crawled up onto my lap so she sat with a leg either side of me, her fingers sliding into my hair. She was so small next to me, her body thin and soft, but there was a supple tone to her muscles that showed how she looked after herself and could hold her own. I still felt like I'd break her if I wasn't careful.

"I take it you liked that?"

"Liked it?" I repeated, incredulous. "You damn near sucked my soul from my body. Fuck, baby, I'm addicted to you and everything about you. And this mouth?" I stopped to touch her slightly swollen lips. "I could kiss you forever."

Tria grinned triumphantly, and I felt some of her insecurities ease. She'd been worried her inexperience would make her less desirable, and I hated that. I slid into her mind and let her see herself the way I did, the way her timid touches and need for instruction made the experience hotter than I ever knew it could be. I wanted her to see how the way she was learning just to please me made me ferociously happy and somewhat cocky.

She was everything.

"I love you too," she whispered.

Grinning, I pulled her down and took her lips in a long, deep kiss that left us both gasping for air before rolling her onto her back, my hand sliding between her legs again.

CHAPTER TWENTY-EIGHT
DIMITRIA

"Wait, so the fact that I'm not putting up a fight makes you wary?" I asked, frowning at my mate as I finished putting my hair up.

"Yes."

"You realize how psychotic that is, right?" I asked, dropping my hands once my hair was up.

He shrugged from where he sat on the bed with his back against the headboard. "All the other Witches tied to my brothers fought the bond tooth and nail. They all looked for ways out of it, tried searching archives and creating spells. But you didn't do any of that. Why?"

"Because I love you?" I offered.

"But is that enough? Cali was in love with Adrik when she found out, and they had a massive fight about it. Sawyer too. She had plenty of time to accept it before she fell in love with Malik, but she fought it. Mika, well, she had it dropped on her out of the blue, so I can't blame her reaction. But you?" Harkyn explained, looking at me with a confused frown.

I laughed and shook my head. "So, what? You want me to fight you on this? You want me not to be so blissfully happy and to look for a way out of an ancient, prophesized connection that three other experienced Witches have not been able to find a way out of?"

"No," he said at once and then frowned. "It's just—you're taking in all of this remarkably well. Too well."

I laughed again. "So? I'm not the others. My life was different, and I learned to survive and adapt to things as they happened. I know you didn't know about the prophecy when we met so I don't feel cheated or manipulated. You almost died keeping yourself away from me to give me safety and freedom, and we fell in love before we knew about it all. Why would I complain?"

"Well…" he sat up. "Don't you feel trapped?"

I frowned. "No."

"Really?"

"No. Freedom is an illusion. Everyone is trapped or controlled by something, some more than others. But I don't feel trapped with you. Yes, there is a price to be paid for what we have, but the good far outweighs the bad."

"How?" he asked, and I shook my head at this ridiculous conversation.

"Let me see… universe approved soul mate? Check," I began, crawling up onto the bed beside him to give him a quick kiss. "A true love that will never leave me, hurt me, or cheat on me? Check. Magic? Check. Sisters? Check. Witches who can help me improve my craft? Check three times over. Eternity to explore the world we live in? Also check."

"Okay, and what about being on the run from Angels, Rogues, and Death himself? Having to live in Hell forever? Never being allowed on the surface without clearing it with me first and never going up there alone? Having to give up your job? I know you love being a bounty hunter. Or what about the impending war between us, the Rogues, and the Angels?"

"Do you *want* me to hate it here?" I asked, slapping him in the chest.

He caught my hand and threaded his fingers with mine. "Of course not," he said and sighed. "I'm just worried you're not properly taking all this in. You know? I'm worried you don't truly realize everything you've given up by saving me and to be here. What if one day, you wake up and despise me for it all."

Understanding seeped in and I squeezed his fingers tightly before leaning in to kiss him. "I promise you, Harkyn, I won't hate you. I love you. I have missed you so much these last four years, and I don't ever want to be apart from you. I know what my life is without you, and I know what it will be *with* you, and I still choose you."

Those incredible eyes of his shone with such love and appreciation, that I felt my heart melt a little.

"You've really thought this through, haven't you?"

I grinned. "Yup. Now, enough stalling. We need to go see your brother and make sure he's okay."

Harkyn groaned. "I already told you he was. I can talk to him from here."

"I need to see him for myself and talk to him. He's probably telling you what you want to hear."

Harkyn rolled his eyes and I got off the bed, tucking my notepad into my back pocket while glaring at him.

"If we go, you're going to hug him, and I hate it when you touch anyone else," he pouted.

I laughed at the almost pathetic look on his face and started towards the bedroom door. "Okay, you don't have to come then. I'll go on my own."

I didn't even make it to the bottom of the stairs before he was there. He hauled me up against him and then pressed me into a wall. "You'll never enter any of my brothers' realms without me with you. Is that understood?"

"What did I tell you about giving me orders?" I reminded, not frightened of him at all.

"You're so good at taking orders. I expect you to heed this one," he insisted. While his eyes were dancing with laughter and I felt the humor coming off him, there was also a piece of him deep down that meant it. He didn't want to acknowledge this part of him, he didn't want it to exist, but it did.

My smile faded and I leaned in to brush a kiss over his mouth. "I promise, Harkyn. If it's not a dire need, then I will never enter the realm of any of your brothers on my own."

He weighed my words, the truth of them, the meaning of them, and finally nodded with a sharp jerk of his head. He was ashamed for needing my word on this, but I understood. Despite knowing we were soul mates, bonded as tightly as any two beings could be... I hated the idea of him visiting the realm of any of the Witches without me there.

"Can we go see Tamas now?"

Harkyn sighed. "Fine, but when we come back, I want to have my way with you."

I grinned. "Like you've been having the last few days?"

"And intend to for the next several thousand years," he answered with a smirk.

My head spun a little at the idea of viewing my life terms of such a long period. I knew what being his mate meant and all that it entailed, but it still threw me that my life likely wouldn't end in fifty to eighty years, but instead last for *thousands* of years. It was enough to make my head explode some days.

Harkyn kissed me deeply before slowly letting me go. We left our realm together hand in hand, and I looked around with interest. I'd been out here, yes, but I hadn't had much time to check it out properly. Harkyn pointed to each door and explained which brother it belonged to.

"Where is Donovan, by the way? Has he come back yet?"

Harkyn shook his head. "He's hot on Trinity's trail, and he doesn't want to stop. He's more worried than ever that the Angels will get her."

"Is she his mate?"

Harkyn looked down at me and I shrugged. "The book with the prophecy was out, and I read up. The line that refers to him says something about finding the woman he has been looking for."

"We believe so, although none of us have asked Donovan what he thinks. Things with Mika's family are a little complicated for Donovan, and it's best if we all just steer clear unless he asks for help."

I frowned and thought that was stupid, but I got the impression there was more I didn't know.

"What about Corvin and Devlin? I haven't met them yet," I pointed out.

Harkyn sighed. "They're on some secret mission they haven't told the rest of us about. Not even their Knights know. Or if they do, they're very good at lying and aren't saying. They do that sometimes. They've always been close, and are each other's backup whenever needed. I guess there's something they're looking into. We'll know when or if there's anything to know," he answered, but I could tell it didn't sit well with him that they were on the outside of whatever was going on.

"They were injured the other day. Are they okay now?"

"Yes," Harkyn assured at once. "A random Witch came upon them; she felt their pain and healed them of the poison in their systems and then left before either of them could get her name. They were lucky she even showed herself, so they weren't going to complain that she left so quickly."

When we reached Tamas's door, we knocked, and almost immediately the door opened. Harkyn gripped my hand tighter as we stepped inside, and I looked around until I found Tamas standing at the fireplace. The fireplace looked identical to the one in Harkyn's realm—our realm—but I wasn't sure. The room was large and spacious, with books and weapons lying about. It was a little messier than our realm, but nothing that made him look like a typical bachelor.

"Come to make sure I haven't offed myself?" Tamas asked as he turned to look at us. He looked a little better today than he had the other day, but that spark I'd come to love in his eyes was absent.

"Something like that," I answered.

His smile grew a little and he nodded. "I understand."

"Do you?" I pressed, stepping closer and letting go of Harkyn's hand. "Because you were going to get yourself killed and I have lost enough people in my life. I would have been thoroughly pissed off if you'd died," I snapped, angry now that I could see he was okay.

"I'm sure your anger is something to fear when dead," he joked.

I raised an eyebrow and crossed my arms over my stomach. "If you don't think I would have found a way to bring you back just to string you up by your feet and use you as a pinata as punishment, then you have another thing coming."

"You don't think that's a little much?" he asked, putting down the drink in his hand.

"No," I answered and glared. "The original plan had you strung up by a much more delicate and favored part of your anatomy." Harkyn snickered, and Tamas stilled for a moment before a rusty sounding chuckle escaped his lips. *There.* There was the smallest glimmer of the Tamas I'd come to know and love.

"Okay, okay. Fine, I promise not to intentionally put myself in a dangerous situation that could get me killed. Happy?"

I sighed and dropped my arms. "For now."

Tamas's green eyes studied me, and I felt the remorse roll off him. "I am sorry, you know? I didn't ever want you to feel my pain, I didn't want to scare you into running away. And then the other day when you saw me, I wasn't in my right mind. I hate that I scared you, that I upset you, and that I made you worry you'd lose someone else you cared about."

Tears burned my eyes at his words and I cleared my throat. *"Brace yourself."* It was all the warning I was going to give Harkyn before I launched myself at Tamas and wrapped my arms around him. He hugged me back quickly and I squeezed my eyes shut as I held him.

"Don't die on me, dummy," I whispered.

Tamas chuckled and slowly let me go before playfully ruffling my hair. "I'll do my best."

"You had better," I warned and knocked his hand away. Tamas's lips quirked up, and then flicked a glance at Harkyn.

"Anyway, I had better keep my hands to myself before your mate decides to play Ping-Pong with my nuts.

"Gross," I replied, scrunching up my face at the visual.

"Says the woman who wanted to string me up by my balls and play pinata," Tamas defended.

I sniffed indignantly. "That was different."

Both males cracked smiles and I wandered back over to Harkyn and let him wrap me in his arms. That itching started almost immediately, the one that made me feel like I needed to rub myself all over Harkyn like a cat to get rid of the feeling of the other male. This bond thing was crazy.

We sat with Tamas for another hour, just talking. Harkyn heard it from Tamas how we met and everything that had happened. Harkyn seemed as concerned as the others that someone was hunting Nephilim, and that Zarak had been so on edge. Apparently, Cali and Adrik were closer to the Nephilim than anyone else, so it was up to them to find out more information. Both were curious about Trinity, and neither too happy when I explained about her Angel friend. While Harkyn could feel how I genuinely believed he was good, I knew Tamas didn't believe me, and considering how powerless he felt now and how damaged his arm was, I figure he had good reason to hate all things Angel at this point. I just hoped one day, my friend would find his way back to us and be as he was before. I hoped that the attack didn't take from us the Tamas we all knew and loved.

~

HARKYN

"So, are you hungry?" Dimitria asked as she stretched her arms above her head. I flicked a glance from her lithe form to the notepad on the table and picked it up, flipping through it. She never let me read it anytime I asked what was in it. Now was my chance. Amusement crept in the more I read and I laughed out loud.

Tria spun to face me, and her eyes snapped to the notepad and she hurried to take it. I lifted it above my head and started reading aloud.

"*Large, open-planned room with never-dying fireplace to the right. Kick ass library to the left with a rolling ladder I can't wait to climb. Candle holders with brass fittings, stone walls like an old castle, velvet drapes along walls I assume are there to add color...*"

Dimitria stopped trying to get the paper and crossed her arms over her stomach and huffed, her cheeks turning pink. "Give it back."

"Why are you describing our realm?" I asked with a small laugh.

"I have a process, okay, a way to let things sink in and get a better handle on them. If I were scoping out a mark, I'd write down everything about them and their home to better make out their character and who they are. It helps me work them," she defended.

I laughed and continued reading. "So, knowing I have *a fucking big bed with pillows you're sure are more comfortable than your mattress* is important?" I asked. She made another grab for the notepad, but I lifted it out of her reach and continued reading. "And knowing I have *one wall covered entirely in climbing ivy* would help you know me better? What about this part about the room carrying my scent? Or the giant couch before the fireplace that makes you think you'd sink between the cushions?"

"Harkyn, give it back."

I ignored her. "What about this part about the rough texture of my red door? Or the fact that you see no cobwebs or power points. Or how you feel like you're in a castle inside an underground cave, but you don't feel claustrophobic or buried under thousands of pounds of stone?"

"It tells me about your character, about your personal tastes so that if you were on the run, I'd know what things to look for when searching for you," she explained, huffing again.

"You can find me anywhere with our connection, you don't need this."

"It's my process."

"Oh?" I replied and chuckled, making sure to keep the notepad out of reach. "So, you don't want to write about my mahogany side tables? Or the brass lamps above the bedside tables? What about the giant mirror fitted to the wall across from the bed? Do you want me to pencil in here how the floor is all stone, but that I have large sections of carpet under the bed, the couches, the table to the left beside the library wall?"

"Details matter!" she hissed.

"You're in another *realm*, Dimitria," I returned, wondering how the hell these things mattered to her when she was literally inside another dimension. "You just learned about the inner workings of Hell. You are standing in the realm of the Fourth King of Hell, just steps away from another door that would take you to The Pit of Hell. The weight of an oncoming war is bearing down on us, and you're stuck on a few details about the layout of a *room*?"

"I like to remember things and get a clear picture," she defended weakly.

"But what can these details do for you now? I'm not a mark, I'm not someone you're going to have to chase, and even if I was, you could find me *anywhere* just by feeling for me. Why do you need all the details?"

"I just... I like it," she replied with an annoyed frown.

"It's not like you're writing a book," I pointed out. "Although, if you were writing a book about me and our situation, but were getting wrapped up in a few details over the layout of my realm and *not* on the big picture, I'd be worried. Your book should detail big things, like the King of Hell who destiny herself has deemed your mate, or the fact that you're a Witch being hunted by Rogue Demons, Angels, and Reapers alike. If small details about my room really registered on your *need-to-know* list, I don't think it would be a book I'd want to read."

"Shut up," she snapped with a hiss, snatching the pad away as I lowered it. "And if I *were* writing a book, I'd write it *my* way and you'd be free to leave a review with your name on it telling me your thoughts."

"Of course I'd leave my name," I muttered and chuckled, watching her flip through her pages to get to a blank page. "Only a coward would give their opinion on something and not take responsibility for it, especially if it was disparaging to the author."

"Well then," she said with an indignant sniff. "If I ever decide to publish my findings, I'll be waiting for your review on my note taking. Until then, can we drop it?" she asked, shoving the booklet in her pocket. I was tempted to tease her a little more about it, but nodded. She'd known she was a Witch since she was seventeen, so magic wasn't really new to her. But who got spirited away to a realm just steps away from Hell itself and got caught up on a bunch of visual details?

"You asked if I was hungry earlier…" I said.

She frowned and turned back to me. "Yeah?"

I grinned, letting all the steamy thoughts I had about her run through my head and watched the heat in her cheeks burn bright and the pulse in her throat began to pick up.

"Again?" She asked, like sex is all we ever did, but I felt the instant heat and response in her body, and she didn't sound the least bit against it.

"Yes, and then maybe we'll get to the food," I answered.

"But you said you were hungry," she reminded.

"I am. Just not for food," I said, lowering my hands to my belt where I began unbuckling it. Anticipation shone in her eyes, and her tongue darted out to moisten her lower lip.

"Oh? Then for what?" she asked, and I grinned at her playing along.

"Run and I'll show you."

"Y-you want me to run?" she asked, her chest heaving with every excited breath.

"You'll never outrun me but give it a go anyway. See how far you get, *cara*."

She didn't move as I slid the belt from my jeans and I bent it in half before snapping it loudly, the sound making her jump.

"Run."

With a shaky laugh, she dropped her notepad and pen and ran. Grinning at her fading figure, I kept the belt in hand and started after her at a slower pace, letting the anticipation rise so that the victory at catching her would be that much sweeter.

EPILOGUE
DIMITRIA

"Almost there, sweetheart. Fuck, you look so good taking my cock, baby." He groaned from behind me, his hand fisted tightly in my hair as he thrust in and out of me.

I moaned, desperate to have him again, to come again, but I knew exhaustion would win out eventually. We'd been at this for hours, and neither of us could seem to get enough of each other. I whimpered with need, and Harkyn shushed me.

"Shh, baby. Just feel. You're taking all of me so well, *cara*. I can never get enough of you. I'm addicted. I need to feel your cunt squeezing my cock and milking me dry."

Holy fuck!

Satisfaction rolled off him at my body's immediate reaction to his words and he began to thrust harder, faster, burying himself to the hilt with every thrust. As exhausted as I was, I felt my body building towards another climax, my muscles tensing, my back arching and heat rushing.

"Please," I begged, needing him to make me come, to feel him release inside me and then hold me like he'd never let me go. Feeling so irresistible to a powerful man like Harkyn was becoming a need. He was out of his mind with lust for me, and I was just as desperate for him. We were feeding off each other's needs to the point where we were fucking each other into complete exhaustion almost every night. We woke up most mornings and devoured each other like we hadn't just had each other less than ten hours ago. But I didn't care. We had four years to catch up on in my opinion, and even though my body was telling me this was the last time tonight, my mind was nowhere near through with him.

"Look through my eyes, cara."

I closed my eyes and did as he ordered. It was disorienting at first, but when my inner gaze finally focused, I saw things the way he could. He was looking down at us, at his long, hard cock sliding in and out of me, stretching me, burying himself deeper and deeper with every stroke. The sight was highly erotic, and he liked watching us share a body like this. His grip on my hair tightened and I cried out when the small sting only added to the experience. It jolted me out of his head though, but I didn't care. I was teetering on the edge, being held purposefully there by Harkyn who could send me over at any moment but was all too happy to keep fucking me like he needed me to survive.

"Harkyn, please," I begged, not above pleading when the situation called for it. A part of him liked it when I did that, and I loved making him happy.

"You want me to make you come, sweetheart?" he asked, his breathing choppy.

"Please."

God, it was too much. I was going to pass out if he kept me on edge much longer. Without touching me, I felt his mouth on my clit, his hot tongue flicking and sucking even as he continued to fuck me from behind. The duel sensations sent me over the edge, and I screamed as I came, my body shuddering and clenching, the orgasm ripping through me and stripping me of the last of my strength.

I felt boneless as Harkyn shouted behind me, coming hard inside me, his body pulsing and throbbing. He collapsed over me, his shaky arms holding him up so he didn't crush me. I was so exhausted at that point that I wouldn't have cared if he had.

"You're going to kill me if we keep this up," I mumbled, my eyes too heavy to lift.

"You can't die. You'd just come back and we'd do it again," he replied, his tone as exhausted as my own.

Groaning, he rolled me onto my side and tucked in behind me, wrapping an arm tight across my belly and hauling me against him.

I smiled at the way we fit, at the way he made me feel, at the strength in his arms and the protection and feeling of safety I found there.

After fearing I'd never find it again, I'd finally found my home. And it was in Harkyn's arms.

~

HARKYN

I was jolted awake when Dimitria jumped on the bed beside me.

"What?" I groaned, still exhausted. How the hell did she have energy right now?

"There's arguing in the hall."

"So?" I returned and struggled to open my eyes. "There's almost always arguing in the hall."

"Yeah, but this is funny. Come check it out," she said, and the excitement rolling off her made it impossible to say no. Sighing, I remembered to clothe myself before letting her pull me out of bed. I smiled down at her and the energy vibrating off her, my heart rolling in my chest at the sight of her. Fuck, I loved this woman. She was everything to me, utterly everything. The last four years were nothing but a bad memory now that she was here in my arms.

"—said it a million times. It doesn't count!"

Was that Mika's voice? Understanding dawned, and I sighed. Cole and Mika fought like cats and dogs, and we rarely went a month without the two of them fighting. I swear, Cole pissed her off just for the sake of an argument, because then the two of them disappeared for several days to screw each other's brains out. This was foreplay.

Dimitria grinned and skipped forward to open our door. We stood there in the doorway and took in the scene. Cole and Tomika were in the Arrival Room, and she seemed pissed. Adrik and Cali were grinning from ear to ear as they watched, and Malik looked like he was thoroughly enjoying himself. Tamas's door opened, and I was relieved to see he looked better than he had the other week, and Cassius stepped out too, his gaze sliding around the room to take note.

"Make it make sense, Mika. We are bound in heart, mind, body, and soul. How is that any different than being married in the way humans are?"

"Because we're *not* married," Tomika argued. "You can't go around introducing yourself as my husband."

"So, introducing myself as your Demon King mate would work better?"

"Don't be a smart ass," she scolded. "We've had this argument a million times but you never seem to get it. We're not married. I know the stupid human tradition doesn't mean anything to you, but it does to *me*. And since we're not married, you can't call yourself my husband."

I looked to Dimitria who had her hands pressed to her chest and was nodding, her large eyes wide with sympathy and understanding. Frowning, I noticed that Cali and Sawyer looked at her the same way too. When I caught my brothers' eyes, they looked as confused as I was. Wasn't being bound by one's soul even more meaningful than being married like humans?

"I just don't get why it's important," Cole argued, throwing his hands up in the air.

"Of course not," Mika snipped and gave something of a feminine growl before stalking back to her mate. "I didn't get a say in being your mate, Cole. I know you didn't either, but I was totally blindsided, and I was the one who had to make sacrifices, who had to give up my life, my freedom and everything I had ever known. I didn't get a say in being your mate," she began, and I began to understand her side.

By the look on Cole's face, he was beginning to see it too.

"Being married means that someone got down on one knee and asked the person they love to choose them forever. That's all it is, *choosing* to get up every damn day and choose each other, to have each other's backs, to be there through all the good but especially the bad. That's what being married means to me, Cole. Not that we were chosen to be together by the universe or whatever, but that *we chose* each other."

Cali blinked away tears, and Adrik was studying her with a worried gaze. Cali and he had fought when she found out about the prophecy, because she felt like he'd manipulated the events and had her fall in love with him before telling her. She felt as though she didn't have a choice either. While Sawyer had accepted it easier, it was still hard on her. I wondered if Dimitria felt the same way.

"Alright," Cole said and I turned back to my brother. "Marry me."

Tria took in a sharp breath, and I watched the train wreck in front of me take place. Fucking hell, even I knew you didn't propose like that.

"What?" Mika choked, looking equally shocked and angry.

Cole strode towards her, his eyes focused on her, his every step filled with purpose. He stopped before her, studying her carefully. Slowly, he got down on one knee, cupped his hands, and when he pulled back, he had a ring in his hands. Dimitria took my hand and we carefully edged closer.

"Since the moment you walked into that warehouse two years ago, I have been choosing you. Yes, destiny had a say in it, and maybe it created the circumstances for us to find one another. But I chose you every day from that moment on, even when it scared the fuck out of me. I've never had a vulnerability before, not one our enemies could exploit, but that was what you became when we met. I'd give up everything for you, Mika, *everything*. I would watch the world burn, hell, I'd happily pour the gasoline and light the match without a second thought if it kept you safe, if it made you happy," Cole said, his eyes only for his mate. Through Tria, I was able to feel the way he meant every single word, and how vulnerable he felt right in that moment on his knees and in front of his brothers knowing full well she could say no.

"I chose you from the first day, Mika. I'm asking you to choose me now. I love you, Tomika, and I'll choose you every day for the rest of our lives. Marry me."

The silence that filled the hall was loud and echoing, and I found myself holding my breath just like everyone else. Mika's wide blue eyes were filled with tears, and she pressed her hand to her mouth and a sob broke loose.

"Of course I choose you, you idiot! I just wanted to be asked!" she cried. Cole grinned, his relief enough to fill the room. Mika threw herself at him as he stood and he wrapped her tightly in his arms, spinning her in circles before putting her back on her feet. I clapped along with my brothers and our mates as he put the ring on her finger and Mika beamed up at him, the way she felt about him printed clearly across her face.

Tria leaned back into me and wiped away a stray tear on her face and I wrapped my arms around her waist, holding her close. I'd never thought to propose in all this time, but looking at how happy Mika was, I made a note to keep it in mind.

I glanced up at Adrik who was looking at Cali with an expectant expression and she beamed and leaned up to kiss him. "Ask me another day, and I'll say yes. But now is their time."

"We should do it sooner rather than later," he encouraged.

"Later," she answered with a smile and a wink.

Adrik beamed down at her, and she grinned right back before turning to face Cole and Mika again. A quick glance at Malik and Sawyer forced a chuckle from me as Malik smiled suggestively down at her and Sawyer was shaking her head with wide eyes. "We're not there yet."

"But we're mates," Malik reminded.

"Yes, and we've been together for less than six months. I think we can wait a little while longer."

"Wait for what?" Malik asked as Sawyer walked towards Mika to look at the ring. "Wait for what?" he repeated.

I glanced down at Tria and she turned in my arms and smiled up at me. "Yeah, don't ask yet."

"I wasn't going to," I said with wide eyes.

"Uh-huh. You had that look," she accused, brushing her fingers over my cheek. I smiled and stilled when another thought occurred to me, something I *hadn't* remembered until now.

"What?" she asked, sensing my disquiet.

"Uh, I'm not going to ask you to marry me, but umm... What do you think about kids?"

Her eyes widened comically and she swallowed. "We can have kids?"

"Yes," I admitted slowly. "Did I forget to mention that?"

"Yeah, I think I'd remember a conversation about kids. Especially since we haven't used protection even once," she added.

"I, umm... I forgot," I answered sheepishly.

For several moments she considered my words, and I wondered if I'd fucked up royally by forgetting. To be fair, a lot had been going on, and I hadn't expected things between us to progress so quickly.

"Okay," she said.

I frowned. "Okay what?"

"Okay, I'm good with kids."

I blinked at her and shook my head. "Just like that?"

"Yes," she answered, and her lips quirked up as she wrapped her arms around my neck to kiss me. "I have always wanted a big family with lots of kids. I want it all, and if it's with you, then I'm happy to do it."

Despite the fear having kids brought out in me, the idea of having them with her was an allure I couldn't ignore. A girl with her eyes and hair? A boy with my smart-ass attitude? The thought of seeing her grow with my child set off something inside me I hadn't expected.

She looked at me with knowing eyes when she felt the reaction going on behind my fly and she sank against me, pressing herself into my chest. I grinned down at her, tracing my fingers down her spine eliciting a shiver from her.

"So… want to go back to bed?"

She smiled and tangled her fingers in my hair. "I'll go anywhere and do anything, as long as I have you."

"You have my word, *cara,* you'll always have me."

THE END OF BOOK FOUR

THANK YOU FOR READING

THE KINGS OF HELL
HARKYN

If you loved Harkyn and Dimitria's story, I hope you'll come find me on Facebook and Instagram to stay in touch and up to date. There will be a story for each of the Kings of Hell!

In the next book, be ready for some bonus content featuring Lilith and Lucifer!

Want to know what happened two hundred years ago when Donovan earned his name, Nova? Stay in touch because a prequel is coming soon!

Did you find yourself curious about the Nephilim? I hope so! **Because a Nephilim spin-off series is in the works!**

Thanks again for reading, and I hope to hear from you soon! As always, please do not forget to leave a review. You have no idea how powerful your words are, or how much authors rely on reviews to keep on writing.

DID YOU KNOW…

I HAVE TWO OTHER PEN NAMES?

I know that seems like overkill, but there is a method to my madness.

Books under the name **Alexis Maree** are for paranormal romances. Not everyone likes to read this genre, so I like to keep them separate.

Likewise, not everyone likes contemporary romances, so I have another pen name for those…**T. Maree.**

Then last, but certainly not least, are my sinfully sexy romances, the ones that border on the line of "*should she really put that down in print?*"
Some people don't like those kinds of spicy scenes, and so I decided to keep those separate from the rest under the name **Luna Maree.**

So, if you'd like to check out what else I've written, go onto my website:
https://thethreemarees.wordpress.com/

Happy reading!

Alexis | Luna | T.

ALEXIS MAREE